In The Absence of Light

C. L. Ferrari

Portal Publishing LLC
Fort Pierce, Florida

Books by C.L. Ferrari

Non Fiction
Enriching Your Retirement - ebook, Amazon 2016

Fiction
In The Absence of Light - first of trilogy -ebook, Amazon 2022
In The Absence of Light - print, Amazon March 2022
The Swordsman - prequel - second of trilogy - ebook, Amazon
fall of 2022
In His Image - sequel - third of trilogy - ebook, Amazon spring
of 2023

Children's Books
Kitty's Life Series - When I Grow Up - ebook, Amazon April
2022

See what's new coming from the desk of C.L. Ferrari
Https://clf-words.com

ISBN-13: 978-1-957769-00-4 (paperback)

Dedication

To my wonderful children who encouraged me to be adventurous and follow my dreams. Thank you Dan, Heather, and Shawn. Your support and understanding have given me wings. I hope my support for you has done the same.

Prologue

On December, 21, 2012, I begin this work, the day when the world was supposed to end, according to many, because of the end of the Mayan calendar. We're still here. And this story has to be told. Because today isn't the end, the world goes on.

This tale revolves around the conflict of forces, and the evil which continually strives for victory. Our world is in turmoil and the battle between good and evil is unending.

In my sixty plus years, I've seen and experienced a lot. Having traveled thousands of miles, been touched by diverse cultures, and journeyed deeper into my faith, I've discovered an undeniable truth. There exists layers of invisible forces through which we each unknowingly navigate every day of our lives. These layers have nothing to do with social class, wealth, occupation, or status among men. No, they're much more than that. They are layers of joyous light and soul numbing dark, purest goodness and terrifying evil.

God did not promise that our lives will be without trouble or strife, tears or sadness. The free will we've been given won't be taken away, but we are promised that a good side to all bad things that happen will be shown to us.

This story is about the consequences of entanglement with souls which are "In the Absence of Light", the critical life and death importance of spreading the light into the dark areas of the world and standing on God's promises, the ultimate victory of good over evil, beyond the pain. And it is about Hope.

This is a work of fiction based on what I know to be true.

For we wrestle not against flesh and blood, but against principalities, against powers, against the rulers of the darkness of this world, against spiritual wickedness in high places.

Ephesians 6:12

I have told you these things so that in me you may have peace. In this world you will have trouble. But take heart! I have overcome the world.

John 16:33

1

The Beginning

HIS EYES jolted open, or did he just think they did?

Blackness. No, he saw darkest blue. The blue of deep space, just a fraction from being black.

Weightlessness. Confusing but not scary.

The boy sleeps, or does he? His dreams, when they happen, are usually detached, like a movie, not involving him. He is an observer of life as he is in dreams, and sometimes it's hard to tell the difference. But this dream is not the same. He feels it.

He hears a voice, one like he's never heard before. It is deep and musical, otherworldly, there-and-not-there, soothing.

"The time is here, Pauley. We're coming. It's almost your time to awaken."

Now he can see, but his eyes aren't open. He is viewing Earth from a great distance, a little ball of blues and greens where all seems tranquil enough, quiet, and peaceful actually. The planet floats in the vast black of space, suspended and slowly, slowly turning with the tiniest glimmers of light flickering around it.

It looks like when he's opening Google Earth on his laptop, except that this dimension is real, it's not a 'program.' This isn't a cool video game. Pauley is zooming in with his awareness, not an icon or button. He is rapidly approaching the planet, and he sees that angels flank him. These overly large beings are golden warriors with expansive white feathered wings and flowing robes that shimmer with a fluorescence, carrying him toward the orb.

"This is the world created by God for his most beloved, the New Ones, your kind, Pauley. You can see all of this because your blessing is the gift of divine vision, and it's time. You can see it now as His battalions of Heavenly Host see it."

Understanding fills him and feels like warm honey flowing through his body, soft and soothing to the depths of his soul, bringing him contentment and peace. But he has questions. As he thinks them, the angels hear.

"Why did God create Earth? Why these rivers and forests, the oceans, and the mountains? Why right here in THIS particular solar system, in this specific galaxy, when space is so big? What is His plan? And why am I here?"

"The plan is known only to Him, Pauley. Fulfilling the plan will be the task of many, but He alone will orchestrate it. And it will be challenging because He gave the New Ones free will. They don't understand yet that His way is the divine way, the best way because He has knowledge of all time, and so they continue to forge on, choosing their own paths. They make bad choices for wrong reasons and then make more bad choices attempting to solve the problems they create. But He loves you, all of you. And even before He created it all, He knew the story of this world and its occupants from beginning to end because time, as you know it, doesn't exist. Yours isn't the only

In The Absence of Light

world He created, but it's the only one you'll know."

"How did it all start?" Pauley asked.

"When He created mankind, He loved you all, and we loved you as well, at least all of us save the part of the Host which would be cast out. Those instead became jealous and hungry for power, something unknown to any of the Host before then. Their rebellion angered Him, and He dealt with them harshly, their ethereal beauty removed from their energy, leaving them as horrible manifestations of all they represent, greed, hatred, envy, anger, and lust. That was the First Great War, and Our Father was the victor, as He will always be."

"He cast these fallen from heaven to Earth, but it is not their final destination. Eventually, they are doomed to spend eternity in the fiery pit, but they are now allowed to test His limits on Earth. They swore vengeance against Him, and to this day, they attempt retaliation, seeking to hurt Him through the New Ones. The Fallen Dissidents learned that they could use His gift of free will to turn the New Ones against Him."

"This planet is rotten with the absence of hope and the presence of evil brought on by the evil ones. Many of the New Ones have lost their way and now blindly act out the instructions of the Fallen creatures. Our Father is watching the struggle, desiring for His New Ones to accept His grace and bring the world back into balance, into a state of joy and peace. That's what He intended for you from the beginning, from the very days when the first two New Ones walked in the glorious garden."

As the angel continues to explain, their journey slows. Pauley watches as the Earth becomes enormous, and the rivers and mountain ranges become clear to him.

"These days of turmoil are leading up to the Second Great War. His Word has already foretold of the days of the world as it is known now. And He knows the details of the final days to come. The timing of this, too, is known only to Him. The Host is His army, and we fight the battles on all planes of existence. When He says it is time, only then does the last creature fall and the beast go to the pit."

"Why are you telling me this? I'm just a kid. What can I do?" Pauley questioned.

"You will be His instrument in battle, Pauley. So, you are seeing much. You will awaken soon, and your real life will begin. For now, just rest. Your part is of great importance, and you will know when you are called."

With that, his mind drifts back into dreamless peace.

~~~

They come from throughout the universe's dimensions and now gather at their designated stations. This small group flies a hundred sets of wings, spread in alabaster spans of ten to twelve feet each, silently carrying the Angelic Army closer to Earth. As they speed through the vastness of space, passing galaxies yet unknown to man, and crossing orbits of comets large enough to dwarf their intended target, the blues and greens of Earth become more defined into places of water and land, and the Host adjusts direction.

The plan of the Dark One is to have his creatures wreak extreme havoc in numerous locations throughout the planet, hoping to thin out the ranks of the Angels sent to quell the chaos. The Evil Ones are skillful and stealth to gain a foothold, then they become more brazen. Sadness and hopelessness are spreading, and the number of believers is wavering. Old generations of strong faith are passing over into the Kingdom, and the new generations are not following in His ways, unseated by temptation and confusion.

Greed and strife are powerful. False prophets abound. Heinous acts against each other grow common, and the New Ones are becoming numb to all the horrors. The Evil Ones have been working diligently; their results are frightening and destructive, leading to further despair and hopelessness.

The Winged Warriors approach their destination, a small area of Earth within the third dimension of existence. This location is significant. Other factions of the Host are being directed to similar sites around the planet to carry out their orders. All are destined to fight for the survival of the New Ones. Toward that goal, each is prepared to be destroyed in a fierce and devastating battle.

The warriors in this group know that they will once again be encountering the Swordsman, one of the New Ones especially favored by Him with a divine gift. This human can see the Host and the demon hordes, and he fights as bravely as any Archangel in God's army. He is a worthy ally.

2

Spiritual Battle

GABE MATHESON sat in his motor home, hands on the wheel, staring out the front windshield. Breaking his reverie with a sigh, he looked at his cell phone to remind himself since day and time seemed to have little meaning. It was ten a.m., Thursday. The parking space at the police department gave him a distant and partial view of the Pacific Ocean on this clear California morning. He didn't remember ever swimming in it though he'd been near enough on several occasions. But then, there was always a job to be done. His tasks that were life or death, every time, left no room for things like splashing in waves or lying in the sun.

Yet another case closed, and the report filed. How many had it been now? He'd lost count. The battles, some small, some involving far too many innocents, always violent. The one that took place here was over, for now. Homeland Security knew Gabe's name as one of the good guys, so the local law enforcement branches had instructions to ask for reports and allow him to go on his way. They knew he fought, but they initially thought it was against the underground al Qaeda making headway into the United States, and now they assumed it was against ISIS cells or internal terrorists. They didn't know if he was CIA, FBI, or some other "dark" agency, and they didn't ask. They did know that he was what they considered undercover and highly classified. And that he brought in many serious criminals whose captures wouldn't be in the headlines because they needed to disappear for reasons only those in charge would know. So, his acceptance was without question. Gabe figured his free pass through their ranks was part of the plan that was his mission. A Divine Plan, he knew.

It was autumn, in other parts of the country, the leaves were beginning to change. His mind raced to Luke, his best friend from college. Gabe had so few that he could call friends. Luke had been in his thoughts because his inner alarm was going off. Gabe felt compelled to travel next to Luke's town. A phone call was in order, and it wasn't news that his friend would welcome.

He closed his eyes and breathed deeply, thinking about the first time they were involved in a battle, twenty years ago. The time when he saw what, not whom, he would be battling. The day he learned the meaning of Principalities. He visualized it behind closed eyelids as if it were happening all over again, and he was an observer. His heartbeat quickened as his memory flashed the raw unworldly scene before him while he sat alone in the RV.

~~~

He was running for his life, dodging and gasping for breath, both terrified and confused at the scene which met him as he opened the doors to leave the gym. Now his lungs were bursting at the physical exertion. His muscles screamed as he whirled, jumping and ducking to keep from being bludgeoned. And his peripheral vision was working at hyper speed.

CLANG! The sound of metal on metal rang out. CLANG, CLANG!! An echoing cacophony of his steel longsword clashing against lead pipes and machetes flailing perilously in the air.

Gabe leaped from the top of a concrete wall to the ground and rolled, lifting his head as he heard a deadly whoosh, something ferociously

7

parting the oxygen as it sped toward him. Another jagged pipe swung heavily in a wide arc, barely missing his skull but grazing his shoulder, ripping his shirt, and opening a gash. Faces, evil masks filled with hate and murder, were behind the arms that wielded the weapons. Grotesque black, scaly, red-eyed demons appeared to be riding the backs of his attackers.

What was happening? No time to think! The air, the sky, filled with bats? Not bats! More of the demons, stinking of burnt sulfur, drooling, panting, soaring pterodactyls, shrieking as they swooped.

His reflexes came from years of martial arts and boxing, creating a taut, muscular build to balance his six-foot-five gladiator-like frame. On a whim, he added a class in Historical Fencing and Weaponry to his curriculum last term. He seemed born for it, mastering the skills needed to wield the lethal longsword, only in his hands now because he'd just left a workout with a fencing classmate.

Behind him, he heard the rapid-fire rat-tat-tat-tat of an automatic weapon and screams, hundreds of screams. Then individual shots; one, after another. People ran in mortal fear knocking down and trampling anyone who stumbled. With longsword in hand and blood trickling from his shoulder, he bolted across the Quad toward his dorm, the last place he'd seen his best friend.

Injured bodies lay scattered across the grass and walkways of the Quad. Puddles of red slowly spread around them, staining the concrete and turning the lawns to a muddy maroon. Those chasing him went after slower targets as he ran across the ivy-laced entry portico to the massive carved wooden door of the dorm.

He heard sirens. And more screaming as a machete sliced the backpack and into the skin of a student who hadn't run fast enough. Bull horns, more gunfire. Clouds of tear gas.

He heaved at the partially open door that someone had tried to block from the inside with piles of furniture. The flying demon bats circled and dipped in the air; their hideous faces contorted and their bodies writhing with glee at the carnage. He could hear no sound from them, but he could hear the fear in the cries of his classmates coming from above on the second floor. He took the stairs three at a time, driven by pure adrenaline, and reached the landing.

For a split second, he stopped, stunned at seeing   a dark shape, mouth in a snarling grimace, riding the shoulders of a bearded man with matted hair and a bloody switchblade opened and pointed at Luke. His friend's back against the wall, a growing red circle claiming the fabric on the front of his shirt as it spread. Luke was in shock, eyes wide and mouth agape, unable to escape as the attacker moved in for a second brutal stab.

Gabe swung his longsword with both hands, slicing the man's arm at the elbow, the force leaving it cut, bleeding, and dangling. Gabe lunged, and his blade opened the man's chest. With his eyes frantic, the assailant tried to make a sound, but only bubbles of blood emerged from his mouth. The creature on his back, in a blur of speed, launched itself from the man's shoulder. Up through the ceiling without even creating dust, it succeeded in fleeing the wrath of the swordsman. But, the bearded man, its previous domination, crumpled heavily, fatally, to the carpeted wooden floor.

If mortal ears could have heard the shrill bellows of the demons, it would have deafened them. Luke's legs gave out as Gabe grabbed him, supporting his weight in preparation to run. But run where? Where in this insanity?

And then, in the hallway before them, a form materialized. A golden, almost translucent, giant warrior with creamy white wings that spread so wide they disappeared into the rooms on either side of the hallway. It brought its wings in, moving them easily through the solid walls, wrapping the two men in an arc of protection, and Gabe looked up into its amethyst-colored eyes as it nodded gravely to him. Without words, Gabe knew his friend was safe, and he needed to save as many others as he could reach. How did he know?

But there was no time to waste; he bolted toward the screams coming from the rooms down the hall. Somehow, he understood that this was his destiny; his training and strength were part of the plan before he ever knew a plan existed. He was called into action, forever changing his life.

Twelve hours passed, but it seemed like days. Gabe sat in the hospital room next to his friend. Luke was still sedated after emergency surgery to repair the internal damage and stitch the wound. His doctors said he would recuperate after several weeks of rest. The slashing was deep but not life-threatening as it missed vital organs. Luke would carry the scars, a lifetime reminder of the attack.

Through the conversations he'd overheard between victims and the police questioning them, Gabe learned that no one else could see the demons which were so frighteningly visible to him. They only saw the people driven by the demons, like the bearded man who attacked Luke. Police, SWAT, and the National Guard were all involved; together, they'd subdued the monstrous invasion, but not without loss of life and hundreds of injured students and faculty. The media called it a possible terrorist event. How else could it be explained? Gabe wondered if the authorities noticed the strange tattoos on some of the attackers. And if so, why weren't they talking about it on the news?

After the angel left them, Gabe went through the dorm, ensuring the other students were safe. He returned to Luke, dropped his sword, and carried him downstairs, where first responders were already making their way into the building. With Luke in the hands of paramedics, Gabe went back for his sword and quickly packed some of his clothes. He knew in his gut that he wouldn't be returning to classes; his institutional learning was over. There were things in this world now revealed to him and him alone. His destiny was ahead, not here.

The look in the angel's eyes lasted only a moment, but it forged a bond. When their eyes connected, he instantly knew things in his soul with utter certainty. However lonely and challenging, this was a glimpse of his future, impossible to deny. He was now a part of something bigger than anything he could have imagined, accepted, and needed in the ranks of the Warrior Angels. His life would be devoted to fighting and defeating the dark forces threatening the world.

~~~

Gabe slowly opened his eyes, sighed, and straightened his shoulders. It was time to move forward. Reaching for his cell phone, he punched the icon with Luke's picture. They stayed in contact several times a year over the past two decades and had seen each other a few times as well when his quests took him across the country and back again. Gabe would have to tell his friend that the next one, and it would be a big one, would be in his backyard.

"Luke. It's Gabe. I think you know why I'm calling."

"Hey, old friend!" Luke said warmly. "I had a feeling I'd hear from you. I've been getting some pretty strange vibes lately. Things seem off-balance, the air is different, things I see every day don't look the same, and I can't put my finger on it, but the hairs on the back of my neck have been trying to tell me something."

"Yeah. It looks like my next mission is right under your feet, buddy. I'll be there in a couple of days."

"I'm ready for you. Your room is waiting." The line went dead.

He felt under the seat for his longsword and, reassured it was there, he put the key in the ignition with one hand and ran the other hand through his longish hair. Moving the gearshift in reverse and pulling out of his parking space, he kicked it into drive and began mile number one to his newest destination.

Gabe was heading into some beautiful country at a lovely time of year. Sadly, his life's work left little time to enjoy God's bounty. Little did he know that as he was heading east, there were thousands of other beings traveling to the same place, some his allies and some his enemies, and this event would do more to change his life than anything he'd been through before.

11

3

Henderson County

A RELATIVELY small rural county in the eastern part of Kansas, Henderson County contained a few little towns and nearly a thousand farms. The closest big city was one county to the northeast, where many Henderson residents shopped at the big malls. It encompassed vast acres of undeveloped wooded land, agricultural farms, lakes, and streams. Two main highways intersected here; a state road running east and west and a county road jogging north and south. The countryside, crisscrossed with rural roads and trails, was used by local hunters in season and adventure seekers riding ATVs the rest of the year. The lakes and scenic streams provided excellent fishing, and most locals were skilled outdoors men.

Many within the population of about twenty thousand had family roots that went back to original settlers over two hundred years ago. Regardless of the town where they resided, they knew each other because many were related, and they often came together for community events.

Families supported the single high school sports activities. 4H clubs were active, and the county fair was the biggest event of the year - no one missed it, just like no one missed hunting and fishing seasons. The two small elementary schools served from kindergarten to eighth grade. There was a PTA; school plays, dances and proms, cheer-leading tryouts, a chess club, and school sports rounded out the busy school year calendar. It was a true picture-postcard all-America kind of setting in all ways except for the dwindling numbers of younger people as the kids graduated and migrated to bigger cities for jobs and higher pay.

Just as everyone knew where to find the few chain restaurants and ice cream shops in the better areas of the towns, so did everyone know where there were some seedier places and what streets and alleys to avoid at all costs. The general population avoided people who lived in those parts of town and frequented the nudie bar, all-night liquor stores, and the adult video store. Parents taught their kids not to go into shady places because danger lurked there.

What mainstream folks didn't realize was that there was a danger they couldn't see. Not all nefarious people are recognizable. Some who appear to be threatening are just stereotyped as bad. And on the other hand, bad guys don't wear black hats to announce themselves. A very clean-cut, All-American-looking guy could be a serial killer, like Ted Bundy. Beneath a believable façade could exist a heartless, cold-blooded psychopath. And the full spectrum of Satan's demons was hard at work to convert humans into those vile ranks.

~~~

Just as with the diversity of angels, some being warriors, guardians, escorts, and helpers of humanity, often perceived as humans or animals, all being of different types and ranks, so are Demons different from each other.

Beelzebub's personal army and inner circle are the most immense and horrific leaders. Their breed is called Gai'Ograh, stinking, drooling, and terrifying giants of dull deep purple warty skin. Of these, two hold the rank of top Princes, Astaroth, and Shemiaz. Together with Satan, they form the Evil Trinity.

Many other equally ominous Princes earned their positions. Balam, Beleth, and Corson command scores of fighting legions. Others control specific humans, critical players in the plans of the Evil Trinity. Mammon, Rakshasa, and Asura are among these. Every leader, every Prince, knows its place, but all scheme for advancement and favor.

The warring ranks, the expendables, are far smaller and slightly less grotesquely imposing than their leaders. What they lack in size, they make up for in numbers. The Legoniaries, the legions, are indeed many. Their sizes and minor ranks vary, but their contribution to the cause is mighty.

Most diminutive in stature are the demons of the species Klazyn. Their specialty is possessing humans through whispered suggestions. These creatures, the size of human toddlers but in nightmarish form, cause chaos and destruction by turning the New Ones away from the Light. The entire plan rests on the success of these mind-benders. They are the termites in the structure of God's will.

~~~

A dozen black bat-winged Legoniaries and Klazyns, ranging from eighteen inches to four feet tall, jostled and rustled about on the roof of a one-story bar ten minutes from the high school in Gibson Glen, the county seat. It was the largest town in the county, named after the founding family, and the home of the blue and orange-bannered Gibson High School Raiders, state football champions.

The Demons communicated with growls and low-pitched screeches. They waited anxiously for something to take place, eyes glowing in shades of orange and red, stinking of burning sewage, and yet invisible to human perception. The tension was increasing. At this point, they were all equals, Indians without a chief, which was volatile. Legions continued to land and with each new arrival grew the probability of friction within the ranks. At last, a large black shadow was cast over them as a foul-smelling Lieutenant settled onto the roof space, talons piercing into the wood and brandishing a wide sardonic smirk which exposed curved black knife-like fangs.

Suddenly still in anticipation, the lower-ranking demons understood the unspoken order. Some of the possessive Klazyns were already attached to their charges inside the bar below. Each demon on the roof awaited the human to whom it was assigned. It then clung to the New One until told to do otherwise. They were to sink their talons into the flesh of the human and position themselves to whisper horrible things into their ears which only that particular human could hear. The evil suggestions would come to the humans as thoughts and, conditioned as they already were, they would then do the bidding of the dark forces.

There was little which could get the demons to abandon their posts, little that they feared. They believed themselves to be a righteous flying army, and their part in the Great Plan was critical to eradicating the New Ones. Once wiped from the face of the earth, those humans who had given up their souls would be torn from God forever and would become the minions of Satan. Yes, those who died proclaiming the Son as their Savior would go to God's Kingdom, but the battles and work of the demons between now and then would shrink the numbers of the saved. It was all about Satan smiting God and his jealousy of the New Ones.

It was going well. There would be a good report for the General, thought the grotesque Lieutenant. He dissolved from the roof and reformed, tucked in a dark corner of the bar below, hunched over and lurking. He was in a good mood.

4

Residents

Kasey

SHE MECHANICALLY cleared the table in the dim light of the bar and grill, wiping up spilled beer from the scarred wooden tables and emptying the overflowing ashtrays left by the lunch patrons. The smells never changed, stale beer and cigarettes, but now it was physically nauseating.

This is where she and Carlos met, just ten months ago. Five days a week, she worked here after school, until at least ten in the evening when she hurried back across town in the dark to their apartment where she did her homework. Serving food and cleaning tables in a bar was legal for a seventeen-year-old girl if she wasn't behind the bar or handling the liquor. It was the family business, and Kasey had to do her part; she was, after all, cheap labor.

But Carlos had paid attention to her. He always smiled when she entered the room and never forgot to leave her a good tip. She guessed that he must have had a good-paying job; he was just twenty-one, and yet he always flashed a wad of cash when he paid his tab. It must be nice not to have to worry about money.

Because of her work, there was little time for friends or high school activities. It was often a struggle to maintain high grades, but she vowed her brains would be her ticket away from this life, which was otherwise her destiny. Those thoughts had always kept her going, even when she could hardly keep her eyes open.

"Kasey! Hurry it up out there! It's almost six, and the Friday night bunch will be here any minute!". Grandma Myrt, 'Gran,' still did all the cooking and was always after her to do this or that; she never seemed completely happy with the way Kasey fulfilled her duties. Even though she and Trisha shared the apartment with Gran, they rarely saw her at home. Gran was either at the bar working or sleeping in her room with the door closed. Kasey and Trisha practically raised themselves after their father walked out ten years ago. In a state of deep depression, their mother drank herself to death a year later.

Saturdays were full days from ten a.m. to six p.m. But on Sundays, she got a break, mostly because she maxed out the hours per week she could work at her age. But Friday nights, she waited tables from after school until midnight, and it was becoming harder to stay on her feet for hours on end. Lapsing frequently into mental tangents helped her keep from thinking about the pain in her back and legs. She thought of Carlos.

She'd started seeing him about a month after their first meeting. He was kind and polite, things Kasey hadn't known before from a guy around her age, and she fell hard. He told her that he loved her soft blond hair and lapis blue eyes that spoke to him with gentleness. They stole a few hours to be alone on Sunday mornings or a weeknight when she would skip her homework and cram to get it done the following day during homeroom. On their third date, she found herself carried away by her passion and a deep longing to be cared for, and they made love.

Life seemed lighter after that, happier, more complete. He told her he wanted to be with her always and made the promises that go hand in hand with a new and consuming relationship. He gave her a beautiful tiny gold cross on a delicate chain which he placed around her neck. Carlos was raised a Catholic but didn't practice his religion. Finally, there was something in her life, a bright secret light; she felt she had meaning, purpose, and worth because of him.

One Friday evening, six weeks into their intimate relationship, she learned that he wouldn't be showing up for their regular Sunday morning time together. Kasey was cleaning countertops at the bar. Grandma Myrt was making idle conversation, half talking to herself, when she muttered something about the cops making a big bust that day. "It's a shame; he was a good customer," Kasey heard. Her curiosity piqued, she paid closer attention.

"Who, Gram?"

"That Carlos fella, he was arrested for drug trafficking," she replied. Seems he had quite an operation going around here. They got a few other guys who worked for him too."

Kasey had barely heard the final part of Gram's sentence. The room suddenly seemed smaller and without oxygen. She remembered how her heart thumped; practically beating itself right through her chest cavity, and then the sweat broke out on her forehead. She had gasped and leaned onto the bar for support, blinking away tears.

On the coming weekend, she'd planned to tell him that she was pregnant. That they were going to be parents to the most beautiful baby and that they would live happily ever after. She would finally be able to tell her grandma and her younger sister about her relationship with Carlos and her impending motherhood. The visions of a cute little house with a swing set in the backyard vanished into the murky smoke-filled room.

She couldn't breathe, but Gram didn't know any of that then and only saw that there was work to be done.

That was seven months ago. Kasey did tell Carlos about the baby, but the announcement went to the prison by letter. She received a bittersweet reply, encased in an envelope full of numbers for the return address. He was both happy and sad, still professing his love but hopeless, having received a ten-year sentence. There were no more messages from him after that. She broke the news of the baby to Gram and Trisha, and as she expected, grandma was chastising and harsh. Trisha was elated. And time marched on, magnifying her insignificance.

Though her belly made her condition undeniable, she had been able to make special arrangements to finish her senior year and graduate, at least on paper. The rest of her class would do the 'walk' next spring, but her teachers had agreed to allow her to do the entire year's work at her own pace and much of it from home after the baby was born. Kasey worked hard at it and would have it finished with a flourish. Opportunities for a bright future may have dimmed, and her hope was all but gone, but she would have her diploma months ahead of her classmates because of her fierce determination.

Kasey spent Sunday mornings in solitude now. The apartment was across the street from a little Christian church, and she often opened her second-floor window to hear the music and watch the people as they came and went. They seemed happy. The inside of a church and what went on there was foreign to her. It was not the way of her family. No one talked about beliefs or faith.

There was a gray emptiness inside her that she couldn't even describe. Carlos brought color, but it faded away in his absence. Her life had never known deep joy. And now, here she was, standing in the bar with a tray in her hand. Her thoughts focused on her present with little hope for better.

The foul black creature clinging to her shoulder grinned, and Insecurity hunched over to whisper more words of loneliness into her ear.

Hearing a familiar sound, she snapped out of her reverie to see the front door opening and the first of the loud and rowdy Friday night crowd began pouring in. She sighed and hoisted the tray of garbage and dirty glasses to carry to the kitchen. The unearthly glow of the streetlights flowed through the door as the sky darkened.

~~~

Jake

Jake Bauer pushed open the heavy wooden door to enter the dark, boozy, smelling tavern. At six foot two and already drunk from a day of tipping bottles, his thin and unhealthy frame swayed toward the bar. The conversation he was having with himself, overheard by some of the patrons already there, continued. "Damn that woman! Why does she always have to spoil everything?" He'd planned to have a good evening here, meeting with friends and knocking back a few. Someone was always hanging around to tell him jokes, share stories, or bitch with him about the women they knew.

So what if he'd already put away a bottle of vodka while Peggy worked. It was boring staying at her place during the day by himself. Why couldn't she put herself in his shoes once in a while?

She was supposed to be happy and fun when she got home, not a nag. And yet, there she was, bitching at him from the first minute because the bottle was empty. Calling him no good and worthless, just like he heard from his old man.

He tried to get a job, but the economy was terrible; that wasn't his fault. They said it was good on the news, but not for guys like him; only the big wheeler-dealers were making money. Big money too! It made it even harder that he wasn't allowed to drive and had to walk or ride a bike to a job.

Those stupid damn cops had been out to get him. They purposely picked him out and followed him home from the bar that night four years ago. Then they said he was drunk! Of course, he wasn't, but he refused the breathalyzer because he knew they could twist the outcome, making him look guilty. The case went to court, and he ended up having to do some time anyway because it was his third DUI. Now, who knew if he'd ever get a license again. "Damn cops! Why aren't they out trying to catch criminals instead of picking on the little guy?" he mentally lamented.

It had been another in their long line of arguments, and Peggy had ended up crumpled in a heap on the floor when he stormed out to come to the bar. It was her fault. She never knew when to stop. Peggy knew he had a temper, so what was wrong with her? Now she'd have to fix that black eye so no one would ask questions again. Damn! He just hated when she caused trouble. He had to be careful not to hurt her bad enough to send her to the hospital. Then it would be just another thing he'd have to explain to the cops, and they already had it in for him.

What was wrong with the world that no one would give him a break? The IRS was after him for not filing his taxes for the past ten years. "Jesus H. Christ! It's my money, and I worked hard for it – they should keep their grubby thievin' mitts off of it. I'm tired of supporting those freakin' illegals, we give them everything, and I have squat! Won't happen anymore, I won't deal with that crap!" were his thoughts, often shared with anyone who'd listen at the bar.

He sat and ordered a straight-up vodka from Billy, the bartender. Billy was a fixture here for as long as he could remember. He was a bit slow-moving due to a deformity in his left leg but a good listener. Grandma Myrt, the owner, employed Billy because she got him cheap, and he didn't cause any trouble; in fact, he probably chased problems away just by being there. Nobody messed with him. That would be stupid since he was about as big as Paul Bunyan and looked like he could and would kill you with one punch. Good guy that Billy.

As he reached for the vodka glass, he noticed the hot little blond bitch cleaning tables and serving food. She was carrying a tray of crap back to the kitchen and looking considerably fatter than he recalled from the last time he'd noticed her. Some dude probably knocked her up. Yeah, that's how these bar bitches work. "Can't trust 'em either. Little sluts, that's what they are. Come to think of it, that's how most women are – just sluts," he assured himself. That's what his old man told him, and he was right. But this one was young, and Billy looked after her. "Leave it alone, Jake," he said to himself. He didn't need that kind of trouble.

The first vodka went down fast and smooth, and he called Billy back over. "Pour another Billy boy and keep 'em comin', gonna be a good night tonight," then he smiled and settled back in his bar chair, sure that all was right with himself and that the rest of the world was off balance. He half-turned to the woman on his right and slid his free hand up her thigh. "And how're you doin' tonight, Sarah?" And Sarah smiled with glazed eyes and her front teeth missing. Jake's demons sneered and hissed and dug in deeper. Abuse, Drunkenness, and Blame were on a roll.

Someone shoved coins into the jukebox, and the sounds of old twangy country music and pool balls smacking together set the night in motion. The darkness inside of the bar somehow became thicker.

~~~

Bobby Jack and Rufus Chaney

"Rack 'em up, idiot," he ordered his younger brother. "We gotta get in some practice before the dupes get here. Need to make some hustlin' dough tonight." Bobby Jack was a regular at the bar and grill on weekends and often made drinking money by challenging some newcomer to a game. He wasn't the brightest bulb in the pack but compared to his brother, Bubba, Bobby Jack had at least gotten to the eighth grade.

The family came from the deep hills of Kentucky, and his Ma ran the clan. The boys could pretty much do as they pleased and found a little work here and there to help support the ramshackle household where ten of them lived, three generations now. It had been four, but old Grams died last winter, and she was the end of that bunch. As long as they didn't piss off Ma, everything was fine. She and her fifth common-law husband would take care of things.

Bubba was born with the cord wrapped around his neck; it took a bit before he got some good color. That's why they said he was slow. Bobby Jack just called him an idiot. Bubba understood enough to have his feelings hurt by the nickname, but he just followed along anyway. Where else did he have to go? Ma always told him that his big brother would watch out for him, and such became his lot in life.

Bobby Jack and his siblings were half brothers and sisters. Fathers had come and gone. Now the two girls were popping out whelps of their own, and who the fathers were was anyone's guess. No one asked; no one cared. Just a new bunch of little snot noses running around underfoot. One of the girls danced in the local strip club, the other did some waitressing and hooked at night. It was best to stay away from the homestead and not talk much when you had to be there.

"Hey, idiot! Go get me a beer," came the order, and Bubba trudged off to fetch a cold one for his brother, passing old man Chaney as he came in wearing grubby denim jeans and a plaid shirt with sweat rings and stains of unknown origin. Rufus Chaney had been a friend of Grams' back in the day. He was old, with a face that always looked like he hadn't shaved in a couple of weeks and a smell that made those near him gag a little and take a big step back. Chaney had some menial job a few hours a week and sometimes found a day or two of work for Bobby Jack. They spent a lot of time doing secret things, things they didn't discuss with anyone else. Bubba left behind for those, and he never questioned; that would have required more thinking than he could muster.

Old Rufus used to leer longingly at the sisters when they were young. Years ago, there had been frequent money exchanges between him and Grams and some odd comments from the girls, but Bobby Jack stayed out of that.

"Hey, Chaney," said Bobby Jack, in a barely tolerating tone, just audible over the noise.

"Hey, BJ," returned Chaney, chuckling.

Bobby Jack didn't like it when Chaney spoke his nickname because years ago, Chaney said it always made him think of a blow job. The nickname was OK coming from his family, but this dirty old man made everything around him just as dirty, and BJ got pissed just hearing Chaney's voice; that gurgly laugh gave him the creeps. Bobby Jack was disgusted by Chaney, but there was a weird attraction at the same time. For all he knew, Chaney could have been his grandfather or even father, for that matter. He hated being around him but just couldn't quit the habit.

Rufus whispered some things to Bobby Jack. Bobby Jack did some agitated whispering right back. The heated exchange went on for a few minutes, and then Chaney suggested that he and BJ should do some prospecting the following day before the garbage collection truck came around. They would ride through the wealthier neighborhoods in town to see what people had put out for the pickup.

Things like old appliances, furniture, fixtures, and even pieces of metal could be collected for scrap and resold for some quick cash. Shit, they'd found some real prime stuff last week and pawned it at the shop by the bar with the scrap metal going to the recycling plant. Got fifty dollars each for that haul, a good day indeed. He had the pawn receipt right here in his jacket pocket. It made him feel good to pull it out and look at it once in a while, even though the money was already long gone.

Bobby Jack nodded when Chaney said he'd be by to pick him up just before six in the morning. Old man Chaney shuffled off, covered in unseen black creatures, leaving Bobby Jack waiting for his beer and thinking about the events of the morning he spent with Chaney. Hard to believe it was just a little less than twelve hours ago. "What a damn mess," he thought, shaking his head.

Bubba was heading back to the pool table with a beer mug in one hand and a piece of paper in the other. When he reached Bobby Jack, he handed him the paper. "What does this say? Billy at the bar said it was a real sad thing and that lots a people were upset. What is it, Bobby Jack?" Bubba couldn't read at all, BJ had a limited vocabulary, so they just stared at the words beneath the big picture of a little girl, Bubba in innocence, Bobby Jack with growing uneasiness. Two creatures flew in and clamped into the shoulders of BJ, joining those already in place. A third sunk it's talons into the back of his neck.

And from a dark corner came a low and sinister chuckle, exhaled with a hot stinking breath smelling like sulfur.

~~~

Pauley

The boy was unresponsive. He was fourteen and had never spoken or looked anyone in the eye with any understanding, yet he displayed a keen savant-like intelligence. He didn't verbally acknowledge when spoken to, but the first time he sat at a piano, he played a short Mozart piece from a TV commercial with no sheet music. When he picked up a pool cue, he completely cleared the table with precision accuracy, and he consistently beat every highest score on the most popular war-themed video games. He did exceptionally well on those which required the player to wipe out evil characters with gruesome violence.

Pauley didn't fit into any school system. He hadn't gotten a formal diagnosis, but numerous medical and mental health professionals had given their best guesses. He seemed to defy all definitions and created his own unique category. Pauley was special. He was a palpable force without a final destination.

To look at his expressionless face was disturbing, but he was handsome. Dark and wavy hair framed a face that was soft with youth but would grow strong. He had a medium build, five foot four, but the promise of his father's height as he matured. If his eyes held warmth, he'd have been considered quite a hunk by the girls his age. Instead, he had no friends. No schoolmates. Only his father, David Kemper, was there for him day after day. Not that Pauley seemed to notice.

David was a single dad by fate, not by choice. Pauley's mother, Sylvia, died in a car accident when her baby was only two weeks old, though Pauley came out of it without a visible scratch. They were coming home from the grocery store and got broadsided on Sylvia's side by a driver who fell asleep at the wheel.

Describing their life as complicated would be a gross understatement. David's feelings fluctuated by the day, even by the hour. Pauley was not a child easy to love, but something in his face reminded David of the wife he so deeply adored, and he didn't give up hope, though that hope had worn very thin.

David was a long-distance truck driver fourteen years ago but needed a business that would allow him to remain at home to care for a baby after the accident. He sold his truck and opened a pawn shop located three doors down from Myrt's Bar and Grill. David and Pauley ate lunch there frequently, so the patrons were used to seeing David with Pauley following close behind. No one talked to Pauley anymore, though they tried way back when he was little. They knew now that Pauley wouldn't respond because he didn't know they were there, or he didn't care. It didn't make much difference one way or the other.

David was personable, though he remained private. Making a living in a pawn shop wasn't easy, but it was a good fit. It wasn't unusual for observers to compare him to a young Clint Eastwood in build and imposing toughness. Talking to him about business was fine, and he did welcome their business. But David wouldn't talk about his family. Speculations swirled regarding the accident and how Pauley became the way he was now. No one really knew anything; they just enjoyed having something to talk about.

Sylvia Kemper was a faith-filled and beautiful young woman. With her death, David went in the opposite direction. He could never resolve the issue in his mind and often wondered how God could have let these things happen, even after all of this time. "God" was not a word Pauley ever heard his father say unless it was followed by "damn!".

This Friday evening, David and Pauley were standing at the takeout counter waiting for the dinner they would carry home. Grandma Myrt always cooked a special meal for them. David was one of her favorites; she pitied him greatly for what life had dealt him. For him alone, she dropped her stern façade.

As the crowd grew and the layer of smoke haze deepened, something caught Pauley's attention. For the briefest second, he turned his head toward the back of the room, his face showing a hint of expression, and the wide pupils of his dark eyes reflected two tiny red flames. No one noticed, and then Pauley's face went blank again.

David picked up the plastic bag containing two dinners packed inside white Styrofoam, paid Grandma Myrt for the food, and turned toward the door. Pauley followed him out of the bar and into the darkening night. Outside, Pauley heard an unusual rustling up toward the bar's roof, but David heard nothing, and Pauley remained silent.

~~~

Crystal

The TV was on, one of the friendly faces of the local evening news channel was talking about something. She guessed that meant it was after six. A glance at the windows proved it true since the sky was a deep, ugly charcoal color.

She was having a hard time making anything much matter since she received the news of Jamie's death in Afghanistan, only a week after he'd left her arms. A cloud shadowed her happiness since that day. Her future changed with a single sentence uttered by one of the two soldiers in uniform standing at her door. He never got to know that he was going to be a father.

Crystal's parents lived in Florida. They wanted her to move there to be nearer to them, but she refused. Henderson County is where she grew up, the place she knew and loved. She had so many good childhood memories. Her mom and dad went south to start a new chapter of their lives that was right for them. But she wasn't ready for a retirement community yet.

Having passed thirty, she figured she'd never meet the right guy or have a family until less than a year ago. A friend invited her to a picnic. She almost didn't go but was guilted into it, so she dragged herself to the park, where she met Jamie. It was so weird because he was four years younger than she, but they hit it off from the first minute. Jamie had just begun his leave from the Marines. He'd already completed three tours but had re-upped for another. After just two more dates, they decided to marry before he was shipped out again. In her last memory, he waved goodbye as he boarded a plane. Only three months together, and he was gone.

Thank God she had so many friends and supportive family members to help her through the grief and keep her focused on the positives. Her belly rolled, and she felt a sharp kick, and that was the most significant positive of all. The baby, their baby, was all that remained of him in her life.

The due date was coming up in another few weeks; she hoped that this little one would look like her daddy. That sandy-colored hair and green eyes with a smattering of freckles across the cheeks. How much she missed his face. What a wonderful gift that would be.

> "...the 7.4 earthquake in Ecuador has devastated small towns within a twenty-mile radius of the epicenter on the northern coast. Severe aftershocks continue, and the death toll is up to three hundred and eighty as of five o'clock Central time today.
> And now, breaking news about a missing local girl."

She heard the words, and they registered. Anything having to do with children seemed to catch her attention immediately.

> "An Amber Alert has been issued for Becky Robbins, a

nine-year-old from Greenville, on the north side of
Henderson County. She left for school this morning but
never made it there and has been missing since seven
a.m....."

A sick feeling hit the pit of her stomach. How could anyone hurt a
child, an innocent baby? What was wrong with people? She didn't
know the family, but that didn't matter. This little one was in trouble,
and her eyes began to fill with tears again. She seemed to cry all of the
time now.

The phone rang. Crystal looked at it and let it ring a second time,
knowing that if she didn't pick it up, the caller wouldn't relent.

"Hello, Jill."

"Hi Crystal! I'm just checking in because I won't be available for a
while. Did you hear about the missing girl? It's all over the news."

Jill and Crystal bonded in second grade and had been fast friends
since. They shared everything; school, Sunday School, church, secrets
about other girls, fantasies about boyfriends, and hopes and dreams of
the future. A few months ago, Jill and her husband found a new
church that they loved. Inviting Crystal to join them was a weekly
thing, but Crystal hadn't attended a church since Jaimie died. Her
friend coaxed and cajoled, but Crystal wasn't ready, even if the pastor
was all of the things Jill claimed.

"I just heard it, Jill. It breaks my heart. Thank you for calling to check
on me. You don't know how much I appreciate you." The tears were
falling down her cheeks, and she didn't reach to wipe them away.
There she was, crying again.

"Several people from church are getting together to join search teams,
honey. We'll be out for a while, but I want you to know that I'll have
my cell phone with me. If you need ANYTHING, please don't hesitate
to call." Jill was such a dear person who cared, really cared, about
everyone.

"I'll be just fine. I wish I could help too. Please let me know if there's any news. Love you."

"Love you too, girl. We'll talk later, get some rest, and eat your dinner! You've been too lax on your meals, and that baby needs food! Bye, honey."

"Bye," Crystal pushed the off button and set the phone down. Some stupid game show was starting. She laboriously rose from the couch and went to the kitchen to warm up a plate of the casserole Jill dropped off earlier that afternoon. So many of her neighbors and friends were still going out of their way to take care of her. She felt blessed despite her sadness.

The bell rang on the microwave. She took her plate and headed back to the couch with a glass of milk to watch a movie. A comedy, something to lighten her mood, but the heavy feeling of oppression lingered, and she mentally whispered prayers for all of the children of the world.

Three creatures dug their talons back into her shoulders as soon as she finished praying. Fear, Self-Pity, and Hopelessness were doing a fine job with this one. Backsliding faith left room for demons of doubt; a little whispered prayer didn't deter them.

~~~

Tom

He'd been pulled off the missing child investigation and dispatched at about six p.m. on a domestic dispute. It was no longer in progress, but the neighbor who called the Sheriff's Department said they needed a deputy. Several other police officers and deputies searched for the little girl. Tom took this call.

He knocked on the apartment door at the reported address, and the neighbor answered, ushering him in. A woman sat there with an eye that was blackening quickly. Her nose was bloody and slightly askew, probably broken. She still wore a stained waitress uniform from her day job, but it now had smears of blood on it as well. What the hell was wrong with people?

She answered his questions through swollen lips. Her drunken boyfriend had given her a face bashing because she made a comment he didn't like. She kept repeating how it was her fault. How many times had Deputy Tom Dempsey seen this kind of thing? Far too many to count, unfortunately, the abuser and the enabler. Sickness, it was all an evil sickness.

Tom felt so fortunate to have Beth. He'd started to get a little too heavy into the booze himself, and then he met her through a friend. The first thing Tom noticed was her curly ginger-colored hair and freckles. She was refreshing, bubbly, joyful, and he wanted to share in all of those things when he looked into her hazel eyes. Beth was so colorful compared to his bland shades of brown. Two years ago, she said she would marry him; together, they started a great future.

Having that balance helped him to get through the days like today. People beating up on people, children missing, and the horrible things that humans do to each other. It was enough to make one lose all faith in the goodness of mankind.

Beth was there for him in that department too. Her family was active in their community and their church. A great group of loving and caring people who had welcomed him into their fold with open arms. A bit of a change from the indifference of his own family. He was pleased to be where he was in life.

The woman, Peggy Baker, would not press charges or even give her boyfriend's name, so there was nothing he could do except file the report. He couldn't even call her an ambulance; she refused the medical assistance. When he left, the neighbor was still trying to convince her to go to the hospital, but Peggy didn't want to cause any trouble. That woman will probably end up dead; he thought to himself as he drove away.

After reporting to the dispatcher and receiving directions to rejoin the search in progress, he snuck in a call to Beth.

"Hi, hon. Just letting you know that I'll be late tonight. We're all working on the missing girl case."

"I knew you would be, sweetheart. We're all praying for a good ending and your safety. Love you." He could hear the love in her voice, and the reassurance would bolster him for the rest of the evening. "Love you too," and he switched off the communication.

Life was a complex thing; Tom thought as he clicked on the flashing lights and pushed on the gas pedal to get back to the urgent task at hand. There was no moon, making the prospects of finding a little girl all the more difficult. He didn't notice that there weren't any stars shining either.

Above him, dark creatures continued to arrive, filling the night sky and adding to the palpable gloom. A foreboding was beginning to seep into the population of Henderson County.

~~~

Luke

In a small neighborhood church on the east side of town, a middle-aged pastor sat in one of the old, smoothly worn, wooden pews with his head bowed. He wore jeans and a T-shirt that boldly stated, "Jesus is not my Religion, He's my Salvation."

Luke was not a stereotypical pastor. He had initiated a new wave of participation in the little church by welcoming people in whatever clothing they chose to wear and offering up praise to upbeat contemporary Christian music. Luke's messages were of love and salvation, not fire and brimstone damnation. The membership was growing, and it included people from all walks of life.

As soon as you walked through the set of arched wooden doors, you could feel the difference; it was physically perceptible, many actually got goosebumps. The place was alive with the Spirit.

Luke hadn't come from a line of pastors; in fact, his life had been on the other end of the spectrum. He understood dysfunction and emptiness. He was the perfect example of God using people right where they are to serve the greater purpose. Luke and God came together at a very low point in Luke's life, and it had been upward and onward since. He was here in this church because of the circumstances and opportunities laid out for him. Still a single man, his life was complete, and he knew that the perfect woman for him would cross his path when the time was right. God's timing, not his, was a lesson learned a long time ago.

Tonight, he was sat in a pew praying for little Becky. Just this morning, she disappeared on her way to school. At this moment there were hundreds of people looking for her. He knew the horrors which could befall an innocent little one in the hands of evil. Part of Luke's ministry was in the county jail; he also did short outreach stints once a month in the state prison with some dangerous men. And so, he prayed hard.

The front doors stayed open to let passersby know that everyone was welcome, even though it was late and other churches were closed and locked. Golden light spilled out of the windows, just plain light to the human eye, but holy light to eyes that could see it. Luke thought he felt a presence as if someone had entered. Opening his eyes, he turned to scan the back of the room. There was no one to be seen. Instead of feeling eerie, his heart filled with peace and calm. He resumed his prayers, thinking he was alone, but *they* continued to enter through the front door in total silence. Soon the little church was filled to capacity with translucent beings clad in heavenly armor, each at least seven feet tall, with enormous wings spread in an arc of protection surrounding the praying pastor. Unaware, he prayed on for Becky to be found and for the safety and salvation of Gibson Glenn.

A car traveled down the street in front of the church. Pauley looked out the window as they passed, his face bathed in the light flowing from the doorway. His eyes grew wide with instant knowing, and within him, a switch clicked on, sparking the energy which would grow to be a force beyond understanding.

The car continued down the street, David deep in thought while he drove, not noticing the change in Pauley. Pauley's mouth gaped slightly open, still staring out the window. Life flickered in his eyes.

The large, winged guardian at the front door of the church watched the car disappearing into the distance and smiled, saying softly, "Welcome, Brother Pauley!"

5

Friday Night

THE BURNER phone rang at six-ten p.m., and he immediately picked it up when the agent saw who was calling. "Yes, Senator, sir, I've completed your instructions to the letter, sir. Thank you for entrusting me, but I assumed you'd be at the fundraiser."

"They'll wait for me. I want to be absolutely certain that this plan is in action and that I am in no way whatsoever connected to it."

"Yes sir, absolutely sir. I am the only person aside from you who can connect the dots. All the other players know their role, but no one knows anything about each other or you. Their further instructions are programmed to go to them at the appropriate times through an automated system."

"Keep it that way. Now dispose of this phone and do not call me for anything. You have an emergency contact who will go through other channels to alert me if need be. Otherwise, we've never spoken to each other. Got it?"

"Yes, sir. Goodnight, sir."

The agent clicked off the cell phone and left the building. He quickly removed the SIM card, which contained all the burner phone activity records, from the cell phone, put it into his pocket, and tossed the phone in a sewer grate. The SIM required more thorough destruction. His car was only a few feet away now. Relieved that this complicated covert operation was over, he thought about getting home early to his family on Friday night. They would be pleasantly surprised. This senator was going places, and to be in his trusted circle could mean promotions to come.

He smiled to himself as he opened the door, sat down, and turned the key in the ignition. His earthly consciousness ended with the earsplitting explosion. In a flaming inferno, a ball of searing red and yellow erupted into the night sky, shattering car windows and sending metal and glass flying in a two-hundred-yard diameter. The SIM card melted beyond recognition, along with the agent's body, both gone forever.

~~~

Kasey finished cleaning off the empty tables just before midnight. She stood up and stretched, tossing her straight blond hair over her shoulders. Even though Gram kept the place open till two a.m., Kasey was allowed to leave earlier since there were child labor laws. There was still a full bar and noisy activity at the pool tables. The drunks could get rough about this time of night, but Gram didn't tolerate fights, and no one messed with Grandma Myrt and Billy.

It was a little chilly outside, so she wrapped her jacket around her shoulders as she headed for her rusty '95 Malibu. Gram helped her get it last year to drive to and from work and school, and it then became her responsibility to transport Trisha.

The car was parked at the far end of the lot, a short block from the bar. Outside of the streetlight glow, the shadows were more profound than she could ever remember, somehow ominous. A tiny flashlight on her key chain helped her get to the door without tripping.

She revved the engine and pulled out into the empty street, fresh air invigorating her as it flowed in through the open window, bathing her face in coolness. At least she wouldn't fall asleep while driving.

As she rounded the corner to her street about fifteen minutes later, she saw the light coming from the doors and windows of the church. Why in the world would there still be anyone there at this time of night? She drove past it and parked in her space in front of the apartment building.

Trisha should be sleeping, so there was no hurry. Kasey crossed the quiet street and slowly walked up to the open door. Was the glow exceptionally bright, or was it just the contrast to the moonless night? Standing in the doorway, it took a few minutes to focus, and then she saw a man. He was sitting in a pew with his head bowed, so still she couldn't tell if he was breathing.

Just as she was preparing to leave, he turned and saw her, offering her a wide smile. "I'm not sure how long I've been sitting here or what time it is, but you're welcome to come in. I'm Pastor Luke." His friendliness was disarming, and she couldn't help smiling back. He was nice looking for an older man and not dressed like someone in charge of a church.

"Thank you, I live across the street and am just getting home from work. I saw your lights on and thought I'd make sure everything was OK. I've never seen anyone here at midnight." The little black creature had held on to her shoulder as long as it could, but when she stepped into the church, it let go and sped into the night with a shriek she couldn't hear.

"How thoughtful of you," he answered sincerely. "Is it really that late – wow! Have I seen you here before?"

"No, sir. I've heard your music, though, and really like it. I don't know much about church. I've never been." This truth embarrassed her, and she looked down at her feet rather than meet his gentle gaze.

"Well, young lady, I'd consider it a favor if you'd join us this Sunday morning. It would be my pleasure to introduce you to some of our members who, I'm sure, will make you feel very welcome. We're a very comfortable and caring family here, and we'd love to see your smiling face."

She looked up and smiled again. "I'll try, thank you. I have to be getting back to my little sister now. Goodnight." She turned and walked back to her building, climbing the stairs slowly to the second-floor door.

After she was ready for bed, she took another look out of her window to see the lights still shining. There was an odd blur of light in a circle around the building. It must be her tired eyes. She rested her hand on her belly, and the baby rolled gently.

~~~

Jake staggered out of the bar at one a.m. with Sarah; neither could stand on their own, and both barely made it, even leaning on each other. Sarah's place was around the block, and they headed in that direction, through the alley. Their swearing, banging into trash cans, and raucous laughter would have woken the dead, but most who lived in this area had passed out cold.

They reached her door, got it open, and fell inside. Jake made it a few more feet and collapsed on the floor. Sarah made it as far as the couch before unconsciousness won out. The stench of booze breath and alcoholic residue seeping out of sweaty pores was overwhelming, but it was not unusual at Sarah's tiny apartment.

~~~

Rufus Chaney shuffled out to his van in the privacy of deep darkness and slid open the side door. He heaved the dark green lawn-sized garbage bag over his shoulder, staggering under the weight. It was so much easier when he was young. Damn, it was a bitch getting old.

"Cleanin' up, always cleanin' up. This van needs to be empty for tomorrow mornin' when I pick up Bobby Jack for some prospectin'. Next time I'm makin that boy clean up his own mess. He's young and strong; why the hell not!" he said out loud to no one in particular.

His mind drifted to the last time he was mixed up in this kind of thing. He and his younger sister's son, Jonathon, played around with a couple of fresh young things from the old neighborhood. That was forty years ago. Rufus was thirty-nine, and his nephew a good twenty years younger. One thing had led to another on that night too. It ended up with them having to dump two bodies in the river. The girls' bodies were found, but they were never connected to Rufus and Jonathon. Damn! Jonathon was good at all that cover-up stuff. He was smart, as Rufus recalled. But he drowned in that swimming accident in the lake. That happened in Jackson County the next Fourth of July after the incident with the girls. Some fisherman found his body a few days later. Hmmm. He hadn't thought about that for a long time, but now his mind flashed over to a metal box they buried. Something about safer keeping was nagging at him, but he couldn't remember.

Then he refocused on things much more current. That was some fine young flesh he scoped out after meeting Bobby Jack at the bar earlier tonight. Imagine just stumbling into a goldmine like that! A Girl Scout troop camping out in the woods near town. He'd have to go back and look at that again, maybe tomorrow after the clean-up was all said and done. He heaved the garbage bag onto the dirt floor of his shed and closed the rickety door.

Two blood-red eyes shone in the blackness of the moldy-smelling shed. And then they dissolved into the inky night.

~~~

Crystal woke abruptly at three a.m. after tossing and turning restlessly, in the throes of a nightmare. An ominous black vulture-like creature had been hovering over her baby girl, with talons out, ready to snatch her from her cradle. The smells were of what she'd imagined hell would be like, intense heat and rotten eggs. Then her baby morphed into a beautiful little child, shrinking in terror from the numerous creatures which had suddenly appeared. Crystal was screaming, but no sounds came from her throat. Then she sat up, realizing the baby was rolling and kicking with great force.

Beyond her vision, a massive golden warrior materialized beside her, sent by prayers of her friend Jill, and the horrid little demons let loose of her shoulders and fled in terror.

She panted and wrapped her arms around her abdomen, and the baby quieted. Calmness returned, and peace prevailed; she said a prayer of thanks for the safety of herself and her baby. Her thoughts ran to Jamie and how she missed him. She didn't remember ever having a bad dream during the short time he was by her side. "Oh, Jamie, how I wish you were here." It wasn't fair that they had hardly even gotten to know each other.

She leaned back against the pillows and closed her eyes. Within minutes she was sleeping soundly. The warrior with shimmering wings who stood guard next to her bed bent over and stroked her hair, and she sighed.

~~~

At four a.m, Tom entered his front door, exhausted to the bone. He and the others had continued the search with flashlights and huge floodlights until they couldn't move another muscle. They were relieved by a new group of officers and volunteers brought in from the surrounding counties. He had orders to sleep for eight hours before reporting back after lunch. Hopefully, the daylight would produce better results, and they would find her by then.

He crawled into bed quietly so he wouldn't disturb Beth. She reached her arm around his shoulders when he settled and snuggled closely. Almost immediately, she resumed her soft purrs of sleep, and he lost consciousness.

Out on the front lawn stood the sentinel. The stars remained blocked from view by the black sky, filled with multitudes of things far thicker than air.

6

Puzzle Pieces

LUKE POURED his second cup of coffee just before six. God had kept him wide awake and in prayer all night. He was starting to feel the weariness in his bones, so the hot coffee was good—time to check the news for any updates on the search for Becky.

> "...so, the speculation is rampant as to who will throw their hat into the ring for next year's Presidential election, still fourteen months away. We can be sure that there will be plenty of announcements within the next sixty days, though. Rumors of secret talks between the RNC and a certain prominent Senator are flying, so stay tuned as we bring you the latest as it happens."
>
> "A car explosion shook Arlington, Virginia last night, in a parking lot right outside of the Pentagon. The Department of Defense and local law enforcement are investigating. Though not confirmed, it appears at this time that the vehicle may have belonged to a DCIS agent."
>
> "On a local note, searchers are still combing fields and forests for the missing nine-year-old girl in Henderson County. A Sheriff's Dept. representative tells us that

roadblocks have been in place since yesterday. We'll keep you up to date...."

Luke clicked off the TV; his prayers, and those of hundreds of others, placed Becky in God's hands. The search would go on, and they would do everything humanly possible to find her, but in his heart, he well knew that God's answers to our prayers aren't always the answers we want. His job as a pastor was to support the flock in rejoicing if Becky was found and returned home safely. His job was also to offer and lead the comfort needed if the result differed. Luke prepared himself for both scenarios.

Several of his church members were volunteers in the search, so he awaited firsthand accounts from them. Taking his coffee in hand, he walked to the front of the church, realizing that the doors were still wide open. He glanced outside through the predawn gloom, and his eyes fell on the apartment building across the street. Remembering the young and very pregnant girl with the sad blue eyes who had stopped by at midnight, he said a short prayer for her safety.

Putting his other thoughts aside, he became fully aware of the odd weather and lack of light. It seemed strange. He made a mental note to watch the weather report. If storms were predicted, that wouldn't help the search crews. Shaking his head, he closed the doors, leaving them unlocked for visitors, and headed back to the kitchen. As he walked, he recalled the words of his friend, Gabe, saying that the next battle would be right here. His hand unconsciously went to the front of his shirt and rubbed the spot where the long scar marked his chest.

The translucent Guards, now repositioned on the church's roof, waited. Some stood, some sat, but all were vigilant. Inaction was not something they cared for, but they had orders. Big things were coming, and it was their duty to stand fast until they heard the sound of the trumpet. Everything was falling into place.

Angels have their ranks and distinct duties, as in any army. There are three types of angelic beings within each of the three groups of angels, called Choirs. Those in the top two Choirs deal more with personally attending to God's directives and keeping peace in the Cosmos. They also assist with miracles and can appear to humans in earthly form.

The third Choir is known best to humanity, containing the Archangels and Angels. Archangels guide the entire world, in charge of managing the earthly duties of the Angels below them in rank. Michael, Gabriel, and Raphael were calling the shots on every battleground around the globe.

Angels, of the type sent to Henderson County, are guardians of people and everything physical. They protect and warn, as well as act as warriors on God's behalf. These are the armies sent to save the New Ones from extinction. These are the heavenly comrades of the Swordsman.

The most prominent Angel stood and watched as an old white van came down the street and passed the church. He could hardly see the van for the number of black creatures clinging to it. His hand automatically went to the hilt of his sword, but he stood his ground and didn't engage.

~~~

Chaney pulled into the grass driveway of the shack where Bobby Jack lived. He was a few minutes early, and the house looked quiet. The door opened, BJ emerged.

The passenger door creaked as he opened it to get in, and he reached to brush empty cans and crumpled cigarette packs off the seat and onto the floor so he could sit. They'd been out garbage picking on several occasions, and usually, each ended up with some spending money for their efforts. But this morning, there was tension in the air.

Bobby Jack didn't like the dirty old man, but he sure did enjoy a good roll in the hay. BJ just preferred his women to be older, while Chaney was lusty for the little ones. No matter what age they chose, the agreement had been that dogs don't shit in their own cages. If they were going to go trawling, it would be on one of their trips out of the area where no one knew them. Right now, he was pissed at Chaney, and at himself, for breaking the rules here in their own county. Now they were walking a tightrope, and he was nervous.

"Let's get goin' before those garbage bastards get all the good stuff," Chaney muttered.

"I don't much feel like prospectin' today, Chaney; in fact, I don't much feel like bein' around you at all. You broke the rules yesterday, and now we're in deep shit."

"You're a wimp, you asshole. If you hadn't lost your temper...."

"Wait a minute! That was all your idea, you fat old pre-vert," BJ interrupted, opening the door to get out.

"Get back in here! Now is as good a time as any to get the clean-up done. Might even be the best time with the garbage trucks comin' and all." Chaney grumbled, starting the engine. "It'll still be dark for a bit; we'll get down the road and outta town before we dump the garbage."

"Dump your own garbage, old man!"

"Oh no, you don't, we're in this together, and you're stronger than I am," Chaney shot back at BJ.

Bobby Jack settled back into the seat, rubbing the injury to his hand, knowing he was part of it whether he wanted to be or not. Chaney backed the van up and headed toward his place. They had to pay a visit to his shed before finishing this job.

The black things swarmed all around the shack and the van like flies on roadkill. From a distance, one of the Guard Angels sat listening in the top branches of a tree, and a tear rolled down its cheek. One of the smaller non-warrior beings from the Second Choir had already escorted the soul of little Becky to her Heavenly Father yesterday. For that, there was great joy and rejoicing. The Angel's tear was for the sadness left behind.

~~~

Through the night, state and local police saturated the area between Becky's home and the elementary school she attended. Her family paced and waited for hopeful news. Media trucks and police vehicles were parked everywhere, and reporters were grabbing the few gawkers awake at this hour off the street just to have someone to talk to on the air.

The cooperation of law enforcement organizations leading the search operations allowed their efforts to proceed smoothly. Everyone focused on a positive result. With many volunteers, a lot of ground was getting covered. The Sheriff's Department decided to set up roadblocks on all major roadways in and out of the county shortly after the original missing report came in, just in case someone tried to run. Trunks would be checked on every vehicle leaving the county as well. They would face swift justice if someone had taken this girl, but finding Becky was the priority.

~~~

Chaney pulled around the back of his dilapidated trailer and right up to the shed. "Now get right in there, grab the big bag on the floor, and toss it into the back of the van here," he ordered. BJ scowled but followed his directions.

There were dozens of dark creatures cackling and drooling with delight as they watched the scene unfolding from their perches on the rooftop and in the trees. The demons riding the backs and shoulders of BJ prodded him to anger and hatred, and bitterness against Chaney. He swore under his breath that he would get back at the old man for treating him like dirt. BJ hoisted the sack onto his back and dumped it into the van with a thump, slamming the doors shut. He was angrier that he couldn't do anything about Chaney than he was about having to do the task at hand.

Once loaded, Chaney turned the van south to get across the county line as quickly as possible. His aim: get to the nearest convenience store where no one would notice them tossing garbage into the dumpster.

The southern county line was only about ten miles from Rufus' place, and they were nearing it now. Approaching a curve in the road, Chaney spotted the blue and red lights flashing through the trees and brought the van to a halt, clicking off the headlights. "Damn and shit to hell!" he cursed. "They've set up a roadblock! Get back there, get that bag outta the back, and haul it over to those woods, fast! I'll turn around and be ready for you."

BJ didn't even question. He jumped out and grabbed the bag, dumping it about ten feet into the tree line, then ran back and jumped into the passenger seat. Chaney chugged off as fast as he could make the old van move, not putting the headlights back on until they'd gone a full mile down the road. Bobby Jack never realized that something had fallen from his pocket when he dropped the bag.

The Winged Warrior stood beside the bag, calmly smiling, watching Bobby Jack retreat. His mission was to follow the murderous humans and act upon anything which might bring information to those investigating. It had been easy for him to dislodge the pawnshop receipt from the jacket pocket. And no demons dared to be close enough to the warrior to see what had happened. Those attached to BJ had temporarily abandoned him when the Angel stepped in. He shot into the air like a meteor, returning to his superior with the news that his task was complete.

~~~

Chaney left BJ at his place and turned around to go back home. That boy did nothing but squawk the entire time. What a wasted morning. He wondered if he should just go prospecting by himself but thought better of it. His back just wouldn't hold up to a lot of heavy liftin', and it was too late for that now anyway. The garbage trucks were already doing their morning runs, and the sky was lightening to a thick and eerie yellowish gray.

Slightly more than twenty-four hours had passed since Becky was pulled into an old white van by two men.

It was Saturday, there was a mall the next county over, and kids liked to hang out there on weekends. Chaney had plenty of time for breakfast at the Waffle House before going there for what he called 'window shoppin''. The arcade didn't open till nine a.m. anyway.

He turned off the dirt road and onto the state highway, heading east. Twenty minutes later, he approached the county line and got to the roadblock attended by a lone trooper. There wasn't any other eastbound traffic at that time of the morning, and Chaney's heart began to pound hard. The trooper glanced inside through the driver's window and let Chaney pass. As the old man accelerated to leave the roadblock, he chuckled, feeling a bit cocky and quite empowered, like he could get away with anything.

He didn't notice when he passed a nondescript camper heading in the other direction.

7

The Swordsman

THE ANCIENT motor home traveled west on the state road from Interstate Highway 35, the closest interstate to Henderson County that connected to I40 coming from southern California. If Chaney had looked, he'd have seen that there was a single occupant, a very large man who appeared to be over forty. His heavily muscled six-foot-six frame filled the driver's space with no room to spare. His longish dark hair already showed gray streaks, adding to the look of concentrated seriousness displayed in the lines of his solemn face.

Gabe Matheson had come to Henderson County to deal with another "situation." And he was concentrating intensely on the days to come, but not so deeply that he didn't notice Chaney's white van covered in black creatures with blazing red eyes, traveling east. Gabe was one of a select few humans who had the gift of multi-dimensional vision, but neither humans nor demons knew that about him. That van was a problem that could wait; it wasn't his first order of business here.

First up was getting together with his college buddy, Luke. They had a lot of work ahead of them, and he knew he'd be here for at least several days. The looming battle gave him great concern.

~~~

A few church members came by to update Luke on the search for little Becky. Unfortunately, nothing was gained for all of the work they'd done, and she was still missing. They were weary and discouraged, and they left to return to their own homes for much-needed rest and recharging. The longer this search went on, the more troubling it became, and the greater the probability grew that the child wouldn't be found alive.

Luke stood in the church's front door, watching them drive away when he saw the old RV. It was both a welcome sight and an ominous one. That camper meant that Gabe was here, and when Gabe arrived, big trouble was already in the making.

They'd spoken by phone two days earlier, so Luke knew what was coming, and it wasn't unexpected. He'd felt the growing dark presence in the town. The war of Principalities goes on, and Gabe was one of the strongest of God's human warriors. He had the innate ability to know where he was needed. Or maybe it was just his hotline to heaven. The experience they'd shared in college had been the turn in the road for both of them, leading them into different directions but each in ways to serve God.

Luke waved, and Gabe pulled into the parking lot, landing the camper at the back, facing the church building. Gabe unfolded his large frame, emerging from the driver's door with a big sigh and half-grin. Despite the dire circumstances, it was good to see his longtime friend. "Hey, Luke! It looks like we're in for a tough time again. Are you with me?"

Luke unconsciously rubbed his chest where his shirt hid the scar. They approached each other, extended hands for a hearty shake, and then moved closer for a brotherly embrace. "Gabe, you know I'm always ready to stand beside you," replied Luke sincerely. They were more than brothers in Christ and good friends; they were comrades.

A dozen more of Archangel Michael's warriors arrived and took their places on the church's grounds. Shudders went through the ranks of the on-looking demons; the grins of the dark leaders suddenly weren't quite as confidant. They knew Gabe as a formidable enemy who frequently thwarted their plans. At the moment, that was all. One lower-ranking creature shot into the air on a mission to relay the information to the lords that the despised Swordsman had arrived.

~~~

Kasey peered out of her window from across the street to see the two men in the churchyard. She didn't have to be at the bar for work till ten a.m., so breakfast and laundry were on her agenda. For some reason, looking at these men, the pastor Kasey met last night, and the stranger who stood a full six inches taller than Pastor Luke, she felt the warmth of complete security well up within her. She lingered a moment more to relish the unfamiliar emotion and then went in to wake Trisha.

~~~

Gabe glanced around the grounds before following Luke across the lawn to the kitchen door of the pastor's apartment. He acknowledged the Host gathered around with an almost imperceptible nod and received subtle signs of recognition in return. Gabe looked to the sky and saw the growing number of black flapping wings blocking out the sun. This would be a big battle, but he was sure that the ultimate victory would be theirs. Not an easy one, though, and that meant casualties.

That was always the hard part for Gabe. It is not so much for those souls leaving to spend eternity with the Father, but for those who would remain eternally lost because they refuse to accept grace or redemption. It hurt him more than the numerous wounds he'd received over the years. He always felt responsible, though He'd learned in his early days of battle that changing the outcome wasn't within his realm of effect. God had the plan, man had free will, and Gabe's job was to fulfill his role.

Luke was already turning the burner on, and the frying pan was ready.

He had expected his friend's arrival, knowing how he could survive and continue with so little downtime. Gabe pulled out a chair and settled at the table, both hungry and a little weary. It was a twenty-four-hour drive from the west coast where his last battle took place, and he drove straight through, taking only a few hours for a nap at an interstate rest stop. There was always another town with different faces but the same enemy to battle in this unending war. He had developed friendships with other spiritual warriors throughout the country, but he and Luke had a deep and special bond.

Their first joint encounter during college was when he realized he had the gift of vision crossing dimensions. It was the pivotal point in his life, the place when Gabe devoted his life to God's service, not to a woman and family. The war, it seemed, only he could see. Luke was his confidant and comrade; he had told Luke everything about that day and what he'd seen. No one else was ever privy to his secret. Knowing that several dimensions exist simultaneously was a huge concept to grasp. At first, Gabe thought that he'd lost all grip on reality. Then he understood that he was the only one who knew the actual truth.

Gabe since met only two others in his travels who were like himself. One, a man in his eighties who'd fought hard and long. Gabe was there for the man's last battle. He went out slashing demons into oblivion, having earned his eternal rest.

The other was a woman. She was a teacher in her thirties. You would never imagine the strength she possessed to look at her, but she was a protector of children. Gabe had witnessed her in battle, and she was fierce. Lesser demons cowered in her presence, and greater Demon Lords sought the celebrity of being the one that would bring her down, a feat not yet accomplished as equally fierce warriors of the Host accompanied her.

Why the Father had chosen these few to receive the gift was not something any had time to ponder. Their time was better spent using their powers to accomplish their assigned tasks. Divine sight came with a hefty responsibility.

Luke placed a heaping hot plate of ham, eggs, and fried potatoes with mushrooms and onions on the table in front of Gabe. "Your favorite, my friend." Luke smiled.

The warm and enticing aroma reminded Gabe that he was here, in the flesh, and his flesh needed nourishment. A fresh pot of coffee completed the fare.

"You haven't said a word while I cooked. Thoughts far away and already making plans for this trouble coming? Do you know what direction it will come from or what form it will take this time?" Luke asked between bites.

"Not yet, but I saw a van traveling east that I'm guessing is a part of the picture; demons covered every inch. And there was a roadblock at the county line. What happened here since we last talked?"

"A little girl went missing yesterday morning, Gabe. The whole county is looking for her. No sign of her yet, though. The congregation has been praying and volunteering to search in shifts."

"Your church property abounds with warrior angels," said Gabe. "And the sky is filling with fighter demons. I saw many of the large higher-ranking commanders on my way into town. This is going to be a big one, and the little girl is probably part of it too."

"I knew the weather looked strange. I guess the darkness of the creatures can somehow seep into our dimension, giving the sky an ominous look like the past couple of days." Luke didn't relish another battle like the one he'd shared with Gabe back in college. It had almost cost him his life. They'd kept in close contact since then, and Luke knew that Gabe had been through many more, but he, himself, had only experienced that one. And it was terrifying.

"We need to start with some scouting and research." Gabe continued, "That will give us an idea of how much time we have and how massive and strategic this battle will be. Then we'll need to rally the saints and organize prayer vigils. Things are OK for right now though, it's still early. And in my experience, this is the time when we're supposed to get rested up. There won't be time for it later."

"Then let me show you to your room. You can sleep and get cleaned up on your schedule. Just let me know when you're ready to start and what you want me to do. Till then, I have some calls to make, a few hours of sleep to catch up on myself, and preaching to prepare for tomorrow's Sunday service." Luke led the way to the spare room of his apartment, where he left Gabe before grabbing his cell phone and the list of his congregation members and their phone numbers.

The church could always on Jill and her husband when needed, and right now, he needed someone to hang out at the church while he and Gabe caught up on their sleep. Knowing that the enormous golden warriors Gabe had once described now guarded the church grounds allowed him to relax in the face of impending danger. He dialed her number.

Jill arrived within thirty minutes and took over the task of communications between volunteers still searching for Becky. Luke retreated to his room, where sleep engulfed him within minutes of his head hitting the pillow.

On the rooftop of the little church, the ever-watchful and protective warriors sat, alert to danger but knowing that the time for battle had not yet arrived. There were still several pieces missing from the picture, and the fighting never started until the picture was complete.

8

Saturday Morning

SATURDAY MORNING, a great day for being outside. The mid-September air was losing its summer humidity, and even though it was weirdly overcast, it was still warm enough to spend the morning riding trails on backwoods toys. A couple of senior boys from the high school fired up their ATVs and headed into the south county woods; it had the best trails for full terrain experience. Hills, a couple of creeks, and all kinds of obstacles were awaiting their arrival, so the boys wasted no time.

~~~

Bobby Jack sat on the porch with his feet propped up on the railing when his ma emerged from their ramshackle home. He was deep in thought about the problem and what to do about it. Though BJ knew she would be royally pissed, he also knew his ma was shrewd and could figure a way out of anything. He just decided to tell her when he looked up and found that she was standing in front of him.

"What's yer problem, Bobby Jack?" She beat him to the punch. "Yer lookin' pretty long in the face, son. You in trouble with the law again?"

"Old Rufus got me into a tight place, Ma, and I can't figure how to get out. No trouble with the law yet, but it could go that way."

"Damn, Bobby Jack! That old pre-vert is bad news, and you know it! What the hell have you gotten inta now?"

Bobby Jack proceeded to tell her about Friday morning with Chaney. "We started out on a can-finding trip on the north end of the county Just wanted some recycling cash. Rufus saw a girl walkin' alone to school and dared me to open the sliding door and pull her in when he slowed down. Ma, he swore he'd just drop her a block from the school and not hurt her. He just wanted to cop a feel to get his day started off good. You know how he is. The old man can't use his crank any more, so he gets off just lookin' and sometimes grabbin' at the young stuff."

"We weren't gonna hurt her, so I saw no harm in it – we weren't close to home, but not across the county line where he usually likes to go. I climbed between the seats to the back and did what Chaney told me to. When he pulled the van over and hollered out the window to the girl, somethin' about finding his lost dog, she walked over to the van. I slid the door open and grabbed her around the middle, and then shut the door real quick."

"I tried to tell her we weren't gonna hurt her, but she screamed. I held her down on the floor, and she screamed louder and tried to kick me too. So I put my hand over her mouth, and she bit me hard, and it started bleedin'.

"Chaney turned around in his seat, grabbin' the girl and makin' it all worse. My hand kept bleedin', and it was getting all over the girl and her clothes. Chaney was almost slobberin' and gettin' all excited like. I hauled off and punched the girl in the head, hard, just to shut her up, but her neck snapped. Chaney just kept grabbin' till I yelled at him to stop."

Bobby Jack continued the memory in his head. Then, the blame started; each pointed his finger at the other for fault. They argued till Chaney realized they had to get out of the neighborhood before things got hot. He fired up the van and drove as quickly as he could. Bobby Jack then told his ma about dumping the bag this morning at the south edge of the county inside the tree line because of the roadblock.

Ma listened through the story and then smacked BJ upside the head. "You damn fool! Neither one of you has the brains of a tree stump! We got to git out there and git rid a that body. Some nature lovin' tree hugger is gonna find that thing, and there'll be hell to pay! As soon as it gets dark tonight, we're headin' out there to fix this shit!"

BJ was relieved. Ma was in charge now. The bat-like demons perched on the shoulders of both Ma and BJ had their talons firmly entrenched in flesh, and filthy yellow grins stretched across their grotesque faces.

~~~

David set the plate of pancakes on the kitchen table and went to get Pauley for breakfast. Pancakes were the one breakfast he enjoyed, so David made them every Saturday before going to the pawnshop.

He opened the bedroom door and found Pauley at his desk, working feverishly over something. David was immediately curious. He didn't remember ever seeing this kind of determination in Pauley. Almost everything he did was emotionless and robot-like; even his piano playing was beautiful but energy efficient. David stepped closer, being careful not to startle his son, and instead, he was the one who was surprised.

Pauley was working on a sketch. His room always had a supply of paper, crayons, markers, and pencils, but David never saw him draw. The picture was of a dark, demonic, hideous creature cowering before a winged angelic giant clad in warrior attire. David was stunned.

Pauley stopped, put the pencil down, and looked up at David, making eye to eye contact. David forgot to breathe.

~~~

Chores finished, Kasey and Trisha left the apartment at nine-thirty. Trisha went to the library for a homework assignment, and Kasey was to be at the bar and grill at ten to help prepare the lunch menu. Several people milled about in the front yard of the little church. Kasey wondered why.

Then she remembered Pastor Luke's invitation for tomorrow morning and thought she just might take him up on it. She was curious about Christians and that stranger she saw earlier too. She felt drawn to them, sensing protection and peace. Whatever motivated her, she would go with it and see where it led. Her life needed to get better. Maybe the church people had the answer.

It was a good thing the little fire-eyed demon on her shoulder couldn't read her thoughts, a skill reserved only for the highest-ranking Princes and even then, only applied to their specific charges. Shudders would have seized this little demon at Kasey's intentions. It had already been dragged up to that church once and wouldn't relish a repeat of the pain inflicted from the mere proximity.

~~~

Crystal woke from a comfortable sleep as if she was emerging from a warm bubble bath. Relaxed and refreshed and soothed, things she hadn't felt in quite a long time. And she was hungry.

She dressed and called Jill's cell phone to see how the search was going. Although she couldn't get out there and walk long distances, she might help on another front. And maybe she and Jill could have breakfast before they got started.

Crystal dialed, and Jill answered on the second ring. "Hi Crystal, glad you called me. How're you doing this morning?"

"I feel terrific, I'm hungry, and I want to help. What can I do?" Crystal replied in a voice Jill hadn't heard since before Jamie's death.

"Wow! That's great, girl! I'm at the church helping out Pastor Luke. He was up all night, so he's catching some shut-eye right now. I'm coordinating the volunteers. Why don't you come over here and help me? There's plenty of food in the kitchen, and he said to help ourselves. I could use the help AND the company."

"I'll be there in ten minutes, Jill. Can't wait to get out of the house and be useful." She had seen the church a few times and knew the address. An easy drive from her house. Maybe it was time to get back into a Sunday routine. She wanted her baby to grow up in a friendly church family as she had; Jamie would have liked that too.

Crystal found her car keys and purse and headed out the front door. As she turned her key in the lock, she thought she saw something in her peripheral vision. Turning to look, she saw nothing there but the front porch swing. It took her a minute to realize it was gently swaying, yet there was no breeze. Odd. Then she maneuvered her bulky baby belly down the three steps to the front walk and the car in the driveway. It felt wonderful to be out in the fresh air, though the sky wasn't bright and clear as it should be this time of year.

A single dark creature braved the wrath of the giant warriors by being on the property. It watched her departure from a perch on the porch swing. This New One had recently been given some special protection, and bringing her down would make the General quite pleased. Despair would stick close to her and wait for its chance to sink talons into her flesh. Its gross yellow fangs emerged from a gruesome smirk.

~~~

Rufus Chaney found a game to play in one of the rear corners of the arcade. It was one of his favorite vantage points; he could see all the activity without being noticed in his dark lair.

He was particularly interested in a couple of girls who looked around twelve, even though that was at the top end of his preferred age range. The problem with that age was that the young boys were interested in them too. The girls were giggling and attracting a lot of attention from four scruffy-looking, heavily tattooed guys playing the next machine.

Well, no harm in looking and fantasizing; a stop back at the Girl Scout camp on his way home was also on his agenda. He was very good at remaining inconspicuous while scoping out potential new victims. Most of his adventures were voyeurism and even exhibitionism, but occasionally he got to touch. Years ago, he could convince some adult to 'lend' him a girl for a little quick cash if he was lucky. BJ's sisters occupied him for a span when he could still use his pecker, but they were of no more interest once they reached their teens.

Chaney was so covered in writhing, drooling, red-eyed demons that he would have been difficult for even Gabe to see. This man was beyond the point of salvation. Not because God had given up on him, but because Chaney chose it and loved his choice. He was the perfect puppet to do the bidding of Demon Lords.

~~~

Tom rolled over and stretched like a large cat. He smelled the coffee and bacon, and his stomach rumbled. Beth, up since five, knew the aromas of a good breakfast would rouse her sleeping husband.

He knew what a lucky man he was. Beth was everything to him. He'd hoped that they would have a family by now, but things didn't seem to be going their way in that area. They discussed the idea of adoption, but neither was pushing the topic, so it was in limbo. Climbing out of bed and reaching for his shirt and jeans, he heard Beth's sweet voice calling him to breakfast or brunch at this hour.

Her back was to him as he rounded the corner to the kitchen, so he snuck up behind her, wrapped her in his arms, and buried his nose in her curly herbal scented hair. He was only a couple of inches taller than her five foot eight; they fit together well.

"Thank you for the food, and thank you for being you," he whispered into her ear.

She turned and put her arms around his neck, kissing him lightly on the lips. Her smile came from her mouth and her eyes, in fact, her whole face. She was the definition of 'joy' no matter the circumstances. This woman walked the walk. "You sit yourself right down here and eat," she demanded. "I'll not have my husband fainting from lack of nourishment while he's doing such important work."

Tom did as he was told. Bacon and eggs never tasted so good. He had to hurry, though. It was already after eleven, and he was due back at the Sheriff's Office at noon.

9

Evil Unleashed

HOMEMADE CHILI and grilled cheese sandwiches were today's feature. Most of the regulars ordered the daily special. Those who only wandered in occasionally usually went for a burger. The food was always of secondary importance to the beer and alcohol. Today was no exception. Ten in the morning was the legal time to begin selling alcohol in this county, and there were always people waiting at the door on weekends.

Kasey sprinkled more chili powder into the steaming pot and stirred. The lunch crowd was already growing, and it was barely noon. They were getting a lot of volunteers from the search today. These guys put in a few hours combing through the underbrush and then had to talk about it for twice as many hours over cold mugs: so much speculation, so much evil. No matter, it was bringing quite a bit of business to Myrt's, and that was good. It was going to be a long day.

The more she thought about it, the more determined Kasey became to make herself cross the street the following day. That little neighborhood street seemed like a six-lane highway full of speeding tractor-trailers to her right now. It would take all the bravery she could gather to walk into a room of strangers who would probably see her belly and no ring on her finger and judge her. But Pastor Luke was kind, and she felt good being around him. Maybe, just maybe, the others would be like him.

Kasey ladled out two more bowls of hot chili and sliced some fresh bread. She carried out the tray to the couple at table number three. Just as she set the bowls down, a nighttime regular came rushing in the front door.

Jake yelled, "Turn on the TV, turn on the TV!" and Grandma Myrt clicked the remote. The news channel came up right away, which everyone was watching a while ago to see if there was any local update on the search for Becky Robbins.

> "...about the prison break at the state penitentiary, which happened at ten a.m. today. I repeat this is a news flash – breaking news about the prison break this morning."

The state prison was just a few hours away by car, and it housed some pretty dangerous men. The news flash announcement caught the attention of everyone in the bar.

> "A riot broke out this morning among the inmates in two of the cell blocks of the state prison. Several guards became hostages, and three prison inmates were killed. Sixty-five minutes later, the guards were released, unharmed. Upon being questioned, each one said that the ringleaders disappeared after causing the chaos. The guards were locked in cells until some of the trustees were sent in with keys to let them go."
>
> "Upon further investigation, a total of twenty-five, yes, I said twenty-five of the most dangerous prisoners were not located. This is the worst incident in the nation in recorded history and further fuels the debate about states privatizing their prisons. Where these prisoners are and how they may have escaped is a mystery at this time. The investigation is underway, with State, County, and City Law Enforcement

joining in. The moment there is any proof of prisoners having crossed state lines, the Federal Bureau of Investigation will take charge. Stay tuned as the story continues to unfold. This station will cancel all regular broadcasts to continue bringing you the news as it happens. All residents of counties near the prison are urged to stay home and indoors if possible. Additional information on how you can ensure your safety will follow this news report."

"The fires continue to rage across Colorado. Five different fires have now burned over three thousand acres; all suspected to be originated by acts of arson. Evacuees are....."

Gram turned down the volume slightly, and the bar began to buzz. Worried looks exchanged, stories shared of someone who knew someone who knew a dangerous person doing time in that place. Speculation about who they were and how they got out. "Had to be an inside job." "Had to have help from the outside." All Kasey knew was that she would be extra aware of her surroundings and careful not to put herself into potentially compromising situations until all of them were caught.

She had orders to take and food to serve and little time for thinking about more than the numerous hours remaining in her day until she could go home and relax. Tomorrow was her day off, and it could come none too soon.

~~~

On the roof of the bar, the lesser demons danced and celebrated, red eyes flashing and slime drooling from the misshapen holes in their faces which were supposed to be mouths. The time drew nearer, and they were busy doing what they did best – wreaking havoc.

Their numbers increased by the day. The Lords arrived in higher ranks, issuing new orders and changing plans. Everywhere, they saw New Ones with at least one demon attached firmly by razor-sharp talons and more circling. It would be their greatest victory!

~~~

Carlos was in over his head, and he knew it. He was a small-time nothing compared to these guys. Lester Byrd, the kingpin, took Carlos under his wing for unknown reasons. A man notorious and convicted for his rampage of murders. He'd heard some of the tough guys whispering that they thought Lester was going soft. He didn't look at all soft. Lester stood about five foot eleven with solid muscle like a bull. His walnut-colored hair had some gray streaks like his oversized mustache. Only the scar running from his eyebrow down his right cheek kept him from looking like a movie star. Unless you knew who he was and what he'd done, you'd never guess that he contained such evil.

Only Lester knew that Carlos reminded him of his own son, born to a Spanish beauty in earlier days before the murders began. He loved her in a possessive way, but she had screwed him over when the kid was only about four years old. That's what started his fearsome rampage, slashing and killing the woman and her lover before moving on to just about anyone else who pissed him off. He was driven by blind rage, and it caught up to him.

The child went into foster care, then was adopted, and no longer connected to Lester in anyone's mind, memory, or records. A friend of Lester's kept up with the kid's progress and secretly took pictures when he could, sending them to Lester under the guise of sharing family photos of his godson. The images showed a happy and handsome young man with his mother's thick dark hair and flashing dark eyes—clearly her Spanish heritage and beautiful features.

Last month, the kid had his seventeenth birthday and was in his final year of high school. That was a significant factor in Lester's decision to pretend as if he'd been the one to mastermind the break when he got the offer. Lester had nothing to lose and two things to accomplish. He wanted to see his son before he died, and he didn't care where or how that end took place or how many he had to take out with him. If Lester had a chink in his armor, his kid was it. And then there was the snitch.

For the time being, Carlos benefited from the physical similarity without knowing it, but he had to be very careful. These men had no loyalty, and one wrong step could cost him his life.

Each of the other twenty-four men who participated in the break knew only of the part they played. No one but Lester had all the pieces to the puzzle. Except for the piece that told him the name of the real mastermind. Without knowledge, no one could rat out the others or the inside and outside accomplices. Lester still had many friends. Once outside, the convicts split up, going in numerous different directions.

Carlos, Lester, and three others had a pre-arranged hideout to lie low for a few days. Lester planned to stay under the radar until some others began to get caught, far across state lines. He figured the Feds would be concentrating the search elsewhere by then and no longer in areas anywhere close to the prison.

Safety in numbers. He didn't have to outsmart the Feds, just all of the others who would keep the Feds busy with their lame attempts to get free.

"Hey, kid. You stick with me till we get where we're going. Then I want you to disappear. Every one of these badasses will get caught and dragged back to the pen. Me, I'll go down fighting. It's my last stand. I got out to take care of a couple of important things. Once those are done, I'm as good as dead," he told Carlos shortly after they settled into the hideout.

Carlos knew that Lester's target was Henderson County and Carlos wanted to get back there to Kasey and the baby. He'd sent her only one letter, and that broke his heart. But it wasn't fair to ask her to wait ten years for him. Nothing would have made him happier than being a father, being her husband, and taking care of them both.

He knew a guy who could give them fake IDs. Maybe he could take her away and start over fresh somewhere. There was plenty of time to think about that. Lester told them they'd be in the hideout for at least a week. Then they would take their time sneaking short distances and hiding out again. It was only about a hundred and fifty miles but on foot, at night, and staying out of sight; it could take them a couple of weeks to make the trip. Lester figured that time was on their side, with so many others to track and catch.

The other three men stuck by the side of Lester because they thought he was leading them to a stash of money stolen from a bank in Henderson County just before Lester's arrest. He never told them that, but he let them believe the rumor. It was presently to his advantage.

After their escape through the sewers, which terminated in exiting a manhole about five yards from the edge of some woods, they entered the thick brush safely. It had enough tree cover to keep them hidden from hovering helicopters. They found a pile of camo tarps and spread them out. Hiding underneath gave them protection until dark. The men saw that Lester had to have outside help, but no one had a clue about the source.

~~~

Crystal sat at the big desk in the church office with Jill. Each had a list of people they were calling to solicit volunteers for the search. Many were not even church members but were business owners, government workers, neighbors, anyone who could lend a hand.

They ate a brunch of cold chicken and fruit salad which neither one finished; the remnants sat on plates near the phones they were constantly using. Hours had passed in what seemed like minutes. Crystal only moved to refresh her iced tea and go to the bathroom. She had to do that a lot now.

Crystal's back was to the office door, so she turned to see who it was when she heard a voice. A very nice-looking man walked in, about six-foot-tall, dark blond hair, piercing blue eyes, and wearing jeans and a t-shirt. She figured he was a volunteer until Jill jumped up and moved toward him, calling him Pastor Luke. He looked toward Crystal, and their eyes met; she took a deep breath.

Luke was smiling; as usual, having just enjoyed a nap and completed his teaching notes for tomorrow morning's church service, he felt good. Jill introduced them, "Pastor Luke, meet my dear friend, Crystal. I told you about her, and she's graciously volunteered to help me organize today. Crystal, this is Pastor Luke."

He was beside her in three steps and took her hand, covering it with his other hand in a gesture of deep friendship and gratitude. When their eyes had met, something clicked, but he was unsure of what had just happened. She was visibly very pregnant and wore a ring on her left hand. She was pretty with her long, wavy, light brown hair and sable brown eyes sprinkled with flecks of green and gold. She also had attractive dimples in both cheeks and chin, evident when she smiled. But it was not like him to have any sudden physical reaction to a woman, especially a married and pregnant woman; he was controlled and focused. The weirdness going on must be affecting him in ways he hadn't anticipated.

"Crystal, how nice of you to volunteer. When is your baby due? You and your husband must be thrilled," he commented.

"My little girl is expected next month, pastor. Unfortunately, my husband died overseas before he even knew about our baby. Jill and many of my other friends have been helping me through the tough times. Today I felt up to giving back a little of the blessings." Why in the world had she told him so much at their first meeting? Good heavens! She was never so open with anyone. She was beginning to understand why Jill raved about this man.

Luke felt an odd sense of relief wash over him and was embarrassed by it. "Well, it's wonderful to have you here, but I am so sorry for your loss. Thank you for volunteering."

Jill stood at the door, trying to hide a tiny little grin that was escaping despite her best efforts. Given time, the world always moved on.

A moment later, Gabe walked through the door. Luke introduced him to Crystal and Jill. He looked a bit less road-worn and ready to do some strategizing with Luke. The men excused themselves and returned to the apartment.

Jill sat back down and looked at Crystal's flushed face. She was hesitant to make eye contact, which confirmed it. There would be many more chapters to this story, and perhaps a very happy ending thought Jill.

~~~

"Let me see if there's been any news about the search before we get started, Gabe," Luke said as he switched on the little TV in his living room.

> "...I repeat, the investigation continues, now under FBI leadership as the first escaped convict is in their hands, captured just over the state line. Many of the twenty-five escapees are extremely dangerous convicted felons. Local law enforcement is advising the public to consider them all armed and is imposing curfews on surrounding areas. If you are just joining us, all regular programming is suspended as we continue to bring you live coverage of this morning's state prison break."
>
> "But now a moment for news on a global level. A second nuclear blast for this year took place today in North Korea as they continue testing against the warnings of the UN....."

Luke looked at Gabe. "The hunt for Becky will get lost with this prison break going on. I'd better let Jill know so she can cope with this too. We have to be careful about volunteers running all over the county with these guys on the loose."

Gabe's face was stone. "There will be very high-ranking demons in this battle, Luke. Someone in power has unleashed this evil; a lot is riding on this for them. Stay alert for clues. It would tip everything in our favor to know in advance what they're up to and how it ties in with Henderson County."

~~~

"The FBI has just released a list of the escaped convicts. We're running the names and pictures across the lower screen at this time. We will continue to do so every thirty minutes until they've been captured. Please tell all your friends and neighbors to watch on the hour and again on the half-hour. These faces need to be committed to memory to assist law enforcement in capturing all twenty-four remaining convicts as quickly as possible as the active search has now spread across five states."

Kasey's eyes were fixed on the TV, as were all other eyes in the bar. The faces and names rolled across the screen, one by one. Some very evil-looking men, a few were very ordinary, even nice-looking men who looked like their pictures had gotten there by mistake, except that they were dressed in orange and had numbers under their faces. Then Kasey froze, and a bar patron pointed; it was the face of Carlos.

He wasn't like these hardened criminals. What was he doing with them? Sure, he had gotten ten years, but he could've gotten out early on good behavior. She cared about him deeply. Where would he go? Who was he with? Did they make him leave? Was he a hostage? Oh, Carlos, what have you done? Her thoughts were racing and jumbled, but her body was paralyzed.

Billy looked at her from behind the bar. His heart hurt for her. He knew how she cared and what kind of a life she'd had. He loved her like a daughter, one he would never have because everyone knew he was deformed, and women didn't want a man like him. He made a promise to himself to be her protector. She wouldn't be alone, ever, neither would her baby.

10

New Vision

DAVID WAS confused. The events of this morning with Pauley had left him speechless. He'd cut himself off from everyone after Sylvia died, now he was without a friend to help him sort this out. No one to share his thoughts with or give him feedback or advice. He was alone with this, and it was too big for him.

He always opened the pawnshop at ten a.m. on Saturday instead of the regular eight-thirty for weekdays. His customers usually needed money on Thursday and Friday and didn't get out of bed on Saturday until noon. It was time for him to take Pauley there now. They could put in some quiet hours, and he would have tomorrow off. Maybe time would give him some idea of what to do. What could he do? This was all happening whether he did anything or not!

"Pauley, time to go to the shop," he called. Always before, he knew that Pauley wouldn't respond to his words. He had to physically go into Pauley's room and guide him out with a light touch. He was turning to do that now when Pauley opened his door and came out by himself. David stood still, staring at his son. This child had changed from a walking mannequin to a, what, a person awakening? "Let's go, son," he said, and Pauley began to walk. It was incredible. He turned and followed Pauley to the door instead of leading for the very first time.

Twelve minutes later, David was unlocking the door of the shop. Pauley went to David's desk and sat down; he began to sketch again with pencil and paper. David left him to draw and started his monthly inventory, shaking his head in wonder.

~~~

Gabe told Luke that there were some things he could use for the upcoming battle. The standard items used to equip the general population were bibles, crosses, tasers, mace, baseball bats, knives, and the like. When demon-led humans were out to harm, innocents needed to protect themselves. Together they looked up possible addresses where they could be found and purchased.

He always began with scouting out the area. Since he could see the demons through dimensions, Gabe traveled around to find where the highest concentrations of Legoniaries and Klazyns were gathering. Though the Host was aware of his gift, the demons were not, and his recognizance went unnoticed by them. They knew he was an enemy, but the only demons who knew he could see them were already dead. Gabe found that how the enemy configured their forces always gave him clues to their battle plan. The Swordsman would use that intel to annihilate them.

He was ready to start scouting, planning to gather the battle tools he wanted. Luke stayed at the church office to work with Jill and Crystal on the list of Saints. Many of their volunteers would qualify; God's Saints were those who had accepted His grace. And from those, they needed the ones who had embraced the task of being prayer warriors. The prayer vigil of the Saints was critical to their success. Prayer empowered the Host and weakened the darkness, but it did not alleviate violence. They expected a large turnout at the church service tomorrow; today, the word passed through the information chains.

Gabe grabbed his keys and left the apartment, pointing a thumbs-up sign toward Luke. He was happy to be working with his old friend on this one, but battle was never pleasant. It was just his way of life.

~~~

The bell over the front door jingled. David looked up from the rear of the shop to see a giant of a man walk in. Longish dark hair, very muscular, chiseled face, and tan from many hours in the sun; he could have been Hercules or something. The man had to duck as he passed through the doorway.

"Be with you momentarily," he shouted as he walked past Pauley toward the front. He glanced at Pauley's sketch and stopped short. This one was of a human man, standing on a hilltop, brandishing a sword as he slashed away at flying demons. The guy in the sketch resembled the guy at the front door. Again, Pauley looked up and made eye contact with his father. This time he put his hand down hard on the picture, his finger pointing to the face in the sketch while he looked at David. David patted Pauley on the shoulder and continued to the front. He was unsettled; this was getting downright scary.

"I'm David Kemper, the owner. How can I help you, sir?" he asked the big man.

"Well, Mr. Kemper. I have a shopping list, and I wondered how much of it you can help me fill?" stated Gabe.

He handed the list to David. David looked it over and slowly raised his wide eyes to Gabe. He'd never seen a list like this before, but he could certainly help him with at least part of it; several of the items were in stock. "I can sure help, but I've got to ask you, sir. Are you planning a religious war? Bibles, crosses, mace, tasers, is there something I need to know about?"

Before Gabe could answer, David felt a nudge at his side. Pauley had come to the front and stood beside him with the sketch in his hand. Pauley looked at his father, then he looked at Gabe, and finally, he stretched out his arm and handed the drawing to the giant man.

"You…" was the first word he uttered, the only word he ever spoke in his life.

Gabe knew that something monumental had just happened from the look on David's face. When he looked at the sketch, he knew he was in the presence of a miracle. He saw himself in battle on the paper, detailed down to the streaks of gray at his temples and the intricate carving on his longsword.

Pauley looked past Gabe and saw the warriors of the Host standing outside the door of the shop. He smiled.

"Mr. Kemper, my name is Gabe Matheson, and we have some things we need to talk about," said Gabe. "You have an extraordinary young man here, and you need to know why. Are you a believer?"

~~~

Peggy sat at the kitchen table in her uniform with an ice pack covering her eye. Her lip was split but no longer bleeding when Jake walked in the door. She looked up as he approached, wary of what he would do.

"Shouldn't you be at work?" he asked with a sarcastic tone.

"I was; they sent me home to take care of my eye. It didn't look good to the customers," she replied loudly. "So now you've made me lose a day of work too," she softly muttered.

Jake turned abruptly. "Smart mouthing me will only make it worse, bitch. You're the cause of all my problems, so you're lucky to be in one piece."

Peggy cowered and shut her mouth. She considered calling that deputy who'd left his card, but she wouldn't.

Jake continued to the bedroom and flopped across the bed. His head still ached from last night, and now his stomach was in knots too. On TV at Myrt's, he saw the faces and names. He knew that trouble was coming, big trouble, and he needed to have a clear head to figure out how to get away from it.

Fourteen years ago, he had been in a fix with the law, and to get out of it, he used some info he'd gotten from an acquaintance to help catch a killer. He learned the whereabouts of Lester Byrd purely by accident. Lester was wanted for multiple murders, and Jake had squealed like a stuck pig to get himself off scot-free. The detectives let him know in no uncertain terms, though that somehow Lester had gotten the informant's name. As long as Lester was in the state pen, Jake felt somewhat safe. With Lester now on the loose, Jake's continued existence was precarious.

He had to get some money and get as far away as possible. Peggy had nothing, no savings, and nothing he saw worth selling. The people he hung out with at Myrt's were in the same shitty boat as he was. Nobody had a pot to piss in, so he couldn't borrow either.

He had to come up with a plan. Someplace he could easily knock off and walk away with a wad of cash to get him far from here, where he could start again. He'd probably need a gun too. Not a legal one, he couldn't wait for all the licensing nonsense, and he didn't want his name associated with one anyway. He still knew people on the dark side, criminals who stayed under the radar. Yep, he'd have to risk a visit this evening to see what he could line up.

Things would work out. He'd get away from Peggy, and things would get better. She had been bad for him since he met her and moved into this dump.

Black claw-like talons tightened in his flesh, and the Klazyns hissed and moaned in delight.

~~~

The ATV came to a stop just inside the tree line, and its driver turned off the motor. His cell phone was ringing, so he waved to his friend to come over and stop for a short break.

"Hi, mom, what's up? What? Well, yeah, we can be back in about twenty minutes. We'll get going right now. OK, mom, quit crying; I'll be there before you know it."

"Hey, Bob! That was my mom. I guess some convicts escaped from the prison and could be in the woods out here, so she wants us to get home, now! It's getting late anyway."

His friend gave him the OK sign, and they both revved up and headed back toward town. About twenty feet from where he took the phone call lay a large garbage bag by the foot of a pine tree.

~~~

David and Gabe sat across from each other at the oversized desk. Pauley stood next to David, hardly blinking, staring at Gabe's face.

"I left all of that God stuff behind fourteen years ago, Mr. Matheson. Since my wife was killed, I don't know what I believe. All I know is that as of early this morning, things got very strange with Pauley, and I don't know why or even what set it off."

"Please call me Gabe; I'll call you David. We should be on a first-name basis because we'll be counting on each other very soon. I'll explain what I can about Pauley."

"How can you explain? You don't know him. Why does his picture look like you? How did he suddenly become an artist, and what is the meaning of these sketches? And he SPOKE! Gabe, he's fourteen; he's never uttered a word until you came in that door! What is going on?"

"Your son has a gift, David. I know it's hard to understand this, but I speak from experience, so please, trust me. If you need a reference, one of my best friends in the world is Pastor Luke at the little church on Morningstar Lane. He's known me since college, and we went through some of what I'm going to explain to you."

77

"However crazy it is, if it helps my son, I want to know," sighed David, feeling overwhelmed and bewildered.

Gabe began, "Human life here on earth is considered a 'plane' of existence. You may have heard the term 'dimension' in science or even sci-fi movies. The third dimension is what we live in, where we can see all around an object. We use two- and one-dimensional terms for art that has dimension on one side or is flat like a drawing. Our world stops there, no fourth or higher dimensions because our eyes and brains see only the 'plane' of our own existence."

"OK, I get it so far," David leaned in to hear more.

"Besides myself, I've only met two others in my entire life who can see beyond our plane, with a multi-dimensional vision. There are things that most people should not know, let alone see. From the look of the sketches Pauley drew, he has the ability. What I have never seen before, though, is someone who has this ability to see through dimensions and time. There are no active battles here right now, so Pauley must be seeing the past or the future. This is new to me and needs to be explored." Gabe was most curious to know more. What gifts had God given this boy? And how did He intend for them to be used to His glory in the upcoming battle?

David's eyes were wide, and he was sitting up straight now. He looked at Pauley. Pauley turned his face to his father and smiled. The veil over his eyes was gone, and there was a person in there, a responsive person. "You've got to be kidding me," he whispered, not taking his eyes off of Pauley.

~~~

Crystal was exhausted but hated for the day to come to an end. She felt so helpful while she assisted Jill; it changed her perspective. She would always love and miss Jamie, and their daughter would be a constant reminder that he'd been a vital part of the future, but it was time to put the self-centered grief behind her and keep going. There were so many needs out there, and most were more extensive than her own. After

Pastor Luke got them started, he left to work on his list of things that required his attention. She decided to come back tomorrow for the church service, eager to hear his sermon.

"Crystal, I'm calling it enough for today. You need to get home and rest, my girl. Tomorrow's service will be a very busy one. Will you come?"

"Yes, I will. You were right, Jill. I do need to get out and start being with people again. I won't argue with you on quitting for today. I'm pretty tired."

They walked out to the parking lot together and exchanged a quick hug. "Now, you lock yourself in tight tonight. With all those convicts on the loose, I want to know you're safe," warned Jill.

"I promise. See you tomorrow." Crystal drove out onto the street, waving goodbye, and turned in the direction of home. What a day, hmmm. What a day. It was only just after four in the afternoon, but it looked dismal outside. She wanted to be behind her locked door and snuggled in a blanket; the air was getting a bit chilly. Maybe she'd watch a good movie before she slept for the night.

~~~

At least three-quarters of his list of battle tools came from David's pawn shop. But the greatest treasure was in finding Pauley! Gabe returned to the church after spending much of the day scouting around town. He had the preliminary details needed for creating his plan, and he wanted to see what Luke had done during the afternoon.

Luke was waiting for him in the doorway with a satisfied look on his face.

"Help me unload this stuff, please, Luke. Then tell me how things are going with your end," called Gabe.

Luke hurried to the camper and began filling his arms with the items his friend had accumulated and brought with him. There had to be at least a hundred used bibles along with various weapons, protection devices like tasers and mace, baseball bats, and crosses made of all sorts of materials from wood to silver and semi-precious stone. One box contained loudspeaker equipment, and there were several individual speakers. They carried them into the apartment; Luke led the way to a storeroom in the church. Once everything was stowed, they headed toward the kitchen to have some dinner.

"Our volunteers have been busy and very productive. Every member has been contacted and will be bringing as many people as possible to the service tomorrow. We'll update them on the search for Becky and the escapee issues. As far as they know at this moment, it's like a giant neighborhood watch effort spread across the whole county," explained Luke. "The prayer chain has been asked to pray specifically for strength to the Angelic Host in overcoming evil. They don't understand the reality or details of the battle thing, but we'll fill them in if the time comes to do it," Luke explained.

"Luke, what they can see is what they'll be battling, flesh and blood, real people. The demons work through the humans they control. These local people will see the danger that comes in human form. Like in the battle we experienced at the college and the man who stabbed you. You couldn't see the demon on his back, but I could, and when the man fell, the demon left him. There will be dangerous people coming here and many here who will become dangerous. You won't see the demons attached to them, but the demon's manipulation will make them behave in brutal ways with anything they can use as weapons."

"It's my job, along with the Host, to battle the demons themselves. When we out them, the humans they were attached to become fertile ground for the next powerful force. If they're to be saved, that's the time to help them when they are most vulnerable. That's where you and the congregation will be most instrumental. Otherwise, the next demon that comes along will snag them again, and the evil continues to grow."

"Even the Christian who is lukewarm is in jeopardy," Gabe continued.

"Though their souls may be saved, they can still do harm. God will not renege on his gift of free will, and if they have turned from Him, the darkness can use their flesh to do evil. As the numbers of the Host increase and the prayer cover grows stronger, the lesser demons with the weakest holds will have to flee. When someone rededicates or newly dedicates themself to Christ, they are at their strongest to repel demons. It's a balance thing, Luke. The demons think they're getting a good foothold, so we have to pull the rug out from under them. That leaves the Host to deal with the great Demon Lords. And the Warrior Angels know how to handle that."

"The thing we haven't discovered yet is the core reason for this to be taking place here. There is always an underlying motive for a location and the people involved. Something they want that ties into a much larger picture. Vast numbers of demons and high-ranking demon leaders can only mean this location is a significant piece of the Dark One's plan." Gabe finished with a sigh.

"We'll have to work smart to figure it out and turn the tables on them," stated Luke. "Our first run-in with this was what changed my course and led me to the ministry. I know it wasn't a random thing, Gabe. In every fiber of my being, I know that we were put on the paths intended for us that day. Just as we are both here for a reason right now, this is probably another life-changing event for us and possibly for the planet. But we're not alone, and we can do what we're called to do."

They discussed the issues over fried chicken and potato salad brought in by some church members. It seemed that no matter the crisis or the celebration, the church benefited from excellent cooks who jumped right in there to offer up their gifts.

Outside, the sky grew darker as the diffused light from the distant sun disappeared. Streetlights began to flicker on, and the activities of the night dwellers came alive.

"Now, let me tell you about what happened at the pawnshop, Luke. You'll want to stay seated for this...."

11

Saturday Night

"GET OUT there to the pickup Bobby Jack," yelled Ma. "It's gettin' dark, and it's high time to go clean up this mess you and Rufus made."

Rufus Chaney would not be with them, by Ma's order. She didn't want him to know what was happening, so he couldn't blab to the law later if it came to that. She didn't much like having him around anyway.

Bobby Jack took the wheel, Ma sat in the passenger seat, and Bubba rode in the truck bed behind them, along with a couple of shovels and a tarp. He started the truck and pulled out of the yard onto the dirt road leading to the paved county road Chaney had taken. Within fifteen minutes, they reached the bend where Chaney stopped. BJ pulled over to the shoulder. The roadblock was still in place where they'd seen it; around the bend and through the trees, they could see the blue and red flashing lights reflected through the deepening dusk off of pine trunks and branches. The search was still on, so Ma told him to pull up into the trees for better cover.

He turned off the motor and climbed out of the truck with a flashlight. Geez! These trees all looked alike now. He'd been in such a hurry; he hadn't had time or foresight to look for any distinguishing landmarks. Bobby Jack walked around in a twenty-foot circle, shining his flashlight beam at the base of the trees in search of the green plastic bag.

Ma was getting antsy; they were still somewhat exposed in the truck, and she wanted this finished. "Found it!" BJ whispered too loud as he rushed up to the truck. "Come on, Bubba, bring the shovels and the tarp," he ordered.

"Bury that thing fast, and don't leave it lookin' fresh!" Ma commanded.

Bubba and BJ ran back to the tree where the bag lay. They spread the tarp about ten feet away from the tree where the ground was soft and fewer roots would get in their way and began to dig. Dumping the shovels full of dirt onto the tarp, they dug until they had a hole about four feet deep. Then BJ walked hesitantly over to the bag.

He saw that an animal had torn a side of the bag open, and there were shreds of material and plastic on the ground. He didn't want to touch it, but he also didn't want to experience the wrath of Ma when she was pissed, so he heaved the bag over his shoulder, took several steps, and dropped it into the hole. Then he and Bubba shoveled the dirt from the tarp back over the bag till the hole was filled again and shook the remaining sand loosely over the area to give it a more natural look. Bubba took the tools and the tarp, and they ran back to the truck.

BJ started the motor, backed out of the trees and onto the road, and waited till he was further away before he turned the headlights on. Ma heaved a sigh, satisfied that they wouldn't be bothered with this problem again.

Black things from hell clung onto the truck and its occupants as it sped back to town, clutching, and rolling, hissing, and dripping, in their silent laughter.

~~~

Kasey was off duty at six o'clock, free now till Monday after school. The first thing on her agenda was to eat the dinner she brought from the bar for herself and her sister and then sit with her feet up until she fell asleep. She hated to even turn on the TV, but it was like a magnet now. Every fifteen minutes, the faces of the escapees slowly rolled across the screen. Her Carlos had been gone for such a long time already.

As she drove home, she passed the church and parked in her assigned space. The church seemed quiet tonight. Trisha ran out to help her take the food upstairs. The TV was already on, still broadcasting the six o'clock news.

> ".... bombing took place in Aleppo today, killing many civilians including women and children. Survivors are digging through the rubble to find anyone else still alive."
>
> "The search goes on by local law enforcement for little Becky Robbins, the nine-year-old who disappeared on her way to school yesterday morning...."

"Was that just yesterday? It seems like days ago already," she thought out loud.

> "Officers previously involved in her search have been pulled off to work on the hunt for the escaped convicts from the state prison. Henderson County's Sheriff is asking for additional volunteers as Becky is still a top priority, and the Amber Alert remains in effect. Please contact the Sheriff's Office or check with your local church. Many are assisting in the coordination of volunteers."
>
> "No convicts have been apprehended at this point, leaving twenty-four dangerous men still at large. We're rerunning the names and photos at this time and will continue every thirty minutes...."

Kasey sat down on the couch, balancing her dinner plate on her round belly. She watched the pictures roll by yet again, almost knowing them by heart. The TV remained on at the bar all day now. Right after

Carlos' face, there was a face that she found herself staring at, again and again. The man was handsome. He reminded her of an actor; what was his name? She stared and thought a minute, oh yeah, Tom Selleck. She remembered him from a private eye show on the old rerun channel. The mustache and thick eyebrows were probably the things that made her think of him.

The news person said this guy, Lester something, was a murderer. How did someone become a murderer? He looked stern, but like any father in any ordinary neighborhood might look if his kid had done something wrong. How is anyone supposed to tell the good guys from the bad guys if they don't look bad? Billy, the bartender, was pretty beat up looking, and some thought he looked scary with his crooked nose and unusual features, but he was the sweetest guy in the world.

Kasey took her dishes to the kitchen and washed them up before getting comfortable in her flannel PJs. There were a couple of good sitcoms on tonight. Humor sure uplifted the spirit, and uplifting was what she needed to take her mind off of things. Just before her shows started, she found herself wondering where Carlos might be at that very moment.

~~~

Not even out for a full day yet, and the men were restless. As soon as it was dusk, they left the temporary cover of the camp tarps and walked on to the first stop. Lester's contact set them up in a decent cabin, deep in the woods; they were unlikely to be noticed as long as they didn't do anything stupid.

He had an agenda; it was a deal with the contact who acted on behalf of someone anonymous. He made it clear to them what he wanted, and the connection made it clear what they expected of him. He was to retrieve a box, kill an old man, and then kill a woman, no questions asked. Someone seriously wanted this task completed to have pulled off what just went down, a twenty-five-prisoner escape. Lester doubted if the feat could have taken place before the privatization of the prison. It would be near impossible to pay off as many as it would take to put on that show. But when you could afford to hire who you wanted, anything was possible. Yep, whoever it was had one hell of a lot of pull and a lot of cash behind this escape. And something this big would tie up the media and a multitude of law enforcement agencies. A perfect diversion, but for what?

Carlos found a corner where he could watch the others and settled in for the night with one of the blankets he found in the hall closet. Lester was calm and seemingly not bothered by the constant yapping and whining of the other three convicts. They wanted to beeline to the money they anticipated and then get as far away as possible, Mexico, Canada, South America. Being holed up so close to the state pen made them very nervous and dangerous.

His beautiful Kasey occupied his mind as he drifted off to sleep. Lester looked like he was sleeping, but he was quietly watching through lowered lids and listening for signs of trouble. He learned to survive with practically no downtime over the past fourteen years. This was nothing.

~~~

Tom pulled evening roadblock duty. He and his partner were on the south border of the county, set up at the county line. It was pretty quiet, especially for a Saturday night, but the escaped convict situation kept a lot of Saturday night partiers much closer to home.

He was walking casually around the cruiser, looking into the woods to see if he detected any movement, being exceptionally watchful because those convicts could be anywhere when he saw headlights approaching the bend through a fairly dense stand of pines. They came to a stop and then seemed to pull off the road into the trees. Then they abruptly went out.

It could be some couple just looking for a place to make out, but still, it was curious. Tom told his partner to stay with the car while he took a closer look at the activity. He walked toward the trees about twenty feet from the road. The darkness increased as Tom walked further from the patrol car's flashing lights, but he didn't want to use his flashlight. The light would give him away if someone was out there, and he wanted his approach to be undetected.

Slowly working his way through the trees, as quietly as possible, he'd gone only a short distance when he saw the beams of two flashlights and faintly heard hushed voices. He worked his way closer.

Two men, one gave directions, and the other answered. The second man put down his flashlight and lifted something, a blanket, a sheet? Then he shook it out and seemed to be spreading sand around. He took the sheet thing, grabbed two tools – shovels maybe – and picked up his flashlight. The two of them headed back to the edge of the woods, out of his sight. There was too much underbrush to hurry after them; he'd have tripped and fallen. He called his partner on the radio as quietly as he could as soon as the men were out of hearing distance. Tom heard a motor start but saw no lights from a vehicle, then the sound of the motor faded out as it sped up the highway. His partner wasn't able to get back to the cruiser and around the bend fast enough. The suspicious characters were gone.

~~~

Jake was on foot, hating that he couldn't drive. He was on his way into a tough neighborhood with nothing but a kitchen knife under his jacket for protection. The contact expected him at nine p.m. and didn't like it when people weren't on time.

Jake knew the address; he'd been there before. This time, he was getting a gun and fake driver's license, and it was costing him everything he had plus a chunk of the job they wanted him to do. But the gun was the tool he needed to get more cash, to get away while he still could. Knocking off a place wasn't on his resume, but this contact set him up with someone who had that experience. If they could pull this off together, even with his share of only twenty percent, that would give him enough to get out.

He stood at the walk leading to the front door, a slight feeling of uneasiness in his gut. The Klazyn Demons perched on his shoulders, hunched over with talons tightly gripping his flesh, and whispered foul things into his ears. Then he took a step toward his new future.

~~~

Five additional patrol cars arrived; the place was swarming with cops. Floodlights lit up the trees, and officers combed the area where Tom witnessed the suspicious activity.

One shouted, "Found something!" A few others headed over to where he stood, shining his flashlight down on some shredded pieces of plastic and fabric.

"Mark this area, take photos, and don't touch anything," directed the Sergeant. Another officer, about five feet away, called for attention there as well. A piece of paper, a receipt of some sort, was lying on the ground. The officer marked that spot too, and the Sergeant bagged the evidence.

It was too hard to see in the deep shadows; even with the floods and flashlights, the air seemed too thick for the light to penetrate, so the Sergeant in charge had the men stretch crime scene tape around the trees in a circle of about sixty feet in diameter. He posted men on the side nearest the road so no one could disturb the area. Fortunately, the press hadn't gotten wind of this yet, so they didn't have tons of people trampling a possible crime scene.

Tom suggested they also tape off the area where the vehicle had likely parked in case they could get tread prints from the ground as additional evidence. He knew the men buried something, but they would have to wait just a few more hours to look further. Tom dreaded what he expected to find. The Sergeant was taking no chances that anything might be missed or messed up in this investigation; they needed daylight. The perps wouldn't walk due to police error if this had anything to do with the missing child.

His shift began at noon, so it was time to check out and go home to

Beth. He needed her right now to calm him and give him strength for what would be uncovered tomorrow. Henderson County had never seen anything like these last few days.

~~~

Luke sat, listening intently to Gabe's retelling of the events in the pawnshop. He hardly moved and could barely even recall breathing until Gabe finished.

"He can see as you do? And he's never spoken before? This kid drew a picture of you before you walked through the door? How do you think this plays into the whole picture, Gabe? I don't know what to think!" exclaimed Luke.

"I don't know, Luke. But God does, and He'll let us know soon enough. Time for me to call it a night though, things are starting to build, and I want to stay alert to the details," replied Gabe.

12

Sunday Morning

AT SIX-THIRTEEN a.m., the sky began to lighten at the cordoned-off scene where a dozen patrol cars were already on site. Most of the officers and deputies were sipping the last of their coffee, waiting for enough light to start searching the area. Two canine handlers waited, their cadaver dogs prancing to begin their search.

The Sergeant summoned them all together for instructions. "Deputy Dempsey will lead you to where we found possible evidence last night. I want plenty of pictures taken and anything found to be cataloged – by the book! Pay attention to protocol. We don't want a case blown because we mishandled evidence," he sternly cautioned. "Stay out of the way of the dogs. They'll be covering the area for anything that may be buried." By that, the officers knew he meant a little girl's body.

The group broke up to start their tasks. Tom led the way to the marked spots and stood aside as the others got busy.

In a matter of minutes, the dogs began pawing the ground and whining. Their handlers gave them commands to stand down, and officers took over, first scouting the area for additional evidence. Then, the shovels came out.

A shallow grave produced a large green garbage bag. Tom's stomach lurched. More pictures, more pieces of evidence marked, and then two officers pulled the bag out of the hole. They gently opened it enough for more photos to be taken. The Sergeant got on his radio to the dispatcher. "Call out the Medical Examiner and an ambulance."

The search for Becky was over.

~~~

A gut-wrenching cry of the deepest imaginable anguish pierced the early morning stillness. In the dim light, two Guardian Angels turned toward each other, understanding clear in the pale violet eyes of each. Little Becky's body was discovered less than thirty minutes ago, and the Sheriff was breaking the news to her parents in the house below the roof where they now stood.

"We must stay very near now; these Saints cannot be lost. This kind of despair brings the New Ones to their knees and leaves them open to attack," one whispered to the other. A crystal tear fell from the perfect smoothness of a translucent cheek in respect for the emotional devastation of this young couple they protected. They stood erect, wings at the alert, ready to defend against the evil which was growing stronger by the hour. Stalwart guardians.

~~~

The only forensic detective in Henderson County was pouring over the newly collected evidence by seven-thirty a.m. So far, he'd seen shreds of the plastic bag and of Becky's bloody clothing, the result of an animal trying to get at the decomposing body. He picked up a piece of paper; it was a receipt from a local pawn shop. Bingo! It had a name and date right on it. If any of the blood found on the clothing could be linked to this name – they had their man, and if this man already had a record – this one was already solved. Somebody upstairs was watching out for them, and he wasn't about to turn down the help.

In a preliminary examination of the body, the detective noticed that one pierced earring was missing, a tiny gold cross stud. He noted his report to ask her parents about that. Pierced ears were the rage now. His eight-year-old daughter had been begging for permission, so he and his wife agreed to it for her ninth birthday. This girl was barely older than his daughter. He shuddered.

A warrior angel stood next to the detective, the same angel from the woods where Becky's body was found. When it was apparent that the detective was satisfied with what he had in hand, the warrior gathered himself and shot through the ceiling of the police station to report the information to his commander.

~~~

Luke got up at five a.m. and was on his third cup of coffee when the first news bulletin came in. He knew where Becky's soul was now and that she was safe, perfected, and forever protected. It was her family that he prayed for this morning. The heartbreak of losing a child, especially to violence, was a dark emotional abyss.

He looked at the clock at seven-thirty, noting that his service would begin in ninety minutes. People would start arriving within the next hour. Most of the members would know about Becky by the time they got here. It would be a morning of consoling and healing. It would also be a morning of education and rallying for those who had never experienced spiritual warfare.

This evil that took Becky was only the tiniest tip of the iceberg that soon would hit Henderson County. And of that, Luke had no doubt. Gabe felt this would be a much fiercer battle than the one they had shared years ago. Luke couldn't imagine the magnitude.

The phone rang, yanking him from his thoughts. It was one of the volunteers asking if he had heard the news. The calls continued to come in, one after another, for the next thirty minutes.

Gabe walked into the kitchen as he finished a short conversation. He clicked the off button and set the phone down on the table.

"The little girl's body was found this morning... and two more of the convicts were caught in West Virginia. Do you think the others have distanced themselves too?" asked Luke.

Gabe poured a glass of orange juice. He took his time answering. "Not likely, Luke. A bad chunk of that evil is probably headed right here from all of the signs I've seen. It's going to get ugly. We should pray right now;   to ban all evil from this property and building. And for people coming here to have open ears, eyes, and hearts to receive God's instructions. Our prayer gives them protection wherever they are through the end of the Battle."

So, they prayed, and angels throughout the county went out to protect the saints. As each massive warrior materialized next to its charge, the fearful demons loosened their grip, and many flew away, retracting in pain, to regroup elsewhere, chattering and gnawing at their claws.

~~~

Crystal awakened refreshed and eager to return to the little church. If she was frank with herself, she looked forward to seeing Pastor Luke and hearing his sermon. He was such a remarkable man, with a wonderfully contagious glow that affected everyone around him.

She called Jill at seven-thirty to ask for a ride. Jill and her husband passed right by Crystal's place anyway, and she thought about the seam-busting turnout expected with so many members involved in the search and now the worries about the prison break. Crystal felt a bit anxious. Being around Jill right now would calm that. Besides, may as well save a parking space. Jill, bless her, was happy to accommodate and promised to pick her up in an hour. They made no mention of the news bulletins; Jill wasn't thinking about them at that moment, and Crystal hadn't even turned on the TV.

She continued getting ready and caught herself singing in the shower, to her amusement. It had been a long time ago when she'd last done that.

~~~

Lester's cell phone rang at seven-thirty a.m. He clicked it on and heard a recorded monotone voice say, "Go now." He hadn't expected the message for several days, but he knew it would be the only one he'd get. Now he had to ditch the burn phone and head out.

The timing had changed, but he committed to following the instructions, regardless. The hour would come for his purposes after satisfying his obligations. If not for his unknown benefactor, who knew Lester well enough to choose him for this job, Lester would still be sitting in that damn shoebox of a cell. The mystery person had orchestrated the entire escape to perfection, and everyone else thought that Lester had done it.

"Well, thanks, whoever you are," he muttered now to himself.

"Time to get moving," he spoke aloud to the others. "We're starting this walk during daylight, so we have to keep our eyes open and our mouths shut." He knew that they'd get assistance along the way. He didn't know what kind, where it would come from, or when he would receive it, but it didn't matter. He just had to keep his eyes open.

Carlos rose from the corner and silently began preparing to leave. The other three were full of questions, complaints, and arguments until Lester turned to them and gave them a look that stole the words from their mouths. It was better not to cross him or make an enemy of him; they had no chance at all to get away and live life elsewhere if they were dead.

Lester stood by the open front door as they filed out wearing the camouflage hunting clothes left for them; the prison garb was buried in the woods. He closed the door and stepped off the porch. In his hand was a map of trails and back roads to follow, keeping them in the woods and protected from view by stands of trees and underbrush. Lester found the map tucked into the fresh clothes left for him at the cabin.

The first stop marked for him was only about five miles away. All it said on the map was "stop." He herded the others in that direction, figuring they could make it in about three hours of moving cautiously.

~~~

"Breaking News – We're interrupting your regularly scheduled programming to bring you this update. Good morning. It's eight a.m., and as we reported thirty minutes age, police have just discovered the remains of nine-year-old Becky Robbins in a wooded area near the southern Henderson County line. The investigation will continue with evidence discovered at the scene. As the Sheriff stated, no one on the force will rest until the killer is brought to justice. Every officer in the county is actively participating."

"And to repeat another earlier news flash – two more escaped convicts were apprehended this morning. Several calls received by the Mountain Valley, West Virginia Police Department, led to the capture. Residents who saw the photos on their local news stations reported the sightings, and the convicts were cornered in a gas station and surrendered after gunfire took place. No one was injured...."

Ma turned off the TV and smacked Bobby Jack upside the head, spilling his coffee. "Evidence was found? I thought I taught ya better! Pack yer things and git outta here, now! Before those cops come lookin' for ya."

"Where do I have to go, ma? I ain't got no money," whined BJ.

"Go visit yer cousins in Kentucky, just git outta here," she insisted, and take yer brother with ya!"

96

BJ went to his room to pack his things. On his way down the hallway, he hollered to Bubba to do the same. Damn that Chaney, this was all his fault. Maybe BJ should stop to see him on the way out and give him a good beatin'. The old man sure deserved it.

~~~

Kasey was still sleeping when the alarm went off at eight a.m. She rolled herself out of bed grudgingly; then, she remembered the invitation to church for this morning, and her world brightened just a little. Last night Kasey pleaded with Trisha to come, but Trisha wouldn't budge. Sunday was her 'sleep all day if she wanted to' day, and she wasn't giving it up.

She knew she had seen people going into the church wearing everything from jeans to Sunday 'best', but she was distraught about what she should wear so as not to stick out in a crowd. What a joke! No matter what she wore, that belly would stick out a mile.

She finally made her wardrobe decision; long jeans, a preggie-top, and a light sweater. Those were definitely 'blend-in' clothes. By eight-thirty, she was cleaned up and ready; she sat down to catch the latest news on TV before forcing herself to walk across the street.

~~~

At eight a.m, Tom got a name and address. He and his partner went to arrest a man on suspicion of murder. The blood on Becky's clothes was not hers; the type matched that of Bobby Jack Taylor, the name on the pawn receipt, and a man with a long history of priors, many violent. Also found were some partial fingerprints which matched those on file for him. It would be at least thirty-six hours before the DNA confirmation on the blood came back from the state capitol, but they could hold him until then, and it would be a slam-dunk. Two unanswered questions: who was the second man in the woods, and how many were involved in the murder? Maybe Bobby Jack would shed some light on that.

Tom checked the address and cringed. He hated that section of town. It always made him feel like he was entering an evil portal when he had to go there. They pulled away in the cruiser, Tom not expecting a warm welcome at the Taylor residence.

By eight-fifteen a.m., according to the GPS information, they were a block away from the target address. Tom slowed down to approach cautiously. As they rounded the corner, an old model pickup was exiting the dirt driveway with two men in the cab. The driver was Bobby Jack, and BJ saw them coming. The demons which had become permanent grotesque attachments to his upper body were frantically giving him instructions.

Almost bald pickup tires spun in the dirt as BJ slammed his foot down on the gas pedal, and the truck lurched forward in a tight turn away from the patrol car, speeding recklessly. Tom hit the gas and switched on the lights and siren as his partner called the dispatcher with info of the pursuit location and requested backup.

Bobby Jack felt pissed and panicked. It was all happening way too fast; he needed time to think. Bubba's eyes were big as boiled eggs, and he had a white-knuckle grip on both the dashboard and the door. BJ sought an escape route, but there wasn't one. The cop car was on his tail. He couldn't outrun them in this old thing. Damn, if he'd just left a few minutes earlier, they would have missed him, and he'd have a good head start.

He was approaching a blind intersection near Myrt's doing about sixty mph and intended to make a hard left and head toward the county road. In an instant, a move he hadn't anticipated, another cop car appeared in front of him, blocking the way. He stomped on the brake and pulled hard on the steering wheel, the pickup skidded sideways, slamming into the patrol car and crushing the right side of his truck.

~~~

At eight-fifteen, Beth caught her breath. She picked up her cell phone and called her parents, "Pray for Tom, Mom! Please pray right now, you and Dad! Something is happening, I can feel it, and he needs us!" They began to pray together on the phone, and the golden warriors following and protecting Tom's car could feel the power flooding through them. They looked at each other and smiled. The prayer cover of the saints was mighty.

~~~

David had awakened hours earlier and was past his need for coffee by this time. If he was asked to name the time of his life which had the most impact on his future, it was a toss-up between the day he learned his wife was killed and yesterday. His head was swimming with what-ifs and recollections of events.

The door to Pauley's room opened, and his son stepped out, hair combed, clean clothes on, and a 'ready to go' expression on his face. David was confused for a minute, he never opened the shop on Sunday, and then he remembered Gabe telling him about the little church and Pastor Luke.

"Do you want to go to the church Gabe told us about, son?"

Pauley stood straight and appeared proud that he had purposely prepared himself without help or prompting from his dad. He wasn't shy about his answer, but words still felt foreign to his mouth. "Yes," he replied softly, choosing no further explanation.

It didn't matter how many years passed or why David stopped believing or attending church. The miracle of his son coming back to him was enough reason to bow to Pauley's desires right now. David went to his room and changed into street clothes. They were out the door at eight-thirty.

~~~

Tom hit the brakes and came to a screeching stop about ten feet from the pickup. The officers in the other patrol car received some minor

99

injuries, but the driver was moving around. Tom's partner radioed for an ambulance, jumped out, and ran to them.

With his gun pulled, Tom carefully walked toward the truck. A small early morning crowd of onlookers was beginning to gather. Bobby Jack slumped over the steering wheel, appeared to be breathing. The other man was crushed and mangled, his head through the windshield, doubtfully alive.

A third patrol car arrived, siren and lights blaring, and the officers hurried to Tom's aid, covering the truck with their drawn pistols. Tom approached the driver's door, opened it, and grabbed BJ by the left shoulder. BJ was marginally conscious and stumbled out of the truck, nose bleeding profusely and a gash above his right eye from flying glass. One of the other officers swung him around to face the truck and handcuffed him, arms behind his body.

Bobby Jack seemed to understand what happened now. He looked through the truck window at the other man, and the officer heard him mutter, "Oh shit, Bubba. Oh, shit"

The air was thick with frenzied, swirling, screeching black ghouls. Hundreds of pairs of red eyes and the stench of sulfur breath would have been enough to terrify the humans witnessing the end of this little drama. There was an excellent reason, so few could see them.

13

Sunday Service

PEOPLE BEGAN filing-in thirty minutes before the service started, tightly packing the pews, leaving no square inch unfilled. Everyone knew there was more purpose this morning than on other Sundays. There was a look in the sky and a feeling in the air. Over one hundred warriors of the Host accumulated on the roof and at the property perimeters, and more were coming.

Pastor Luke was at the door, greeting everyone as they entered. He had asked Gabe to sit off to the side but in the front row so he could come to the front quickly when Luke would call on him later to address the congregation.

Cars packed into the parking lot and overflowed to line the street for blocks in both directions. Atop each arriving vehicle rode an angel. Because the prayers of Luke and Gabe were strong, many lesser demons fled from their human hosts when the angels arrived. Guardian Angels now protected them; the Klazyn demons were furious, but they kept their distance growling and snarling, yet in silence to the human ear.

Some church members took over the greeting task so Luke could step outside to assess the situation. He walked to the street just as Kasey was crossing from the other side and went to meet her.

"I'm glad you decided to join us today," he said warmly as he took her arm to walk her across. Her face glowed. This sincere welcome felt good.

"Thank you so much, Pastor Luke. I am a little nervous," she confessed.

They stepped onto the sidewalk, and he found himself face to face with Jill and Crystal. "Well, this is opportune," he smiled. "Hello ladies, I'd like to introduce you to Kasey. Kasey, this is Jill, and this is Crystal. Kasey lives across the street and is visiting us today for the first time. Will you two take her inside with you and make her feel at home?"

"Of course, Pastor. So nice to meet you, Kasey. It looks like you and Crystal have something in common," smiled Jill. "Let's get inside before all of the seats are gone. Don't want you two little mamas standing."

Kasey looked down at the sidewalk, slightly embarrassed. Crystal took her hand and gave it a little squeeze. "No need to be shy, sweetie. It's my first time here too, except for yesterday afternoon when I helped Jill do some organizing." Kasey and Crystal felt an instant bond which would be helpful in the days to come.

Four teenage boys from the congregation set up the speakers and instruments inside. Luke arranged with them on Saturday to connect the extra sound system components Gabe procured. He was following a feeling, and he knew where those came from. Several men were setting up dozens of additional folding chairs in the yard for the same reason. The little church only held about two hundred and fifty, and when God worked in a powerful way, they knew enough to be ready for it.

With ten minutes to go, he went back inside, satisfied that the men had everything under control. Latecomers would have seats and could hear the sermon, and the weather was accommodating. The front doors would remain wide open. Luke checked the boys in the band, made sure his notes were in order, and gave the nod to Gabe.

The place was abuzz with chatter and disjointed sentences as voices rose and fell, but at nine a.m., the talking stopped, and every face looked toward Luke, standing at the pulpit. He took a moment to survey the packed room and noticed a couple of new faces next to Gabe; a man to his left and a teenage boy between them. The church was filled with a fifty-fifty ratio of new faces to familiar ones.

He stepped up to the microphone and began, "Thank you all for coming this morning. I asked each of our members to bring friends and family today because it's a significant day. You all have outdone yourselves and my cup runneth over." His smile broke the tension. Light applause and a wave of chuckles washed through the pews.

"This is a house of worship and praise, and our church family loves to do both. Let's begin with prayer; then, we'll raise the roof with song. Being in the right spirit is vitally important to the seriousness we have in front of us today."

He bowed his head, and the people in front of him followed suit. "Father, we've come together today with Your guidance and protection to be gathered in accordance with Your will. We ask that You show each of us what You want us to do and where You want us to be. We sense evil permeating our towns and neighborhoods, and we know that You and your Host are far stronger than the darkness. May our prayers empower the Host to fight strongly in battle, and may we be victorious in bringing Your light to the world. In Jesus' name, Amen." And a few hundred amens echoed through the building and across the front yard.

Electric guitars, keyboard, and drums went to work on a rousing version of 'Our God is an Awesome God," and the believers jumped on the musical soul train with enthusiastic voices.

Jill and Crystal sang, but Kasey just watched and let it all soak in. She'd never been in a group of people like this, and it was strange but good, very good.

David remembered the words and began singing without realizing he was even doing so. Pauley's eyes danced, and his grin covered most of his face. His feet tapped to the music, and his body swayed to the strong bass beat. Gabe looked to his left and watched the happiness pouring out of Pauley and the joy radiating from David. For the first time in his life, he felt what it must be like to be a father; love, pride, and fear for this young man who was so much like himself. But God's peace settled over him, and his thoughts moved forward.

Several more energetic praise songs had the people from the front row to the furthest back row in the yard invigorated for half an hour. Then the band slowed the beat and broke into worship with 'It Is Well with My Soul.' Tears often follow when the Spirit moves, and many a cheek wore wet streaks by the song's last strains.

Luke waited until the music faded to quiet before he began again.

"We are here today because this is our church home, or because someone has invited us, but most specifically because things here have changed for us, and we commonly seek God in times of trouble. Our community has been on an emotional roller coaster for the past two days—devastation, fear, anticipation, hope, expectation, and sadness. We were called to work together in finding a lost child, a parent's worst nightmare. And despite our efforts, we've heard this morning that we did not change the outcome of the terrible drama which occurred. We are slammed with the reality that we are mortal, and our hearts are in pain."

"A child was taken from her parents, her schoolmates, her friends. She was taken from this earth. How and why we may never know. But what we know, and is most important, is that she is now beyond any harm or hurt. Becky is in the loving embrace of our Father. It's now her family members who need our help and our prayers. They need God's peace to carry them across the abyss of loss and grief."

"Please reach out to them with love if you know this family. If you don't, well, we're a small community; everyone touches everyone in some way. Our responsibility is to turn the light on in every dark corner of the world where we live. A tragedy like this can put the light out permanently for some. Where darkness encroaches, evil gains a foothold."

"Until the person responsible for Becky Robbins' death is caught, and even for a time after, we'll be watchful and concerned for our children. We'll look at those we don't know, maybe with suspicion and maybe even silent accusation. Unfortunately, in our natural need to 'profile' people, we automatically group those with certain looks together, which is the same as condemning the innocent with the guilty. We, as Christians, need to be sensitive to the needs of those less fortunate than ourselves. We must follow the example of Jesus and extend our love and charity."

"So, what is the answer? Who do we trust? We trust our Father. He is the protector of our souls. God has given us, each and every one of us, free will, and He will never take that away. The free will of someone walking in darkness could certainly be a danger to our flesh but never to our souls. Evil is always nearby, always crossing paths with us, always just a moment ahead or a moment behind. And there will be times when the call comes for us to stand up for good in a spiritual battle."

"We've just recently been alerted to yet another danger. Twenty-two men, most are violent criminals, are still at large and could be anywhere. Are we walking through the valley of the shadow of death? Maybe so, but we're told to fear no evil. But how long has it been since our quiet little county has had this much major criminal activity? Never! The Police Department will also confirm that there's been a huge increase in lesser crimes like theft, sex crimes, domestic violence, assault and battery, and illegal drug use."

"Our environment has been changing, at a rapid pace. Have you noticed the unusual color of the sky lately? At this time of year, it should be clear and sunny with a hint of crispness in the air. The moon and stars aren't visible, and the dark of the night is thick and smothering? How about the strange feelings of foreboding that creep up on you before you can pray them away?"

"All of these things are like déjà vu for me. They happened once before in my life, twenty years ago. They were the preface to something I'd hoped I would never have to experience again. The fiercest spiritual battle I could ever have imagined, though it manifested in real life, in the flesh. A college friend of mine, who is here with us today, shared that experience with me. I'm here because he stood by my side and saved my life. Much was revealed to me then about powers at work, powers beyond our vision. But the most important thing I learned was that our Father is always there, and even our darkest days serve a purpose."

"This is my friend, Gabe Matheson. He is a true spiritual warrior, anointed by our Lord. He has devoted his life to fighting the darkness. I'd like him to come up now to explain what this means and why it is so important to us here in our town," Luke said as he held his arm out to welcome Gabe to the front.

The congregation was silent. Most everyone had expected some talk about Becky Robbins and perhaps a little memorial and thanks to the volunteers. This led to far more than they had imagined, yet what the Pastor said was right on target. Things were strange. Many who thought they were the only ones who felt that way were relieved to know they weren't alone. And then they were worried again because this validated those feelings and made the strangeness a real threat.

Gabe rose from his seat and took a few strides to the microphone. He and Luke briefly embraced in the way of comrades wishing each other well before going to the battlefield.

Gabe turned to face the believers and began in his deep voice, "I do a lot of traveling. Luke and I haven't seen each other much in the past several years, but we're as close as twins, and he knows where I go and what I do when I get there. I called him a couple of days ago to ask him if he had been sensing anything unusual here in Henderson

County because I felt it where I was on the Pacific coast."

He paused. "Luke told me about the change in atmosphere here, the sky, the uneasy feelings, and the wariness that was growing like a knot in his stomach. Tell me, how many of you have felt the same thing?"

Almost every hand went up. Gabe continued, nodding, "I was in California when I made this call, and yet, I knew what was beginning here, over one thousand miles away. You might wonder how that could happen. Just know that there are things beyond our understanding that are, things that exist, and we have to accept them."

"I am a spiritual warrior. What does that mean to you here in this quiet little part of the country where nothing much usually happens to change your day-to-day lives? It means that I am called to go where God directs me, to places where evil and good are at war. Fierce war. My job is to prepare God's people for the battle. And I am called to this place," explained Gabe.

The congregation began murmuring, and people looked at each other with worried expressions. "Don't be afraid," Gabe boomed, catching their attention again. And in a softer voice, "But be prepared."

"The abduction of Becky Robbins and then the prison break; these are just the beginnings of the bad things we will see in the days ahead. How do you protect yourselves and your families? Be vigilant, be watchful, band together for safety in numbers. Take your children to and from school in carpools. Be there if they have after-school activities, or better yet, suspend those activities until this is over. If you are an employer, give extra time to your employees to take care of their families. Your business will not suffer."

"Meet with law enforcement and have open lines of communication. Organize neighborhood watches and report any unusual activities or strangers in the area. Don't take unnecessary risks."

"But at the top of the list – pray. We will need many prayer warriors. You will probably never know the magnitude or importance of your prayers, but I can attest that I am alive today because of the prayers of others. Pastor Luke will be organizing prayer chains and groups, and shifts. What I expect to happen here will likely occur over the next two weeks, maybe much sooner. Stay in touch with each other. When the critical time is near, we'll all know what to do. We will get through this together and show the evil that this is not a place for it to take hold. The people of this county are strong of faith, and we will resist and conquer."

"If you are curious about specifics – I don't have any. These kinds of things are never revealed to me until they take place. I can tell you that the evil you will need to fight against is evil you will be able to see in the flesh. Like the person who killed a little nine-year-old girl here just two days ago. Like the escaped convicts. But I also caution you. Evil often wears a less frightening mask. Follow the urgings of the Holy Spirit, who is with you always. If something doesn't feel right in your gut, get away from it. If you feel depressed or worried, pray it away, those feelings are not from our Father. If you are unsure about taking action, don't. Pray for protection around your loved ones, church family, and community. Pray for discernment to have a clear vision about God's will."

"God has already overcome the world. We just have to stand on His Word."

Gabe paused again and then returned to his seat. Pauley put his hand over Gabe's and smiled. No sound, not a cough, nor even a rustle of papers came from the congregation.

Luke took his place at the podium and spoke slowly and clearly, "The Lord is my shepherd; I shall not want. He maketh me to lie down in green pastures: He leadeth me beside the still waters. He restoreth my soul: he leadeth me in the paths of righteousness for his name's sake."

"Yea, though I walk through the valley of the shadow of death, I will fear no evil: for thou art with me; thy rod and thy staff they comfort me. Thou preparest a table before me in the presence of mine enemies: thou anointest my head with oil; my cup runneth over. Surely goodness and mercy shall follow me all the days of my life: and I will dwell in the house of the Lord forever."

"These words are in the book of Psalms. They are particularly significant today because God wants us to trust in Him, in ALL things. He gives us safe places to rest, and he revitalizes us. If we follow Him, he will lead us to be better people and accomplish great things to His honor and glory."

"Never fear when facing difficulty or darkness because God has your back! He will fight for you and care for you, giving you all you need and more. No matter what may happen to your flesh, as long as you carry the banner of God in your arms and the Son of God in your heart, you will spend eternity in His presence."

"While we're here on this earth, in this form, in these bodies, we've been directed to have love, faith, and charity. We're to serve and care for one another. But we're also to stand fast against evil and those who make friends with the terrors of darkness."

"Our greatest defense against evil is in Jesus. Recommit yourself to Him today. Do it now if you haven't opened your heart to a personal relationship with our Lord. Pray with me, "Father, I want to begin or strengthen my relationship with your Son. I accept Him as my savior and ask you to forgive my sins. I want to become a new person in you and put the flesh behind me. Please give me your strength and your peace, Father, as you write my name in the Book of the Lamb. In the name of Jesus, Amen."

"Take God's peace with you today. Spread His love, rebuke the darkness, and good shall continue to be victorious. Let His light shine through you, and others will want it, and it will illuminate the world. If you don't already own a bible, there are stacks of them on the tables outside. Take one and begin to read. The New Testament book of John is a great place to start. Then share the Word with anyone you know who has not yet become a believer. You could be the one God sends to lead them to a much better eternity. The stronger the forces of God, the surer we are to have victory over the evil coming our way."

One of the boys in the band, the lead vocal singer, began to sing solo with no backup music. After the first line, the other three joined in, and then they added music as the congregation began to sing too. "This little light of mine, I'm gonna let it shine...."soon, three hundred and fifty voices rose to the heavens with the proclamation that their light would drive away the shadows in every corner. Over and over, they sang the verses.

Numerous translucent warriors of the Host, which had filled the grounds and the rooftop, began to glow in brilliant golden rays of light. Their angelic voices filled the air in praise for the newly saved souls, including Pauley's.

Involuntary shudders rippled through the ranks of the fearsome demons circling high in the sky overhead, and they began to shriek and writhe from their pain.

Pauley's ears registered the deafening shrieks and the ethereal voices of the angels. But he was so overcome; he didn't know if he imagined or actually heard these new, otherworldly sounds.

14

More Trouble

AFTER THE service, people were milling about, talking, getting their names on lists for prayer shifts, and carpooling. Almost no one had left the church grounds yet, even now, twenty minutes after the service ended. Luke walked from one group to the next, listening to the conversations and commenting.

This mighty family of believers was not running scared or abandoning a pastor who had suddenly lost his mind. They were putting on their battle armor and facing the challenge. Luke was humbled and grateful.

Jill and her husband took charge of organizing again and sat at a folding table with pen and paper in hand, surrounded by people waiting to volunteer. She was a natural, and her gifts would be well utilized here.

Gabe stood talking in earnest with the man and boy who were sitting with him during the service. The boy was as alive as a downed electric wire but didn't seem to be speaking. Luke realized there was no question, this had to be Pauley, the miraculous young man who Gabe had described, and the man was his father, David. Amazing. He would make it a point to speak with them.

On the sidewalk stood Kasey and Crystal, lingering deep in conversation. Luke was glad they were together. Perhaps these two single mothers-to-be could be of comfort to each other through the births of their babies. Crystal's auburn hair fell around her shoulders in soft curls, and she looked angelic. He shook his head a bit, took a deep breath, and then moved toward another group of people, among whom was the Chief of Police. How beautifully God's plans always came together. There was still a lot to do, and talking with the head of the police was a good place to start.

~~~

Kasey was like a broken dam as she spilled out her story to Crystal. It just felt like she should, like it was the right thing to do and the right person to listen to her. Keeping all of her joys and disappointments bottled up inside with no one to talk to who would be able to understand had been more challenging than she thought. Crystal was so empathetic. Even the fifteen-year difference in their ages shrunk to nothing though Crystal was almost old enough to be her mother.

Then Crystal shared her story, and Kasey felt her troubles shrink in comparison. They stood on the sidewalk across from her apartment building, getting to know each other but somehow feeling like they'd already known each other for years.

"Please come visit. I don't live very far away. You must be busy with work and school, but if you find time on Saturdays or Sundays – I'd love for you to be part of our lives," she said, rubbing her baby belly. "Maybe our kids can grow up to be best friends," Crystal offered.

Kasey had tears in her eyes. She'd never felt so welcomed, ever, by anyone. If this being a Christian, it would suit her fine. She agreed to visit Crystal the following Saturday after work and have dinner together. Then they would see each other at church on Sunday. They hugged, and Kasey said her goodbyes as she headed across the street, followed by her invisible warrior. She had prayed the prayer.

Crystal walked back toward the crowd surrounding Jill, meeting several more church members along her way. Everyone welcomed her with open arms. "Put me on your list, Jill. And count on me to help you with organizing too," she called. She turned quickly and bumped into Luke. He caught her as she wobbled and steadied her, "I'm so sorry, Crystal. Are you OK?"

"Of course," she laughed. Luke hesitated to take his hands off her shoulders, and they were both awkwardly silent for a few seconds. He allowed one hand to fall to his side but trailed the other down her arm to take her hand. "Would you have coffee with me one morning this week?" he blurted.

She was momentarily speechless. Had he overstepped his bounds? "I'd love to, but I'm not drinking coffee now. OK, if it's juice for me? And my appetite is growing, so you could even throw in breakfast with that."

His heart began to beat again, and he laughed. "OK with me, we'll talk later. May I call you?"

She nodded and blushed. He was captivated.

"Pastor Luke, may I introduce.....," one of the church members interrupted. Crystal shyly smiled at him, tilted her head slightly as though she understood, and walked away.

~~~

The Girl Scout camp was set up in a meadow the size of a football field. Tents on one side, campfires in the middle, and activities took place on the opposite side. The perimeter was brush and woods. Three troops combined for this weekend camping excursion: a total of thirty-nine girls and nine leaders.

There was a rustle in the bushes near the tents, and two little girls looked up. All of the others were at the campfire doing their best to make an edible breakfast that would earn them their badges.

Back in a clearing, about twenty feet away, stood a man dressed only in a long coat. He held it open with one hand and touched himself with the other. They screamed and ran toward the Scout Leaders fifty yards away.

Rufus Chaney lumbered off in a hurry, back to his van before they had the presence of mind to chase him.

~~~

They reached the 'stop' spot just before eleven a.m. These men were not hunters or outdoors men. The three 'extras,' as Lester thought of them, had already used up all of the water in the first of two canteens they were each given. Carlos kept a low profile and had barely touched a quarter of his water in the first one.

Walking cautiously into the open area first, Lester saw the vehicle before the others did. He approached it slowly, signaling to the others to hold back. A man, dressed in farmer's clothing, sat in the driver's seat reading a worn paperback book. He looked into the rear-view mirror and saw Lester nearing his door.

"I'm the transportation arranged for you," he said to Lester in a low voice. "Your map says this is a 'stop'; I'm the assistance you get. I don't want to see you; follow the directions you got."

Lester looked at him suspiciously, but no one else would have known about the map. The vehicle was an open-back truck filled with hay and covered with a tied-down tarp, a common sight in this rural area. The driver opened his door and got out. "Follow me," he said, leading Lester to the back of the truck while looking only at the ground. "You people will get in under the hay; I'll make sure you're well covered. I can drive eighty miles over back roads, avoiding two county-line roadblocks, before I can go no further. Then I leave you per my instructions."

Lester knew the man got a good amount of money for the task. He waved the others out of the woods, and they clambered aboard and then burrowed within the hay piles. Five minutes later, the truck was on its way toward Henderson County. It would be a long eighty-mile ride traveling on bumpy roads at twenty-five miles per hour, but it was much faster than walking.

~~~

By noon Tom was sitting at his desk in the Sheriff's Office. He'd booked Bobby Jack and began the questioning about the murder a couple of hours ago. It was slow going, though. BJ was still not putting it all together, and Tom knew there was a lot more to the story that he needed to know. So far, BJ hadn't lawyered up nor even asked for his phone call.

The detective took over the questioning, and Tom was relieved to get a break. The past couple of days had been grueling. First the search, now the constant calls coming in, totally out of character, this was usually a quiet place. People in the community reported various crimes happening all over the county and the sightings of unsavory-looking strangers walking the streets. Each report needed to be looked into by one of the deputies. But it was a small force, and most officers and deputies were part of the chase, so they were behind on the follow-ups, and still, the phones rang.

He picked up the messages on his desk and saw a report from a Girl Scout leader with the group camping east of town. A flasher in the woods had been close to the camp and scared a couple of the girls. These were girls about the age of Becky Robbins. "Good Lord! What is going on in this county? We're going to have to expand the force - fast - if this craziness keeps up!" he muttered to himself. He put out an APB to all officers in the county; be on the watch for an older man wearing a tan trench coat and nothing else. Seriously? A tan trench coat? This guy watched too many old movies. They would check out the wooded area near the camp as soon as they could get to it.

Another report was dropped on Tom's desk. The dead man in the getaway truck was Bubba, Bobby Jack's brother. A background check on Bubba gave them little; he was a small-time criminal with minor entries on his rap sheet. Bobby Jack said that his brother was 'slow,' so Tom figured he had been an assistant, maybe even just for the disposal of the body. There was still something Bobby Jack was holding back.

Bubba's body was extracted and taken to the county morgue. Both wrecked vehicles were locked up in the yard of the towing company. The family notification was in order, but the Lieutenant suggested it wait. There was a chance that other family members were involved; letting them know what had happened to Bubba would send them running.

It seemed like all hell was breaking loose. Tom didn't know how right he was.

Beth would be home soon. She usually stopped for lunch after church with friends when he was on duty. He wanted to talk with her for just a minute, but he'd text instead. They'd talk soon. Then he realized that there was a text waiting for him from her. She was worried.

~~~

He sat alone in the study of his Tudor-style mansion. Massive mahogany furniture was all custom made. One wall filled with bookshelves from floor to ceiling contained leather-bound first editions, expensive decor, and artifacts he gathered during his world travels. Oriental rugs on the floor, original paintings hung in museum fashion; all of this was his because of who he'd become. Because of the deal he made years ago with the people who had it all. Now he danced with the devil himself, and it didn't bother him a bit.

His fingers rose to the sides of his face, around his ears and hairline. They could afford the best, and it was only the best who had created the face he wore. No one, not even his own mother, would ever have been able to look at him now and know who he was. That hillbilly kid died decades ago and would never be resurrected, at least not if he could help it. But he had to fix this mess on his own because if 'they' knew what he'd exposed in a drunken stupor to some bimbo he'd had a fling with, the whole plan could come tumbling down. They had a lot of years invested in him. If he screwed it up, it would mean his life.

She vowed to remain discrete when they began the affair a year ago. What the hell made him think he could relax and let down his guard with her? She was nothing but a good lay, a diversion from the stress and pressures of keeping up the facade of an upstanding politician with a perfect family and life. She was no sworn confidante or one of 'them,' but somehow, he'd felt enough trust to be himself, to let his guard down for just one weak moment. She was that good.

Then she disappeared two weeks ago, right after he let those dark secrets slip out. At first, he'd thought that "they" had found out about his loose lips and had taken her. But it was worse, she was a plant, and he'd been too stupid to know it. He suspected where she was going with the knowledge she now had, but he would get there first. And she would pay. In the meantime, he was going to one hell of a lot of trouble and expense to tie up these loose ends. It annoyed him greatly.

He scowled and rubbed his perfectly smooth temples near the perfect streaks of gray in his flawlessly styled hair.

Odors of sulfur and brimstone hung in the room like heavy fog beyond his senses. The creature, crouched behind the desk next to the five-thousand-dollar leather chair, towered above the man, narrowly falling shy of the fifteen-foot ceilings. This beast was a warlord of high rank, a Gai'Ograh, and he was permanently attached to the Senator.

Dozens of smaller but no less grotesque creatures hung about, awaiting the Demon Lord's next command. The ultimate plan belonged to the darkness, and taking over the country preceded taking over the world. Any error not immediately corrected would critically affect their timeline, and the Dark Master would not be pleased

~~~

Chaney sped down a back road to get to his place. He got sloppy again and too close to home with his bad choices again. Was he losing it mentally? Did he just not care anymore? The sound of a siren broke into his consciousness. Oh damn!

Chaney slowed down and pulled the van over. The window was already down. He pulled his registration out of the glove compartment and waited for the cop to come to him, and watched in the side mirror. The deputy wrote down his license plate number and then approached the window; Chaney anticipated the phrase "Your license and registration, sir."

He was unprepared for the look on the cop's face when he peered at Chaney through the window and then pulled his handgun, ordering Chaney out of the van. Now he was in trouble. How would he explain why he was wearing a tan trench coat, with nothing under it, and with his clothes bunched up in a ball behind the driver's seat?

~~~

Tom got a call from dispatch. An officer was bringing in a man fitting the description of the flasher. Tom gave the instructions to bring him into the Sheriff's Station for questioning. He sent a quick text to Beth telling her the day was complete chaos but that he was fine and would see her this evening.

It was time to check on Bobby Jack and the detective in the interrogation room. They'd been in there for a while now. Tom wanted to know if the time produced any leads.

The detective stepped out of the room as Tom approached the door. "BJ's talking about how his mother was in on the body disposal; in fact, it was her idea. This guy isn't the brightest," he confided as he called for a car and a couple of officers to arrest the mother as an accomplice. Tom suggested he send two cars; these people were volatile, and caging a she-wolf was no easy task. Then he went to the kitchen to make another pot of coffee; he'd need it.

Ten minutes later, a deputy took Chaney to interrogation room number two. The Sheriff's Office only had two, and BJ was waiting for the detective to return in room one. As Chaney passed the door to room one, the detective opened it to go back inside. At that moment, Chaney and BJ made eye contact, Bobby-Jack's eyes popped open, and he began to yell. "You som-bitch! Yer the reason I'm in here and Bubba is dead! You lousy pre-vert som-bitch!"

"That's it!" Tom said to the detective, slamming the door to BJ's room. "That's what he was holding back." Tom had another deputy put the visibly shaken Chaney into the holding cell. He'd talk with Chaney after calling dispatch to find out where the arrest occurred. When Tom got his answer, he asked another deputy to meet the tow truck driver and bring the white van to the compound. He was pretty sure it would turn out to be evidence.

~~~

The library was open from one till four on Sunday afternoons. She stood in front of the big wooden door with her hand on the knob and pulled. This was where she hoped to find the information that would corroborate what she already knew so she could move forward with what had to be done.

She walked up to the librarian and asked where to find forty-year-old newspaper stories. "We have those on microfiche, dear," answered the elderly lady with her gray hair pulled back in a bun, an Aunt Bea from Mayberry look alike. "Right this way. You can look through the catalog files to your heart's content," said the nice woman, leaving her to her search. She settled in for the afternoon. With the large machine in front of her and a box of rectangular plastic cards on the table, Cheyenne Pierce was on a mission.

The librarian didn't remember having seen this pretty lady before. One was unlikely to forget her. She was very tall and slender, but that long, straight, raven black hair and those stunning turquoise eyes set her apart.

The thought faded as soon as she returned to the check-out desk, where the next person awaited her assistance.

~~~

Jake woke up in a decent mood but felt like an army of muddy boots had marched through his mouth, and inside his head was a dull thumping. After scoring the gun last night, he had made plans with a shady guy named Rocco to knock over a small bank branch this coming Friday between noon and three o'clock, as soon as the Wells Fargo truck had delivered a load of cash for covering payday checks. He had to wait until Thursday to get the fake ID custom-made for him, so he planned the job the day after, which worked out perfectly. No sense in waiting around for trouble.

Then Jake went out for a few drinks to celebrate. He knew where Peggy kept her tips, and her tip money was always his drinkin' money. With the job done, and his cash in hand, he could high tail it outta here and not look back.

He rolled over and looked at the alarm clock, one twelve. Good, he could go to Myrt's for some decent food and a cold beer. God knew that Peggy couldn't cook squat and likely had nothing in the house to eat anyway. He lay still for a minute, listening, no sounds. That meant she was probably at work; he wouldn't have to argue with her when he left.

Peeling off his stinking shirt from yesterday, he put on a clean but rumpled one from the pile on the floor. Showering wasn't a concern; he wasn't especially hygienic. Two minutes later, he was out the door with his new gun tucked into the back of his belt, under his shirt. Jake and a weapon were a dangerous combination.

~~~

Over a thousand miles away, on a beautiful estate near Washington DC, a conglomeration of monstrous-sized Demon Princes gathered with their attached elite humans. Giant dragon wings, burning red eyes, green slimy drool, sulfurous stench; all in good form and eager to get on with the plan. "A new world order is the ultimate goal. It is time for our dark forces to overthrow those not in line with us. Piece by piece, the plan is coming together," spoke a Demon Prince, the words coming out of his mouth just fractions of a second before being spoken by a human in a fifty-thousand-dollar business suit. The other Gai'Ograh nodded enthusiastically as the details were unfolded before them.

Each of these vile creatures, the upper echelon in the ranks of demon royalty, commands a prominent person in world leadership within the political and financial fields. But only the highest-ranking command those humans who are the global puppeteers, who pull the strings but remain unseen by most.

Humans are only attached to demons of this rank after they prove over and over again that they are fully compliant to a lesser demon's suggestions and have no remorse about the actions they take to follow those instructions. It is a sort of graduation; the more they can be used by the darkness, the more prestigious their position in leadership, and the higher the ranking of the demon who commands them. The humans are pawns and, ironically, the reason that the whole spiritual war had started in the first place. Victory will be sweeter because humans are the primary weapon used to eradicate their own kind.

They coordinate battles in scattered locations across the country and the world from this base. Success is almost guaranteed with the strategy to conquer from within. The plan is simple, as they gain more and more of the non-conspicuous areas of the country, these cities and counties and states will eventually overwhelm the entirety, and the whole will fall to darkness. With the United States under their control, the rest of the world will go down predictably like a row of dominoes.

One Demon Prince here commands a prominent politician, a Senator who was chosen as a promising boy and grew into an asset of the best kind. One who they created from scratch and who had shown no hesitation for personal gain and no guilt about those he destroyed. Much time and effort are invested in this human as a pivotal and critical part of the operation. He recently jeopardized it with an indiscretion; thus, they zeroed in on the county where he was born in a Mid-Western state. A piece of lingering evidence tied him to serious trouble, and it could kill his candidacy for the top position in the country. But they will make it right with a few revisions to the plan; too much was at stake to let it go. This location will be theirs soon, despite the news that one of their most vigorous human opponents and obstacles had recently arrived. Now is the perfect opportunity to remove Gabe Matheson from the face of the earth. The battle will eliminate him and make room for the infusion of more false prophets.

The corruption of Christians is the biggest bonus in the war and that single thing that makes everything else more enjoyable. The more "God lovers" they turn into money-hungry zealots for wealth and power, the more innocents get taken with them into the ways of evil. The media is a huge asset, and televangelists are the golden trophies. The warlords encounter few dangerous humans who cannot be turned. But Gabe Matheson is one of them. So, his death will bring celebration.

When this victory is theirs and all loose ends are disposed of, the Senator will have a clear path to the Presidency, which will become a perpetual dictatorship.

The discussion was over. The human puppets, who foolishly thought themselves the puppeteers, left the meeting, smugly satisfied that they would soon run the United States government. And with them went the Crown Princes of the Army of Darkness. They knew the truth of who was in charge.

~~~

For fourteen years, Pauley listened to people talk. It wasn't that he couldn't speak; Pauley did not need to communicate. It was like he had been at a movie theater, sitting in the dark, watching everyone else going through their lives. He was just an observer.

But recently, he saw something which reached out of that movie like it was in 3-D—burning red eyes in the dark. He mentally retreated from them but was curious. Then he began to hear and smell things differently. The same night, when they passed the church on their way home, he saw the light and the warriors of the Host. The light flowed over him like soothing water in a hot shower, waking the part of him that had been dormant. He became conscious of a desire to live. Pauley was finally compelled to step out of the movie theater as an observer and jump into life. Then the visions began. He tried to put them all on paper but could only capture a few so far; they came so fast.

He sat here now with Gabe, the warrior in his visions. Gabe was explaining things so he'd understand what was happening. He and Gabe and only a few others in the world could see the angels and the demons. But Gabe said he would be Pauley's mentor and protector because he had a lot to learn.

Pauley's words were coming more easily now too. He'd found his voice, and he knew what the words meant; it was just getting his mouth to produce them for the first time. It was still his place to listen and learn, though, so his speech had time to catch up.

"I don't know if your visions are past or future, Pauley. The fact that you have them is new to me. I never know what's coming; I just get feelings and thoughts which lead me to where I'm supposed to go. That's God's way of communicating with me. We'll have to do some research and experimenting to learn more about your gifts and how God wants you to use them," explained Gabe. I believe that God will direct you, maybe by using the Angels or me, or maybe by laying His words on your heart. But don't worry, you aren't alone in this.

The two of them and David were sitting in a diner where they'd gone for burgers after church. David asked questions, and Gabe answered to the best of his ability. Pauley saw the vast, dark clouds of demons in the sky and those lurking from rooftops and telephone wires on the way there. He saw demons attached to people walking on the street and even sitting here in the diner, just tables away. But golden warriors accompanied the three of them and all the people from the church. The demons seemed to shrink from the direct blazing sight of the warriors.

"Never make eye contact with the demons, Pauley. I know it will be difficult, but they shouldn't know that you can see them," cautioned Gabe. Of course, the Host knows our secret, and that's good, but any apparent contact with them will also alert the demons, so be covert about this."

Pauley nodded in agreement, he knew the meaning of 'covert' from the spy shows on TV, and he could do that with no problem. Looking at the burger and fries in front of him, his mouth watered. Pauley went to work on consuming everything the way a fourteen-year-old boy should.

David marveled at how normal Pauley had become compared to how he was just a few days ago. Normal? Well, maybe he passed normal in one giant leap and flew way beyond it.

~~~

Two cruisers pulled up into the yard where Bobby-Jack lived. It seemed deserted. Deputies cautiously circled the shack, peering into windows and checking out the storage areas. The occupants had vacated in a hurry. They radioed in their findings.

The message came to Tom, who issued an APB for the second time that day. This time for Bobby-Jack's mother. There were still roadblocks in place because of the escaped convicts. Chances were good that she wouldn't get far. Several surrounding counties had set up roadblocks, and they were also receiving the APB.

It was time for him to chat with Rufus Chaney and discover what happened to Becky. Then he could put a couple of bad guys away. One good thing about placing child molesters behind bars is that the prison population didn't like those crimes either. The punishment doled out by inmates was harsh justice.

Tom had Chaney taken to the interrogation room. He walked to the door and opened it, steeling himself with a deep breath. There sat a smelly, old, balding, fat man in a trench coat. Tom thought of him touching a little nine-year-old girl and the terror she must have felt. It made him want to retch. This man was going down.

~~~

Five men crawled out from under the hay: hot, cranky, and dusty. The truck lumbered away with no conversation between the men and the driver. His job over, he wanted to get as far from them as he could.

Lester pulled out his map and looked around, orienting himself by the noted landmarks. It was about three in the afternoon, and they were to shelter for the night in a big hunting blind nearby. It didn't sound cozy, but Lester had undoubtedly had less to work with. He started walking in the direction of the blind, and the others followed behind him, Carlos in the lead.

Ten minutes later, they found their destination, a large platform up in a substantially sized tree. Lester climbed up first. There were some shabby blankets, a couple of gallon jugs of water, and several packets of dried beef jerky piled up for their use. He handed down the water and jerky and told them to go easy; it could be a while before they got more food.

The three 'extras' started to hoard the jerky until Lester climbed down and put a stop to it. He took it all back, gave them each one piece, and handed the rest to Carlos to hold. Carlos cringed; Lester painted a bull's eye on his back in doing that. Now he had to depend on Lester's protection, or these guys would do him in without a second thought.

They filled the canteens and put the rest of the water aside for their use tonight. The canteens would be for tomorrow's travels again.

"Best you all settle in and get some rest. We'll be doing a lot of walkin' tomorrow to avoid roadblocks," ordered Lester. "If you need to walk around a bit, just don't go too far. If anyone sees you and you lead them back to us – you're dead." No one needed clarification. "We'll climb up in the blind at dark. Till then, sit or sleep your choice. Just be quiet."

Two of the other men settled on the ground and started chatting. The third wandered into the woods. Carlos sat under a tree in the shade and thought about Kasey. His life was a mess. Did he have the right to pull her and a baby into it too? He had time to decide. It would still take a few days to get there.

Lester sat in the blind, looking out in all directions. They had a few hours to kill until dark. He saw nothing moving, but things were moving all around them, black vile things.

15

Cheyenne

SHE GOT her hair and build from her Indian blood. After tracing it back herself to confirm her mother's claims, she found that she was one-quarter Native American from the Cheyenne tribe. That explained her mother's clever choice of 'Cheyenne' for her only daughter's name. Where she got the eyes, who knew? The other three-quarters of her heritage was like the United Nations.

Hers wasn't a good childhood. She was an only child, bullied by other kids in the trailer park. Her mother was an enabler to her father's alcoholism and turned a blind eye when, in his drunkenness, he progressed to sexually abusing his daughter.

Cheyenne ran away when she was fifteen and had been on her own since. She waitressed her way through her GED, a BS degree in criminology, and a black belt in Karate before the FBI recruited her. With her looks, most of Cheyenne's work was undercover, pretending to be something she wasn't – dumb. The assignments she got were high-level corrupt men who thought they were entitled to it all and had long ago crossed the line. She was good at her job, and they were terrible at keeping secrets from beautiful women whom they greatly underestimated.

The FBI had a suspicion about Senator Gregory Manning, but those details were above her pay grade. They wanted something on him, though, and that was her job. Her assignments were long-term; she was to take whatever time needed to get close enough to her targets to dig out their secrets. This time it took a little over a year before she got what she needed. Now she was on the trail of evidence that would derail his career path.

She preferred to be a loner. A few acquaintances at the bureau talked with her in passing, but she had no real confidants and no relatives who mattered. One other agent had tried to get close to her, and he was genuinely a good guy, but she wasn't looking for friendships or relationships, though he was someone she felt she could trust in a pinch. Working alone didn't disturb her, but the older she got, the more the solitude crossed her mind. She toyed with thoughts of having someone around who was entirely in tune with her, like two superheroes in partnership to rid the world of bad guys. She chuckled to herself. "Thirty-five years old, and I have a fantasy in a rural library about being Batman and Robin with someone who doesn't exist," she thought.

The librarian rang a little gold bell that had been sitting on the check-out counter. Cheyenne looked at her watch; it was three fifty-five p.m., and the library was closing in five minutes. Her work here, done for today anyway. The microfiche search uncovered the news headline she was looking for with the detail she needed to put this case in a closed file once she found the physical evidence.

To that end, she now needed to find a person, Rufus Chaney. After putting away the items she had been using, she walked back to the desk. "Thank you for your help," she said softly to the librarian. "I need one more thing though, would you happen to have a local phone book handy before I go?"

The librarian reached behind the desk and handed the book to her. "Dear, you don't look familiar. Are you new in town?" she asked.

"Yes, ma'am. I'm doing a little research on some history here, which won't take long."

"Well, if you need a place to stay, there's a lovely little bed and breakfast just around the corner on Old Oak Ave," she said, smiling warmly. "My sister owns it and would be happy to have you stay for as long as you want. It's very quiet, and the rate is reasonable. It's called the Settle Inn."

"Why, thank you. I will do just that as soon as I leave here, and I appreciate the information. A quiet place in this part of town would be just perfect." She found the number and address for the only Chaney in the phone book, jotted it down in her spiral notebook, gave a little wave goodbye, and left the library. Standing on the front steps, she pulled out her cell phone and touched the app for the GPS. Chaney's place was about four miles away. She'd check into the B&B first and then see about this guy.

The four-wheel-drive, hardtop Jeep she rented under an FBI approved alias would stay in its space at the library for now. Cheyenne walked around the corner and entered the Settle Inn. The aroma of baked chicken and homemade apple pie filled her nostrils, and her stomach rumbled.

An hour later, full and comfortable in her room, Cheyenne began going over her notes. Her mark, Senator Manning, the man whose life she was assigned to infiltrate, had told her that there were two girls in their early teens. He and Chaney raped them and then strangled them, dumping their bodies in the river. The newspaper said that two girls ages eleven and twelve were found in the river, partially decomposed. There had been evidence of sexual activity which the Medical Examiner wanted to call violent but was unable to reach a definite conclusion due to the condition of the bodies.

That part of his story was a check. Now, this Chaney guy, how did he connect to the Senator? She needed to talk with him as soon as she could find him, but she needed to do it in a way he wouldn't catch on to or be frightened off. He was the clue to the buried box, the evidence that would tie it all together with a pretty bow.

Reaching over to put her notebook on the nightstand, she saw the bible sitting there. Had she ever really read one? Not really, but she'd gone to Sunday School a few times when she was little, and one of her college professors was a Christian. He shared some thought-provoking stories from the bible one afternoon when she went to him for some assistance. How they'd gotten on the subject was a lost memory now. Though she'd always felt a higher power existed, there wasn't a solid belief base supporting her feeling.

The Klazyn demon on her shoulder laughed out loud, a wheezy, raspy, gasping sound that she couldn't hear. It could sense her confusion, and her uncertain quasi-spirituality was ripe for the darkness. Satisfied with the job it was doing, it flexed its talons and gripped her tighter.

"Time to go," she thought and grabbed her purse and her handgun.

16

Word Spreads

THE SHERIFF'S Office was busier than Tom had ever seen it! Deputies, dispatchers, clerical workers, even right down to the custodial staff. It would be only a matter of hours, probably less, before the media would be beating down the door about the arrested suspects. And how they'd kept it under wraps, this far was a mystery to Tom.

He was still interrogating Chaney at five p.m. Rufus wasn't spilling his guts like Bobby Jack, though. This was like pulling teeth; the old codger was cagey. Tom asked another deputy to return Chaney to the holding cell. They'd start over again tomorrow.

The detective emerged from the room where Bobby Jack still sat. He related to Tom how BJ explained how he and Chaney picked up the girl and killed her. Also, how Chaney planned the first dump, and BJ's mother, Ma, had orchestrated the final burial. And now, the whole confession was on videotape.

They still needed something physical to tie Chaney to the murder; BJ's confession wasn't enough to convict him without evidence. Tom told the detective that Chaney's vehicle was towed from his arrest location to the compound. They would start tearing it apart tomorrow.

BJ was cuffed and shackled for transport to the jail. Tom finally called it quits to go home to Beth. "Has this been only one day? Lord! It sure seems like a week has passed since this morning," he said to himself, grabbing his jacket and starting for the door. The phone rang again, but he left it to the next shift to answer.

As he exited the building, the young man who did the floors at night leaned against the wall, talking on his cell phone.

~~~

"Hi Aunt Nettie, it's Duncan. Yeah, I'm at work. Wow, this place has been jumpin' today. It looks like they caught the guys that killed the little girl. I don't know them, but they live right here in Henderson County. Some guy named Bobby Jack and another one named Chaney. Real low-life guys, if you ask me. Guess we'll find out more tomorrow. OK, tell Uncle Joe I said hi, and I'll be over next weekend for some of your apple pie. Bye."

~~~

Cheyenne stood at the desk, waiting for Miss Nettie to get off the phone. She wanted to make sure that she knew the right place to park when she got back. Getting the car towed for parking illegally would not be good.

"Hi, honey, you at the Sheriff's Station? – pause – Do you know them? – pause – Do they have any details yet? – pause – I will, Duncan, see you on Saturday." "Well, what do you know," she said, looking up at Cheyenne. "They've caught the men who killed that poor little girl. Someone named Bobby Jack and another man named Chaney. I sure hope they put them away forever. Imagine killing a nine-year-old girl; God rest her little soul," she clucked, shaking her head.

Cheyenne's ears perked up at the mention of the name Chaney.

"Where is the Sheriff's Station, Miss Nettie?" she asked. "That's one of the places I have to go for my research while I'm here."

"I'll draw you a map, sweetie. Won't take you but a few minutes to get there, but I hope you're planning on going tomorrow. Bein' that it's Sunday and all, most of the daytime deputies who would know anything are gone for the night."

"Yes, ma'am. Tomorrow is good for me," she answered with a grin. GPS wasn't something Miss Nettie was apparently fond of using.

Now she had an evening with nothing to do. She'd seen a square with a gazebo when she came into town. It was only a couple of blocks away, and a walk would be nice. Even though the weather was weird, with the streetlights coming on during the daytime, and it was a decent temperature. Two blocks east on Old Oak Ave and take a right on Morningstar, then it was just three blocks down. Miss Nettie said that local musicians often had free concerts in the park on Saturday and Sunday nights.

Cheyenne set off on her quest to find the square. Not a challenging pursuit, though. She was already able to hear the music when she turned onto Morningstar. She passed a little church set well back with a large front lawn in the first block. The double front doors stood open, and the lights were on. "Wow, if this was in the city, that church would be ransacked in a heartbeat," she thought to herself.

~~~

His lunch with David and Pauley lasted about three hours. They were all pretty tired and needed time to process the information he'd shared. Pauley's 'awakening' was happening at breakneck speed, and he didn't want to burn the boy out before he'd even gotten started. Gabe left them and returned to Luke at the church to catch up on the afternoon's events. Luke had some more visits to make afterward, and Gabe retired to his room to go over his notes.

Sometime later, a gurgle in his stomach reminded Gabe that he was human and did have to eat again. He meandered into the kitchen, opened the fridge, and pulled out some leftovers. Music floated in through the open window. He stepped to the side screen door and peered out; the dusk was heavy, and the streetlights were already on, illuminating a solitary stroller on the sidewalk, moving toward the source of the sounds.

Maybe a walk would be good. The tension was mounting, and any minute or two of unwinding Gabe could grab was precious. Once he did his dishes and put the food away, he pushed open the screen door and followed the path of the stroller, three blocks down, to the square and the gazebo. The boys from the band in church this morning were putting on a concert; they were pretty good. Some light rock and some contemporary Christian tunes kept the small crowd entertained. Neighbors took the opportunity to sit in rockers on their front porches as the music wafted by on thick night air.

Benches sat scattered around the small park, illuminated by old-fashioned-style lamp posts. Most of the listeners brought blankets to sit on, which they spread around the lawn. One bench near the gazebo held some available space for him, so he walked toward it. As he approached, he recognized the person he saw on the sidewalk a few minutes earlier.

"Hi, is this seat taken?" he asked the pretty woman with raven hair. The imp attached to her bared its fangs and hissed, knowing who he was immediately and being very uncomfortable with the warrior trailing Gabe so close in proximity. She watched him walk toward her from between her almost closed eyelids, pretending to be concentrating on the music.

"The seat is available," she replied unenthusiastically, fully opening her eyes. It was hard to take her gaze away when she looked directly at him. The man was very tall, standing in front of her, and his hair was long-ish and dark with some gray streaks. His build, very apparent in his T-shirt and jeans, and his overall look, reminded her of a gladiator. But it was his eyes that reached her soul. Eyes that were tired but yet full of deeper energy. Eyes that seemed to have seen so much but still sought to see more. There was far more in them that she struggled to put into words; deep, friendly, trusting.

"Thank you," he smiled, leaning back into the bench and stretching his long legs out in front of himself. "I'll bet this place is picturesque at Christmas time. Kind of Norman Rockwell-like." He was more aware of her than he'd been of any woman for as long as he could remember. His life held no time for relationships or romance. His lifestyle certainly didn't give him much opportunity to get to know people. But that didn't mean he couldn't appreciate beauty when he saw it.

They both sat, just listening, aware of each other for the next few minutes but neither wanted to make the overture since both were used to being alone. Cheyenne broke the silence, "I'm sorry if I sounded abrupt. I just got into town, and I'm a little tired from traveling."

"No offense taken," he replied. "I just got here yesterday after a long drive, so I know what you mean." "Are you visiting friends or family?" he ventured.

She shook her head. "I'm doing some history research which will only take a couple of days. Then I'm off again." For some unusual reason, she wanted to talk with him. She turned toward him on the bench and extended her hand, "I'm Cheyenne."

His large hand engulfed hers warmly, and he replied, "I'm Gabe; nice to meet you, Cheyenne. Can I assume your name comes from your heritage? Your height and hair are certainly characteristic."

"I'm surprised that you know about the Cheyenne, Gabe. Yes, you're right. Native American tribes are not a hot topic; they're often overlooked in the scheme of things. I researched because my mother said I had the blood. I wanted to find out for myself," she paused. "May I ask what your heritage might be? I would have guessed Roman gladiator if that qualified," she laughed.

Her comment made Gabe laugh as well. "I never really did any digging. I'd guess I'm a mutt, too many things mixed in there to sort

135

them out." A few moments of silence passed.

The band played a favorite of Gabe's, 'You Came for Me,' by All Things New. He started singing along in a soft but rich baritone voice, "Wandering through the darkness, searching for the light, I was buried underneath, broken pieces of my life…. But even in my emptiness, my sin, and my greed, that's the man You came to deliver, that's the man that You set free…" he could see her demon's pain as it heard his words. She sat quietly as he sang, listening to the lyrics as they pierced her heart, and a tear rolled down her cheek.

"I think there's a reason we ran into each other here tonight," he said softly. In my experience, there are no coincidences."

~~~

Pauley was in an agitated mood. Since they got home, he had been drawing almost constantly, save for a dinner break. David checked on him periodically but left him alone. He felt sure that Pauley would come to him when it was time for David to know what was on his mind.

A short time later, Pauley did emerge from his room with papers in hand. David looked over each of the two professional-quality pencil renderings, wanting to absorb every detail. Clearly, Gabe was the male figure in the first one. He was standing, facing the right side of the page, in a clearing surrounded by tall trees. The figure wore jeans and a t-shirt, but Pauley had managed to capture what appeared to be the outlines of almost transparent armor over his clothing. And he held up a sizable sword in his right hand; arm raised to the sky. There was a broad ray of light shining down, spotlighting him.

The second drawing contained several people. Gabe was there again. This time there was no armor visible and no sword. But he was the central figure facing the viewer, and he held up a large cross, straight in front of himself and in both hands. Beside him to his left was a beautiful woman with long black hair. On his other side, shown only from the shoulders up, was Pauley. Behind the three of them were many indistinct people, but they looked up as if to see something above the viewer's head, above the cross.

David looked at Pauley and smiled. "You have become quite the artist, son. Can we show these to Gabe tomorrow? I know that he wants to learn more about your gifts. These might help."

"Yes, dad. Cheyenne needs God."

"What do you mean, Pauley?" David asked, his heartbeat speeding up a bit. "Who or what is Cheyenne? How do you know this?"

"He'll know," Pauley answered matter of factly, still keeping to a minimum use of words. He patted David on the shoulder and returned to his room. David heard the light switch click and saw only darkness under Pauley's door; it had been a pretty exhausting day.

~~~

"...and in Henderson County, we have an update in the murder of nine-year-old Becky Robbins. Two suspects are in custody, and the Sheriff's Office has another person of interest who they are attempting to locate at this time. We'll bring you additional details as information comes in. Stay tuned to WTTV and 'News at 11' for a complete story."

Billy poured another shot for Jake, who was shit-faced already. Billy allowed him to have this much liquor because he knew Jake didn't drive. Sunday nights were usually slow, but Myrt's was busy tonight. When there was trouble, everyone was spiritual. Some people sought their spirits in liquid form; those were the people Billy dealt with daily. No one knew that he never touched the stuff. Billy was a believer, and his spiritual infusions came from a much higher bartender.

Jake threw back his head and downed the shot. He slapped some bills on the bar, then grabbed it to steady himself as he did his best to stand up and stagger to the door. It was four blocks back to Peggy's but only a short walk through the alley to Sarah's place. He opted for Sarah's and turned toward the alley. About five feet later, he fell into a pile of garbage next to a dumpster and passed out.

Billy saw the handgun outline under the back of Jake's shirt. He was unsure what to do about it, though. It probably wasn't a problem tonight in Jake's condition, but it could be soon.

~~~

Gabe was on his way back to the church after walking Cheyenne to the Settle Inn. They'd talked for over an hour. He told her about how he had reached a point of giving up on everything after his parents died in a car crash; he was sixteen. In his grief, he thought there was no one to turn to and no money to live on until the parents of his best friend next door took him in. The insurance money paid his way into college, where he met Luke. And he told her how he'd felt a void in his gut, feeling like there was something more but not knowing what it was. Until he read John 3:16 and accepted God's grace, what he didn't tell her was how his life had changed since that acceptance and that it had become the life of a traveling warrior.

Cheyenne listened intently, asking a few questions here and there. She'd thanked him and told him she had a lot to think about. "I'm staying at the church with my friend, the pastor. Can I see you again before you leave town," he asked? Cheyenne nodded, smiled, and disappeared into the Inn.

The door was open, and now God would let him know if he was to play a further part in this woman's life or her salvation. Gabe entered the church through the front door and went to Luke's apartment. Luke was in the kitchen, talking on the phone with someone Gabe couldn't identify from the conversation. If it was something important, Gabe would find out later. He needed time right now for some introspection and prayer anyway. He was experiencing feelings, and a good dose of discernment would help him sort them out.

He took his cell phone out of his pocket and saw a text from David.

"More pics fm Pauley. Need 2 see u tomo. Who's Cheyenne?" Gabe chuckled. God never ceased to amaze him.

~~~

Cheyenne sat on the edge of the bed staring at the bible. It was still early for her, and she had the evening free. After about fifteen minutes, she picked it up and turned to John 3:16 in the New Testament. The Klazyn demon pulled its talons from her flesh, shrieking as if she was acid to its touch, and fled into the night.

17

Madness Monday

THE MEDIA had been swarming all night, trying to get information on the suspects. They knew that the Sheriff would give a press conference at seven a.m., not before. Most of them were camped out in their cars and vans in the Sheriff's station parking lot, waiting. This was big news.

~~~

Jake labored back into consciousness with a fierce headache. He looked around, disoriented, and slowly realized that he was in a garbage pile. Pulling himself up using the dumpster, Jake took a moment to gain his balance and then began the four-block walk to Peggy's place. Remembering his gun, he felt the back of his belt and was relieved to find it still there.

Four blocks seemed like four miles. There was the building ahead of him, but it appeared to get further away for every step he took closer. His body felt sluggish and heavy, and he was nauseous.

As Jake slipped further and further into darkness, the number of demons he acquired grew. The foul black creatures covered his body, and they thoroughly enjoyed their task. The more they whispered in his ear, the angrier he got. By the time he reached the apartment, he was furious and blamed Peggy again for all his troubles.

His pockets were empty – no key to let him in the locked door. He banged on the door, yelling obscenities.

The screaming, yelling, and banging accosted Peggy's ears at six-fifteen. She jumped out of bed, terrified, knowing that it was Jake and that he was in no mood for a face-to-face confrontation. Grabbing her cell phone, she dug the policeman's card out of her underwear drawer, dialing frantically....no answer. It hit his voice mail at the office, so she left a quick message and went to the door to open it for Jake before he woke everyone in town.

~~~

Crystal opened her sleepy eyes to the sound of her cell phone ringing at six-thirty a.m., the caller ID spelling out Jill's name. "Morning Jill, what's up?" she yawned.

"It's been all over the local news since about ten last night. They've caught two guys who they're pretty sure killed little Becky. I just wanted you to know, and I'm sorry if I woke you."

"No, that's OK! Wow! Good work, police department. Now we only have to worry about the convicts. Hey, do you need some help today? I'm available," she said, smiling.

"As a matter of fact, yes, I do. Can you meet me at the church at nine? I have some errands to run first."

"I'll be there," answered Crystal as she mentally reviewed all of the clean clothes in her closet and tried to decide what to wear. She pressed the 'off' button and swung her legs over the side of the bed. Her thoughts returned to yesterday after church. That made her smile again, and she hauled herself out of bed and into the bathroom.

~~~

The sky held only the faintest beginnings of light when the men woke. Lester stood below the blind, flashlight and map in hand. Carlos climbed down in a hurry; he didn't want to be near the cons when they were awake, at least not without Lester being nearby.

"You have thirty minutes to get ready," Lester said loudly enough for the men in the tree to hear. "Carlos, give them each another piece of jerky. Finish the water in the jugs. The canteens will be for the road." Lester gave his orders and then walked into the woods. Carlos handed out the jerky and walked to the edge of the clearing where Lester disappeared, distancing himself from the others. One of the men sneered at him. The other two just let it pass.

The thirty minutes went by, and Lester reappeared. "There's a roadblock one mile from here and a couple of miles of open fields on each side of it. We'll have to make a wide arc to the north and use the trees for cover. Once we get far enough past, we'll stop for a break. I figure it to be about a two-hour walk if we don't drag our feet. Now get movin'."

They followed him with no complaints, for now.

~~~

The moment the door lock clicked, Jake shoved it open, smacked Peggy in the face knocking her out of the way. She fell backward onto the coffee table and rolled onto the floor into a fetal position, cowering out of Jake's reach. Passing her, he walked toward the bedroom and fell face down across the bed. She still didn't move. Ten minutes passed before she dared get up. Then she heard him snoring.

Rising slowly and quietly, she slipped into the bedroom for her clothes and hurriedly dressed in the living room. A last grab for her purse, and she rushed from the apartment. The picture of a handgun sticking out of the back of Jake's pants etched in her brain.

~~~

Kasey pulled herself out of bed, not looking forward to school today and work tonight; her back already ached. Good thing she came home after church yesterday and rested all afternoon. Her feet were swollen enough as it was. Sweet, dear, Trisha had taken pity on her and done all the chores.

During the night, Kasey had a dream about Carlos. He was in danger, but she could only sense it, not pinpoint what it was. She rubbed the gold cross she wore around her neck and wished she'd get some word about him. Trish was already up and had the TV on. The station was running the names and faces across the bottom of the screen to resume regular programming. No word of more convicts captured yet. How could twenty-two men stay in hiding this long? Good Morning America was starting.

"I'm Lana Spicer, and this is Good Morning America. We're going immediately to our sister station in Oregon, where there is a hostage situation taking place as we speak. Five of the escaped convicts from the massive prison break last Saturday morning have taken hostages in a local diner. We go now to our reporter on the scene, Mark Farmer. Mark, what's happening in the diner?"

"Thank you, Lana. The FBI just arrived on the scene. Two of the convicts went in to get takeout food; a waitress recognized one. It's only five a.m. here, so very few people were in the diner. The waitress visibly panicked, and the other convicts rushed the diner with weapons. One person, the cook, got out the back door to safety. The cook is in protective custody in one of the squad cars now. I believe that the police are questioning him."

"Another person tried to escape but was shot and is lying, presumably dead, in the parking lot between the massive numbers of police cars and the front door. The man is too near the diner to approach until the danger is past. We believe that four others are being held captive. As

you can see, the parking lot and surrounding areas are blocked, and there are police cars and flashing lights everywhere. The police have evacuated the immediate area. I don't believe this will be over in a short time, Lara. We could be here for many hours to come."

"Thank you, Mark; we'll check back with you later. Now, back to the other news for today...."

They didn't give any names yet. Would God listen if she said a prayer? She was so new at being a Christian and had so much to learn. "Maybe I should tell Pastor Luke before I leave for school. God listens to him, I'm sure," she thought. She hurried, getting dressed to go over to the church before she and Trisha had to leave.

Getting down the stairs today was a chore. Kasey sure wished they lived on the ground floor some days instead of up a flight. No one was on the street this early. She headed for the side door of the church, where the light shone through the kitchen window. Pastor Luke and his friend Gabe were sitting at the table. Now she was embarrassed but forced herself to tap on the screen door anyway.

Luke jumped up and opened the door for her. "Kasey! Good morning, what brings you here so early?" he asked, ushering her in.

"I was hoping you could pray for someone for me," she answered, and suddenly tears welled up in her eyes. "I don't think God will hear me, but he listens to you."

"Sit down here; let's take a minute to talk," he said, pulling a chair out for her between himself and Gabe. "Kasey, God listens to ALL prayers. Now, who is it that we can pray for and why?"

Kasey told him her story about Carlos, their relationship, and her fears for his safety. "Let's all pray in agreement, Kasey." They joined hands and prayed for Carlos and God's will in the outcome of his circumstances. A wave swept over Gabe; it was the 'feeling' he always got when the battle was getting close.

~~~

Beth was reluctant to let Tom go. After he'd related yesterday's events to her last evening, she silently prayed for hours for his continued safety.

His cell phone rang, and he put down the glass of OJ to answer it. A call came into the station that the Sergeant passed off to Tom to handle. "Yes, sir, I'll stop by there on my way in." He turned to Beth, "the day is starting early. I have to make a stop on my way to the office. Don't worry, hon. I'm going to talk with a pastor, can't get any safer than that, right?" he smiled and went to the bedroom to finish getting ready.

It was five minutes after eight when he pulled into the church's parking lot. The pastor was at the side door and welcomed him inside, offering a cup of coffee. Tom accepted. "So, pastor," he began ...

"Call me Luke, please," Luke offered.

"OK, Luke, I'm Deputy Tom Dempsey; Tom is good. Now, why am I here, Luke?"

"I had a conversation with a young lady earlier this morning. I'm not betraying any confidences, Tom, because we discussed my call to you. It seems that she had a relationship with one of the escaped convicts before he went to prison and is now very pregnant. The young man is aware of the pregnancy; she's afraid for his safety. He's not a dangerous, hardened type but may have thrown in with some hard-core criminals to get out of prison for her and the baby."

"Thank you, Luke. I'll need to get names to handle this as gently as possible. If there's a way to keep her safe and her boyfriend from being killed by the other convicts, I'll do my best to find it."

Tom scribbled details in his notebook as Luke talked. He'd do some research before he called in the Feds, and he made a note to himself to see Kasey this afternoon where she worked at the bar and grille. He

145

wanted to assure her that she had done a good thing by sharing the information.

~~~

At eight-ten, Crystal pulled into the church parking lot. A Sheriff's Deputy car was pulling out. She hoped there wasn't any trouble. Pastor Luke was standing in the front doorway, and he walked to her car to greet her.

"Is everything OK, Pastor?" she asked, concerned.

"Fine, the detective was helping me with an issue involving Kasey, and she asked me to speak to you about it; it's good that you're here now. We can go inside and talk."

"Sure. Is Kasey in some trouble? By the way, I'm here to help Jill again. She's meeting me at nine," she informed him.

"Kasey is good; it's more about her boyfriend." They reached the door, and he led her inside to the office.

"You mean Carlos. She told me a little about him. He's in jail for drugs, right?"

"Well, he was in jail, prison really, but he's one of the escaped prisoners. She's afraid he's in danger, and so we decided to involve the police to help protect him, if possible. He's not one of the tough guys. She thinks he may have taken up with them to get out for her and the baby."

She was speechless. She'd only just met Kasey yesterday, but she felt a protective instinct toward her. "How can the police help if they don't know where he is?"

"By watching for him and giving him a chance to save himself." Luke knew that God was capable of anything, but he also knew that the free will he gave us often led to bad choices in tight situations.

"Hello!" Jill called loudly from the front door. "Guess Jill is early too. Time for me to get to work," Crystal whispered, smiling but sorry that their time alone was so short.

"Me too, but how about that breakfast tomorrow?" he asked.

"Sounds good; I'm hungry by seven-thirty. Is that too early?"

"Not at all. Can I pick you up? I thought we'd go to Miss Nettie's place. It's a B&B, but she serves a delicious breakfast to the public, and it's only two blocks from here."

"I'll be ready. You can bring me here afterward so I can help Jill again. She'll take me home later," she finished.

Jill stuck her head in the door of the office. "Hi, you two. You didn't answer; I wasn't sure anyone was here." She had a funny little grin.

"Sorry, Jill, we were discussing a mutual friend. Come on in – I'm about to leave so you and Crystal can use the office," Luke offered. "See you both later. By the way, I appreciate your help. Coordination of our resources is critical to getting through the troubles we're facing. Thank you again." He disappeared around the corner, giving a quick nod to Crystal. She tried to stifle a giggle.

~~~

At nine a.m., Tom finally sat down at his desk in the Sheriff's Office. "Time to get that scumbag back into the interrogation room," he thought. His desk phone rang; it was the front desk clerk.

"I just saw on the news that the standoff with the escaped cons is still going on in Oregon, sir, and a woman is here to see you about one of the prisoners."

"Geez! I don't want to talk to the media!" he said to her.

"She's not from the media, sir," came the answer.

"OK, I'll be right out."

When Tom stepped into the reception room, he was pleasantly surprised. The woman stood up to greet him. "Hello Deputy Dempsey, I'm Cheyenne Pierce." She was striking—probably five feet ten in flat shoes and eyes that could have hypnotized the most stoic person alive. "Can I talk with you in private?" she asked and discreetly showed him her badge.

They stepped outside. There was a small pavilion with benches and tables for civilian employees who wanted to smoke or eat outdoors. He led her to a seat, and she began, "I'm working undercover, deputy; our conversations are classified. My case carries a national security level, so I can't give you details about my investigation, but I've just learned that you have a man in custody that can be critical to the outcome. His name is Chaney."

18

Countdown Begins

CHEYENNE DIDN'T finish with the microfiche until about three p.m. She was so focused that lunch hadn't crossed her mind once. The search produced an article about a local teen, Jonathon Chaney, visiting a lake in Jackson County with some friends for the 4th of July. He went missing. Five days later, his body was found by a fisherman. The cause of death was drowning.

She wondered if the actual police report could shed additional light on the death. Maybe she could take a drive over there this afternoon, but she hated to have to reveal her identity or presence to anyone else. Maybe Tom would make a call to them for her? It was worth asking.

She waved goodbye to the librarian and called the Sheriff's Office from her Jeep. Tom sounded a bit frazzled when he answered. "Hi, deputy, this is Agent Pierce again with a favor to ask."

"Sure, agent. What's up?" Tom replied.

"I need a police report from archives over in Jackson County, but I don't want to let anyone, but you, know who I am or that I'm here pursuing an investigation. Any chance I could get you to request it for me?"

"I can take care of the request for you right now, but I have no idea how long it will take for them to find it for you. Give me the details."

"July, thirty-nine years ago, accidental drowning of an eighteen-year-old named Jonathon Chaney. I need the full report including the Medical Examiners notes and the kid's fingerprints – oh, and who identified him." Cheyenne had a hunch, and the file on this case could help it turn into a fact.

"Got it. Consider it done," Tom said. "It usually takes a day or two, but this is old; it could be longer. I'll let you know when it gets here. Do you have any reason to believe he may have had a record here in Henderson?"

"Good thinking deputy, would you check that for me too?"

~~

The restaurant was slow on Mondays, so Peggy could leave after the last lunch patrons were gone. While cleaning up, she confided in her co-worker, "I'm terrified to go back to my apartment, Missy. He's getting meaner. It's weird, but I can see him getting worse every day."

"Why not come home with me for a couple of days? I have a guest room. You and I wear the same size. You can borrow some of my clothes for after work and wash up your uniform in the evenings; you'll only need the one," suggested Missy.

Peggy hesitated but agreed and felt somewhat safer and more relaxed for her decision, but there were some things she'd need. Maybe she could sneak back in when Jake wasn't there to grab just the essentials.

"Let's just get these tables wiped down and the flatware rolled into napkins for tomorrow, and we're outta here," Missy said as she finished table number six.

~~~

The men made their way through the underbrush, keeping to the woods as they trudged toward the next hideaway. Occasionally they were forced to cross some smaller open areas, but those fields were pretty remote; even so, Lester remained vigilant.

Four hours passed when the 'extras' began grumbling about needing a break again. The underbrush was exceptionally thick and most of the clearings far too exposed, making this part of the journey very slow.

They were nearing a dirt road but remained concealed, so Lester called a ten-minute halt for water and rest. With only two miles to their destination, he hated wasting time. Carlos found a tree trunk near Lester's position and sat so that he could keep an eye on the others. Two of them wandered into the woods; Carlos figured they had to take a leak.

Moments later, the remaining three were startled by the sound of something crashing through the bushes. The two convicts broke through into the small clearing, panting and red-faced. Lester was on them immediately, "What the hell? What's going on?" he growled.

"People out there," one of them panted. "We ran into people, and we hauled ass. I think they saw us!"

"Oh shit," Lester almost whispered. He was the only one with a weapon. He didn't know if 'the people' meant the law or just some farmers, but the plan was now in jeopardy. "What did they look like? Did they get a good look at you?" he grilled the other con.

"They had an old truck pulled to the side of the road. Just a hillbilly woman and man, they saw us good, though. We walked out of the woods about thirty feet from them and then hightailed it back here."

"You three stay here, and I mean RIGHT HERE!" ordered Lester. "Carlos, you come with me." And he turned and headed into the woods where the men had just emerged. Carlos followed silently and quickly.

They jogged about fifty feet, then Lester stopped and turned around. "I wanted you here to keep you away from them," he said, gesturing in the direction of the men they'd just left. "If anything happens to me, you're on your own. Stay away from them and find your own path. Remember what I said before, kid, disappear!"

Carlos nodded. Lester resumed his direction. They were at the edge of the wood line within a minute, peering at the truck and its two passengers. The woman shouted orders and berated the man, something about stopping and now being seen. Maybe they were hiding too? No matter, they were now a loose end needing to be taken care of.

The woman was closest, about twenty feet away, with her back to Lester. The man was pouring gas from a small red container into the gas tank, and it looked like he was almost finished. As he removed the funnel and tossed the empty red container into the back of the truck, Lester raised the handgun, took aim on the woman, and squeezed the trigger. She crumpled to the ground with a hole in her head. The second shot rang out, bringing the man down, face in the dirt, to lie in front of her.

Ma would not be escaping the consequences of her involvement in BJ's bad decisions. She was no longer a threat to anyone. The men dragged the bodies into the woods and pulled the truck undercover. Then they walked back to the clearing. There was one more task to attend to before continuing.

Lester reached the clearing first. The three cons were crouched at the edge, uncertain of what would happen next. Lester approached them, but Carlos hung back instinctively. The cons stood. "I told you that if you brought danger to the plan, to the rest of us, you were dead." Before his last word faded, he had thrust a knife into the gut of the closest con with his right hand. He drew the gun and shot with his left hand. The bullet sped into the chest of the standing man. He fell, face frozen forever in an expression of disbelief as the bloodstain quickly spread across the front of his shirt.

No one would find these bodies any time soon unless they were paying attention to the vultures. Lester thought for just a split second about leaving the gun to make it look like the two dead cons might have killed the old couple and then each other in a fight, just in case some hunter might stumble on them sooner than expected. But the gun was critical in carrying out the rest of the plan, so he stuck it back into his belt and wiped off the knife and his hand on the back of a dead man's jacket.

The remaining con stood statue-still, holding his breath. Lester looked at him, said nothing, and turned back to Carlos. No words were necessary.

Carlos picked up their things and followed Lester into the woods. The other con followed too, but at a bit of a distance.

The several black, foul, grotesque creatures riding the broad shoulders of Lester were maliciously joyous.

~~~

Jake slowly opened his eyes. As he stared, the face of the bedside clock came into focus. Three-thirty. Already? He checked his pockets and found eleven dollars and some change. Barely enough to pay for food, let alone to have a few drinks. He had to survive until Friday; then, he'd be free and clear.

He hauled himself up and plodded to the closet 'hiding spot' where Peggy kept her tips. Only the few dollar bills which he'd left there yesterday remained. "Crap!" Jake thought. He counted it all out again, and it totaled fifteen dollars and thirty-three cents. As he raised his head, his eyes settled on Peggy's CD player. There was a pawn shop just down from Myrt's. He looked around to see what else he might be able to use for spending money to tide him over, being constantly encouraged and reassured that he was in the right by his foul, dark companions.

~~~

A conference call was taking place. Not the typical kind of business call in any corporate office, but a high security, high tech 'for your ears only' kind of call between leaders. The leaders who thought they manipulated the world, but in fact, were themselves puppets.

Driving these men were demon warlords of the highest order, dark Princes who reported directly to the Master, to Satan himself. This group of human men was called The POETS, but none of them knew where the name originated. They knew only that they were in charge as POETS and could make anything happen. Anything.

The gruesome Princes knew what the name stood for, and they also knew that they were at the top of the heap. They took an oath, were crowned, and thus dubbed the Princes Owned ETernally (by) Satan, POETS. This meeting was of their design to discuss the revised plan. What they spoke, their human puppets repeated.

"We'd like a report on the political plan and its progress," came a demand barely cloaked as a request from the Vatican member, who was unknowingly mimicking the words of the Vatican Demon Prince.

"This is playing out as designed with a bonus," proudly growled the North American counterpart, "The eradication of an arch-enemy, Gabe Matheson." He paused to hear the audible satisfaction of the other members. "This part of the plan, and this human, will be history within four days," he finished.

With human eyes on every battle, and spies and instigators reporting back through channels, these men had learned long ago that Gabe Matheson had some kind of unexplainable connection. He was always found in the middle of their plans, thwarting their efforts, making their lives difficult. Up to now, his demise had eluded them.

"The plan is in place to fire the Vice President on Wednesday of this week. His egregious sexual misconduct will hit the news this evening, and the President will have no choice but to appoint a new VP from the most esteemed members of the Senate, our groomed substitute. On Friday afternoon, he becomes the VP, an urgent expedite since the President will be flying to the UN shortly after that to give a speech, but he will not arrive. Air Force One is going missing. We will have our temporary leadership of the United States in full charge by the following weekend, and the dust will settle within forty-five days. Then it will be a clear path for our man to begin his campaign for the election next year, and we all know how that will turn out. The United States will solidly be ours within fourteen months. And then the rest of the world will follow."

The POETS all nodded in their respective locations. Their demon Princes snorted and drooled in anticipation of the soon-to-be victory in their grasp.

~~~

They reached the shack just before four p.m. Lester motioned Carlos to hang back as he approached the door. The place was empty, so the two of them went in and saw from the cobwebs and small animal tracks that it had probably not had a human inhabitant since the last hunting season. One set of faint footprints, likely from the person setting up the hiding place.

It was a single room. The walls had spaces between the boards from the weathering and shrinking of the old wood. There were two sets of crude bunk beds and a ratty-looking blanket on top of each thin and lumpy mattress, no pillows.

In one corner of the shack stood a makeshift counter and a couple of shelves. An old can opener, some plastic spoons, and half a dozen cans of Pork 'n Beans were there for them. Also, two jugs of water, nothing else. The men were not supposed to remain here for any length of time.

Behind Lester and Carlos, the other con entered cautiously. "You can bunk over there," Lester motioned to him. "Open up three of those cans for us; we'll be back in a minute," Lester ordered, and he nodded to Carlos to follow him outside. The con obliged without hesitation.

Carlos walked with Lester to the edge of the tree line, about fifty feet from the shack. Lester didn't want the other man to overhear. "OK, kid. We're close now, only two more miles to the county line, where we each have a different agenda. I know what I have to do, and it doesn't include you. I want you to cut out tonight when you hear that guy snoring," he nodded toward the building.

"Get as far away from us as you can, but don't let anyone see you. Lay low for a day or two before you make a move to see your girl. I've got some final things to take care of, and I don't want you getting spotted and having the law swarm the area." Lester paused. "It's been one of the few pleasures of my life to know you. Now stay out of trouble and get a new start somewhere. Not many of us ever get the chance to turn things around. Don't waste it, kid." He stuck his sizable fist into his pants pocket and pulled out a roll of cash. Handing it to Carlos, he abruptly turned and walked back to the shack, leaving Carlos standing there with his mouth open.

Lester had made an oath to obtain an object and sever a connection. It was important enough to someone else to have put together this entire elaborate scheme, someone with connections on a scale Lester had never seen or experienced. He committed an address and a map to memory when he was back in prison. The time was now to act on the information and fulfill his commitment. Once done, he was free to take care of the snitch and see his son before they caught up with him and took him down.

He entered the shack and looked at the other con. "You joined this little group because you thought it would lead you to cash. The thing is, you figured you'd have to split it and hoped it would be enough to fund a new life. Those other two, they screwed up. I don't want or need the dough, so when we get where I need to be, I'll tell you the location, and it's all yours. You just have to get the hell out of my way and not look back, got it? In the meantime, do as I tell you."

156

The big guy dressed in camo with the scar on his face just nodded, wondering if it was a trap of some sort or if he'd just won the lotto. He took his open can of beans and retreated to the bunk Lester had assigned. He'd follow directions until something felt wrong just in case he was the lucky winner. Not havin' to split that stash sounded pretty damn good.

~~~

Jake pulled open the door and heard the announcing jingle. He had the CD player tucked under one arm and a bag of CDs and DVDs in his hand. If this went well, he could scrounge up a few more things from the apartment to pawn before he left at the end of the week.

David looked up from the back counter as Jake approached. "Can I help you, sir?" he asked casually.

"Yeah, man. I need some cash, so I want to pawn a few things," Jake explained as he laid the items out on the counter.

A movement he saw in his peripheral vision caught David's attention. It was Pauley. He had left the chair and was hiding behind the big desk. Even though Jake's demons couldn't hang on to him when he came into the pawnshop because of the guardians, Pauley still knew he was trouble. David became very wary due to Pauley's new ability to 'see' the angels and demons.

"Don't I know you from Myrt's?" David asked, looking Jake in the face.

"You could; I'm in there a lot to catch a bite to eat. My girlfriend doesn't cook much," Jake offered while evaluating the situation. It certainly wouldn't hurt his plan to be recognized here. The place he was planning to rob wasn't too near, and then he'd be gone. What the hell. "I'm Jake," he stated.

"Well, Jake, I don't take CD players in for pawn, but I'd consider buying it outright from you. It is yours, right? You know there is a law about selling or pawning stolen property."

"Yeah, yeah, it's mine," Jake answered with a touch of nerves. David wasn't sure if it was because Jake was committing a crime or if he was pissed off, but he had a distinct feeling that he should tread lightly.

"Then I can pay you twenty for the player. People don't generally come in here looking for used music or movies, but I can give you another dollar for each of those CDs and DVDs. Will that help you?"

That would be forty-five dollars in Jake's pocket right now. "You got yerself a deal, Mr." agreed Jake.

Instead of going to the cash box, which he kept hidden, David pulled fifty dollars in bills out of his back pocket and counted out forty-five for Jake. Handing it over the counter, he chuckled, "Guess business has been taking things in more than selling things lately. Looks like you left me with a five-dollar bill to end my day. Must be time to go home," and David smiled the least intimidating smile he could muster.

He'd learned that trick in his early days of pawn ownership. Leave them thinking you have little or no cash on hand, and keep the guns and gold locked up and out of sight, and any potential problem person will generally leave you alone.

"Thanks, mister," Jake said as he turned to leave. David saw the gun tucked in his belt under his shirt and breathed a sigh of relief when the door closed.

"Pauley, it's safe now; you can come out," David called. Pauley emerged and came to David at the counter. "Were you afraid, son?"

"No, the angel said to hide but that it was OK," he stated matter-of-factly. "That man is bad and will do a bad thing, but not today."

David was dumbfounded. Will there ever be a time when things his son says and does won't blow him away? "Get your things, son. It's time to lock up and go home."

~~~

Kasey looked up as Jake entered Myrt's and made a b-line to the bar. She finished clearing the table and retreated into the kitchen, utterly unnoticed by Jake. After the visit from the deputy earlier that afternoon, Billy asked her if everything was good. She assured him that it was and added, "He's a real nice man, Billy. Someday he'll make a great dad."

Billy was already getting a beer from the tap, anticipating Jake's order. He slid the beer over as Jake sat. "Thanks, Billy! Nice to be back where everybody knows your name if you know what I mean," he laughed out loud at his own joke.

"Hey Jake, we got some homemade soup and fresh bread back there. Whaddya say? On the house? You look like you could use a good meal," Billy offered. He figured that food would soak up alcohol Jake would be consuming, helping avoid or delay trouble.

"Well, that's damn nice of you there, Billy. Dish it up!" Jake felt good, money in his pocket, free food, looked like he'd be able to hang in there till Friday, and freedom! "And pour another beer too, would ya. This one will be empty in another two gulps."

Kasey had been on her feet for almost three hours, and she was just about in tears. She didn't know that Billy convinced granny to hire another waitress who was just coming in the front door. Billy stepped into the kitchen to get Jake's soup and saw Kasey leaning against the sink. "Hey, kid. It's time for you to go home," he said, gently patting her arm.

"I can't, Billy. Gran expects me here for a few more hours. I can get through it for a little while longer." All he could think was that she was so brave, so sweet, never complaining. How he wished he could make things better for her.

"A new waitress is starting tonight. She's here now, and she knows how to handle things. I talked to your grandma and told her you needed time off, that baby is close. Now grab your purse and go home!"

She looked up at him and smiled. There was still a hint of the old twinkle there. Her arms encircled his neck, and she hugged him with all the energy she had left. "Thanks, Billy."

Kasey was in her car and out of the parking lot in less than three minutes.

~~~

Crystal got home a few minutes after two in the afternoon. She had a little cleaning and laundry to do before she quit for the day. Those darned contractions continued to clutch her sporadically, and that was sapping her.

Chores done, dinner eaten, she plopped onto the couch about the time the six o'clock news was to begin and put her feet up on the coffee table. "Holy Cow! Look at those monsters!" she thought. Her feet were swollen halfway up her calves. "I'd better wear slacks tomorrow, or Luke will think I have a disease," she muttered to herself. That pillow was so inviting. She poofed it and put it behind her head, and in sixty seconds, she was asleep. Crystal had forgotten to lock the front door in her hurry to get to the bathroom.

The golden sentinel stood by the door. Nothing would come near this saint.

~~~

Tom pulled into his driveway at six, knowing that Beth usually put dinner on the table at six p.m. It had been an afternoon of increasing calls reporting everything from mischief to someone hearing gunshots and an increasing number of strangers in town. An APB was still out on BJ's mother. There was no more word about any other escaped prisoners, and he was beat to the bone. But his brain was stuck in overdrive.

Meeting the FBI agent brought unexpected intrigue to his little corner of the world. He hoped he could continue to help her through the conclusion of her investigation so he could find out how Chaney connected to Senator Manning. It was one of those things he'd love to discuss with Beth, but much of his work was off-limits as far as conversation with civilians, including his wife.

Tomorrow was another day, and it was already promising to be busier than today had been. Tom got out of his patrol car, locked it up, and went to the house for a night of just being Tom. On his way in, he thought for a brief moment about Kasey. Now that was a topic he could share with Beth.

~~~

Cheyenne finished another wonderful home-cooked dinner in the dining room of the little inn. The notepad she carried was open beside her plate, and she studied while taking in the last mouthful of warm cherry cobbler covered with a scoop of fresh churned and melting vanilla ice cream. This was a dangerous assignment. It could force her to gain ten pounds if she didn't wrap up this case soon.

Between leaving the police station and dinner, she'd done some reading not related to her investigation. The Gideon Bible sat open on her bed at this very moment. There was a lot she didn't understand. Not one to leave mysteries unexplained, she decided to take a little walk to see if Gabe was at the church. Something about him urged her to seek him out, and the exercise would do her good even if he wasn't around.

The dark skies were smothering, even with a slight breeze. Streetlights gave her ample lighting, but it was like the rays emitted from the lamps were stopped short, not reaching a normal distance. Eerie. Anyone who had claustrophobia would undoubtedly be having a hard time tonight.

She covered the two blocks in a couple of minutes. Cheyenne stood in front of the open church door, wondering if she should enter or call out or go to the back of the building where the Pastor must live. While she pondered, Luke stepped into the church from the rear door to his apartment. Seeing her standing there looking uncertain, he called out a greeting, already knowing full well who she was.

"Hi, there! You're a new face and a pretty one," he said smiling. "Won't you come in?"

"You must be the Pastor, Luke, I believe?" she replied, advancing two steps inside.

"Well, you seem to know me. From your description, I would have to guess that you would be Cheyenne?" he said as he proceeded toward her.

"So, Gabe told you about me?" she returned, trying to hide the pleased look in her eyes.

"What little I know did come from my very good friend, Gabe. Might you be here to see him this evening?" He was now standing in front of her and reached out to shake her hand in welcome.

"Yes, I am. Is he around, or is he out on a mission?" This time she couldn't contain the smile that took over her face. Luke was charming.

At that moment, Gabe entered the open door behind her, and she turned quickly at the sound and awareness of his presence. "Not nice to startle your guests," she winked.

"I'd be surprised if you were startled. You have the reflexes of a lioness," Gabe observed. "So, Luke, I see you two have met. Now, if you'll excuse us, I believe that a walk is in order." He took her by the hand and led her back out the front door. She went willingly, waving goodbye to Luke.

"I am surprised and pleased to see you. You don't mind the walk, do you?" he asked after the fact.

"Not at all. I need it after the food I ate at the Inn. You're going to have to roll me out of town."

A block went by with no more talking. "I came to see you because I've been reading the bible, and there's a lot I don't understand. I felt compelled to ask you to talk with me about it. One thing I cannot do is leave something unexplained."

In Gabe's mind, he thanked his Father for setting this up in His way and His time. "Tell me where you want me to start," he said, and they continued to walk and talk.

It was nine p.m., and they had finally made a full circle of the neighborhood, reaching the door to the lobby of the inn. Cheyenne couldn't remember a time in her life when she'd share private things. She never felt comfortable enough with a person to open up. But now, she told Gabe about her childhood, the abuse she'd suffered, and her fears and loneliness. This history turned her into an undercover agent who did whatever was necessary to accomplish the task with the FBI.

It was like the opening of floodgates which then couldn't be closed again. She stopped at the details of her current assignment, though. It was dangerous to involve a civilian. He was too nice a guy to understand how seedy her work life could be and the darkness of the characters in her assignments.

Gabe shared some of his experiences as a spiritual warrior but kept a tight rein on most of the details in order not to scare her. She was just opening her eyes and heart to salvation and had no idea how demonic the dark side could be.

Neither of them had a clue that they were standing face to face with one of the only other people on the planet who could so wholly understand themselves. That was for them to discover soon, but not this night. Pauley's drawing flashed through Gabe's thoughts, and he knew God was not finished with them yet. This was a road they would travel together.

Tall as she was, Cheyenne looked up at Gabe's face and deep into his eyes. Standing in the light of the front door, she could see the passion for his beliefs in their depths and the steel determination and sincere caring. He was a man like no other, but they'd just met, and she had things to think about.

"Good night, Gabe. I'll probably be having breakfast here about seven-thirty in case you were curious."

"Good night, Cheyenne. Interestingly, you chose this remote spot when I had already made reservations here for myself at that exact time. Perhaps our paths will cross again." He smiled back at her beautiful grin and left her watching him retreat into the darkness.

Cheyenne went straight to her room, threw on her pajamas, and flipped back to the first verse she'd read last night. She wanted what he had. Her eyes closed, her head bowed, she opened her heart for the first time and invited Jesus inside. A divine peace settled over her.

The glowing warrior on the roof above stood to his full height. It lifted its head, spread its alabaster wings wide, and emitted an angelic song of praise so beautiful that no one in the dimension of humans could have comprehended, even if they had ears to take it in.

Except for Pauley.

He heard it immediately from a distance of miles. It was as clear as if he had been standing in front of the angel. He recognized it as the same he'd heard in church. Tears flowed down his cheeks at the ethereal beauty of the otherworldly sound, and he began speaking words of prayer in a language foreign to him. Yet he was able to understand every sentence. His ears were now as open as his eyes. Yesterday, Pastor Luke prayed the prayer with him, and now he could hear because that's what he was born to do.

Demons gnashed their teeth and shrieked, fleeing as if the sound was acid in their ears, with the painful knowledge that another soul was saved.

~~~

"Good evening, and welcome to the WTTV eleven o'clock news. Big headlines and breaking news tonight! An unnamed source came forward yesterday with audio and videotapes and documents containing clear and indisputable evidence of sexual crimes on minors and child pornography distribution committed by a top government official. That official is none other than the Vice President of the United States! He is unavailable for comment as he's been whisked away by the FBI to an undisclosed location. The word from the White House is that the President is looking into this and will take immediate action once satisfied of truth in this unexpected turn of events."

~~~

At two a.m., Carlos quietly lowered himself from the top bunk. There was no light, no moon, or stars to show him the way, so he'd memorized it before going to sleep. Shoes at the edge of the bed, next to them his pack with some water and the remaining jerky he'd stashed, and five long steps to his right was the wall directly next to the exit door. As Carlos slowly opened the door, he turned back for a second and imagined he saw Lester's open eyes. But it was just his imagination. In a moment, he was gone, finding his way into the woods and closer to Kasey.

Demons of all shapes and sizes were thick in the air and the trees. Evil saturated everything. The foul creatures now numbered in the hundreds of thousands. Lester heard every minute sound made by Carlos while he was leaving. He knew it was over for himself; these were his last days. Good that the kid got out. Maybe for some, there could be a happy ending. Not for most, he was sure, and he was anticipating the worst for himself.

19

Tuesday Morning

PAULEY SAT up in his bed; the illuminated clock numbers displayed five sixteen on his ceiling, and the sky outside was still pitch black. He'd heard the ethereal sounds of heaven last night, and then the warrior angel that was now always by his side spoke to him. He explained that the Angelic Host rejoices when souls are saved and that what Pauley had heard was the voice of an angel singing praise.

Now he remembered the song and the angel's words clearly; it was real, not a dream. He had to tell his father and Gabe as soon as possible. He had learned something important, something that hurt the demons.

~~~

Jake woke disoriented. It took a full five minutes of thought to realize he was on the couch at Sarah's place. Safe enough and in no hurry to get anywhere, he closed his eyes, patted his gun, and returned to unconsciousness.

~~~

After a whole night of slumber and almost twelve hours of being off her feet, Kasey felt like a new person. She could take her time getting ready for school.

Something felt different today, though, almost electric, and her senses were working overtime. There was a need for urgency, but she couldn't put her finger on why. It made her very aware and a bit uneasy.

A hot shower would help, and then she'd figure out what was going on. Maybe she could talk with Pastor Luke again after school. Gran told her last night that she didn't have to go back to work till after the baby was at least a month old. That must have been Billy's influence. Dear Billy. He was a constant in her life, a supportive and solid rock. She clicked the T.V. on and saw that there were still fifteen minutes before the six o'clock news would begin. "Shower first, news later," she thought and headed into the bathroom, totally unaware of the man sitting in a car about half a block away who was watching for her.

~~~

It remained inky dark around him, but Carlos knew the dawn would be coming soon. He hadn't gotten far during the night but far enough to get himself out of the way of Lester for now. Once it was light, he'd be able to travel faster.

He remembered a place that would be good for hiding, where he could stay out of sight for the rest of today and most of tomorrow. By Wednesday evening, it should be safe to contact Kasey. In the meantime, he had to get there and find some other food along the way to hold him over.

Hunkering down into the camo jacket for as much protection as it could offer, he leaned back against the pine tree trunk to wait. At first light, he would be up and gone.

First light was already underway, but the density of the creatures would block it for another hour. Blood red eyes watched him from every tree branch, and his demons clutched deeply into his shoulders.

~~~

The digital numbers on his clock told him it was finally six a.m. It was time to talk to David. Pauley walked across the room, opened the door, and turned to the only other bedroom in the house. He heard a slight clink and redirected himself to the kitchen, where the sound originated.

David was making coffee. He reached for a bowl and the cereal box and then went to the refrigerator for milk. As he turned, he spoke, "I heard you moving around earlier, and I couldn't go back to sleep. Are you ready for some breakfast, son?"

"Not yet. We have to call Gabe." Pauley said as he sat down at the table.

"What's up? Did you do another drawing?" asked David.

"I know how to hurt demons. I hear them now. I can hear angels too."

David paused, trying to absorb this new revelation. "What do you mean, Pauley? Take your time. Tell me slowly." David was standing there, staring at his son with the bottle of milk in his hand. He'd forgotten entirely about what he was doing.

"I went to my room last night. Then I heard a song, different, not a person singing. The angel told me someone was saved, so they sang. I heard screaming. In my head, I saw demons flying away screaming."

"Were you dreaming, Pauley? Or did your angel speak to you?"

"I wasn't asleep yet. The angel was standing right next to me when he was talking."

David plopped into the wooden chair across from his boy, his mouth agape, his head spinning again. Changes were taking place so fast he could hardly keep up. Pauley now speaks for the first time in fourteen years, not just words, whole conversations! He can see angels and demons and is supposedly a spiritual warrior in the making. Pauley is one of only a few people on earth who can see through dimensions. And now he can hear things too? What in God's name happened in that car accident? If he could only talk with Sylvia.

No. Sylvia would tell him of the miracles of God and that he should believe. She would be glowing in the new knowledge that her son now played such an essential role in God's plan. Sylvia would calm his fears and show him how to count his blessings. And she would pray for his salvation as she'd done during the few years they'd shared.

Pauley repeated himself slowly to make sure David heard every word. "Angels sing when someone accepts the Light, Dad. It hurts the demons bad. They scream and fly away. People need to be saved."

Pauley had called him 'Dad.' It was the first time he'd ever heard that term from his son's mouth. In the few days that Pauley had been talking, he'd never referred to David at all. His gratitude and his love for this child soared, his heart swelled to bursting, and his eyes welled up with tears.

He understood what his son was saying, what Sylvia was always telling him. It was time for him to give it up and accept the grace which had always been there for the taking—the gift God held out to him every day of his life.

It didn't matter that it was only just after six o'clock; he picked up the phone and called Gabe.

~~~

Gabe was in the kitchen, just starting his second cup of coffee when his cell phone rang. He hadn't seen Luke yet. The caller I.D. showed David's name.

"Morning, David. You're getting an early start. What's up?" he began.

"Hi, Gabe. Pauley has more to tell us. Things happened last night, and we need to see you as soon as you can get here. I think it's vitally important to your strategies and my future."

"That was a little cryptic. Can you tell me anything more over the phone?"

David hesitated. "Can 'they' hear our conversation?"

"They're not omniscient, David. That's reserved for God alone. They can only hear like we do if they're within earshot. The host is protecting you and Pauley from any of them getting that close to you," David explained.

"OK then, Pauley can hear now too," David explained, hoping that Gabe was as blown away as he felt. "Salvation is a critical part of the solution. Last night around nine-thirty, he heard something, and his angel told him it was a song the angels sing for a newly saved soul. We need to talk, Gabe. You need to hear it from Pauley. There is more, but you should get the rest of it in person."

"I'll get there as soon as I can. How about just before nine at your shop?" Gabe considered his breakfast plans to meet Cheyenne at the Inn. This new revelation excited him, but he had a powerful feeling that she also had something of vital importance to share, and he was led to go there first.

"We'll be expecting you then, friend." David put down the phone and put his large hand over the smaller hand resting on the table. "I wish your mother was here to see what an incredible young man you've become," he whispered, his eyes misting again at the thought.

~~~

Crystal lay there staring at the ceiling. Her feelings were so mixed. The absence of Jaimie was fading her mental picture of him more every day. She didn't ever want to forget him, but she understood that she had to move on, that he would want her to find happiness again.

Luke had impressed her from the start. Sure, he was good-looking, but it was more than that. He had an inner glow. His essence projected the spirit of God, the love of His son. Yet, he was a man, flesh, and blood, one whom she was sure would be everything she thought a man should be as scripture described the traits of a husband.

Could she be so blessed to have two great loves in her lifetime? She glanced at the clock on the nightstand, six-thirty, time to get ready. He would be here in less than an hour to pick her up, and after breakfast, she'd be helping Jill again.

"How are you two looking today?" she asked as she looked down at her ankles. They didn't reply, but they pleased her anyway with their return to almost normal shape overnight. "Nice," she said to herself. She made a promise to the reflection in the mirror over the sink, "After this little stinker is born, YOU are getting back into shape, lady!" Then she giggled at herself and dove into the closet for a quick wardrobe change.

Finishing her teeth, hair, and makeup took the better part of the hour. She was standing at the front window when Luke pulled up in the driveway behind her car. When he knocked, her heart skipped a beat.

"Hi there," she greeted, opening the door.

"Good morning," a smile wide across his lightly tanned face. He looked so much more like a surfer than like a Pastor in jeans and a t-shirt. His hand was held out to her, "Are you ready, my lady?"

"I'm starving, if that's what you mean," she laughed, giving him her hand as she stepped out. He closed the door behind her; she locked it. And they walked across the veranda, down the steps, and out to his car. As they began the short drive to the Inn, he started the conversation.

"I didn't watch the news or even talk to Gabe this morning," he said. "You are my first human contact of the day."

"Well, how flattering," she pretended to blush. "But on a serious note, Luke, before we get too busy later, Gabe talked with Jill and me yesterday. This is some heavy stuff, this spiritual battle. He didn't explain a lot, but as I understand it, the forces of evil work through men just like God's love often works through men. We're in for a whole lot of violent crime and danger in the next few days. Are you concerned? Should I be afraid?" She finished the last sentence unconsciously, rubbing her belly.

"The experience I had years ago with Gabe was intense. That's why you need to understand the power of prayer cover. You and that little one will be fine; I'll make sure of that."

She sat silent for a moment, staring at the road ahead. "I feel like there's something more I'm supposed to do to prepare for this," she said softly. "Will you keep that in your prayers for me? If God wants more from me, I want to hear it, to know it. I want to help win this so we can go forward without fear."

"What a courageous woman," he thought to himself. "Agreed," he answered, nodding. "I guess we'll get to know each other at hyper speed in light of the current circumstances," he said, taking and lightly squeezing her hand.

He steered the car into a parking space at the Inn with his free hand. Breakfast awaited.

~~~

Gabe walked into the small dining room. There were only six tables, each covered with a blue and white checkered cloth and surrounded by four chairs. He chose the one by the wall with a vase of bright white daisies. Cheyenne appeared at the entrance from the lobby at precisely seven-thirty. With a sweeping glance, her eyes settled on his large frame and dark, handsome face, and she walked across the fifteen feet of space separating them from each other. He was already standing and pulling out a chair for her to sit.

The rest of the dining room was empty, but they weren't paying attention.

"Thank you, Gabe." She was golden. He could feel the divine energy she emitted, and he recognized it immediately, like a heady perfume.

"I detect something distinctly different about you this morning," he teased, waiting for her to divulge her secret.

"Not fair!" she pretended to pout. "My secret is out just because you have superpowers!" As soon as she said it, her mind immediately flashed to her thoughts from some days ago when she had imagined herself as part of a superhero team. Was he her Batman?

"So, do tell, Miss Cheyenne. How are you today?" He couldn't contain his joy. Anytime a soul came to the Light was a time for celebration, but this soul was hers, and she was something different.

"I have it, Gabe. The salvation you described to me. And I'm filled; with energy and joy and peace. And the desire to wipe all of the bad off the face of the earth. I went back to my room after you left, and it hit me. I wanted what I saw in you. So, I prayed. And I felt it. And I'm happy."

He was elated. Cheyenne was incredible. This mission and the future took on a whole new meaning. Then the timing dawned on him. "Was that about nine-thirty?"

"Yeah, probably. Why?"

Out of the corner of his eye, he saw two people enter the room. Luke and Crystal had come for breakfast at the Inn. Are there any coincidences in God's plan? He knew there weren't.

Luke caught sight of Gabe and Cheyenne a second later. He turned to say something to Crystal, she nodded, and they walked toward Gabe. Gabe leaned in close to Cheyenne and whispered, "I'll tell you in a bit. We're about to get unexpected company."

"Well, what a surprise!" Luke spoke first. Gabe stood and welcomed the newcomers. Cheyenne immediately invited them to join the table, receiving a nod and a thankful smile from Gabe. Luke introduced the two women who hadn't met before today.

"An interesting group we make," observed Gabe. "Since God is in charge, I think we can all agree that there is no such thing as a coincidence." The others nodded in agreement. "So, what could He have banded this unlikely quartet together to accomplish?"

Crystal spoke first, "I don't know about you three, but he brought me here to eat! Food first, solving the problems of the world second. You have to have your priorities straight."

At that moment, the waitress stepped up to the table, ready to take their orders.

Three voices chimed out simultaneously, "Coffee!" And then Luke added, "and juice for this lovely lady, please," motioning toward Crystal.

Someone turned on the small wall-mounted T.V., and the morning's news commentary filled the room.

> *"Yes, the DOJ announced an incredible turn of events late last evening, and an emergency Grand Jury session was called at midnight last night. With the evidence presented, after four hours of deliberation, the United States vice president has officially been indicted on numerous charges ranging from Child Endangerment to Rape of a Minor and Child Pornography Distribution. This evidence comes from a deep and lengthy investigation into a global crime ring known for these atrocities. An inside source tells us that the Vice President has had an emotional breakdown and*

admitted to the charges. The President is preparing to name a new V.P. by Wednesday evening and does not plan to cancel his international trip to speak at the U.N. Indeed, no one saw this coming!"

The four of them looked at each other with their thoughts shooting off in different directions, but somehow all knew this tied into the war they were facing. Cheyenne was the only one who knew about the dark political goings-on that brought her here, and her stomach lurched, ruining her appetite.

~~~

Carlos was on the move now. He was getting his bearings and planning his route to the old barn. It was a place he'd found on a hike one day a couple of years ago, about two miles out on the southern side of town.

There was no sign of use by anyone else back then. Carlos returned several times, and the only footprints he ever saw were his own. He set a few 'traps' to see if he could detect anyone else visiting the place. Other than animal tracks, there was never any sign of life there.

Of course, he would approach cautiously when he got close, but it was his best bet to stay out of sight. By his guess, it would take him most of the morning since he had to make a wide circle around populated areas and be very discreet in his travel. It was a good feeling just to have a plan.

~~~

Prisoners in the Sheriff's Office holding cells weren't required to rise early like in the County Jail. Chaney lazed around till about eight before a guard brought him a breakfast tray. It didn't look terrible, but it wasn't the stack of hot griddle cakes dripping in syrup and butter he would have ordered at Waffle House. He took his time picking through the eggs and toast, figuring it was still better than he'd be getting when they transferred him over to County.

While he ate, his thoughts wandered. Yesterday, some things had come to mind that he hadn't thought about in many years. The kid, his nephew, was a wild one with a real evil streak. He knew that Chaney liked the little girls, and he played his uncle big time. Chaney wasn't violent by nature but put him in a bad situation, and anything could happen. He wanted the sexual stimulation; Jonathon wanted blood.

When it happened, Chaney was forced to continue his part in the drama through the final stage, the dumping of the bodies. Just like this time with B.J. He was at least smart enough then to protect himself from the possibility that Jonathon might blame the whole thing on him later.

Jonathon told Chaney that they needed insurance. Something that would incriminate each of them so they couldn't turn and run to the cops in a fit of rage. He took a piece of jewelry from each girl, a ring from one, and a bracelet from the other. Then he dumped them in the river. Then he added the handkerchief he had used to wipe the blood off his hands. Some of the blood belonged to the girls from where he bashed their heads with rocks. Some of it was his from scratches he got as the girls fought for their lives. And finally, he added Chaney's sunglasses, making him first put a thumbprint on one of the lenses.

He put the items in a small metal box. They buried it under the tree next to the river, where they dumped the girls' bodies. Chaney didn't know that it was Jonathon's original intention to go back and get the box later, remove anything that could link himself to the crime, and use it for future blackmail. Chaney snuck back a few days later, dug up the box, and moved it. Before reburying it, he removed the sunglasses and tossed them in the garbage. Jonathon never knew that his uncle had moved the box because Jonathon drowned, and it didn't matter anymore. "Hmmm," Chaney muttered to himself. "I wonder if that box is still where I left it?"

~~~

Tom waved goodbye from the cruiser as he backed out of the drive.

Beth was such a gem. Being the wife of a law officer was no easy task.

It was good to share some of the things that weighed on him. Last night they'd talked about Kasey. He could see the longing in Beth's eyes when he told her that this seventeen-year-old girl was pregnant and due soon with so many troubles to face. As he knew she would, Beth suggested he invite Kasey over for some 'family' time, maybe a cookout next weekend.

Every day he thanked God for her. Beth was the best thing that had ever happened to him. A child would make their lives complete, but whatever God's plan was, that was what mattered. If God intended it, then it would be. Until then, they'd keep pouring out their love and caring on whoever needed it.

After parking the patrol car in the gated lot, he crossed the grounds and entered the station. No one expected him for another half hour, but Cheyenne was coming back at nine, and they were going to question Chaney for a while again before sending him over to the jail.

A large, sealed envelope was sitting on his desk with his name handwritten on the front.

Tom purposely walked past it to the coffee pot and got himself ready to start another eventful day. Someone's phone rang, but it wasn't his, so he ignored it. His cup full, creamed, and sugared, he carried it back to his desk, sat down, and took a deep breath.

The office stamp on the envelope was from the police department in Jackson County. "That was pretty darned fast," he thought. He decided to open it before Cheyenne got there.

The message light on his phone was blinking, so he checked his messages before touching the envelope. There was one from the night clerk at the front desk.

"Hi Tom, an officer delivered the package to your desk about four a.m. He said to call the number on the business card inside if you had any questions. And hey, did you hear about the Vice President?"

Tom replaced the receiver of his phone. He hadn't watched the news this morning but made a mental note to catch up with it today when he had time. He ripped open the top of the envelope and removed copies of the paperwork he'd requested yesterday afternoon—a yellow sticky note adhered to the first page and a business card attached with a paper clip.

The note read: "This case has been a thorn in my side for too many years. I could never quite settle myself with the way it ended. Please call if you want to talk." And it was signed by the Chief of Police. "Well, a new mystery," he said out loud, speaking to himself. "I wonder what Cheyenne will make of this?"

"I wonder what Cheyenne will make of what?" she asked. Engrossed in the envelope contents, he didn't hear her come in. Since he'd left instructions with the front desk to send her back on arrival, she wasn't announced.

"Hey, good morning, Agent. Your request lit a match on someone's front burner. We have a reply already, delivered this morning in the wee hours. Never have seen anything like that!" he remarked, shaking his head.

"And the note, what does it say?" she questioned as she sat in the chair opposite him, putting her tablet on the desk.

He pushed it over to her, and she read it for herself. "Hmmm. We'll definitely have to call this man. There's another story behind the story, and this is getting just too interesting. Can we take time to go over the papers before we get back to questioning Chaney?"

"Sure," he was a little confused. "Do you want me to read them too?"

"Why not. These aren't classified, and there might be something in here that could help you in some way."

She pulled the paperwork apart and sorted it, giving him several documents, and keeping some for herself. "We're looking to see if there is any positive proof of identity, who did the I.D. if there was one, and who else was involved, names of witnesses, officers, etc. What looks kosher and what stinks. Then we'll give the Chief of Police a call and find out what he wants to tell us."

They both dove into the task at hand with relish. Cheyenne could feel it in her bones, this was the hunt, and they were close to the target.

After about ten minutes of reading, Tom spoke up, "Found something!" She raised her eyes, staring at him with anticipation. "Good reason for the Chief to be interested; he was the first officer on the scene to see the body. He must be about ready to retire now and would love to have his questions answered before he goes."

"Bet he would," she replied. "Unfortunately, I don't think we'll get much help from the M.E. since he's dead. I just looked him up on the Internet. When this happened, he was an old guy, and he died a couple of years later of an apparent heart attack. His report says that the body was almost unrecognizable due to the decomposition from being in the lake. They got some fingerprints but not good ones. The M.E. called it an accident. Have you run across any names of witnesses yet, deputy? Or who did the I.D.? And did you have a chance to see if he had a record here in your county?" she asked.

"Says something here about the fisherman who found the body being an out-of-towner. Some hot-shot state politician there for a weekend of bass fishing. And his record here was short, mostly teenage minor incidents."

Cheyenne's ears perked. "Does it give a name?"

"Yeah, it's right here. Geez! It was Carlton Ryan; he was Lt. Governor at the time. Youngest one this state ever had. Didn't he just retire from the Senate as one of the top dogs?"

"Yes, Tom. Yes, he did." Her mind began to spin with possible connections.

"OK, and here's the name of the person who gave the positive I.D. Oh, Lord! It was his uncle, Rufus Chaney."

He looked up at her with wide eyes. She handed him the business card, and he dialed. She picked up another phone, pressed the button for the same line out, and just listened.

"Chief here," answered the Chief of Police of Jackson County on the first ring.

~~~

The ride from the Inn to the pawnshop gave Gabe just a few minutes to think. They'd had an eventful breakfast and some on-the-edge conversation to go along with it. Gabe and Luke could discuss anything, but knowing just how much to say in front of Cheyenne and Crystal was touchy. The news about the Vice President tied into this whole thing; he was sure. But it wasn't yet clear how.

He had wanted to tell Cheyenne about the angel singing at the same time she had given herself over to God, but then he'd have to explain how he knew, and that was too deep. He wanted to tell them both about salvation being like poison to the demons, but then he'd have to explain about demons and dimensions. Also, not a breakfast topic for the general public. Last Sunday, what he'd alluded to in church was still more of a concept than a detailed picture. They had to cross these bridges soon. He saw that he and Cheyenne would be in this battle together. But the Inn was neither the time nor the place, so he let the conversation flow and knew that God would show him when and where.

Cheyenne had to hurry off to an appointment, though she shared no details, and he had to get over to see David and Pauley, so they said their goodbyes in the parking lot with just a "See you later," and no definite plans made.

The bell jingled as Gabe entered; they were both waiting eagerly. He was barely two feet inside the door when Pauley burst out in the most urgent voice he'd yet expressed, "It's the salvation that sends them away, Gabe! It hurts them like fire!"

David was practically dancing; he was so eager for Gabe to hear the whole thing.

"Whoa, Pauley. Let's calmly start at the beginning and take your time. I want to put this thing completely together. If it helps us in battle, we have to understand it as fully as possible." Gabe gentled him, and they all sat in chairs around the desk that David had already arranged.

Pauley began, "I went to my room."

"That was just after nine," interjected David.

"I put on pajamas. The pencils were messy, so I put them away. I looked at my drawings. Then I heard a sound. It was different, not a person, not scary. More than beautiful. Loud like it was just outside." He took a deep breath and continued, "My angel said, 'Do not be afraid,' he said it was a song. He told me with each salvation, the angels sing," and he paused.

"Wow, Pauley, that's incredible! I've never heard them make sounds at all, never! And I've never heard stories about the few who can see them, like me, being able to hear them," whispered Gabe in awe. "Is this the first time your angel has spoken to you?" Gabe had seen the guard Host on the roof of the pawnshop when he arrived.

"No," Pauley said firmly with no explanation. "But then I heard screaming too, screaming and shrieking that hurt my ears. I saw in my head; the flying demons were leaving fast. Like they were hurt or burned, and some turned to dust. My angel said, 'Listen and tell Gabe.'"

They were now verbally communicating with him through Pauley, helping him with battle strategy. Giving him an edge by revealing secrets about the demons he'd never have known nor even imagined.

~~~

Crystal and Luke walked into the church together. Jill was waiting and said nothing when she saw them, but her eyes followed their every gesture. They were far enough away that Crystal could speak softly, and Jill wouldn't hear.

"That was nice, Luke. Thanks for feeding me," she smiled sincerely. But I feel a real need to talk with you at length. There was an undercurrent in the conversation, and I know you and Gabe have something going on. Something you don't want to tell the rest of us. Something about what's going to happen. I feel strong enough to handle it, Luke, I really do."

He looked at her and wondered. "When I share things with you, it's because I'm sure the spirit has told me it's OK to do so. I'm not sure about the things I haven't shared yet. I can't take shortcuts with God's will until I am. Please be patient and understand. This is a war bigger than any earthly war. We're all reporting to a higher power to lead us. I'm a soldier following directions."

He took her hand reassuringly. "You have responsibilities every bit as big as mine. You are gathering the saints for prayer cover, which is life and death critical, and you are making another saint to join our ranks."

She smiled and nodded and went to join Jill, who couldn't wait to ask for every detail of every second of the morning.

~~~

"Chief, this is Deputy Tom Dempsey in Henderson County, sir. Thank you for the speedy reply," opened Tom.

"I couldn't have been more caught off guard, deputy. I thought this thing was buried decades ago and that I was the only one who stewed over it. I assume you've read over the paperwork by now."

"Yes, sir. I have Rufus Chaney in custody associated with a recent crime here in our county, and his nephew's name came up in interrogation. I'm just trying to be thorough. Chaney made a reference that could be a possible lead on a cold case involving your drowning victim."

"Well, I didn't see that coming, but this thing stunk like rotten fish from the beginning. I couldn't get anyone else to go along with my thinking, so if there had been a crime back then, it could make some sense." The Chief mulled over some things in his head as he hesitated before finishing. "Do you have some specific questions to ask, or do you want me just to tell you what I saw and what bothered me about the whole thing?"

"Please just talk to me, sir. If I have questions, I'll ask when you're finished."

"The call came in that a body was found floating at the edge of Spooner Lake. I was just a patrolman back then, and I was first on the scene. The caller wore fishing gear, but it was all new like he'd stepped out of the pages of a sports magazine."

"Now, I'm a fisherman son. My daddy taught me as a kid, and I did it all my life. The way this man walked, talked, and handled his gear, he was not a fisherman. His face was clean-shaven, and his nails manicured. And he was wearing aftershave! Who the hell puts on aftershave for a fish?"

Tom chuckled.

"I called in the M.E. without touching the body. It was clear he was dead, no need to check for a pulse. The decomp was pretty bad, and he stunk to hell and back. That was my first dead body experience, and those things stick in your memory. While we were waiting, I questioned the caller."

"His name you've already read, and you know who this guy is now.

He was a pretty high-up muckety-muck in the state even then, and once everyone else found out who he was, they fell all over him, making asses of themselves. No real investigation ever got done because they all wanted to make it smooth for the politician. No scandal, know what I mean?"

Tom was smiling at Cheyenne. He mouthed the words "I like this guy," and she nodded.

"Well, I asked him how he found the body, and he said it was when he was walking around the lake looking for a good spot to fish. What a lame-ass answer! I asked him how he saw a body hidden in reeds when he was so far up the bank. He said he must have glimpsed the clothing, and then he got down closer and saw it was a body. He had his "assistant" drive back to town to make the call."

"In all my life, I've never had a fishing "assistant." That guy never did sit well with me, but I was the low man, and there was nothing I could do about it between a state politician's word and the M.E.'s report that said it was an accident."

"I remember that Rufus Chaney fella coming in to do the I.D. I guessed him to be about twenty years older than the kid. I asked him afterward what he saw that confirmed it was Jonathon Chaney. He said it was the bathing suit and the St. Christopher medal. Well, Holy Geezus! Anyone could have those. So, there was never a positive I.D., but the old Chief closed the case. I always wondered if someone had manipulated that whole affair."

"That's about the end of it. Don't know any more except that it never digested for me. Sits there like a bad oyster in the pit of my stomach. Maybe you can shed some light on it now, son. I'm retiring next month, and I gladly turn it over to you," finished the Chief.

"That was a complete recount, sir. I've made notes to add to the information you sent. If I have anything else I need to ask, may I call you again?" asked Tom.

"Sure can, son. I want to know how this turns out."

Tom thanked him and ended the call.

Cheyenne was on a high. Senator Manning and Jonathon were the same age. Jonathon's body was never positively I.D.'d. Another politician was heavily involved, and the police department had buried the case. It looked like corruption in its juiciest form. Now she urgently needed to find that box, and fast! The source of her final answer was in Chaney's memory. The tricky part was extracting it without having him get suspicious and clam up.

~~~

Senator Manning sat at his massive mahogany desk with a plain, 10x13 yellow envelope in his hands. The kind used for interoffice communications. He opened it and extracted the contents, a single sheet of paper containing one short paragraph—eight small words that had powerful meaning.

R.C. in custody. Girl in town. Thor arrived.

He sighed, hating the task of cleaning up messes, especially his own. It had taken a lot of doing to coordinate everything to get the man with the code name 'Thor' there. Manning was confident that what he wanted could be done, but unforeseen complications were always possible.

It was Thor's problem to retrieve the object and then eliminate Chaney. How many times had he chastised himself for not going back to remove the box of evidence after his faked death? He should have killed Chaney, too, just for good measure. No telling what that old man remembered, even if he thought his nephew was dead. It would have been so easy to destroy it all and prevent this, but he was willingly sucked into a life of wealth and glamor and just assumed with his cocky attitude that it was all behind him and that his new mentors would protect him from everything.

What Manning had to decide was the fate of the girl. Who would he assign to carry out the elimination, Thor? They had broken contact, and to reconnect would cause suspicion. Or should he involve another puppet?

Having had that thought, the perfect person came to mind, and it was someone Thor would be taking care of anyway, for a personal reason. That would work splendidly. Thor would take out this guy after the hitman killed the woman, and the last loose end would be tied up. Except for getting the box and destroying the evidence, of course.

Oh, he was very pleased with himself. He picked up the phone and dialed. When someone answered at the other end, he spoke, "Work order for dispatch. Coding: schedule J, message to arrive at ten hundred hours." Then he replaced the receiver and opened his laptop.

He entered his security codes, pressed the keys to obtain Encrypting Schedule J, and typed.

> Hire – Jake Bauer,
>   Mission: Eliminate agent X-1,
>   Deadline: 48 hours
>   Over

Then he scheduled the message for a ten a.m. delivery and logged out.

It was time for his limo to be at the front door. He had a meeting and a lunch date with some highly influential people with bottomless pockets. He couldn't keep money waiting when there would soon be contributions and funding needed to boost his position as high as his aspirations.

A monstrous Gai'Ograh Prince stood over Manning, instructing the Senator in a low growl what he then accepted as his own thoughts. When Manning left the room, the lesser demons who served the high ranking one cheered and danced, slobbering and snorting foul substances. The Demon Prince bellowed, and five of the more minor demons propelled up through the ceiling like rockets. Their destination, the new assassin, Jake Bauer.

20

The Box

CARLOS DIDN'T have a watch, but he figured it to be about eleven o'clock from the sun's position. The barn was near now; he was watching for landmarks. There, behind that stand of trees, just a bit of the weathered roof was visible.

After ten minutes of remaining as still and as silent as he could and not seeing or hearing anyone else, he left the shelter of the bushes and walked to the ancient structure. It hadn't changed since his last visit over two years ago. There were no footprints around the building, and nothing seemed to have been disturbed. He approached the big door and pushed hard, opening it just wide enough for him to squeeze inside.

Entering the dark interior, the temperature around him dropped at least ten degrees. Dust particles slowly moved in the shafts of light that pierced through the spaces between the old wallboards as he made his way toward the stalls. It smelled of damp earth, but it wasn't unpleasant. If his memory served him, there were some old blankets in one of the stalls. Finding one in useable condition would be a bonus. He planned to position himself up in the loft where the vantage point was the best, and a blanket would make his stay a bit more comfortable.

As he entered the stall closest to the back of the barn, he tripped over something slightly protruding from the hard-packed dirt floor.

~~~

A boy, small for his age, ran in through the big door and straight to the last stall where he kept his strawberry pony. He ducked down behind the pony and partly covered himself with the fresh hay covering the floor.

Horrible noises were coming from the house near the barn. Yelling and crying and things breaking. He covered his ears with his hands, but that didn't block out all the sounds.

This was a typical evening for the boy. He knew that in a short while, the man would come looking for him, and he'd likely get a beating again. But for now, he was protected by the pony, the only living creature that ever loved him.

Chaney was yanked out of his reverie by a guard unlocking the cell door.

"You're wanted in the interrogation room, Chaney. Let's get goin'," ordered the guard.

Chaney rose to his feet. There was a great heaviness in his chest. "I really loved that pony," he muttered to himself while passing the guard. The officer looked at him like he was crazy and then escorted Chaney down the hall.

~~~

Cheyenne planned to pull out all the stops and make this go fast. She had a strong feeling that her time was shorter than she might hope, that Manning was somehow going to catch up with her and all hell would break loose. The timing would be right. Gabe told her that hell would, in fact, be breaking loose here within a couple of days.

She went into the observation room as Tom entered the interrogation room where Chaney sat. "How're you doing today, Chaney?" Tom asked the man. The old guy looked like he'd aged another ten years overnight. He just looked up at Tom and shook his head.

"Are you ready to answer some more questions?" Tom asked.

"Yeah, I guess I can do that," he answered. There was no fight in his voice, no caginess. He was off his game today for some reason. Tom wondered what had happened. The old guy just seemed exceptionally tired.

"Well, today, I'm not going to ask you any questions about B.J. Is that OK?" Tom waited for a reply before continuing.

Chaney nodded but had no strong reaction.

"Yesterday, you mentioned someone I want to talk about today. You mentioned Jonathon."

Chaney raised his head but said nothing.

"You also mentioned that Jonathon had done something bad and dragged you into it, just like B.J. did, right?"

Chaney nodded again.

"I'm going to ask for your help here, Chaney. I know you don't have to answer this, but I do believe that somewhere deep down inside of you, there was once a good person who may still exist. I'm going to ask you to help me close out a terrible hurt for two families. Two families who lost little girls a lot of years ago."

Chaney sat up a bit straighter and looked slightly more focused. He saw the girls laughing and playing as young, healthy children in his mind. And he remembered the evil look on his nephew's face as they watched the girls from the car parked nearby. It had made him tremble then, and he was feeling the same reaction at just the memory.

Tom heard Cheyenne's voice in his ear, "Ask him how he felt when he I.D.'d his nephew's body. I know it's jumping ahead, but I think he hated that kid, and we need to get that negative emotion going."

"You were the one who went in to make the I.D. on Jonathon's body Chaney. How did you feel when you saw him?" Tom asked.

Cheyenne saw the expression on Chaney's face. "I was glad he was dead," he answered flatly. "He was bad, really bad."

"Ask if he was afraid of him," urged Cheyenne.

"Did he ever hurt you, Chaney? Were you afraid of him?

"He hurt me. He hurt a lot of people. I'm still here; a lot of them ain't."

"Did he hurt those two girls?" Tom knew what to ask before Cheyenne spoke.

Chaney had been looking past Tom into his own memories. Now he focused on Tom's face. "Yes, sir. He killed 'em."

"Ask if he can help us prove it," Cheyenne almost yelled.

"Can you give me some way to prove that? I can tell the DA that you've been very cooperative in closing a cold case, Mr. Chaney. It could go a long way to helping you in the B.J. incident." Tom tossed that association in for good measure, careful not to make any promises.

"Don't know why but somethin' made me think that night that I'd have to take special care to protect myself. We put some things in a box. The way that boy's mind worked, I wouldn't have put it past him to try to blame me for everything. I went to where we buried it, and I moved it. He was evil and a conniver. I was glad he drowned. But after that, I didn't have to worry anymore."

"What did you put in the box?"

"Some things that belonged to the girls. One of the rocks he used to bash in their heads. His blood on a rag," answered Chaney.

"Where is the box, Mr. Chaney?" Tom asked, hoping his voice wasn't shaking.

"Firecracker is protecting it," he answered. "She's been keepin' it safe all these years."

Chaney told Tom he was tired. "Can I have a rest now?" he asked in such a soul-weary way that Tom agreed.

"We'll get back together after lunch, Mr. Chaney. Thank you for your cooperation."

Tom opened the door, and the guard took Chaney back to his cell.

Cheyenne was sitting in a chair staring at the one-way glass. "Are you OK with how that went?" he asked as he entered the observation room.

"Yeah, perfectly OK," she answered. As soon as we have the box, we're done."

"What are you thinking? How do Jonathon and Manning connect?" He was asking if she'd come to the same conclusion that he had.

"They're the same person," she said, turning her head to look at him. "Manning is the murderer, and we're going to bring him down and find out how high this corruption goes."

"But what about the dead body? Who was that? And the Lt. Governor? How does that fit in?" he asked, dreading the answer.

"Someone way up on the top of the heap got the Lt. Governor to come here and make the story look credible. They figured that no one would question it much with a politician of his rank. Remember, this was about forty years ago. They probably abducted some kid, killed him, and set it up to look like Jonathon. That would mean that they'd been watching Jonathon and then recruited him or something. They wiped him off of the face of the earth and started him from scratch with a new identity to mold him into their man. We can prove most of this with that box. But until we have it in our hands, it's just wild speculation. And remember," she said, looking him in the eyes with a straight poker face. "This is all classified."

Tom rarely felt fear, but it began wrapping its tentacles around his spine at the impact of her words.

"Now, who the hell is Firecracker?" she wondered out loud.

"Someone's nickname? The name of a pet?" He was guessing.

"But what pet would live forty years? Does he have a parrot or an elephant?" she chuckled. "Or did he have a pet then that he doesn't have now?"

"Do we have to go digging in a pet cemetery?" he asked, making a disgusting face.

"Don't think so. But if your pet dies, where do you bury it? Most likely, in your yard. Where did Chaney live forty years ago? Where did he live when he had Firecracker?" She knew they were onto something but not quite there yet. "I need to find all of his past addresses."

"I can check that and have the information ready when we question him again this afternoon," he volunteered. "I'll check for arrest records on the kid too." If he could get Chaney's cooperation on closing this cold case and on the current matter with B.J., he could put both of them away, and Cheyenne would have her man too. Does it get any better?

~~~

Carlos bent down to see what it was that had tripped him. Sticking out of the ground about an inch was a bone from a rib cage.

A shudder ran through him. Grabbing a couple of the old blankets, he climbed up the ladder to the loft as quickly as he could.

~~~

It happened when he was twelve. His sister was two years younger than he was. His older sister had gone to live with his aunt quite some time before. The fighting and the beatings were escalating to the breaking point.

The man was his stepfather. His mother was a doll, broken by life and beatings, and with the courage of a mouse. She couldn't stand up for herself or her children. The man beat Chaney for years and sexually abused his little sister since she was only seven. Beating his mother was a daily thing whenever the man was drunk, and that was practically all of the time.

Chaney was in the barn brushing down Firecracker when he heard the fighting and his sister screaming. He bolted to the little house about a hundred feet from the barn. Throwing open the door, he saw the man ripping the dress off of his sister. His mother lay on the floor next to the table. She was perfectly still, a pool of blood around her head.

Chaney wasn't a big kid, but he whipped that man around and punched him in the face. The man fell to one knee, giving Chaney time to grab his sister and push her out the door. "Run!" he yelled.

She escaped, but the man cornered Chaney and pummeled him. Chaney couldn't get up. He saw the man take his rifle from the wall and go outside. A few minutes later, a shot echoed from the barn, then nothing. He crawled across the floor and out the door and hid in some bushes till dark.

Then he made his way to the barn and Firecracker's stall. She was lying in her own blood, a hole in the middle of her forehead. He laid down next to her and held her, sobbing, until he could weep no more.

Then he got himself up, feeling the intense pain of his cracked and bruised ribs, and quietly walked to the house. The snoring was audible twenty feet away. The man had passed out again, probably not even realizing he was in the place with his dead wife, bludgeoned by him for the last time.

Chaney took the half-filled gas can they used for the tractor and emptied the container by splashing the contents around inside of the house. He stepped out on the front porch and pulled a box of matches from the pocket of his overalls.

Striking that match and tossing it into the house was the first thing he'd ever done that made him proud of himself.

As the house burned, he buried Firecracker in her stall. The man didn't get out.

~~~

Minutes later, Cheyenne stood in front of the same librarian. The woman smiled, "So nice to see you again, dear. How can I help you today?" she asked.

"Just a quick question, ma'am. Do you know anyone who is still around that might have personally known most of the families living here in the 1940s?"

"Well, that someone would have to be at least in their late 80s or early 90s, my dear. I'm not quite there myself, but I can direct you to Amos Jones. He's an old farmer who used to have a small place out on the southeast side of town. Knew most everyone, as I recollect, and he does love to tell stories. I believe he's about ninety by now."

"Where can I find Amos, please?" she asked, obviously in a hurry.

"He's usually in a rocking chair on the porch at the old feed store on the corner of Jefferson and Adams. I can draw you a map."

"No, thank you," Cheyenne smiled as she hurried toward the door. "I have one."

She pulled out her cell phone and clicked on the GPS as soon as she hit the sidewalk. The feed store was about six miles from there. Running toward the Jeep, she crammed the phone back into her pocket.

~~~

Lester packed up the few things he had and prepared to start the unknown portion of his journey. He knew he had first to find the location of a metal box buried by a tree about forty years ago. Then on to find Rufus Chaney and kill him. His final task for the benefactor was to leave the box in a prearranged location for someone else to pick up.

When finished, he would be on his own to take care of the snitch, a little weasel named Jake. If he made it through all of that alive, it would be time to seek out his son, just for a look. He had no intention of disrupting the kid's life. Someone was bound to recognize him by then, and he figured he'd die in a firefight with the law.

The other con stood in the doorway, almost afraid to speak, but he couldn't let Lester pack up and leave without finding out where to find the money. "Are we leaving?" he asked tentatively.

"No. I'm leaving. I decided I don't want company on the rest of my trip," answered Lester.

The con waited. Was this guy reneging on his promise to give him the location?

Lester pulled out his map. "Come here," he said. The con approached him cautiously. "I'll show you where the money is, but I'm keeping the map, so you better have a good memory."

Lester pointed, "Here's where we are." He indicated the northeast area just outside the county line in relation to where the town sat. "Here, this is where the money is hidden." He randomly picked a spot on the opposite side of where they were now, the far south side of the county. There was so much farmland around that he felt safe in the story he was making up. It would keep the con busy for a while, looking for a place that didn't exist.

"The money is stashed in the bank bags. It's in an old, abandoned barn. There's a grain bin inside with a false bottom. It's under the floorboards beneath that bin."

"I'm leaving now. You can stay here, go for the money, or go somewhere completely different, your choice. Just stay outta my way, or you're dead." The con had seen him in action, so he believed the sincerity of Lester's words.

They parted ways, Lester going to his doom, the other con striking out on a pointless mission.

~~~

Cheyenne found the corner. The feed store porch and the rocking chair out front were empty. She parked the Jeep and went inside. A couple of old guys sat at a little table playing checkers, a vision that made her feel she'd stepped back in time a hundred years. She approached, donning her most charming smile.

"Hi, fellas. Could either of you direct me to Amos, please? The lovely lady at the library told me that I could find him here."

They looked at her and then at each other. "That must have been Miss Edna. I always figured her to have the sweets for you, Amos."

Amos' grin revealed his remaining two tobacco yellowed teeth. "She's too young for an old codger like me, Theo. What can I do for you young 'un?" his question directed toward Cheyenne.

"I'm researching some history of the area, sir. I was wondering if you could help. You knew pretty much all of the longtime families that were here back in the 1940-time frame, I believe?" she paused.

"Yes, missy, I do believe I knew all of the locals then. A far cry fewer than what we have here now, though. Who do you want to know about?"

"Well, I actually have the name of a pet. I heard the name but don't know who to associate it with. It's pretty different, and it might jog a memory for you. The name is 'Firecracker.' Do you recognize it?" she was hopeful.

"Hmmm. Yes, yes, I do. A strawberry-colored spunky little pony, she was. Belonged to Rufus Chaney as a kid. The two of them were inseparable. I'm a bit older than him, and I remember how bad it was when he lost that pony. Late forties, I think it was, a tragic thing. Same day his mom and stepdad died in a fire that took their farmhouse. After that, he and his little sis had to go live with their aunt. So much lost in one day. It changed that boy. He was never the same again. Grew evil, he did."

"Where was the fire, sir? Where was the farm back then?" She was so close!

"That farm was out 'bout two miles. Dirt roads don't have no names back there, but Miss Edna would be happy to draw you a map, child. Tell her it's the old Chaney place that burned down, and she'll know what you mean." The men chuckled, "Miss Edna loves to draw maps for everything." Even Cheyenne laughed at that.

"Thank you, Mr. Jones. I'll go see Miss Edna again. You've been very helpful. I hope to see you again, and I'd love to hear many more of your stories." She waved as she left the feed store.

~~~

An officer rushed over to Tom's desk, where he sat munching a homemade meatloaf sandwich. "Tom, you've got to get back to the holding cells, fast!" the officer whispered urgently.

Tom choked down the bite in his mouth as he jumped up and followed. They almost ran down the hall to the section containing the four holding cells where a guard waited with the master door open. Another guard was standing by Chaney's open cell door. A third was on the floor doing CPR on Chaney.

"The paramedics are on the way, but I think he's already gone. Looks like a heart attack or a massive stroke," explained one of the guards

"What could possibly be next?" Tom asked himself. "You three, please take care of the paperwork when the ambulance gets here." He pulled his cell phone out of his pocket and dialed Cheyenne.

"Hi Tom, I'll be back there shortly. What's up?"

"Chaney just had a heart attack. He's dead," Tom spoke into the phone in as low a voice as he could manage. He stepped away and headed back to his desk so the guards couldn't overhear. "What do we do now, agent?" he asked, not sure what the next step would be regarding her case but knowing that he still had B.J. on the murder with no problem. "How do we follow up on this Firecracker thing?"

"I've got it, deputy. I've got the answer. I have to make another quick stop at the library, and then I'll be back. Wait there for me, please. I'll tell you everything when I get there."

~~~

The sound of loud knocking broke through Jake's stupor. He opened his eyes to the sights of a dumpy apartment, none too clean, and realized again he was on Sarah's couch. The knocking persisted.

He pushed himself to his feet and went to the door, wondering where the hell Sarah went. She didn't work. He looked at the clock on the wall and saw that it was close to two in the afternoon; it must still be Tuesday. Maybe she had forgotten her key.

The door swung open; a smallish balding man stood there wearing round spectacles. He looked like the stereotypical office nerd from nineteen fifty, a weak, weaselly, bookworm. Jake just glared at him.

"Mr. Bauer, I had some difficulty finding you, sir. I have something I must deliver directly to you," he said, handing Jake a large manila envelope.

The man turned and hurried away before Jake could comprehend what had just taken place. He looked at the envelope in his hands and closed the door.

Tearing the edge open as he sat on the couch, Jake could feel the weight of the bulky package. He turned it upside down, and the contents fell into his lap. The large bound stack of ten-dollar bills was first to catch his attention. Holy Shit! Was this really meant for him? And who would have sent it? How would they have found him at Sarah's? He didn't know anyone with this kind of dough. Forcing his eyes from the cash, he saw a single sheet of paper and a photo lying by the money.

He picked them up simultaneously, one in each hand. The picture was of a beautiful black-haired woman with eyes like he'd never seen. OK, this was getting weirder by the minute. The paper contained a short note.

> Mr. Bauer,
>   It has come to my attention that you require some funds and some long-distance transportation. I can supply both for the exchange of a favor.
>   I know you have the necessary tool to eliminate the problem described in the photo. Once you complete my request (you have 48 hours to do so), additional funding of ten times the amount enclosed and transportation information will be forthcoming

through the same channel that brought this memo to you today.

You can find the problem at the Settle Inn. I will know when you have finished. Consider the enclosed as a deposit.

Jake tore off the paper which bound the bills and began counting. One hundred. Someone had sent him a thousand dollars as a deposit to whack this broad. Someone who knew he already had a gun. And someone who was willing to pay him an additional ten thousand dollars. They wanted it done by Thursday morning. That meant he could do the job, pick up his new I.D.s, and use this person's transportation plan to get far away from this county. Hell, he could go to another country! But he'd have to leave the other guys hanging on the bank job. They wouldn't be happy.

There was no signature or return address; there was no way for him to get back in touch or ask questions. It said that the person sending the message would know. Was he being watched? Was this a trap? Did it matter? He was already living on borrowed time. Here was an opportunity to get what he needed, cash and an exit. It took him only moments to decide to accept the anonymous offer. Now he had to have a plan. The first thing was to find the Settle Inn.

~~~

They had barely put the food away from lunch when Jill heard the phone ringing in Pastor Luke's office. She ran to answer it while Crystal finished cleaning up.

"Hello," she stated simply.

"Hello, I'm looking for the Pastor, please. I'm Pastor Clancy from His Grace Church."

"Oh, hello, Pastor. I'm sorry, but Pastor Luke hasn't returned from his visits yet." Jill looked up to see Luke entering the office. "Wait a minute, sir. He's just coming in. Please hold while I get him for you," she said as she motioned for Luke to take the receiver. "It's a Pastor Clancy for you, Luke."

"Pastor Clancy, what can I do for you today?" Luke asked while he put his things down and lowered himself into his chair.

"Please call me Dan. I have several members of my congregation pleading with me to get together with you, Pastor Luke. It seems that many family members and friends of ours were in attendance as guests to hear your Sunday message. We are on the same wavelength from what's been described and related to me. I want to invite you to come to our Wednesday evening service to give us the same information you gave on Sunday."

"I'd be honored to do that, Dan, and calling me Luke makes me a lot more comfortable as well. I'd be bringing along at least one friend who is critical to the issues, is that OK?"

"That would be your college buddy, Gabe, correct?"

"Yes indeed, he is a spiritual warrior in every sense of the word, and it's the battle which he is called to fight on our turf that is the big issue right now," explained Luke.

"Then it's set. Our service begins at seven, but if you could come earlier so we can talk, I'd appreciate it."

Luke hung up after good-byes were said and turned to Crystal and Jill, who both stood in the doorway waiting to hear what was happening. In reply to their expressions, Luke said, "Gabe and I will address the congregation at His Grace Church, across town, for tomorrow night's service. Would you like to come with us?" as he updated the calendar on his desk.

~~~

Cheyenne jumped out of the Jeep and ran up the steps to the library. She immediately sighted Miss Edna behind the front counter and walked briskly toward her.

The motion caught the elderly librarian's attention, and she raised her eyes to see the stunning out-of-towner approach. "Back so soon? You're in quite a hurry, young lady. How can I help you this time?"

"Please draw me a map, Miss Edna. I need to know how to find the old Chaney place that burned down about forty years ago."

Miss Edna's eyes sparkled as she reached for the paper and pencil.

~~~

Tom hit the print button on his keyboard. The printer began whirring as it placed ink to paper to produce the information he'd requested. He had the old arrest records on Chaney's nephew and was printing out the fingerprint card from Henderson County to compare to the one in M.E.'s records.

The print was complete, and Tom pulled it from the machine and put it on the desk next to the one taken from the corpse. He expected it to be a difficult match due to the decomposition, but there were often at least a few swirl markers that were usable. Tom studied each sheet for a couple of moments and shook his head. These prints were not from the same person, not even close.

His cell phone rang. The caller I.D. told him it was Beth. "Hi, hon. What's up?"

"I just got a call, and we need to be at tomorrow night's church service at seven o'clock. It's important. Can you go with me?"

"Absolutely! What's the urgency, though?"

"Things are going on, Tom, on a spiritual level, and they're affecting people on a physical level. Another Pastor is coming to speak, a Pastor Luke. He's been through this kind of thing before."

"I can attest to the 'things affecting people.' This place is a madhouse with all of the calls coming in about crimes and fighting. In fact, Pastor Luke and I met already, and I'd like to see him again and know more about whatever it is that's going on right now. He seems to be a good guy. I'm your date, Beth!"

"Thanks, sweetie, see you at dinner," she ended, and he could picture her smile.

Someone hurriedly approached his desk. He looked up to see Cheyenne with flushed cheeks and a paper in her hand. "Come on, deputy, we have a map, and we probably need a shovel."

"I can get a shovel in just a minute; I want you to see this first, agent. He slid the two sets of prints to her, and she studied them intently. She raised her head, and they locked eyes. "No doubt at all," he said. She nodded her head in agreement.

Tom grabbed a shovel, and they ran to the patrol car.

~~~

The directions were explicit. Lester was at the right spot, without a doubt, but there was no metal box where it was supposed to be. For at least an hour, he'd been digging around that damned tree. Lester hadn't anticipated anything in the plan being inaccurate after the perfection experienced so far. He had no one to contact or go to for a Plan B. It was time to ad-lib.

The benefactor would know something was wrong this evening when the box wasn't in the arranged drop-off location. Lester started walking in that direction. He'd go there and leave a note saying the metal box was missing. Then, his next task was to eliminate Chaney.

~~~

"Hi, Aunt Nettie. Yep, I got the phone call, and I'll be there tomorrow night after work. It's crazy here! That Chaney guy they arrested for the murder, well, he just up and croaked right here in the jail! The news people got wind of it, and they're swarming the place. Me? I'm just trying to stay outta the way. OK, see you tomorrow."

The young janitor hung up his cell phone, put it back in his pocket, and went back to mopping the floor in the kitchen of the Sheriff's Station.

~~~

Tom and Cheyenne bounced along the dirt roads as fast as they could without giving themselves spinal injury. Miss Edna's map drawing was good, though, full of landmarks since there were no formal streets or even county roads.

As they neared the last bend in the road before reaching their target, Tom slowed to a stop. "We should approach on foot to make sure no one is around," he explained.

"Good plan, deputy. I'll take the front; you go around the back. Call out when you're clear."

They walked toward the barn as quietly as possible with guns at the ready. Cheyenne found the barn door ajar with some footprints and scuff marks which looked pretty fresh. Tom found nothing around back, not even a door, so he returned to the front to join her. She pointed to the marks and put a finger to her lips to indicate silence and caution.

Carlos had heard the car engine from his hiding spot in the loft. He dug himself deeper into the shadows and hunkered down, barely breathing.

Tom went to the right and Cheyenne to the left, exploring every space where someone could be lying in wait. Nothing. Cheyenne whispered, "Those scuff marks and footprints must have been some kids playing here. I think it's clear."

"We didn't check the loft," he replied.

"I haven't seen the slightest movement or heard the least little sound. I think we're OK. Did you see anything in any of the stalls that looked suspicious? Anyplace where Chaney could have hidden the box?"

"I didn't check the last two on the right yet but so far, no. Remember Chaney said that Firecracker was guarding it. What do you think?" he asked.

"Maybe in the stall where he kept the pony?" They both entered the last stall on the right, and Tom caught his foot on the same protrusion where Carlos had stumbled. He pointed his flashlight at it and flicked it on. Bones. Rib bones were sticking up from the dirt. They looked at each other and said in unison, "Firecracker?"

Tom ran to the car for the shovel.

They didn't have to dig far. Chaney had positioned the box in the center of the ribcage, where the pony's heart would have sat. It crossed Cheyenne's mind as she reached for it that maybe even the bad guys had a heart somewhere. After all, we all start out as innocent babies.

She lifted it out of the hole, making sure to touch only the very edges so as not to destroy any evidence. The box was locked. Tom quickly broke it with the shovel handle. Cheyenne opened it gently, and just as Chaney had said, the box contained a bracelet, a ring, a bloody rock, and the icing on the cake, a bloody handkerchief.

She took pictures of the stall, the hole, the box, and its contents with her cell phone. They scooped up the box with the shovel and took it to the patrol car, placing it in the trunk. "Guess that's all I need here," she said. "Let's get this into a forensics lab for testing before anything else happens." They got into the car and headed back to town.

~~~

An encrypted message flashed across his laptop screen. He hit the keys for the code, and the garble became words he could read.

R.C. dead, girl has box, Thor useless

How did that happen? He had it planned to perfection! Imbeciles! They were all imbeciles! What good did it do to have enough pull and money to pay for eyes everywhere if those eyes were set inside incompetent heads? He owned people! He owned law enforcement, judges, politicians. He demanded loyalty, and he paid top dollar for the best results. How was this getting so out of control?

The mammoth demon bent over, drool dripping onto the Senator's immaculate suit, and spoke into his ear. Manning's next thought: he'd have to handle this himself.

He pressed the intercom button for his personal secretary. "I need travel arrangements for a fishing trip. Step into my office now." His tone was not politically correct.

His secretary replied, "Sir, a message from the President just came in. He's expecting you in his office tomorrow morning at ten a.m. I believe it has to do with the Vice President position."

"Have my private jet ready to leave here at eight a.m. and a limo in D.C. waiting for me. I'll be leaving from there for the fishing trip. You'll get the details shortly. Message back when you have it all set up."

~~~

Lester had a thick beard growth already, and in his camos, he was far less recognizable. With his reasonably unique build and the fact that he was a stranger here, people would likely be suspicious. He followed the road but stayed far enough off to the side in the edges of the woods that he felt he wasn't noticeable. Still, extreme caution was warranted.

He'd already seen three different small groups of people walking toward town, dirty, shady-looking men and women. Some with identical tattoos on their hands or arms, a code he couldn't decipher, below two red eyes. A new cult he didn't know about since he'd been in prison for fourteen years. But they paid him no mind at all.

The arranged drop-off point was at a nearby crossroads. The instructions were to place the box, unopened, into the back of an unlocked metal newspaper distribution stand. Since it would be filled with newspapers early tomorrow morning, Lester knew someone watched for his delivery tonight.

Someone was talking a short distance ahead; he slowed his pace, moving further into the woods line as he continued following the direction of the road. The voices grew louder as he approached, and it dawned on him that the sound was from someone's T.V. Across the pavement, set back about fifty feet, was a small cabin. A woman was hanging clothes on the line with the T.V. turned up high enough to hear it outside. No car sat in the yard; she appeared to be alone.

Lester leaned against a tree trunk to listen for a minute, well out of her line of vision.

"...those stories and more after this commercial break on your News 5 at 5."

OK, it was five o'clock, and the news was just starting. Lester could afford to sit here for a few minutes to see if there was any mention of the other escapees. The pace since early morning was pretty steady, and he was feeling it. He leaned his head back against the tree, closed his eyes, and listened to the jingles and hype of products being peddled over national airwaves.

"Tonight's top headlines in local news: One of the alleged murderers of the nine-year-old girl in Henderson County has died in his jail cell. On a national level, the President will be naming a new Vice President in a news conference tomorrow afternoon, and three more escaped convicts were captured in the state of Washington. In world news: the *war in Syria escalates, and a major earthquake has occurred off the coast of Japan. The tsunami threat is at a high level. More on that after the complete local news."*

"Rufus Chaney, who was arrested yesterday on charges of lewd behavior and is a suspect in the murder of nine-year-old Becky Robbins, has died of natural causes in his jail cell this afternoon. The Sheriff's Office issued a statement saying they would give us more details after the Medical Examiner does an autopsy and makes his report. At this point, there is no reason to believe that any inmate mishandling occurred."

"The FBI reports that three of the escaped convicts led police on a high-speed chase through the heavily populated city streets of Spokane, Washington today, endangering other drivers and numerous pedestrians before the convicts' car went out of control and slammed into a bridge abutment. Armed State Troopers and local police descended on the wrecked vehicle, carjacked just hours before. All three convicts were dead. That brings the number of remaining escapees to fourteen. All viewers, please continue your vigilance and call your local FBI if you've seen any of these dangerous men. With the amount of time that has passed, they could be anywhere in the country."

That was enough. He didn't need to hear anymore. The escaped prisoners were doing what he expected, and there were still plenty of cons on the loose out there to keep the Feds busy. Lester picked himself up and trudged on toward the drop-off point. The irony of the target already being dead didn't escape him; it just saved him the trouble. For a split second, he wondered how the orchestrator of this whole thing felt with two parts of his plan screwed up. Once by natural causes, once by mystery. Lester didn't care. All he had to do was leave the note, and he was free to concentrate on finding the snitch. He just might make it to his final goal, seeing his son for the last time.

~~~

The box sat on his desk, unearthed after almost four decades, contained in a marked plastic evidence bag. "I should call in to have it picked up," Cheyenne said as she and Tom just stood on opposite sides of his desk, staring at the bag. "I guess this wraps up my mission."

"It's late," Tom replied. "Wouldn't it be better to let me have it locked up for the night and start fresh tomorrow morning? I've got to call Beth and get home; I'm sure she's been holding dinner. Would you like to come along? There's always enough, and she'd love to meet you."

"Thanks for the invite, deputy. I'll have to pass, but I agree that locking this thing up for the night is wise. I have some things to take care of before I leave town, and this evening seems like the opportunity to get it done." She shook his hand. "I couldn't have done all of this in such a short time without your help. You're definitely detective material, and I plan on including that information in my report. This town and the people I've met have had a major impact on my life. I won't forget it. I'll be here in the morning for the official hand-off to the FBI courier." She smiled and turned away, walking out the front door as Tom carried the bagged box to the secure evidence room where the deputy on duty logged it in; Tom knew him well. The Chief had started bringing on more forces to help with the extreme overload of cases, so there were several new faces in the building. Thank goodness. They could use all the help they could get.

21

Gathering Darkness

DARKNESS WAS descending as Carlos finally emerged from his hidden corner in the loft. There hadn't been any other activity or noises since the two cops found what they were looking for and left. What were the chances that someone besides himself would have visited this barn on the same day? It had probably been years since anyone was here.

He climbed down the ladder quietly and pushed through the door. It wouldn't be wise to stay here now just in case someone decided to come back for something they may have missed. Could he risk contacting Kasey yet? Lester told him not to do it till tomorrow night. He knew where to find the guy who could make the new ID, but he didn't want to spend the money on one for Kasey if she wasn't interested in leaving with him. Why should she be? He really messed up her life.

She was so close to having the baby by his calculations. If she wasn't working now, he might be able to catch her at home. OK, he'd take the chance. Her answer would help him to decide what to do next. He could reach a reasonably private payphone a little over a mile from the barn. Then he'd find a place to hide for the night after he called her—one step at a time.

Carlos looked around at the deep inkiness and shuddered. He had never feared the dark, but this was ominous. The stillness wasn't normal. Even at night, there were usually the sounds of animals or insects, and he hadn't seen a single firefly. He began walking as fast as he could while still being careful to feel his way along the route the cop car had taken. Dozens of red eyes watched him from inside the barn and even more from the tree branches. The hair stood up on the back of his neck and his arms, but he didn't know why; he just hurried away as fast as possible.

~~~

Forty-eight hours was the time frame, and the clock was ticking. This hit job would be so much easier than a bank robbery with another guy. And it paid more—no one to screw things up for him. He'd need to do a little bit of checking out the lady and her habits, a quick whack with the gun, and an afternoon exit out of town. The note said the money man knew all and would send the little bald guy to deliver the rest of the money. Easy.

Well, one thing was sure. Jake got instructions to visit the Settle Inn, and he now had some money in his pocket, so that seemed to be the logical first step. Find the place and check out the target.

Jake had been at Sarah's all day, and she still wasn't home, no matter, it was better that way. Putting a few of the bills in his pocket, he stuffed the rest back into the envelope. It went inside the back of his loose-hanging shirt next to the gun. The phone book was on the kitchen counter under the wall phone. After jotting down the address he was looking for, he crammed the paper slip into his pocket with the loose bills and called a cab. No walking tonight!

An image of the dark-haired beauty flashed across his mind, and he wondered if he could have a little fun with her before he did her in. Maybe a quick stop at Peggy's apartment to shower and change clothes would be a good idea. If he wanted to blend in with the crowd, he needed to do some cleaning up first.

Jake was unaware of the gleeful pleasure he was giving the numerous demons attached to his body. They became more robust with every unsavory thought he had, and more of him slipped into the darkness.

~~~

It was refreshing to get out of school and not go to the bar to work. She took advantage of the extra time to go to the library to do an assignment and ended up being there till dark. A quick stop at the grocery for a few things, and then she hurried home. The night was just so creepy lately. Kasey barely got in the door, looking forward to putting her feet up, when her phone rang. Who would be calling her at this time of night? No one but Gran and Billy knew she wasn't working.

"Hello," she answered.

"Hi, Kasey! It's Crystal from church. I wasn't sure I'd catch you in, not knowing your work schedule. Am I interrupting anything?"

"No, actually, my grandma let me quit the job at the bar until after the baby is born. I just got home. Is everything OK?"

"Absolutely! We're doing mass calling to invite church members to visit another church tomorrow night in support of Pastor Luke for the same message we got on Sunday. He's going to speak, and I wondered if you would go with me? I don't want to drive alone, and we could wow everyone by having our big bellies walk in together. Would you?" Crystal asked, hoping Kasey would trust her enough to venture into even more unknown territory.

Kasey hesitated.

"I could pick you up at five-thirty, and we could catch a bite to eat and visit a bit before the meeting starts at seven, what do you say?" Crystal gently tried again.

"OK," Kasey agreed reluctantly. "Only because it's with you, Crystal."

"It's essential that this message spreads quickly, sweetie. The more we all know, the better we can deal with the problems to come. I'm so glad you said yes. I'll see you tomorrow at five-thirty. Bye till then!"

"Bye, Crystal," Kasey said and hung up the phone.

A half of a block away, a man sat in his car wearing headphones and making notes as to where Kasey would be going on Wednesday. The phone in his shirt pocket rang. Taking it out, he saw his girlfriend's name on the caller ID. "I told her not to call me while I'm working," was his first thought, but he answered anyway.

"Hi, baby! Yep, you betcha! I should be off this surveillance in a couple of days, and that promotion looks like it'll be a shoo-in when I'm done!" he boasted, patting his new Gen 5 Glock 19 on the seat beside him.

He didn't tell her that he had been fired for misconduct, which was totally unfair. But his assignment before that had been to track these escaped convicts. Once he got some info on the kid being in town, he knew he could bring him in and get reinstated. He'd show them who was a good agent and who wasn't. And in his mind, he was the best.

~~~

The taxi pulled up in front of Peggy's apartment building. Jake told the driver to wait and gave him a ten. "If you're not here when I come out in fifteen minutes, I'll find you, and you won't ever screw anybody again," he said as he exited, slamming the rear door.

He couldn't tell if the bitch was home, but he didn't care. He had money, he had a mission, he was somebody, and she was nothing. She wouldn't be in his way for very long. Just the thought of her made him seethe.

Jake slammed through the front door as if it was his enemy. No sound, no lights on; he was alone. He grabbed some clean clothes and jumped into the shower. A quick one would do just fine, he wasn't going to the prom or anything, but if he had been going, it would be great to be taking a beauty like the one in the picture.

Five minutes later, he was toweled off and mostly dressed when he heard a noise. He turned off the bathroom light, grabbed his gun, and cracked open the door just a bit to see who was there.

He could hear two voices, one was Peggy, and the other was a woman he didn't recognize.

"He must have been here because I didn't leave the lights on," Peggy whined.

"Well, count your blessings, honey. The son of a bitch isn't here now. Let's get your stuff and get out before he comes back," said the other woman.

"He probably took all of my tip money again. How the hell did I get hooked up with such a freakin' looser?"

The more Jake heard, the angrier he got, and he still had the loaded gun in his hand. He waited until the women got into the bedroom before he emerged through the bathroom door, blocking their exit.

Peggy heard him first and swung around to see him standing there pointing the gun in the direction of her face. Before either of the women could give thought to escape, Jake pulled the trigger twice.

Both women crumpled to the floor. Peggy with a bullet in her head, her friend took one in the neck, severing her carotid artery. Blood gushed into the grimy carpet.

Jake turned off the bedroom light and closed the door, never feeling calmer. He sat down on a kitchenette chair, put on his shoes and socks, picked up his money and the envelope, returned his gun to the back of his waistband under his shirt, and left the apartment. There would not be a reason to return. Jake's demons were ecstatic with empowerment from his growing evil. More foul demons attached themselves to his body. "Good gun," he said to himself.

It was a neighborhood where crime was not uncommon. No one paid attention to the sound of two gunshots.

The taxi waited.

~~~

Lester waited an hour to see if anyone showed up to get his note but realized it didn't matter, and it was now too dark to see. He was obligated to do two jobs. They were either done or impossible, so he considered his obligation fulfilled.

As he walked, keeping to the edge of the road pavement in the darkness, he had two things on his mind; finding a place to hole up and finding the snitch. The first one would be relatively easy. He was still in a rural area, and sheds and barns were available. The second would take a bit of finesse since he couldn't risk exposure while hunting.

Rounding a curve in the road, he saw the faint silhouette of a large barn behind some trees on his right. He headed that way as quietly as he could to check it out. No one was around, nothing to indicate that it got regular use; this was as good a place as any.

In the morning, he'd have to find a phone book to see if the snitch had a phone or an address. For tonight, he'd chew on a piece of jerky and finish the water in the canteen while he thought about how he was going to kill Jake. Food and water would also have to be a priority for tomorrow.

~~~

216

The TV was still on, but Kasey had dozed off on the couch with her head on the comfy armrest. She opened her eyes, knowing something was calling her, but she was a bit disoriented. The phone was ringing again.

She reached for it, clicking the on button. "Hello," she answered in a sleepy voice.

"Hello, Kasey," came the response in a soft murmur.

She paused, knowing the voice, but her head was still foggy. Then she knew.

"Carlos? Carlos, is that you?" She was wide awake now, and her adrenalin surged with panic.

"Shhhhh, whisper. Be calm. Is anyone with you?" he questioned.

"Trisha is asleep. No one else. Carlos, are you OK? Where are you? Are you a prisoner?"

"I'm OK; I just had to hear your voice. I can't talk long, but I will be in touch soon. How's the baby?"

"We're both fine, Carlos. She's due in just a couple of weeks."

"I know; I've missed you so much. I have to go, but I'll see you soon. Don't tell anyone you spoke with me, please. I love you." Carlos hung up the phone before he couldn't. Being so near and not being able to go to her was breaking his heart.

Kasey sat there stunned. Did that just happen? Was it part of her dream? No, the phone was still in her hand. Carlos had called her. She was torn and confused. Should she tell the deputy for Carlos' good and go against his plea? Should she keep it to herself and take the chance that he could get killed? She had to decide tonight. Tomorrow would be too late, and she had a foreboding feeling growing in the pit of her stomach.

The man with the headset was on his phone. No, there wasn't enough time to trace the call. Too bad. But he knew Carlos would be here soon and he could wait.

~~~

In her room, deep in thought, in a town where she was a stranger, Cheyenne didn't expect a knock on her door. She cautiously approached the peek hole and peered out to see Gabe uncomfortably standing on the other side, staring at his shoes. That made her chuckle.

She opened the door with great flair. "To what do I owe the honor of this unexpected visit, sir?" Standing there in bare feet, wearing leggings and a loose T-shirt slipping off of one shoulder, hair cascading like a black waterfall, she looked more like a teenager at a slumber party than a spy.

"I hope I'm not disturbing you, but I'd like to have some time to talk about things that are happening, things you need to understand. I was hoping you'd have time now," Gabe explained seriously.

"Well, of course, Gabe. Do you want to come in?"

"Can we take a drive instead? My truck is outside. I want you to meet someone, nothing formal, so you can wear what you have on." He looked too serious for her to do less than he asked.

"Let me just get a jacket and pull on my boots, and I'm ready," she said while she was already moving to do just that.

They were in the camper sitting in the parking lot in less than five minutes. He had wanted to explain more to her back in the restaurant at breakfast, but it wasn't the time. Now he felt the need to tell her what he had held back and introduce her to David and Pauley. According to Pauley's visions, Cheyenne would be playing a significant part in the upcoming battle, and he hoped that might also mean she would be a part of his future.

"What is it, Gabe. You can't tell me anything I can't handle, I promise you," she said, knowing that she had so much held back from him about herself.

Slowly, Gabe began to explain. "I am trusting that what I've learned about the future is true and accurate. I'm trusting that you need to know what I'm going to tell you because you will be playing a part in all of this. I'm trusting that because you're a new believer, you'll have an open mind about the unusual nature of the subject matter."

"OK, you've got my attention, now talk."

Gabe put the truck in gear, and as he drove, he explained his ability to see through dimensions. Then he told her about the battle brewing and the amazing story of Pauley. She sat silently through the explanations on the drive to David's home. When they pulled up in the driveway, she turned to him, "That is fantastic stuff, Gabe. On the way back, I'll tell you a little something you don't know about me yet. Now, let's go meet Pauley."

~~~

The taxi dropped him off at the Settle Inn parking lot. It looked old and dumpy, but it had a porch and white picket fence. Jake guessed that was supposed to have some appeal. He entered the lobby, saw no one in attendance, approached the check-in counter, and rang the bell. An old woman with a big, stupid smile came out from a little room behind the staff desk.

"Hello dear, can I help you?" she asked. The sparkle in her eyes was not quite as bright as when she welcomed Cheyenne. She sensed something a bit off with this young man.

"I need a room for a couple of nights. I'll pay cash, no luggage, it was lost by the airlines. I'll need ta get some new things tomorrow," he explained flatly.

"Well, we do have a couple of vacancies. Shame about your luggage, though. You must be here for something important; the airport is two counties away!" she went on, prodding for more information about the stranger. "The room is fifty-five dollars per night, and you have your own bath."

He pulled out the cash for two nights and handed it to her. "I'm here to meet an old school buddy. Short stay, have ta get back ta work and the little lady, ya know."

All of the cash was in ten-dollar bills, which the woman thought strange. She started to give him the key to room number two, right across from the one where that pretty Cheyenne was staying. But for some reason, she thought better of it. He got the key to room number eight on the other side of the house, the side that wasn't remodeled yet.

Jake took the key and walked toward the hall to the right of the dining room. "Take the hall to the left, sir!" she called out, and he changed direction.

A good night's sleep in a comfortable bed, and he'd be able to track down the target tomorrow. If all went well, he should have her out of the way by Thursday, get paid by Mr. Anonymous, and be on his way to a new life by Thursday evening. He knew his life would be so much better without Peggy.

22

A Night of Revelation

GABE TURNED off the ignition. He looked over at Cheyenne eagerly exiting the truck, and he followed suit. They quickly walked to the front door where David stood to welcome them.

"Evening, David," offered Gabe as they entered. Pauley was just inside, eyes wide and sparkling with instant recognition as he watched Cheyenne. "David and Pauley, I'd like you to meet Cheyenne in person. I've told her most of the story, but I wanted her to meet you and get to know all of us."

David extended his hand, and they shook in greeting. Pauley stepped closer to Cheyenne and embraced her before David and Gabe knew what was happening. She returned the warm hug with a slight misting in her eyes. Sincere hugs weren't exactly things abundant in her line of work. Her new understanding of Pauley made it all the more special. "Pauley, it is so good to meet you," she said with great sincerity. Pauley led her to the living room by the hand, where they all took seats to begin sharing their discoveries.

Earlier in the evening, Gabe called to set up the meeting with David.

Pauley's drawings showed that Cheyenne would be an integral part of their future, so he knew that it was time to bring her into the knowledge of all of it, one hundred percent, nothing held back. God knew she was ready, and that was enough for Gabe.

Before anyone else could speak, Pauley made a single statement that left them without words for a few seconds. "I'm supposed to tell everyone about me, about why I didn't talk for a long time, and about why I have to talk now because saving people is the only way to make the evil lose the war."

Gabe was first to respond. "Tell me more, Pauley. Did your angel tell you to do this?"

"Yes, he said that tomorrow night, at the church meeting, I'm supposed to tell about the angels rejoicing and the demons dying when people get saved. He said it will open their hearts, and they'll want to help." Pauley looked confident but a little shaky. "I know I can do it, but I'm a little afraid."

"I didn't know about a church meeting tomorrow, but if your angel said it was time, then you'll have the strength and confidence to tell exactly what you're supposed to tell, Pauley," comforted his father. Then David looked at Gabe and said, "And it's about time I joined the ranks of the saved, Gabe. I hope you'll pray with me tonight so that my soul will eventually join those of my wife and son in eternity. I want that more than anything else in the world. What's happened with Pauley has proven to me that miracles are real and that God exists."

"I'd be honored to pray with you, brother. Pauley, when you heard the angel sing for the first time, it was for Cheyenne. God opened your ears for the praising of her salvation, and you saw that we are a team. Now, listen for the angels again. I wish we could hear what you do." Gabe lowered his head, and they all joined hands to pray the prayer for David as he accepted God's grace. Above them, the angel's songs rose to the heavens, and tears fell from Pauley's eyes because of what he alone was hearing.

With the energy and excitement of three new believers in the group, the four of them talked late into the evening. They asked and answered questions, looked at Pauley's drawings, went over the background only Gabe knew, and listened to Pauley tell them what he would say to the congregation. When eyelids began to droop, they called it a night.

Cheyenne decided she wouldn't be leaving town right away. She had to see this thing through. At that moment, she didn't realize that the decision wasn't hers to make. It was a part of the drama yet to unfold.

~~~

It was late, and the station was still busy with calls but with fewer on duty to handle them. Three night shift officers were new hires; the fourth was on the original staff. The Chief scheduled them for those hours, anticipating less need during the night and using his seasoned officers to handle the chaos during the day. He was wrong.

A lone man in a uniform removed the box from its marked container on its designated location in the evidence room. He placed it inside a larger bin for a different case on a shelf at the back of the room. It would hide there until he could remove the damning items one at a time to hand them over to someone who was coming to get them, as instructed. The plan was in play.

~~~

Gabe dropped her off at the Inn at eleven twenty. He walked her to the lobby door, where she turned to him, raised up on her tiptoes, wrapped her arms around his neck, and kissed him on the cheek. His arms went around her back and pulled her to him for only a moment, but it was enough.

"Thank you, Gabe. You've changed my life, and my heart is bursting with hope. I have work to do tomorrow but will be at the church in the evening. I'm a part of this mission now. And I feel like my whole life has been building up to this."

"Then I'll see you tomorrow," he said as he pulled slightly back to look into her eyes. "And many times more since it seems we have a future already planned for us."

"I'm ready." She flashed him a glowing smile, released herself from his embrace, and walked through the door to find Miss Nettie still behind the check-in desk. "It's kind of late for you, isn't it, Miss Nettie?"

"Yes, dear, but I just got a call for three reservations for Thursday night. Such short notice, but it seems an important Senator is coming and has invited another Senator and our Governor to spend a day or two fishing here. Who would have thought that a Senator from another state would even know about my little place? I was so excited! I wish we'd finished the room renovations. I only have two of the nicer rooms available, so I'll have to do some shuffling. Now that you're in and I feel a bit calmer, I guess it's time for bed."

Cheyenne bid her good-night and walked toward her room with a sick feeling in the pit of her stomach. It was time for her to leave. Manning was on his way, and he was bringing others with high-level demons, as Gabe had warned. She had told Gabe some more about herself and her work on the ride back, but she still hadn't revealed the full details of her current assignment to him. Now she was rethinking that disclosure and wishing she'd said even more.

Deep in thought, she didn't notice the tall skinny man in the shadows of the hallway to the other wing as he watched her unlock her door and enter her room. Nor did either of them see the massive warrior angel stationed at her door, but Jake's demons saw him clearly, and they shuddered.

~~~

Carlos hurried out of the phone booth and down a dark alley. He had to be careful not to be seen because everyone posed a threat to his safety and freedom. Now, finding his way to the guy who could make the fake IDs was his goal. He'd decided to go ahead and get one for

Kasey with the photo of her stashed in his pocket. It was the only thing he'd brought with him when they broke out of the prison, a good close-up he took when they were on a Sunday picnic. The guy could photoshop out the background; he was a pro.

He had the route etched in his mind; getting across town tonight in the dark was his plan. Seeing the guy in the morning would be tricky, but Carlos still had friends he could call in a pinch. At least they were his friends before he went to prison.

What he didn't know was how much his face had been on the TV and that his friends weren't his friends if it meant putting themselves in danger. His mind was solely on Kasey and his baby, which could lead him to make a disastrous mistake.

~~~

Tom answered the phone on the second ring. His brain was reeling from all of the day's activity, and sleep wasn't being his friend tonight.

"Hello," he said quietly, trying not to wake Beth.

"Officer Dempsey, it's Kasey. I'm scared to death and wasn't sure I should call you, but I decided it would be best. I got a call from Carlos, sir. I think he's here."

"It will be OK, Kasey. You did the right thing. What did he say?"

"He asked how I was, told me not to tell anyone he called and said he would see me soon. Please tell me what to do. I don't want him hurt."

"I'll do everything in my power to make sure he isn't hurt. Would you please let me know immediately if there is another contact? The more I know, the better I can head off trouble. OK, Kasey?"

"Yes, sir. Thank you for being there. I trust you, Officer Dempsey, and if anything were to happen to me, I know you'd do the right thing. Good night." She hung up the phone and wrapped a blanket tightly around her. There would be no sleeping for her unless she passed out from sheer exhaustion. Right now, she was aware of every sound in the night. But not aware that her guardian stood over her, protecting her from all harm. It wasn't her time, and she was safe.

Tom put his cell phone down. Her statement had taken him off guard. If anything should happen to her? What was she expecting? And she said she knew he would do the right thing. What was that?

Beth's breathing was still that of the sleeping, so he crawled back under the covers and snuggled her warmth while his thoughts raced.

~~~

The foreboding feelings wouldn't leave her. Now, every thought was about the baby and ensuring its future would be safe and secure. She went to the desk and got a pen and paper. No one else ever needed to know she was writing this unless something terrible happened to her. But she knew. And knowing that what she wanted would be known to everyone in that scenario brought her peace.

Kasey crawled into bed to sleep for the rest of the night.

~~~

Outside of Kasey's apartment, down one block, and parked at the curb, sat the ex-FBI agent who had been listening to her call. Damn! He hoped she wouldn't report it and that she could be considered an accomplice. Oh well, she was still bait, and that was all that mattered to his reinstatement and promotion. He just hoped the local police would stay out of his way so no one would get hurt. This was his case, and he was bringing this kid in, "no one else is going to get the credit. No one!" he shouted to himself inside the parked car as his fist slammed the dash.

The man's demons gurgled out silent laughter as they tightened their grips.

~~~

Lying on his back and staring at the dark ceiling, Luke's thoughts jumped back and forth from the battle he experienced to the one they faced. There was no fear in him, but there were questions. Multitudes of questions. Unlike before when he was on his own and had no one else's safety to consider, he was now constantly concerned with the wellbeing of one lovely pregnant lady who had so recently entered his life.

Luke believed that God would reveal her in His own time and way if a life partner was God's plan for him. There was no doubt in his mind that time had come, but he never expected it would be at a time of such peril. Crystal was more important to him already than he could have ever imagined.

Luke closed his eyes and began praying for her safety and for victory over all of the evil they faced. Within moments he was flooded with the specific understanding that he was to reveal everything to her, that she was strong and protected and the exact right person for him and the blessed future they would have together. He relaxed, and sleep came on a peaceful wave to pull him under.

Many blocks away, Crystal was sleeping soundly, and, in her womb, her baby sucked its thumb contentedly while the angels watched over both.

23

Wednesday Morning

IT WAS still dark, but Cheyenne woke with a start, abruptly and completely. The first thought in her head was to get away from the Settle Inn. Illuminated numbers on the alarm clock told her it was five-thirty. The angel was urging her to swift action, but she thought it was of her own volition.

She hurriedly got out of bed, changed into her clothes, brushed her teeth, and threw on a minute's worth of makeup. She always lived out of a suitcase when she traveled for work, so a fast exit was easy. The room was paid in advance and in cash, another thing she'd learned through experience. Grabbing a piece of stationery from the desk, she scribbled a note thanking Miss Nettie for a wonderful stay. She said that she could book an early flight and was already on her way back home. Should anyone ask, it would seem that she had left town. She dropped the note on the counter on her way out of the lobby. The front door locked from the outside but not for those leaving.

In the Jeep, she took a moment to run a brush through her hair, thinking about what to do next. She'd have to be careful about being seen for the next couple of days. Gabe was her ally, and she needed to tell him the rest of the story and about the new guests coming to the Inn, even if it meant waking him up this early. He might also have some good suggestions. They were intertwined now, and she had to trust that they would find solutions together.

She pushed the key into the ignition, turned it, and the Jeep came to life, taking her the couple of blocks to the church parking lot as quickly as she dared drive. As she rounded the corner, she saw through the kitchen window that the light was already on with Gabe's camper parked next to the building, and she breathed a sigh of relief.

The Jeep slid in on the far side of the camper, hidden from street view, and she climbed out. Dark was getting so much darker every day; how could that be? But being on the grounds of the church somehow made her feel better, safer, as she walked to the side kitchen door and lightly knocked.

Luke heard the Jeep pull in, so he was opening the door as her knuckles touched the wood, not knowing what to expect. "Cheyenne! Is everything alright? It's barely six a.m. Please come in; I have fresh coffee, and tell me what's going on." He ushered her in and shut the door behind her.

Gabe was just entering the kitchen from the living area with a concerned expression at her surprise appearance. "We all need coffee. I have a feeling there is a story that needs to be told. Please sit down, Cheyenne; we're here for you."

She sat, and Luke poured, and the story of her current mission emerged with fine detail, and more emotion than Cheyenne knew she possessed. When she finished, Luke asked for her keys. He went to put the Jeep into the large shed at the back of the parking lot before it got light out so no one would see it in passing. They needed to hide her presence now to see how things would play out. But her story had explained so much. The Angels had masked the visibility of the Jeep while still in the parking lot of the Inn. None of the demons saw it travel to or stop at the church.

They now knew how Gibson Glen tied in with the brewing battle. The level of corruption went all the way to the peak of wealth and politics in the nation. Probably even in the world. The most evil of men were involved at its highest level, so the highest-ranking Demon Princes would also be players. Yes, this would be a terrible battle unless they could somehow break it into smaller pieces.

Gabe reached over and took Cheyenne's shaking hands into his own. "I know you held back on your story because of your job, classified info being a big part of it, and because you didn't want me to know the kinds of things, you had to do. All that matters is that we're both warriors in this, and we're on the same side." He looked into her eyes and saw so much of himself. Gabe's heart now included her. He wanted her with him and knew this was the way it was supposed to be for both of them.

Luke walked in the door and tossed her the keys. He poured fresh cups for all of them and sat down across the table from Cheyenne. "I know the next step," he stated confidently. "As soon as it gets light, I'm calling Crystal. She has three bedrooms, and Cheyenne can stay there for a few days, undetected. When you need to go anywhere to finish up your FBI business here, Gabe can take you," he said directly to her. "No one needs to know you're still in town."

The Host that gathered on the roof nodded to each other. Tension was building, but the believers were growing in number and taking care of each other. The evil ones were in for a surprise if they thought this place would be easy pickings. Surprise was a vital element for their forces against the demons. It would take more than they could do to topple the world that the Father had built.

~~~

Sleeping on the wooden floorboards of an empty store with only some newspapers covering wasn't Carlos' finest moment, but it got him safely through the night. He was just two doors down from the place where he could get the IDs he needed. You couldn't call it sunrise, but the sky was lightening, so it was time to stretch his muscles into wanting to move again.

He expected that stores on the street would begin to open about nine, even in these sketchy areas where businesses weren't exactly on the up and up. Having run out of food and water yesterday afternoon, he would have to do a bit of scouting to curb his thirst and the growling in his stomach. Carlos knew of an open market just a couple of blocks away. On his way to his hiding place last night, he had managed to find a black hoodie jacket hanging on a clothesline, and his beard was coming in now after a week of not shaving. With luck, he could buy what he needed this morning with a small portion of the money he got from Lester and not be recognized.

A quick look at the photo of Kasey steeled him to accomplish the task at hand. He peeked out of the storefront windows to see if anyone was around. Groups of three or four people were sleeping on the sidewalks in the doorways up and down the street. He'd never seen this in his years here. Where did they all come from? Someone had spray-painted graffiti on the wall. Some odd writing he couldn't read with two evil-looking red eyes above it.

~~~

The crowing of a rooster sounded through the still morning, but Lester was awake and waiting. Waiting until his intuition told him it was the right time to get up and move; until he had a clear idea of his next steps in finding the snitch. Waiting until he was sure no one was around to watch him exit the barn.

He found a plaid hunting jacket and cap hanging on a nail, along with some knives stowed in a worktable drawer. The surprise was that the owner had to have been a big man because the clothing fit him well. His look was a unique combination of size and coloring, but his hair had grown longer, and the mustache he used to sport before going to prison was filling in nicely with new streaks of gray that were not in his televised photo. He was showing his age. With the change in attire, he just might get mistaken for an out-of-towner on a hunting trip.

He pocketed a couple of the small knives, should he need a quiet defense that would also save bullets. Then Lester slowly pushed open the barn door, just enough to pass through. There were no sounds, no movement, and the light was still very dim, so he was confident that he was not seen. He moved in the direction of the town. How to find Jake there would take some doing. He had a contact in a seedy part of town who was still in the business of robbery, selling illegal arms, and drugs. This guy was bad news, but Lester's reputation for "bad" was much greater. Lester knew the guy was still in business because prisoners have ways of keeping up with things going on outside. He'd go there first.

~~~

The bed was the most comfortable one he'd ever slept in, but when he opened his eyes and saw it was six a.m., he knew he had work to do. There were no clean clothes to put on, so he wore what he had on yesterday. Jake didn't bring any personal items, so he made a mental note to stop at a store for a toothbrush later. Coffee was what he needed right now. Coffee and a plan.

Jake walked from his room to the lobby, thinking on the way that he'd sit in the dining room till his target came out and then follow her. Somewhere along her path had to be a good place to shoot and dispose of her without being in public view. He had all day today to accomplish his goal, just so it was done by tomorrow morning. Finally, things were looking up, and opportunities were coming his way.

The old lady was reading something to the housekeeper standing next to her, dusting off the desk at the counter. "She said she booked an early flight and was sorry to leave without saying goodbye. Oh my, I will miss that young lady. I wonder where she came from. Very distinctive looking with that black hair and those unusual eyes." She turned, tossed the paper in the garbage, and handed the room key to the housekeeper to change the bed and linens. "I'll bet she was leaving early so we'd have the third room we need for tonight's guests."

Jake was in shock. His mark had just flown out of his reach, and he had no name, no address, nothing. He envisioned thousand-dollar bills flying away into the clouds with their own wings, and he was sick to his stomach. Coffee, he still needed coffee. Then he realized he still had the majority of the deposit and a job to pull on Friday. He'd be OK, but now he had a free day and evening before he could get the new ID tomorrow. Maybe one more trip to the guy who sold him the gun to confirm the arrangements for Friday's heist. That would be a good idea. He had a plan, and it was still early, so he strolled into the dining room and ordered himself a lovely home-cooked breakfast.

~~~

Crystal was getting ready to make a bowl of oatmeal when her cell phone beeped. The caller ID was Luke. What a lovely way for her day to start. "Good morning, Luke. So nice to hear from you."

"I wish it were just social, Crystal, but this morning I'm on a mission."

"How can I help you? You know I can handle it for the cause," she answered, smiling at the thought of being part of his team.

"I need you to come over to the church. A few of us should have some conversation about recent events. How soon can you be here?"

"I'm dressed and ready, so if you promise to feed me, I can be there in about ten minutes," she said as she picked up her purse and keys.

"Great. And on a personal level, I'd like to talk with you a bit too. I have so much I want to share with you."

"Well, Luke, you make it impossible for a lady to refuse. I'm on my way out the door. See you in a few." She closed and locked the door behind her. The guardian on duty escorted her to her car and rode on top. No demon would touch this woman on his watch.

~~~

They sat in the kitchen, Cheyenne, Luke, and Gabe.

"I'm here because I found out last night that Manning and some others, big demon guys, are coming Friday. This morning I woke with a feeling of frantic urgency to get out, so I ran here, the only place I know to be safe. I have to call Tom Dempsey. He's the officer I've been working with on the case. I have to tell him what's going on and get him to bring the box to me to hand it off to an associate. I also have to call this into the home office, so they'll send someone out here to meet up with me. But how do I know who to trust? The corruption is massive, and the evidence is crucial." Was Cheyenne's career crumbling around her with the new knowledge they'd attained? "If I let them know I have the evidence, how do I know they won't send someone to kill me and dispose of the only proof of Manning's crime?"

"All good questions, Cheyenne. We need to proceed one step at a time and think this through before acting. I met Tom Dempsey and believe him to be trustworthy. Let's start with that step." Luke pushed her cell phone toward her hand on the table. She picked it up and punched the icon for Tom.

"Tom Dempsey here," he answered. "Agent?"

"Yes, Tom. It's Cheyenne. I need to talk with you but not by phone. Can you go to the church where you met Pastor Luke as soon as possible?"

"I'm getting ready to head out the door. I'll come by on my way to the station."

"Thanks, Tom. I wouldn't ask if it wasn't vital."

"See you in about fifteen minutes." He pressed the 'end' button and pocketed his phone. "Gotta run, Beth. A quick stop before the station again today. See you here this evening so we can go to the service together." He kissed her puckered lips and hurried out the door as she made shooing motions to get him going.

~~~

At seven-thirty, Kasey woke. The window was still open from last night, and the breeze was too cool, so she pulled herself out from under the covers to close it. She lowered the window and saw a police car drive into the church parking lot. Another car was there, and Crystal was getting out. Uneasy feelings shot through her gut. She didn't mind if Officer Tom told the others about the phone call; she trusted them all. But there was something else, some other thing resonating below their arrivals that put fear into her as she stood at the window. Her anxiety from last night returned with more strength.

The warrior angel had been on the roof but materialized at her side immediately. He felt the fear emanating from her, so he waved one hand over her head. She began to calm and returned to her bed to sleep a bit longer before preparing to leave for school, she had so little more to do there, and her diploma would soon be in her hand.

Her angel saw his comrades across the street, filling every space on and around the church. More had arrived, riding on the vehicles of the officer and the woman. The church property and everyone on it were safe. But the sky above was dark with demons, more so than at any other time he had seen. The battle must surely be very near. Very near.

~~~

Tom pulled into the lot as Crystal walked toward the door. Luke stood in the doorway, waiting for both of them and taking Crystal's hand as she entered. He led her to a chair and got her a glass of juice. Tom sat in an empty chair as Gabe handed him a cup of steamy coffee.

"Agent, Cheyenne, if I may, I got the call from you, but now I'm confused because I thought you had to keep everything under wraps and classified. So, what's going on?" Tom asked, looking around the table at the other four.

"I'm a bit confused too, officer, and I don't think we've ever met," said Crystal, offering her hand for a shake. "I'm Crystal, and I'd like to know what's going on too."

"That's why we asked both of you here. Crystal, meet Tom, a very good man, and deputy for the Sheriff's Dept. You both know a part of the big picture which the rest of us have just pieced together, but you need to know it all because we're all right in the middle of it." Luke spoke, taking the initiative to get it all out in the open. "There is a background that is pretty unbelievable unless God has opened your eyes and ears to be able to receive the truth. Crystal, I'm quite confident that you're ready. Tom, although we haven't directly addressed it, I feel that you are a believer, or you wouldn't have been brought together with Cheyenne to work on the case. Am I right?"

"Yes. I am. I believe that you're speaking at our church this evening; my wife and I will be there."

"I didn't know you attended that church, Tom. God's plan never ceases to amaze me. OK then, we are ready for some truth-telling, so Gabe, please start with the battle that began for us a couple of decades ago." Luke motioned to Gabe to begin speaking with his tale of the event at the college and how he saved Luke's life. Gabe proceeded with a brief recounting of battles since, other warriors he'd met, and how he could see the Host and demons though most humans couldn't. Cheyenne had heard it, so she listened again, awaiting the next portion where she would have to fill in her part. Crystal and Tom, paralyzed with the incredible tale, said nothing.

Luke opened the front of his shirt so they could see the scar. "I wouldn't be here if it wasn't for Gabe and God's plan. It was the beginning of an education and faith experience for me that changed my life." Crystal reached over and lightly ran her fingers over the ugly welts. Then she looked into his eyes with both sorrow and compassion. "Now, Cheyenne, please tell everyone how you came to be in Henderson County and what your mission has brought to light." Luke turned the floor over to her.

"A brief history first. I was recruited into the FBI for undercover work because of my appearance, education, and skills. My job is to bring a bad element to justice. I was used primarily in busting important people who break laws and take advantage of their power. My current mission is to gain the confidence of a very high man on the political ladder. I dig out secrets that show him to be something other than what he appears. Then I report all findings to bring him down if that's what's needed. That man is Senator Gregg Manning, positioning to run for the presidency next year."

She paused. At this point, Crystal was the only one who didn't know about this, and her mouth fell open. Cheyenne continued, "I came here because of something I discovered, and the evidence to prove it is in Henderson. Tom and I found it, and it's presently locked up in the evidence room at the police station. The dilemma now is who do I report it to so that Manning can be brought in and prosecuted for two murders. With the corruption running so high, I don't know whom to trust in the FBI. And I just left the Settle Inn in the dark of night because I heard that an important man from Washington DC was arriving Friday for a fishing trip. It's Manning, but he has never fished in his life. This story ties in with his past and how he disappeared as a teen to be remade into his present persona by someone bigger than him. Maybe several someones, people who pull the puppet strings on a global level. I believe he is coming to kill me himself and destroy the evidence because he knows who I am now and how badly he screwed up by confiding in me during an intimate moment of weakness."

"Oh my God!" whispered Crystal.

"And since David and Pauley were mentioned, let's cover that next. Gabe, would you fill everyone in on their story, please."

Gabe nodded at Luke and began, "I met them only a few days ago at David's pawn shop. You'll hear Pauley tell a bit about himself tonight at the church meeting, so I won't steal his thunder, but I will tell you that this is one extraordinary young man. I have never met anyone who God has entrusted with so much. He sees the Host and demons as I do. But Pauley also sees visions of the past and future regarding God's will. He began drawing and produced pictures of me, of battles, of my very unique battle sword, and of Cheyenne before even meeting us. And we just found out he can also hear the Host and the demons.

This is all new to me. I've never heard of anyone having all of these gifts before. The important part is that we now better understand how to defeat the forces of evil that have come, and are still coming, here to Henderson because of what he has found out and shared.

"I'm still trying to get used to the idea that there are angels and demons all around us that you can see, and we can't," gasped Crystal. Tom nodded, then shook his head. This was a lot to hear in one sitting.

"I'm sure you'd love to see the Host, but you are blessed not to see the demons," Gabe replied in a low tone. His face was mixed with his own emotion of the good and evil which accompanied his gift. "All of the other things which have been going on are a part of the evil descending here. The increased criminal activity you're experiencing at the station, Tom, the murder of the little girl, the escape of the prisoners, it all ties in. Some of it is a distraction. Some of it is part of the plan revolving around Manning. But make no mistake, the dark side does have a master plan. They never do anything haphazardly. What's to our advantage now is that they still don't know about the gifts possessed by Pauley and me, even though they've encountered me many times. That knowledge is shielded from them."

"If the prisoner escape is also a part of the plan, I have something to add to this discussion that you all don't know yet," offered Tom. "I got a call from Kasey very early this morning telling me she received a phone call from Carlos last night. She believes he's here. I was preparing to call the FBI with the info this morning, as a formality, because I know they are monitoring her phone and already know about Carlos. But, this means that the FBI will be covering our county like flies on stink. There may be even more cons in our area. The assumed leader, a killer named Lester Byrd, was caught and arrested here about fifteen years ago. He could also have a reason to be coming here, be it vendetta or contacts he needs to help him get far away. It also means that with all of the additional FBI coverage, if anyone in their ranks is on Manning's payroll, Cheyenne could be in serious danger. There could be a lot of loose triggers roaming the streets."

"Crystal, if it's OK with you, can you put Cheyenne up for a couple of days. You are completely off the radar, so she'll be safe there," Luke asked.

"Of course! You'll come home with me from here. I keep a guest room ready."

"Thank you, Crystal. You're right about danger from unknown angles, Tom. I have one person I can call and be reasonably sure I'm safe. Please keep the evidence locked up but make sure the description has nothing to do with anything current, so no one happens across it by accident, and no one who may be looking can find it. I'll let you know when we need to get it out and to the right people." Cheyenne rose from the table. "Until then, I need to use your office if I may, Luke. I have some work to do."

Gabe excused himself to take Cheyenne to the pastor's office. Tom rushed back to the station.

Luke continued to sit with Crystal. "Are you handling all of this, OK, Crystal?" he asked her, still holding her hand. "It's a lot to have dumped on you all at once."

"I knew you had things you weren't sharing, but I figured it was just personal history. Stuff you'd tell me as we got to know each other better. Then Gabe told us a bit about a spiritual battle, and I thought faith was involved, of course, but it was more about faith when confronted with flesh. Now you've told me so much more is out there. I don't think it's sunk in yet."

"The part you'll see is in the flesh, as Gabe explained it. Actual people doing horrendous things, making terrible decisions. We don't see, and he does, that demons are directing those people. They made their own choices to open themselves to the demons, but the deeper they get into it, the less of themselves remains, and the more demonic influence becomes them. God gave us free will. They've chosen their path. But many can still be saved, and that's our mission in this battle."

"A lot to absorb. Since I'm here, what can I do to help you prepare for tonight?" Crystal offered.

"Jill will be here soon. She'll have things for you to do from home, I'm sure. And if you'll allow me, I'll take you to dinner before we go to the church service. We'll just ride together." Luke rose from his chair. "And speaking of food, I promised you breakfast if you'd come early for this meeting, and I haven't fed you yet."

"Luke, I promised Kasey I'd pick her up for tonight, and we were going to go to dinner. I'm sorry. But I'd bet she wouldn't mind if we all went together; she's quite fond of you, you know."

"Then we'll leave it up to her, and if she'd like me to be the third wheel, we'll make it a threesome. I'll get her first, and we'll pick you up at your place. She usually gets home from school at 2:30. We'll watch for her." Luke tended to eggs in the frying pan with his back to Crystal. She just sat there and grinned.

~~~

At eight a.m., a small but luxurious jet took off from a private executive airport, headed for Washington DC. At ten a.m., Senator Manning was escorted into the Oval Office, where the President gave him the news.

"I don't like you, Manning, no surprise to you, I'm sure. But there are powers far greater than this office, and for whatever reasons they have, they've decided you will be the next Vice President. Neither one of us is fool enough to think the world is run by anyone other than these powers."

"I have about sixteen months left of my second term, so I'm betting they want you to run for my job in the next election. I know you'll accept VP because you're a climber and power-hungry, and it's the next stepping stone for you. You'll be sworn in on Friday at four p.m. Whatever you have to do to prepare for this, whatever you have to clean up, do it between now and then. Do not bring me another embarrassing mess like your predecessor dumped in my lap. There's the door."

At eleven a.m., that same private jet took off toward the Midwest. The Senator was going fishing.

24

Loose Ends

CARLOS ENTERED the door of the shabby office, setting off a little jingle from a bell above. He heard movement in a back room, but no one was in front to see or threaten him with exposure. "Be right out!" Came a shout from the back. He paced.

A young Hispanic man, about mid-twenties, emerged. No one else seemed to be there. "What can I help you with, my man?"

"I need IDs for two people: driver's licenses, passports, and social security cards. I have one picture you can use, the other one is for me. You'll have to take my picture. My buddy, Manuel Rodriguez, told me you could do what I want, and I need them tomorrow."

"Well, tomorrow's a rush order; that'll cost you more, man. A thousand for each person, you got that?"

On the first day after leaving Lester, Carlos counted the cash he had in his pocket, just shy of fifteen grand. For only a quick moment, he wondered how Lester had come across that kind of money, but then he remembered all of the travel arrangements that someone made to get them to Henderson County. His next thought was "Why?" but he decided he didn't want to know.

"Yeah, I can cover that," answered Carlos.

"Then come into the back room so I can take your photo. Give me a 50% deposit now, and I'll have them ready for you by noon tomorrow. Where you go then is up to you, I know nothing. Do you have preferences on the new names, or should I just make them up?"

Carlos followed the guy to the back room and sat on the chair in front of the camera.

~~~

Phones were ringing off the hook when Tom got to the station. He shook his head at the number of calls, messages, follow-ups, and reports to finish. At eleven-thirty, Tom was finally able to come up for air. That's when he remembered the box; he needed to ensure it was securely hidden amongst all the other case boxes, as Cheyenne had suggested. A quick trip to the kitchen for a cold can of Coke, caffeine was critical, and he headed to the evidence room.

"Hi Steve," he greeted the officer on duty, the same one he saw when checking the box in yesterday. He and Steve had been friends for years, so trust was no issue. "I need that box I brought in yesterday. Can you get it for me?"

"Sure, Tom, hold on a sec and let me get the evidence file number. Have it for you right here." Steve went to the shelf where the box should have been, but it wasn't. "OK, that's weird. This space is empty. I put it right here myself just yesterday afternoon, Tom. You saw me do it."

Tom's stomach lurched. "Yeah, I did. Has anyone else been on duty here, like last night or this morning?

"I clocked out at six p.m. and was back this morning at nine. There's a backup with a key, but no one attends the room at night. That would be Rico Flores. I think he leaves his key locked in his top drawer. There's nothing in the log about removing anything either. He knows enough to log things in and out if he does it."

Tom hurriedly walked to the desk of Officer Flores, who was off duty. No one else sat at the desk because all officers were out on calls. Tom jiggled the top drawer and found it unlocked. He saw file marks where someone jimmied the lock on closer inspection. His heart was no longer beating correctly, and his breaths came in gulps. There was nothing to be done but call Cheyenne and tell her the bad news and pray.

~~~

She leaned back into the sofa and closed her eyes to think. Her life was in hyperdrive, and she had to get a grip. Crystal brought her back to the house after the morning gathering in Luke's kitchen, where they had all decided that going to the church meeting this evening was not a good idea for her. For now, staying in hiding was critical, but sitting still was not something Cheyenne was very good at doing.

At ten a.m. her time, she put in a call to Agent Marc Adams and left a cryptic message to call her on the QT. He hadn't called back yet, and it was almost noon. She could only wait.

Crystal was in the other room making phone calls to church members with a message from Pastor Luke. Gabe was scouting for some more items they wanted to distribute this evening. Luke had gone to the hospital to visit an ailing older woman from the choir. She was alone with her thoughts until her cell phone beeped with an incoming call. The screen told her it was Tom.

"Hi Tom, what's up. Make it good; I'm bored to death."

"You asked for it," he replied. "The box is gone."

"Not funny, Tom. My nerves are already raw, and I'm jumping at unexpected noises."

"Not kidding, Cheyenne. I went to get it at eleven-thirty to change the log number and put it in an unlikely place as you suggested. It was gone. The night shift guy usually keeps the evidence room key locked in his desk. The drawer lock was jimmied while he was out on a call. It wasn't an accident, and we have several new hires due to the increased activity."

"Oh crap! There's a mole in your station. Someone has been watching and knows exactly what that box is and is probably reporting back to Manning." A pause. "But could they have gotten a box out of the station with no one seeing, even at night?"

"It would be difficult but not impossible. But if caught, it could blow up, and everything would be out in the open. Would that someone want the risk?"

"Probably not. Tom, there's a good chance it's still in the station somewhere. Have you reported it missing?"

"No, I wanted to call you first. If I report it, I have the same problem as the thief. It will be out in the open. I'm guessing your FBI people wouldn't like that either."

"I'm guessing you're right. I'm waiting for a call back from the only person I could think of who could help and whom I could trust. Let me run this by him and get another opinion and suggestions or info that he has, and I don't. In the meantime, is the day officer in the evidence room someone you can trust?"

"Absolutely, I've known him for years."

"Then tell him you need him to search all of the evidence boxes to see if someone moved ours somewhere else. Feel free to tell him you think there's someone inside working against us but that he has to keep quiet and can't know any other details except that the FBI is involved. Call me back later, and thanks, Tom. This isn't your fault either; it's so much bigger than us." She hung up.

~~~

It was time. After finding out that his target had left the Inn, Jake made a call to set up a meeting with the accomplice he'd have in the robbery scheduled for Friday. They needed to go over the plan, so there weren't any slip-ups. Instead of walking, Jake had the cash for a cab and treated himself again. He had the cabbie stop at a convenience store for the toothbrush he needed on the way there. Jake had reached a limit on how low his level of hygiene could get.

The cab rolled to a stop in front of the house at exactly noon. Jake exited and tossed the cabbie a couple of small bills through the window. Coming to this place always gave him the creeps, but it was a means to an end, and he needed to get this part over so he could quit looking over his shoulder.

~~~

He'd cautiously walked into this end of town, knowing that with its darker element, his presence would be less likely to be noticed. Lester was about to round the last corner to reach his destination. A cab came to a stop in front of a poorly maintained old house, the place where he was headed. He stepped behind a wide tree trunk to wait. The guy getting out paid no attention to anything going on around him, to his peril. Lester immediately recognized the tall skinny form and exhaled slowly, relishing his good fortune. He found the snitch, served up to him on a silver platter or a bright yellow one if you took in the symbolism of the cab.

Now all he had to do was wait. The cab pulled away. That meant Jake was planning on being here more than a few minutes and would have to call another one or walk when he left. Either way, Lester had him now. He didn't want to be conspicuous, even though most who lived here wouldn't look twice at a stranger because they knew to mind their own business and because there were so many new strangers in town. There was a bus bench down the street on the next corner. Lester walked to it, sat, and positioned himself to watch the front door that Jake had entered.

Thirty minutes later, Jake emerged and walked to the sidewalk as another cab pulled up. Lester noted the company and cab number. The cab pulled away from the curb, carrying Jake directly past the bench where Lester sat, and Jake never noticed. Lester walked to a public phone on the outside wall of a convenience store another two blocks down the street. The phone book inside was pretty beat up, and many pages were missing, but he found the cab company's listing. A nasally sounding man's voice greeted him in a monotone. "Hi, I just used cab number 1307 and think I left my wallet in the back seat. If you tell me where it is now, I can go there and get it from the driver."

"Let me check that for you. It's on its way to Settle Inn at 703 Old Oak Ave. I can have the driver leave the wallet at the check-in desk. The lady who owns it is real nice and trustworthy," offered the voice.

"That would be great, thanks." Lester hung up the receiver. These small towns were so different from big cities. He hoped his son had the chance to grow up in this kind of environment with these kinds of trusting people. He also hoped his son was nothing like him.

Lester turned back to the old house where he was initially headed and started walking. He still had business there. If Jake had been there, they had the information he wanted.

~~~

Tom's desk phone rang again. It had been ringing since he walked in the door, and it was now one p.m. Luke and Gabe were right; the amount of criminal activity was escalating at record levels. BJ was tucked away in County for now, and he could sit there till this calmed down. The State Attorney's Office had pretty much what it needed to proceed with formal charges and a clean-cut case to prosecute for Becky's murder. The box was the big focus right now, and the mole or moles. Who knew how many had infiltrated?

"Officer Dempsey," he said into the receiver.

"Tom, it's Steve in the evidence locker. I wanted to call you on the regular line because it's not likely to be tapped with the call traffic we're getting. I found your box, Tom. Someone moved it to another evidence container. This was deliberate sabotage, no accident."

"I didn't think it would be, Steve. Thanks for your time and confidence on this. Now I need to get it out of here and secured elsewhere till the agent can turn it over to the FBI officials."

"If you can bring something in here to carry it in, something that wouldn't cause suspicion, you can have it. You don't know who's watching, though, so use caution."

"Didn't you want me to bring you my lunch bag, Steve, since you forgot yours and can't leave?" Tom said as he eyed the thermal bag sitting on the floor under his desk. "I'm on my way in with it right now."

Tom reached for the bag and headed back to evidence. Steve was ready with the box. He handed it off to Tom through the window, and Tom handed him the container Beth had filled with sandwiches and snacks this morning. The evidence box was zipped up into the lunch bag, hopefully, safe from suspicion. The two men made eye contact and understood each other. They had a problem that needed a solution, but other issues came first.

Back at his desk, Tom slid the lunch bag under his desk again and took a couple more calls. When sufficient time had passed, he told dispatch that he was leaving to take statements from a caller who had reported gunshots. He purposely started away from the desk and then turned around to retrieve the bag, hoping that if anyone took notice, the lunch bag would seem an afterthought instead of the most crucial thing in the room.

Once in the patrol car, he pulled out his cell phone and called Cheyenne on speakerphone so he could drive while talking.

"Hi, Tom. Anything to cheer me up? I still haven't heard from my contact."

"Yes, most definitely yes! I'm headed to the church right now. I know you're not there, but it seems the safest place. Gabe and Luke told us this morning the angels protect it. I have the box."

"Oh My God!!! I don't know how you did it, but you are the most wonderful person in the world!" she exclaimed. Then she heard a beep for an incoming call. "Have to run, getting a call. I'll call you back shortly."

A few minutes later, he pulled into the church parking lot for the second time that day. When he parked the car, he sat with the box in his lap for a moment. This box held things that would immediately change the country's course. With the box tucked under his arm, he went to the kitchen door and knocked. The fact that he, and this handful of saints, were playing such monumental roles in this world-changing event was enough to overwhelm him with breathlessness as his heart pounded heavily in his chest.

Gabe opened the door. "Hi, Tom. I didn't expect you back today. Is that what I think it is?"

~~~

Millions of televisions across the nation were tuned to various news stations when the President made his brief announcement from the Oval Office.

"Good afternoon, fellow Americans. We've just experienced an unprecedented emergency in our country, as you're aware. The second-highest government position has become vacant due to reasons criminal in nature. A Vice President is the second in command after the President, so having that position filled with a person of integrity and responsibility is critical to the functioning of

the United States Government.

There are many qualified people from which to choose within our esteemed Congressmen and women. After deep consideration and with the expediency required for this situation, I have asked Senator Gregory Manning to step up and help me lead America for the remainder of this presidential term. He accepted this morning, and the swearing-in ceremony is on Friday afternoon.

All scheduled meetings and travel, including my essential trip to the UN, will continue as planned, proving once again that the USA can handle the worst and not miss a beat.

Thank you, and God Bless America."

~~~

"Hello." Cheyenne didn't identify herself on purpose.

"Agent? It's Marc."

She exhaled, "Oh, Marc, I am glad to hear from you! What took you so long to get back to me?"

"Meetings all morning. You wouldn't believe the chaos going on here. It's like preparing for Armageddon!"

"Marc, you have no idea how close to the truth you are," Cheyenne replied. "I need you, Marc, on the most important case you will ever work. Tell me, in your opinion of the current activity, are any superiors acting unusual? I've been on a case for over a year that turned out to be way bigger than at first glance. Things are going down, big things that involve big people. I don't know who I can trust. I need your eyes and ears to help me. What I have has to get to the right people because if it falls to the wrong ones, we're doomed."

"This doesn't sound like you, Cheyenne. You don't get rattled. What the hell?"

"I've never had anything like this to get rattled about before. But this is the thing that will do it. So, tell me what you know and see."

"Right. Well, your boss seems to be handling things with a good degree of normalcy. She is getting flak from all directions, though. I've not heard your name mentioned, but probable references to you, and she is taking a hard stand in defense. I hear things like 'pull her in' and 'no longer an asset' and 'rogue agent.' Since there are other women in your division, I didn't put it together with you, but now I see it probably is you they're talking about. Of those she reports to, there is one who is acting especially off the charts."

"Marc, I need to know, above her, who can I trust with information that will rock the Congress and White House?"

"It goes that high? Holy Crap! Do you trust me to talk to your boss and get her opinion? I could do that and call you back this evening."

"Yes, please. I'll be waiting. Until then, it's not just me that knows about the information in my hands. There are six others. If anything happens to me, they know what to do. They'll bypass the FBI and go to the media with everything, and "everything" means indisputable facts and proof. Thanks, Marc. Time is of the essence. This bomb has a very short fuse."

Cheyenne hung up and found Crystal standing in front of her. "Are you OK, Cheyenne? You're scaring me with the panic in your voice."

"Yes, better than ever and worse than ever if that's possible," she replied.

25

Wednesday Afternoon

SCHOOL WAS out for the day, and Kasey's assignments required for graduation were complete. All that was left was to take her finals and her high school years were over. Her teachers would administer the finals, one at a time, in the public library with the teacher present and in charge of proctoring the exam. She would set up the appointments with them individually, so there was no need to return to the school for anything.

Kasey had a date with Crystal this evening to go to the other church where Pastor Luke would speak. It made her nervous to think about it, but she had promised. The other thing making her queasy was hearing from Carlos. It was such a brief call, and she had no idea when he'd call again, but she was frightened for him. What could the future possibly hold for him now and for her and their baby as well? Her imagination couldn't conjure mental pictures of her future. That wasn't reassuring.

It had been a few days since she'd been to Gran's bar, so she decided to stop in on her way home to let Gran know she was going out this evening. Billy was behind the bar, as usual. It cheered her to see him and how his face lit up seeing her walk through the door.

"Hi, Billy! Miss me?"

"More than you could know, Kasey. The new waitress is working out good, though, so you don't worry yourself a bit," he replied to assure her.

"Well, I'm done with school except for finals. And this little one will be popping any time now. No rest for the weary, right? I wanted to let Gran know that I'm going to a church service tonight with some friends. I'll be home before she gets there but, just in case anyone should wonder where I am...."

"Church service? That's new." Billy tried to hide his great satisfaction at her words which filled him with joy. Her comment answered his many prayers for Kasey; to find the Light, ease her struggles, and have a better life, especially now with the baby coming soon. Finding a home in a church family was a promising new direction for her. He smiled and nodded, and she elaborated.

"Yep, I visited the church across the street from the apartment last Sunday. The pastor is speaking at another church tonight, and several of us will be there too."

"That would be His Grace Church, and you're talking about Pastor Luke," he added to her surprise. "I heard about that and might go myself."

"Billy, in all these years, I didn't know you go to church. You never said anything."

"No one ever asked," he grinned. "But I'm very pleased you're going. Maybe I'll see you tonight."

She walked around the bar to hug him and kiss him on the cheek. "I love you, Billy. You're the closest person to a dad I've ever had. See you soon." She smiled and left.

Billy's eyes misted, and his heart swelled. He smiled again, this time to himself.

~~~

The cab stopped in front of the inn. Jake had the rest of the afternoon to kill and hadn't decided what to do yet. As he passed the check-in counter, the cleaning woman waved at him with something in her hand. She hurried to him with a large manila envelope. Jake dismissively took it without thanking her and proceeded to his room.

Behind his back, the cleaning woman gave him a dirty look. Jake was far different than the usual kind and friendly guests at Settle Inn. And he had already become very unpopular.

When his door was closed and locked, Jake opened the envelope. A single sheet of paper was inside, and on it was written just a few short sentences. "Target in hiding. Local address. Seal deal tonight." And below that was an address. He didn't know who was watching this unfold, but he welcomed their help. Now the cards were back on the table, and he was in the game. First, a short nap, and then he'd attend to his evening engagement. That address was only about a twenty-minute walk. What a great way to settle a tasty home-cooked dinner in your belly. A walk in the evening air, and no cabbie to report where he had gone. Then, he might just find a bar and celebrate. He folded the paper and put it in his pocket.

The universe was a strange thing. Some days it seemed to like you.

Minor demons of little consequence filled his room, but some repositioned to make space on his shoulders for a more powerful Klazyn demon. Jake now had a task that deserved a higher rank.

~~~

After leaving the box in the care of Gabe, Tom went to take a report on those shots fired. He hadn't noticed before; the address was the same building as the waitress who'd gotten beaten up by her boyfriend. This was not a good neighborhood. The building reeked of desperation, short-term tenants, and lives teetering on edge. He knocked on the door of the 911 caller.

Once their conversation was over and he'd gotten the information he needed, he went to the door belonging to Peggy just to check on her. He could see lights on by the glow from under the door into the darker hallway, but no noise came from inside. The caller had been sure the shots came from inside the building; Tom's senses were on edge. He put his hand up to knock on the door and saw that the door wasn't fully closed.

Pushing it open just a crack, he called in, "Peggy, this is Officer Dempsey. Peggy, are you here?" And that's when the smell hit him. He backed up a step and gulped fresh air. Entering was something he had to do as a part of his job, but this part just made him sick. Soul sick. He pushed open the door, holding his breath, and cautiously walked through the living room to the bedroom. The women were clearly dead, bled out at least 24 hours earlier.

He retreated to the hall and called dispatch for the coroner, and Tom knew he wouldn't be back to his desk this afternoon. The Chief and the coroner would take up the rest of his time on this shift at the crime scene.

~~~

They needed to be at the church at six-thirty to talk with the pastor before the seven p.m. service. Luke was out on his pastoral duties for his members. Tom had been there and gone earlier, leaving the all-important box with Gabe. Cheyenne would stay at Crystal's house and wouldn't be going to the service.

Jill used her remaining time in Luke's office, contacting people in the various groups and chains to see how things were going and help keep them vigilant.

Gabe did his thinking at the kitchen table. The box. He knew the church grounds were safe, but he'd feel so much better if he could hear it from the lips of the Host. He picked up his cell phone and called David.

"Hi Gabe, what's up?" answered David on the first ring.

"I need communication from the Host guarding the church. Do you think Pauley can do that from there through his guardian, or can I get you two to come here?"

"Let me ask him. Pauley, Gabe is on the phone." David shouted into the other room. Gabe heard a muffled voice in reply. "I'm still getting used to this," said David. "He says his guardian just said to tell you, 'It couldn't be safer' if that answers your question, which I didn't even get to ask him."

Gabe laughed out loud. Working with Pauley was going to be a new experience. "Thanks, man. That is my answer and a big relief too. See you at the service tonight."

He wished Cheyenne was going with them tonight. Her safety was a top priority, and he knew that she had a couple of warriors at her side, so he need not worry. He busied himself with moving some of the items from the storage to his van for distribution this evening. Bibles and some tasers and mace would be available for the church members. As he worked, it dawned on him that he wasn't fully utilizing the information that came from Pauley. How does a war get won when the enemy numbers in the millions? Not by going one on one. By dividing and conquering. The Host communicated with him through Pauley, and he hadn't been paying attention.

Gabe knew what he had to talk about now. What he had to tell them to do and how to prepare. Not just in this church. Not just in His Grace church where they were going tonight. But in every church in the county. In every household and every business. The weapons they needed weren't mace and guns and knives. They needed to send the enemy fleeing for their lives and cause great enough pain to make them not come back.

He'd been given help, in the form of a young boy with divine powers, to win a very decisive battle in a war that he'd been fighting a long time. It would bring them even closer to defeating all the dark forces.

The greatest weapon against evil was the salvation of souls and the praise songs of the Host. Numbers of people coming to God in continuous waves. If the salvation of one could drive away tens or hundreds of demons, the salvation of one after another, in strategic places all over the county, could drive away tens of thousands. That would clear the path for the Angelic Host to deal with the demon Lords at the core of the chaos and avoid the dreadful carnage he'd seen from the lesser demons in so many other battles. It was time to expand the focus of their memberships to outside the county, everyone they knew far and wide who could bring friends and relatives who were ready to accept Christ.

As he ran into the office to talk to Jill, he remembered Pauley's drawings. In one, his armor was almost translucent, as if it was disappearing, and he had street clothes on underneath though he was still brandishing his sword. Symbolizing those fighting methods were changing? In the other, he and Pauley and Cheyenne were leading masses of people, holding up a cross, and following someone not drawn in the picture, but of course, it would be Jesus. In the background stood the saved whose salvation inspired angels to sing songs of praise and demons to die.

It was making sense. There would still be some fighting. There were too many men wholly devoted to evil in this war. But winning this time was about saving people and souls, not about blood flowing and his sword drawn.

And now he knew the climax point of this battle. The highest-ranking demons would arrive in the entourage when the Senator arrived with his henchmen. Cheyenne said that would be mid-day Friday, but things had changed. Manning would become VP on Friday. Where was he now? The Senator hadn't appeared with the President during the announcement. He had to find out how the timeline changed.

He had to make another call to David to ask Pauley if the angels sang those praise songs that hurt the demons at any other times or even at will. Gabe's heart expanded, grateful for Pauley's divine connection. His confidence about the success of this time, this place, and this battle grew stronger.

~~~

Luke returned to the church at three-thirty in the afternoon. He saw Kasey's car in her parking spot, so he walked across the street and up to her apartment before doing anything else. It took a few minutes for her to get to the door after he knocked, but when she opened it, she granted him her beautiful smile.

"Hi, Pastor Luke. What brought you over here? Won't I see you at the church service tonight?"

"Yes, you will, and maybe before that if you'll have me. Crystal told me that you two have a date for dinner before the service. I was wondering if you'd mind if I joined you?"

"Of course not. I would love your company."

She was such a sweet-spirited person. He could see why Carlos had fallen in love with her. "Then I'll pick you up first at five-thirty, and we'll go get Crystal from here if that's OK with you? See you in a couple of hours."

She watched him go down the stairs and across the street. Once again, she had that gloomy feeling in her belly as if something terrible would happen. Pastor Luke told her that God hears all prayers, and she had prayed on Sunday to have the same Spirit within her that the others in the congregation had. Kasey proceeded, trusting that her words would find their way to God's ears. "Dear Father, please don't let anything happen to him," she whispered.

He noticed a car about a block away, which had been there often in the past couple of days. It didn't escape him that it was probably law enforcement of some kind watching Kasey's apartment. He sighed. The world was very complicated.

Two hours later, Luke had his car by her sidewalk as she descended the stairs. She insisted on the back seat so that Crystal could sit upfront with him. It was only a ten-minute ride to her house. When they got there, Crystal was coming out the front door. Once she fastened the seatbelt, they took off for the nearest restaurant between them and the church. You don't keep two pregnant and hungry ladies waiting for food. The conversation was pleasant, and laughter lightened their time together. It was just the kind of respite they all needed.

~~~

The quaint older home turned into a bed and breakfast in a good part of town was easy to find. He had been cautious, wandering around close by but waiting until just after dusk to approach the place. He needed to find out which room Jake was in and if he could access that room other than through the front door. If Jake wasn't coming out, Lester had to go in. There wasn't a lot of activity, probably not many rooms either. Through the front windows, he could see a check-in desk and beyond it a dining area. A waitress moved around, but he couldn't see all of the tables from this angle.

A creep like Jake wouldn't be happy hanging out here long. He'd be looking for the nearest bar. Lester just had to wait for the right time and opportunity. Patience. A harsh lesson he learned in the pen. Bide your time, and don't rush into things. It got dark earlier this time of year, but now it seemed much earlier than usual. He figured it to be about five-thirty, dinner time for some. He'd managed to find some food and water today. Not much, and not great, but his life was winding down, and enjoying big, sumptuous meals hadn't been a part of it for many years now. There were more important things.

Instead of waiting nearer the entrance, Lester strolled around to the side of the lodging. He noticed the public library just around the corner. There was a plot of ground between them with trees and a bench. For outdoor reading pleasures, he guessed. He took a seat and leaned back. Too bad there weren't any stars. He liked stars and fireflies. Come to think of it; he hadn't seen any of either since they broke out. Now that was a shame. His last days, and he couldn't even enjoy some of the things he liked.

What he didn't like was the number of strange people milling about. Most wore dark-colored hoodies; none spoke loudly or acted in a way to draw attention. Their presence alone did that. They stayed in small groups of two to five and were all reasonably nondescript except for the strange tattoo he saw on several, just like those he saw on the people walking on the road into town. Dangerous. That thought kept popping into his head.

Lester sat like that for an hour. Calm. Quiet. Waiting. Then he heard the front door as someone left the building and all of his senses came to attention. It was Jake. He watched the skinny figure pause at the sidewalk and then turn to the right and start walking. His pace didn't seem haphazard. Jake had a mission. Maybe it was that bar he needed. Maybe it was something more nefarious. Regardless, this would be Jake's final stroll.

26

Wednesday Night

BETH HAD dinner on the table for him at six. He knew he was behind schedule, but not so much they would be late for the church service. She met him at the door, and his face told her this wasn't the time to talk about it. They wanted to leave by six-thirty to get a seat, so he scarfed down several bites of the meal she'd made and jumped in the shower. The foul smell of death is not easy to get out of your nostrils. Even when others couldn't detect it, it lingered for him. Tom and Beth walked out of their door, hand in hand, at six-thirty as planned. He never wanted to let her down, and he'd do whatever it took to make sure he didn't.

~~~

Since Cheyenne wasn't going, he made arrangements to pick up David and Pauley for the service. Gabe focused on what he would say to the congregation. Preparing a town with an explanation wasn't something he ever did. His previous way of handling these battles was to ride in and fight with no allies. Now he was telling them what was about to hit them. It went well last Sunday, but even those people didn't hear all that needed to be said tonight. Once again, trust that God would put the words into his mouth was all he could do.

He parked in front of David's house and watched his friends lock up and walk toward the camper. Pauley was a little pale but didn't seem shaky. David was more nervous than Gabe and Pauley together. Poor guy. He'd sure been through a lot in five short days.

"Hi David, Pauley, squeeze in here so we can get going."

"Thanks for picking us up, Gabe. It makes sense since there will be so many cars there. Save a space." David was rambling a bit with his nerves.

"No problem, guys. I wanted to ask Pauley another question before we get there, anyway."

Pauley looked at Gabe in anticipation of the question but didn't say anything.

"Could you ask your guardian if the angels sing any other kind of songs at any time that affect the demons as the praise songs do?"

Pauley paused as if he was concentrating. He was listening to the answer from the Guardian on the top of the camper, and then he repeated it as he heard it from them. "When they are sad, like when the girl died, they sing, but that doesn't hurt the demons. When they are going into battle, they have war cries that sound like thunder, but that makes the demons yell back before they clash. When the saints pray, it lights up their bodies with power, and they kind of hum like high voltage electric wires. That sends the demons running, but nothing hurts them like the praise songs. Then the demons can actually vibrate so fast that they turn into dust."

"Can the angels sing the praise songs at any time or only when a soul is saved?"

Pauley didn't answer right away. "They can only start this kind of praise when a soul is saved,' but the song can go on as long as they want, and there's no limit to the number of angels that can sing for each soul."

"Can you ask your guardian where Senator Manning is or when he'll be here?"

"He's here. Arrived at the big airport this morning and coming to Gibson Glen tomorrow. They are staying at the Settle Inn Thursday night."

Pauley didn't understand the enormous significance of the answers, but that was precisely what Gabe needed to know. Pauley was the biggest blessing in Gabe's life.

The church was easy to find. The youth members were directing the parking. Gabe kept the camper on the side of the street due to its size. They walked across the lawn toward the open doors and encountered several people they knew, greeting all with welcomes and handshakes. Luke was in the doorway, motioning them to enter. The pastor here wanted a few minutes' chat before the service started. He looked around once more and saw Crystal and Kasey walking with a big man who had a limp. Tom was there too, with a woman holding his hand and talking with a circle of people. Cheyenne was the only one missing, and her absence left a gaping hole.

~~~

Jake had pretty much memorized the route. He had no reason to think there was any hurry. When he got there, he'd look around a little, see if she was alone, and then shoot her. That's all. There would be no fanfare, no fooling around, no wasting time. It wasn't going to be something that could go south. Simple. One-shot. Get out.

The demons covering his body were high with anticipation and their euphoria transferred to him. He was feeling somewhat unstoppable and immortal. Things were going so well; he could see himself in another state by Friday night, whistling a happy tune, with plenty of cash in his pocket.

Jake was so deep in his fantasy that he didn't hear footsteps following him by about a block. Lester could be so very quiet for such a big man. He didn't know Jake's destination, but he had time to go along for the stroll. Residents on their route had no clue that such great danger was passing by their homes in the night. But the demons were having a party, and the angels watched the drama unfold.

There it was, the address he was given, clearly marked on the front wall near a porch swing. The lights were on, but drawn drapes covered windows in most of the house. None on the kitchen window, though. Jake walked through the grass to peer in there and found he could see through to the living room, where someone was sitting on the couch watching the news. All he could see were legs but only one person. He quietly walked around the house. No other lights were on, no sounds except for the TV; she was alone. He needed to see her face to be sure, though. He didn't want to waste a bullet on the wrong person and alert the neighborhood.

When Jake left the sidewalk, stepping into the yard to circle the house, all demons left his body. Two great sentinels stood atop the house with expressions of warning. The demons hovered but didn't come closer. Jake suddenly felt his energy ebb. He wasn't so brave now, but there was a job to do and a payoff he needed. His greed urged him on. Jake approached the living room window to see if he could peer through any gaps in the drapery panels. That window was just a few feet from the front corner of the house. The entrance porch was on the other side of that corner.

Lester watched as the door opened, and a woman emerged with stealth movements, holding a handgun with both hands like a professional. Jake didn't see or hear her; she was not in his line of vision. Lester had a moment of thought and then stepped from the shadows into the streetlight. He had no idea why Jake was stalking her, but he decided that this woman wasn't going to take out the snitch; that would be his own doing, as well as the satisfaction that would go with it. She saw him and retreated into the porch shadows. Jake was still trying to see in the window.

Lester approached within twenty feet of Jake before he sensed Lester's presence and turned, his gun in his hand but not raised. The woman with the gun was watching Lester. Jake was watching Lester. Recognition hit Jake like a train, and his eyes widened as his lungs filled with their last gasp of oxygen. His feet tried to move, but Lester's single bullet was fast and accurate. Jake crumpled forward to the sidewalk, blood pooling around his chest onto the white concrete. It was a straight shot to the heart, and Jake would die within a few minutes. His demons screamed and fled into the night.

The woman was still there, the gun in her hand, but she hadn't raised it toward him. He lowered his weapon as soon as the bullet left the barrel. This wasn't a night for killing anyone else. He looked at the woman, stuck his gun into his belt, then nodded and blew her a kiss on two fingers before he walked away. Jake knew who it was that sent that bullet into his heart, and that was all Lester needed. Now, if he could make it to see his son.

Cheyenne backed into the house. She locked the door again and turned out the lights. The TV was still on, so she hurried to turn it off as well. It was a nice neighborhood, and someone would have called the police at the sound of the gunshot. Their response time could be a little longer, though, with all of the criminal activity spurred on by the demons Gabe and Luke told her about. They also told her she was protected here, but her first instincts were to protect herself.

The bizarre thing about this whole event, she knew who the shooter was. She was a trained FBI agent and noticing details, identifying, and profiling; those were her stock and trade skills. She didn't know why this escaped con came to this neighborhood to kill someone trying to kill her. Lester had no other agenda and walked away peacefully. She also didn't know why the dead man was after her or who he was. There were always more questions than answers.

Since she was hiding, she had to make it look like no one was home. When the police arrived, they were bound to start canvassing the neighborhood, and she couldn't risk being identified. Her laptop was on the end table. With it, she hurried to the bedroom closet, sat on the floor, and with the door closed and the light on, she proceeded to research Lester Byrd. There would be a lot to tell the others when they came home.

The distant sound of sirens was drawing closer.

~~~

His private jet sat in an exclusive hangar at the international airport, and he had checked into the Airport Hilton for the night. The Governor and a junior Senator would be meeting him shortly to plan their fishing trip, as they called it in the press releases, and they would proceed to Gibson Glen tomorrow. This episode had to disappear in one fell swoop. He had to be in DC Friday afternoon for the swearing-in ceremony.

An encrypted message was coming through the cell phone. Manning entered the acceptance code.

Thor erased hit man, mark safe, box gone

His private persona held no checks on his deplorable behavior and language.

"Damn it!!!" he shouted at his phone in the plush surroundings of his executive suite, slamming his palm on the oak desk. "Is there no one competent to carry out orders without screwing up? This bitch has escaped me for the last time. I'll do it with my own hands if I have to!" As popular as he was with his base, he'd bragged about it out loud in a public rally; he could shoot someone in the street, and his public would still love him. They laughed and applauded him then, mindless sheep, but as much as he deplored them, he needed their votes for next year's election.

The drooling mountain-sized demon attached to the Senator whispered to him, telling him things to force him to continue with the plan, but the monster felt the first grip of concern as his confidence in

Manning wavered. If he couldn't pull this off and it screwed up the plans of the Princes, there would be hell to pay. Literally, and that hell would reverberate throughout the dimensions.

~~~

His Grace Church was about twice the size of Luke's church, but it was a capacity crowd gathering, and new arrivals would be standing at the rear and sides of the interior. Crystal and Kasey took seats held for them on an aisle near the front. Billy and David sat with them, David wringing his hands for his son, who appeared calm. Pauley had never been anywhere but at David's side, not even speaking or interacting with people until just a few days ago. Now he was next to Gabe, about to stand and give testimony in front of hundreds of people. Life was changing. Luke, Gabe, and Pauley were seated in the front pew on the left side so that they could easily reach the podium when it was their turn to speak.

Members and visitors continued to file in, filling every seat and lining the walls with people on their feet. The teens directing the parking entered the front door and signaled to the pastor that no one else was waiting outside. He stepped to the podium. The room grew silent.

"Welcome. Welcome to His Grace Church. I don't believe I've ever seen our sanctuary so bursting at the seams." His arms spread wide as he spoke. "We are foregoing our regular Wednesday evening service to have three very special people speak with us tonight. Some of you attended Pastor Luke's church last Sunday and asked that he bring his important message here. I had a brief conversation with him just a few minutes ago, and much has happened in the past three days. The urgent need for our participation in a battle of Principalities, the war between good and evil, is growing. You all need to be informed with some background information and some insight as to what we will need to be doing, starting this very night."

"You may ask, 'Father, why would you bring me into such deep and angry waters when you've given me such a tiny boat?' And our Father would answer you, 'Because your enemies have no boat at all and cannot swim.' Please help me begin this evening with a song of praise to our Father who will be with us in all our trials and tribulations."

There had a small musical group, including a keyboard and two electric guitars. They played the intro to What A Mighty God We Serve, and the congregation joined in with words and emotion to match the passion of the music. Songs of praise by the saints were like prayers. They filled the Host surrounding the church with glowing power. When that piece was over, the invigorated congregation sat, and their pastor continued with his introductions.

"I'd like to give all of our time tonight to our three guests. We'll close with a hymn of thanks when the message has been delivered in full. First, Pastor Luke will be addressing us. He'll introduce his friends as we go on. Pastor Luke, please," he said as he held out his arm and open hand to welcome Luke to the podium. They shook hands and then embraced before the church pastor took a seat.

"Thank you all for inviting us here this evening. Thank you for taking to heart the message of last Sunday morning. There are powerful forces at work in this world all of the time. We don't see too much turmoil here in Henderson County, or at least we hadn't till just lately. But there is much evil permeating humanity across the globe, and it has now come to our doorsteps."

"I want to paint a mental picture for you, to share a concept that might be frightening. The scripture in Ephesians 6:12 tells us this: 'For we wrestle not against flesh and blood, but principalities, against powers, against the rulers of the darkness of this world, against spiritual wickedness in high places.'" He paused. "That conjures images of hideous things. The scripture doesn't tell us outright that these powers of darkness do get inside the human flesh. Not like in a horror film, no one is going to snatch bodies. But when human beings accept the darkness by their own free will when God's light is purposely shunned, then, in the absence of light, the darkness of this world will rule that person, and we will have to fight against flesh and blood."

"Things have happened this past week. It became obvious that evil was growing when a child was abducted and murdered. Then while the search was still underway, a prison break took place, and dangerous men spread across the county, the state, and further, putting lives in danger and taking some as well. The FBI became a presence in our neighborhoods. The normal level of small nonviolent crimes and calls to our police station have escalated beyond measure. Isn't that right, Officer Dempsey," Tom stood and nodded his head with a grim expression, then resumed his seat next to Beth, "and now our county has had many more murders, drug crimes, shootings, robberies, break-ins, road rage, and assaults. There is a reason that evil is concentrating on Henderson County, but similar things are happening all over the country. Our challenge is the physical violence it will bring to our neighborhoods within the next forty-eight hours."

"There are physical manifestations in nature of the spiritual wickedness that has set upon us. Have you noticed the changes in the night? There are no stars, no crickets, no fireflies. The sky gets dark earlier than it should, the streetlights seem stifled, their light doesn't carry as far. The daylight hours seem subdued and have a sickly yellow cast when this time of year should be bright, clear, and crisp days with the beautifully colored leaves of fall? There's a distinct difference. You can feel it. It's heavy." Heads nodded all across the room.

"We shouldn't feel doom in this, though. God has told us he has our backs. Read the 23rd Psalm for comfort. But take the words of John 16:33 and let them sink into your soul. He tells us, 'I have told you these things so that in me you may have peace. In this world, you will have trouble. But take heart! I have overcome the world.' You will hear more things tonight from my friends, one who saved my life in college when we learned together what battles against the principalities entailed. And one who is a new friend. A friend who has supernatural gifts and who will be a great warrior for God. That he came to us right here is a true miracle at this time of need. But his gifts will ask much of him. Luke 12:48 'For unto whomsoever much is given, of him shall be much required.' You may have a hard time understanding the things you hear, but you are being given the truth in large doses."

269

"Let me first ask Gabe Matheson to give you some background. Then Pauley will tell you what has happened to him and what he's learned. And finally, Gabe will fill you in on things that have just come to light today. Thank you."

There were nervous looks, and some murmurings and applause as Luke took a seat and Gabe went forward. Then quiet expectation once again came over the crowd.

"Thank you. I'm Gabe Matheson; I'm a spiritual warrior. Luke and I were in college together some twenty years ago when something so life-shattering happened that we bonded and have been like brothers ever since. We found ourselves in the middle of a battle on our college campus. One where many people were killed and injured. Luke spent several days in the hospital due to his severe injuries."

"The evil that Luke just talked about, that infects a human when that human welcomes it in, will turn that person into a force of darkness. That person becomes capable of horrible acts beyond your imagination. Those infected humans, in large masses, overran the campus that day with guns, knives, iron pipes, wooden bats, and anything they could use to hurt innocent people. Hate fueled those groups, like the white supremacists, who rain violence on individuals of color or different lifestyles, like Nazi hatred of Jews, and they fed off of each other until they were in a frenzy where all moral thinking and values ceased to exist. And it is this chaos that the forces of darkness use to tear us apart."

"You will see only flesh and blood with your eyes. Your vision is limited to the here and now, this immediate present. But behind the human aggressors, you can't see that the evil, too, has form. It is the opposite of the ethereal beauty of the angels you can imagine. And you are blessed not to have the vision to see the manifestation of evil. *But not seeing it doesn't make it not real*. When needed, you can arm yourself with weapons to defend against the flesh and blood attackers. I'm not encouraging anyone to go out looking for trouble. But if you or your loved ones are in danger of attack, pepper spray, mace, and tasers are good distractions giving you time to get away from the danger. If you have a gun for home protection and know how to use it, you know what to do, but with caution. Be prepared, be aware. *Those who might be seeking to harm you can be stopped.*"

"But even before it gets that far, the greatest weapon you have in your arsenal is prayer. Your prayers to our Father greatly empower His army to do battle. Your saved soul grants you Guardian Angel forces to protect you. Salvation does not give you a guaranty against physical harm. But even in the worst-case scenario, if the flesh is damaged to the point of physical death, our saved souls cannot be touched by the darkness. *This is a call to all; we need to be warriors for the Light. We need to win this battle against darkness, against demons, against humans who have chosen the wrong path.*"

"Did you hear me say demons? You did hear me right. If you believe in angels, you must also understand there are demons. Wrap yourself around that truth because what Pauley will tell you requires that belief from you. I told you that I'm a spiritual warrior. I've spent the past twenty years of my life traveling from one place to another, wherever God sent me to battle demons and the flesh and blood humans that were attached. But dealing with them isn't your task in this war. The part that's yours will be explained shortly. But now, let me introduce Pauley, who has an incredible story for you tonight." Gabe walked toward Pauley as the teenager stood to do the most adult thing anyone could ask of a fourteen-year-old, to bare his soul. To share his truths in the face of possible ridicule and unbelief of strangers. He bravely walked forward.

The congregation waited and watched; most were stunned by what they'd heard so far. Now a young teen was going to share something even more incredible.

"My name is Pauley Kemper. Until last Saturday, I never spoke a word in my life. Never. My mom was killed in a car accident when I was two weeks old. I was in the car too, but not hurt. At least not the kind of hurt a doctor can find. But it made me different. I knew words in my head. I heard people talking, asking me questions, even talking about me. But I didn't speak. It was like I was in a fog. Or maybe in a dark room with a movie playing that I was watching, but I wasn't in the movie."

"Last Friday night, I saw something. I didn't know what it was, but it got my attention. I saw two burning red eyes in a dark corner. It made my heart beat really fast, and I didn't feel like I was watching a movie anymore. Then, in the car a few minutes later, I saw something else. It was nighttime. My dad drove by a church, and the lights were on. But they were special lights. They touched me inside, and I felt real. And I saw tall men standing on the roof. Not men, they had wings and armor and swords, and I could kind of see through them, but I wasn't afraid. A big one smiled at me when we passed. Then I wanted to talk and tell my dad but waited until the next morning. I needed to draw something to show my dad these pictures that were going through my head. On Saturday afternoon, Gabe came into my dad's shop, and I saw that the drawings I did were of him. I don't know how this happens, but what I can hear and see is helping Gabe and Pastor Luke. And the angel that's always with me now told me to tell all of you that the thing that hurts the demons the most is when the angels sing because someone got saved. I wish you could hear them sing." A tear ran down his cheek, but he smiled, and he was the most beautiful human being at that moment.

How many hearts he touched is uncertain, but there were tears on many cheeks. Pauley returned to his seat, and Gabe stepped to the front again.

"There are parts of that story I hadn't heard until now. God works in such incredible ways. Pauley can see and hear things we can't, and the accuracy of his gifts has been tested and found true. What Pauley has told you is right. The thing that hurts the demons most is the singing of the angels when a soul is saved. If a demon is killed, the person it has attached itself to is free. That person suddenly feels weak and becomes vulnerable because the demon isn't energizing him. Those are the critical moments when a person can go either way. They are fully aware of what happened to them. Some will want to go back because they loved the dark power; others want to come to the Light. Be ready with the word and the prayer of salvation for these. The task of the

Host is to fight the demons in their realm. A dimension few humans can see. Our work here is to lead souls to salvation. When we all work together, the dark forces will have to retreat."

"The way to win a war against millions of enemies is to divide and conquer. If you have family members and friends not yet saved, no matter where they live now is the time to talk with them about their eternal future. Talk, not coerce. Salvation is a free will choice. But we need to reach out. The right time for someone to choose to receive God's Grace isn't something we know. We just have to be ready when it happens. The most damage we can do to the evil that wants to control our world is to have places all around the county where people can come to accept Christ one after another. As the angels continue singing, the lesser demons will perish, leaving the leaders to be dealt with by the Angelic Host."

"Holy places, such as your church buildings, are like acid on the skin of demons. If a demon is attached to someone who enters a church, the demon must flee. Reading scripture does the same thing. When a person with demons attached begins to read scripture, the demons must let go. Though in these cases, the demons hover, just waiting for their opportunity to latch back on when the danger to them is passed. When a human becomes free of the demons, that is the time for them to invite the Light."

"Because certain pieces of the puzzle will be falling into place between now and Friday afternoon, I expect the worst that is to come will happen between then and Saturday. It is the time to be ready, be strong. Our greatest weapon is acceptance of God's gift. Each salvation can mean hundreds of demons destroyed. With souls saved one after another, the songs of the angels will obliterate tens of thousands of the demons. I know it is soon. And I know this is frightening."

"But our Father will be the victor once again. We have more forewarning and more knowledge in this battle than in any other I've experienced. We have to protect ourselves from harm from physical danger while feeding power through prayer to the angels in the spiritual battle against principalities. If you have any questions, please go to your pastor. Our church families will coordinate efforts and reach out to other places of worship. Spread the word. Thank you for being here, thank you for standing up, and thank you for taking your rightful place in this coming, critically important battle."

Gabe walked back to sit with Luke and Pauley. The church pastor took his place, his face a little pale, and motioned for the congregation to stand. "Let's pray." The heads in front of him bowed. "Father, we ask for the guardian angels to be put in place for every person here. We ask that if anyone here has not accepted Your Grace, that they feel a burden on their heart to come forward between Friday afternoon and Saturday evening at one of our salvation locations to save themselves while destroying demons of the dark forces. Thank you, Father, for bringing these warriors to warn us of the dangers ahead. In Jesus' name, Amen."

"To all of us, do not despair! Our Father is with us, for us, in us, and we can never be truly broken or overcome. The closing hymn will be in praise to our Father whose armies lead us in this battle and who protects our souls for His kingdom." The music started with the intro to Onward Christian Soldiers, and every voice raised as the words rose to the heavens.

~~~

Members and visitors filed out into the church grounds. The teens assisted with cars leaving the parking lot, but people lingered, talked, grouped, planned. Luke led Gabe and Pauley to Crystal and Kasey, standing with David. Tom and Beth approached the group. Introductions all around brought nods, smiles, and handshakes.

"We should get back to the church office. Several of our members attended here this evening, and we might start getting calls. Crystal, can you call Jill and ask her to come over tomorrow morning to coordinate again? We all need a good night's sleep, though. We're going to be very busy for the next two days." Luke's nervous system was on high alert, and he needed the peace of his sanctuary to get everything in order in his head again.

"Drop me off, and I'll call Jill right away. We'll come first thing, and I'll bring my house guest. She won't want to be alone at my house. She couldn't be safer than at the church," Crystal offered. "Kasey, are you OK at your apartment?"

"My sister is there, and Gran will be home after midnight. I'm right across the street from Luke and Gabe. I'll be fine," Kasey replied. Besides, she wanted to be at home in case Carlos called.

"David, Pauley, I'd like for you to get together with all of us tomorrow. I know it's a day when your shop is open, but could you manage it?"

"With all of the things happening, we'll be there for breakfast!" David laughed. "The store can stay closed for a couple of days. I'll just put a sign in the window."

~~~

Tom and Beth said goodbye to her parents and drove out of the parking lot. "Thank you for introducing me to Kasey, sweetheart. She is such a wonderful and dear girl, and I can see why you admire her." Beth took his hand for a moment.

"She is a special person. But I'm worried about her. I'm glad she's connected with Pastor Luke and Crystal. These events are sapping her vibrancy and weighing heavily on her."

Tom's cell phone rang. He saw it was one of the station numbers, pressed speaker-phone, and answered. "Officer Dempsey, what's up?"

The dispatcher's voice came through, "Sorry to bother you when you're off duty, Tom. We have a one eighty-seven we need you to attend right away. It happened about eighteen thirty hours, and there are a couple of other officers on the scene, but they're green."

"Right, text me the address, and I'm on my way." He looked at Beth. "Sorry, honey, I have to do this."

"I know. And after tonight's service, I know why. My prayers and your angel will follow you everywhere." She squeezed his hand.

Two bodies early today, another one found tonight. Beth couldn't imagine the darkness he had to face daily. She pulled him to her and kissed him deeply before she left the car to enter their home alone.

The text appeared on his cell. The address was Crystal's house, but Tom didn't know that yet.

~~~

Luke drove first to Crystal's house to drop her off. Approaching her street, they found two squad cars, the ME's vehicle, and an ambulance, all with flashing red and blue lights. Luke and Crystal immediately thought of Cheyenne's safety and were sick with worry. Luke parked his car on the street, and they approached on foot. Yellow tape cordoned off the area.

"Officer, this woman lives in that house, and we're just coming home from a church service. What happened here?" Luke addressed one of the officers.

"I can allow her to go around this way to get in, sir, but the side and back of the house are crime scene areas. A man was shot out here on the sidewalk. We're waiting on additional investigators before we can determine more."

"Was anyone else hurt?" Luke was anxious to know.

"At this time, we don't have any evidence of that, sir."

Another car approached and parked behind Luke's. Officer Dempsey got out. Seeing Luke, Crystal, and Kasey, he was confused. "What's going on?" he asked.

Luke spoke up, "This is Crystal's house. Someone was shot on the sidewalk. We just arrived."

"OK, Luke, please get her inside to safety and check the house before leaving her alone. I'm here to examine the crime scene before we call the Fed's in." Then he whispered, "This may have a connection to the prison break. I'll let you know in the morning. Till then, we'll have an officer stationed here at her house to keep them both safe."

Luke nodded and walked Crystal into the living room. "You and Cheyenne just hunker down and come to the church early. I'll have more details on this for you then. Maybe Cheyenne knows more. If so, feel free to call me. I won't be sleeping." He looked in the house quickly but already knew it was protected. Then he hugged her and made sure the door was locked when he left.

Luke and Kasey left Crystal's neighborhood the way they came. Within ten minutes, they were in the church parking lot. Gabe's camper was already there. "Wait a minute right here, Kasey. I want to get Gabe before I walk you across the street." She remained sitting in the front seat.

Gabe and Luke stepped out of the kitchen door. They talked for a minute, and Gabe looked at the apartment building. He patted Luke on the shoulder and smiled, nodding. Luke walked back to the car and opened her door. "It's clear. You can get out now. I had to make sure Gabe saw the Guardians all over your building. They're in place, and you are safe." He smiled, offering her his hand.

Kasey waved goodbye from the top of the stairs and turned to unlock her door. What a wonderful feeling to know that you were being watched over and cared about. She'd make some hot chocolate and wrap up in front of the TV to see if there was anything important on the news. She needed to have a talk with her sister in the morning. That girl's salvation was now a top priority. Kasey couldn't imagine eternal life without her.

".... after the President's announcement naming him as the new Vice President, Senator Manning has been

unavailable for comment. Rumors abound that he has gone into seclusion for meetings with other government officials before his swearing-in which will take place in less than forty-eight hours.

Further developments in the hunt for escaped convicts after the forecast with Bob Nesbit, our local station weatherman. Bob, can you explain this unusual weather we're having?"

Kasey turned the channel.

~~~

Tom lifted the sheet off of Jake's body. "Has anyone touched or moved the body?" He asked the Officer who first spoke with him.

"Just to retrieve his wallet for ID, Officer Dempsey. Then we just covered him up and started looking around. The whole neighborhood was quiet. Only a few neighbors looked out of their windows or stood in their front doors, and then they disappeared. From what we could see of him, it looks like there was a single bullet to the heart. He had been standing in the grass. We didn't walk into the grass to avoid trampling any possible evidence, but with flashlights, we could see the grass had been flattened in front of the windows as if he was casing the place. There was a gun lying next to his hand. We bagged it for fingerprints and powder residue."

"Good work, officer. I'm going to check his pockets." Tom knelt and reached gently into Jake's pants pockets with gloved hands. He removed a wad of ten-dollar bills and two folded pieces of paper and then opened the wallet retrieved by the other Officer. No driver's license. No credit cards. A couple of business cards for men's bars in the next county and one for a pawn shop in town, along with a receipt for a CD player with a name on it, Jake Bauer. Tom unfolded one of the pieces of paper. Then he unfolded the other one. He had the guy's name and the story; calling in the Feds was next.

~~~

Crystal peeked out between the drapery panels. Tom Dempsey was examining the body. He knew she wasn't home when it happened, so he wouldn't likely bother her with questions tonight. He also knew Cheyenne was here, but he wouldn't arouse suspicion on that front. The noise she made moving around the house and her voice whispering, "It's OK, I'm home, and you can come out now," alerted Cheyenne to open the closet door.

"I'm here, Crystal," she said softly. After checking that the drapes covered the windows, Crystal sat down on the edge of the bed.

"What happened? Did you know that guy was outside? Was he here for you? Oh my God, we were so afraid when we saw the police lights!" Crystal was worried and overexcited. Cheyenne was calm by now.

"I'll give you the short version, but just know that everything is OK, and we're all safe for the time being. We can talk details tomorrow with Luke and Gabe. When I heard noises outside, I got my gun. I went out the front door while this guy was trying to look in the window. Before I could go around the corner, another man appeared in the street and shot the guy at the window. The shooter didn't threaten me at all; in fact, he smiled and blew me a kiss when he walked away. I high-tailed it inside, turned off the lights and TV, and hid in the closet so no one would know anyone was home. But I think I recognized the shooter, and I did some research on my computer. I'll bet I know the ID of the body too. It ties in with the prison break. That's all I know so far, and I really am sure that we're safe here for tonight."

Crystal sat there with her mouth open. After what all she'd heard tonight, learned before tonight, and found when she got home, she was speechless and practically paralyzed.

"Now that you're home, no one will question lights and the TV being on. Let's see if anything else is on the news." Cheyenne got to her feet and went to the living room. "See if you can pull the blind down on the kitchen window; it's the only one not covered."

Crystal followed her into the living room and then did as directed. The TV was on, and they heard the same bulletin that Kasey had heard.

"Holy Crap!" Cheyenne exclaimed. What she thought Manning had been working toward but wouldn't happen until the next election was happening right now before her eyes. "He's going to get sworn in as VP! Do you know what that means? It means that the President is now at terrible risk. This plan is monumental. No one who can do anything will even know what's going on. We have to stop him here. We have to!"

~~~

Luke walked back to the church. That car was there again, a block away. He hoped that Carlos would run off somewhere else now that he'd heard Kasey's voice. He didn't want the kid to get hurt, and protecting Kasey from more harm was becoming an important focus for him. She was part of the family now. Gabe had the TV on for news regarding escapees and anything else that might affect them. Luke entered the living room as the broadcast began.

He sat down to listen. He and Gabe looked at each other, thinking the same thing. The trouble brewing here was full of vengeance and desperation, and the implosion would happen sooner than later. Gabe's alarms about the impending battle set off nervous system reactions all over his body. They didn't even know yet about Lester and Jake.

"I'm thinking I won't be getting much, if any, sleep tonight. Want some coffee?" asked Luke.

"Yeah, make a big pot." Gabe put his head back, closed his eyes for a few seconds, and sighed heavily.

~~~

David sat at the kitchen table, a cold jug of milk and a box of cookies in front of him. Pauley got two glasses and sat down too. They just sat, and breathed, and calmed. David reached for the milk and poured a half glass for each of them. Pauley opened the cookies and pulled a few out.

"I am so very proud of you, son. I had no idea what was happening with you, inside of you, for all of those years. We lost a part of our lives because we couldn't communicate. That makes me so sad. But yet I'm delighted at who you are now, at how we can grow together. You have an exciting future in front of you. I miss your mom every single day. And I love you both so much." Tears were freely flowing down David's face.

"People don't go away, dad. You just can't see them anymore. Mom has always been with us, just like the angels. She knew everything would be OK. I can see her sometimes now, but like she's see-through. The angel told me that our souls are all energy. When we die, our soul becomes free of our body and joins God's energy but remains separate like Jesus. Some people can see the energy but wouldn't know what it is, so they see a form they recognize, like when I see mom, and I know it's her because of her pictures. Souls recognize each other without form. I think that's pretty awesome!"

David looked at Pauley and shook his head. "I am the most blessed man in the world. And all of this time, I thought I was the most abandoned and worthless. We'll both be with your mom again, in God's time."

~~~

Lester found an empty house with a for sale sign out front on the western edge of town. He popped the lock on the front door and went in. There was some furniture, but no personal effects anywhere. He supposed it was for effect when viewed by a potential buyer.

The first bedroom he came to had a bed, and he claimed it. Lying down on a mattress that had some stuffing was something he hadn't enjoyed in many years. Not having to watch his back, well, that was decades. Right now, he was just too tired to think about it.

Lester's last thought before unconsciousness was that his son was playing football for his high school in the next county, info he received from his friend before the prison break. There was a game Friday night, and Lester could be there to see his son without anyone being the wiser. Sleep came softly.

~~~

A panicked call came into the Sheriff's Office at one a.m. from a man who had a farm on the south side of town. He'd heard his chickens being restless, and the dog started barking, so he went out to see if there was a predator. He caught a glimpse of a big man in camo sneaking into his barn. He decided to lock his family inside and call the police because of the warnings.

Two patrol cars left the station to check it out. They apprehended a man who had no weapons but matched the description of one of the escaped cons. The man was sitting in the holding cell awaiting the FBI, handling that case nationwide. It would be on national news in the morning. Millions would view Henderson County and Gibson's Glen on their home TV screens.

27

Thursday Morning

EIGHT O'CLOCK a.m. in the church kitchen, Gabe and Luke were on their second pot of coffee, and the news station was on in the living room. David and Pauley enjoyed a breakfast of eggs, bacon, and toast that Luke had just prepared. Crystal and Cheyenne walked in the side door.

"Oh, that smells so good. Is there some left for me?" Crystal batted her eyelashes at Luke.

"Leftover, no. But I'll make you some right now. A hot plate of eggs coming up! Cheyenne, how about you?"

"Sure, I can do some damage to a breakfast like that this morning!" she answered. "Now, who's going to start so we're all caught up to date? We have a lot to do today."

"First question, have any of you seen this morning's headlines?" Gabe asked the new arrivals. David, Crystal, and Cheyenne all shook their heads to indicate they hadn't.

"We jumped out of bed and rushed over here. What's up?" asked Crystal.

"We saw it about six-thirty. At seven, we called Tom to ask him to be here this morning. He had to go to the station to see if he was needed first but called back and said he'd be here shortly. So many things are happening at once. Police caught an escaped con south of town last night. He's in custody and being questioned by the FBI now," explained Luke. "That means more attention and activity because if one is here, more could be here too. They already suspect Carlos to be in the area. The FBI presence will be more prominent, meaning potential danger for Cheyenne increases. Cheyenne, you'll have to stay here at the church now, where we know the Host has the greatest protection for you until we can hand over the box and be sure you are safe. You can have my room. There are twin beds in the guest room where I'll bunk with Gabe. I doubt we'll need the beds much till this is over." He set plates on the table in front of Crystal and Cheyenne.

"May as well eat and catch your breath. We'll start recapping what everyone knows when Tom arrives," added Gabe.

"Oh, I forgot to tell you, Jill will be here at nine. I think the phones could start getting busy any time now," Crystal added between bites.

They heard tires in the gravel parking lot. A minute later, Tom walked in. "Morning, Tom. OK folks, David, you're first. Did anything happen after church last night?" Luke asked.

"Nothing more than Pauley telling me he's seen his mom, but that can wait till much later." Pauley grinned. The rest of them lost a beat, with mouths momentarily agape, and then regained control.

"OK then, we will table that for later. Cheyenne, what happened at the house last night." Luke wanted to get this out right away so Gabe could relax. It was evident that Cheyenne's well-being had become very important.

She gave the brief story to everyone and then elaborated. "I did recognize the shooter thanks to my training. It was Lester Byrd. So now we know that three escapees came here. But he seemed to be on a mission and was no threat to me. I had to know why so I hid in the closet and did some internet digging until Crystal came home. Lester was arrested here because of a snitch offering the info in exchange for a free walk on his own crimes. The FBI made sure that the snitch knew Lester had his name. Name of the snitch, Jake Bauer. I'll bet that's the ID of the dead guy. I don't know for sure why he was at Crystal's house. He must have known Lester had escaped and would come looking for him. Why didn't he find a hole to crawl into? Was he looking for me?"

"I can answer that when it's my turn, but go on for now," interjected Tom.

"OK. Now here's the biggie and this one makes my stomach turn over. Did we all see the news last evening about Senator Manning being out of reach for comment about becoming VP?"

Tom and David admitted having missed it. Luke and Gabe nodded and knew where she was going.

"The now-former VP was arrested for involvement in sex trafficking and rape. He will be replaced by Manning at the official swearing-in on Friday in DC. Arresting or impeaching a VP has never happened before, ever! The President is due to fly to the UN in a matter of days. If anything were to happen to him, Manning would become President immediately. No waiting for a pesky election or spending money on a campaign. He'll already be running the country. Winning next year's election with minimal effort and expenditure is practically a given. With that power so close at hand, those demon lords must be drooling all over themselves. Gabe said the dark guys had a master plan. This is it."

"The sitting President is in grave danger. The manipulators can make things happen at will. How hard would it be to have the President done away with so Manning could take the oval without a vote. And with their power, everything this country has stood for would crumble. Swastika tattoos and shaved heads would rule with AK-47s, and everyone else would run for the borders."

"Part of our discovery proves Manning's involvement in a murder. Add to that his faked death and recruitment by people aiming to manipulate the government by giving him a new persona. I'm guessing he's linked to many other deaths and even the prison break with more digging. We know he's been after me with intent to kill, that links him to the dead man who was likely stalking me at Crystal's house, and with the shooter who I'm sure is escaped convict, Lester Byrd."

"The last thing, which I haven't spoken about to anyone yet, is something I know from my very close dealings with Manning as an undercover agent before he confided in me about the murders. He has a tattoo. Not where the public can see. I never asked him about it, but it's just come to me that his tattoo is the same one now being worn openly by many who are on the FBI and CIA watchlists as homeland terrorists. This branding is a recent brazen display on his cult followers. He is a part of them, he panders to them for votes, and the manipulators intend him to be their leader, and ours."

"We have to stop this here," Cheyenne continued, "while he's in this town. But to do that, I have to know whose hands to put the evidence box in so it will take him down and not get filed away in a warehouse of suppressed evidence, and I haven't heard from my contact yet, which is really concerning."

"It is all coming together now. Thanks, Cheyenne. Tom, what can you add to the picture?" asked Gabe.

"Let me go back a bit. I took a domestic violence call the day Becky went missing. The woman wouldn't give the name of her abusive boyfriend, but a neighbor gave me a description. I found that abused woman and another woman, presumably a friend, in her apartment yesterday, dead for over 24 hours. Both shot in the head. I suspected but had no more than a description to go on, so it went on the back burner. Last night, there was a gun found next to the body. When I saw him, I immediately asked one of the officers to test the bullets inside against those found in the women. The results came in last night. It's a match.

So, this guy stalking you, Cheyenne, had just killed two women and was, as you discovered, Jake Bauer, the snitch. He also had some interesting things in his pockets. Two folded pieces of paper and a wad of ten-dollar bills, just under a thousand dollars. The papers, well, one was offering him a deposit on a hit, on you Cheyenne, and it referenced a photo of you, but that was missing. The other was giving him an address, Crystal's house. I can only guess that the hit order came from one wealthy person who needs you dead, but there's nothing to tie him to this legally. However, it does show us who has been doing the orchestrating. He had to know the Lester and Jake connection and that Lester would be out to kill Jake. Hiring Jake for the hit would take out Cheyenne, and then having Lester there to take out Jake offered a few solutions for him. He has to be furious that the box slipped from his grasp and that Jake got shot right in Crystal's yard before he got to Cheyenne. After what Cheyenne just told us and all that we've separately confirmed, he probably does have enough pull to have arranged the prison break too. And it's clear that he can afford to have eyes everywhere."

"He'll likely be coming for you when he gets here and may have other hits out there, so he doesn't get his hands dirty. You need to stay hidden right here." Tom finished.

"Thanks, Tom, but he's too prideful and vengeful to hand it off to someone else now. This is who he is; he wants to see me bleed out, painfully, with his own eyes. To answer your question, yes. He has the connections, the pull, and the money behind him to have arranged the prison break. And it could have all been to tie up the loose ends of the box and Chaney, so he had no skeletons to put his presidency in jeopardy. When I became part of it, his life just got more complicated, and erasing those connections became critical."

The oven clock read eight fifty-five. "Hello!" A voice from the front of the church.

"In here, Jill!" called Luke.

"I've got to get back to the station. Find out what, if anything, they found out from the escaped con." Tom bid his farewells and hurried out the door.

"Have I missed something important?" Jill asked.

"Just breakfast and some chatter about last night at His Grace church. Sorry, you had to work. It was a huge gathering. I'll make you some eggs and bacon if you're hungry." Luke smiled and held up the frying pan. How could she refuse? Gabe put on another pot of coffee.

~~~

Tom sat down at his desk with a cup of coffee from the station kitchen. The message light was blinking insistently. He had to finish the report on the murders of the two women and one on the body of Jake. A write-up on the evidence found and tested was due. Then the interrogation of the con. He just wanted to go back to bed, but he knew that the next couple of days would be like this until the worst of it hit them, and they survived the horrors to come.

His cell phone rang. Caller ID said it was Kasey. "Hi Kasey, how are you?"

"I'm doing good, but I think I'll be going to the hospital today. The little county one because I'm basically on welfare. I just wanted you to know where I am and that I didn't hear from Carlos again."

"Are you feeling OK? Do you have someone to take you? You shouldn't be alone." Concern in his voice warmed her.

"I'm fine and can drive myself. It was nice meeting Beth. She will make a great mom one day. Maybe I can bring the baby over after I'm home and rested?"

"That would be wonderful. Beth would love to see you both. In fact, why don't I ask her if she can meet you at the hospital, so you're not alone while you go through this? Having someone there could be comforting."

"That would be so nice. I'd appreciate Beth's company but don't want to be a bother. I'm getting ready to leave now, but I understand if she can't make it. Thank you, Tom. You two are such a great couple."

"You won't be alone, Kasey. See you soon." Tom hung up and called Beth. She didn't answer the home phone, so he called her cell phone. She didn't answer there either, so he left a message. He'd check back in a few minutes. First, the message light. Time to see what emergencies were on the agenda.

~~~

Carlos had to wait until noon to get the IDs. He made his way to Kasey's neighborhood but knew better than to reveal himself. He could see the front of the apartment building and better than a block in each direction from where he hid. There was a car a block away. It pulled in just minutes after he arrived an hour ago, and the driver just sat there. He had earphones on, and once in a while, he put binoculars up to his face. No doubt about it; this was surveillance. They must have tapped her phone and heard his call. Her car was right out in the open, or he would have climbed into the back seat and waited until she was going somewhere, then gently he'd let her know he was there, so he didn't scare her to death.

Someone was coming out from the stairs. That blond hair, Kasey, was unmistakable. She was so pregnant! That was his baby. That was his family. She went to her car but stopped and talked to someone across the street; a man and a kid. They got into a car and pulled over to where she stood. She grabbed her belly and bent over a little. They weren't talking loudly, but he could hear bits of the conversation. County hospital. Labor. She got into their car, and they drove away. He had to get to the hospital. His baby was being born!

The car that had been surveilling her moved out to follow. They would watch her at the hospital too, but he had to take his chances.

~~~

Luke came rushing into the church office. "David and Pauley were just leaving to get some things from the shop, and they saw Kasey outside getting ready to drive herself to the hospital. She's in labor! They took her and will stay there until one of us can get there for her."

Crystal jumped up and down gently. "Oh, I'll go! We're like sisters already. I can stay with her as long as it takes. You can get someone to replace me here, right Jill?" She was already grabbing her purse and keys.

"Take it easy. The nurses will get Kasey checked in and settled. I'll call David and tell him you're coming, then as soon as he lets us know she's in a room and where to find her, you take off for the hospital. We don't want to overwhelm the place. It's pretty small." Luke was laughing as he spoke. "It is awesome that despite all of the chaos and darkness, life and hope continue to go on. We have to make this a good world for children." She got the message.

"Please hang here with me till I can get one of the other volunteers to pop in to answer phone calls. It should only be fifteen to twenty minutes." Jill was already dialing from her list for help.

~~~

On weekdays, Billy's morning schedule had him up usually by nine a.m., so he was already alert when his phone rang. Kasey's name was on the screen.

"Kasey, are you alright?"

"Yes, Billy. I just wanted you to know that some friends are taking me to the county hospital. I'm in labor. But don't worry, this could take a while."

"Your Gran stayed at the bar last night. Did Trisha get off to school? I can go get her."

"No, I told her to take the day off and sleep late. Her niece or nephew is being born today. That's a special occasion. Can you bring her over later?"

"Sure, sweet girl. I'll get her at about eleven, and we'll come. Then I can go back to the bar for the noon lunch rush. You have someone with you till then, right?"

"Yes, Crystal just called me, and she'll be there by the time I get into a room."

"Good. What a nice lady. You take care now and know we love you." He pushed the off button. If he were her father, he'd be there for every minute of this and be the first to hold that new little life. Well, he could still be secretly as proud as if he was. How he longed to be called "dad" and "grandpa."

~~~

The ex-FBI agent didn't try to be stealthy. He just followed a couple of cars behind the one with Kasey in the back. The way she bent over and held her belly by the vehicle, he suspected their next stop would be the hospital, but he'd seen other agents get tricked by things like this, so he was being alert. She could be trying to throw him off so she could meet her con boyfriend, and that little shit wasn't getting away. Little black drooling imps rode on his shoulders, laughing and whispering in his ears. His greed for recognition and his jealousy of the other agents who had passed him in the line of promotions grew ugly.

The car ahead pulled into the parking lot for the county hospital. He parked on the street just a few cars down so he could walk in and check things out without seeming obvious. He had to see if she would have any means of communication in her room and didn't know at this point if she had a cell phone. But chances were that if she did, Carlos didn't have the number, or he would have used it to call her instead of the house phone.

There she was. A kid helped her from the car to the door while the driver went to find a parking place. It would take them some time to get her into a room, so he walked to a convenience store a couple of blocks over and got a coffee and donut. It seemed like ninety percent of his life was spent waiting for someone else to do something. He bought a newspaper too.

~~~

Beth loved doing favors for everyone. This morning, she got a call from a real estate agent friend. Today, there would be an open house on one of her listings, but her friend left some important papers at the office. Still with a few stops to make on the way, she didn't have time to go back. If Beth could get them, they could visit over the coffee and pastries she was taking for potential buyers to enjoy while looking. Beth gladly offered to pick them up and take them to the house. She got the address and left for the office.

"Hi, Jim! I'm here to pick up a folder of papers for Janet on that open house she's doing," she announced on entering.

"We appreciate this, Beth. Janet is a little forgetful lately, and I can't leave the office unattended."

"It's no problem." She smiled, took the folder, and headed back out to her car. "Have a blessed day!"

The house wasn't too far away. She looked at her GPS and memorized the route. She also turned the sound off without knowing it. The phone ended up in the seat next to her with the folder on top of it.

It rang a few minutes later but made no sound. Tom left a message.

28

Thursday Afternoon

MANNING AND his entourage checked into the Settle Inn at two p.m. with little fanfare. Within ten minutes, he was in his small, country décor room with one king-sized bed and a desk with a wooden office chair.

"I want a spin on my trip, and I want it in the news. No, it's not a real fishing trip! For God's sake, I don't fish! I'm here for a photo op with the head of the FBI; yes, I know he's called the Director, so set it up for him to meet with me. Yes now! No excuses. We're going to make a big deal out of the con they just caught. He's in a holding cell, and before they move him, I want pictures! Headlines will say that Senator Manning's law enforcement bill makes every state safe for residents without a shootout. Got it! Now get it done. I want headlines tonight that say I'm here to visit the good people of, wherever it is, and include in the first paragraph how I'm making time to do this despite how busy we are cleaning up the mess of the previous Vice President who is a criminal. And include that my swearing-in Friday afternoon is in DC at four o'clock. Make it happen!"

Manning hung up on his Press Secretary. He called his assistant next.

"Are you sure this little shit hole hotel is the only place I can stay for the night? I know it's a small county with nothing to offer distinguished VIPs. Yes, I know that it's better press for me if I mingle with the people. Damn it! I'm above all of that low-class crap. Hotel sheets give me a rash, and that makes me irritable! Then get some quality sheets and towels for my room, and I want them there before dinner time."

Manning hung up on his assistant. One night here would be torture.

His wife called. He saw who it was and declined the call. When she realized he had no intention of answering, she fumed. Instantly changing her mind, she smiled. If that prick didn't care what she had to say, she wouldn't tell him she'd heard through her gossipy social grapevine that government employees of some annoying type had been poking around and asking questions about him. Let him find out on his own; she was going shopping and would pamper herself with extravagant spending in retaliation.

Manning knew whoever had the box had nothing without the story that went with it. But she knew. That raven-haired woman had entrapped him, and she knew. No one else would even think to put him together with the box or with two murders that happened decades ago. He was confident. Killing her would end this problem once and for all. He could go on with his plans to run the country for a very long time. Manning didn't need to spend time or resources to find the box, it was right here, and he had eyes everywhere. He saw everything through his vast network of connections.

He had company in his suffering. The Governor, a junior Senator, and the Director of the FBI were here in adjacent rooms. They all coveted his favor, but some power positions were still critical to his plan that were not in his grasp. The second highest guy in the FBI. What was his title? Ah yes, Associate Deputy Director. ADD. It sounded like a learning disability. Titles were such garbage. He'd have someone work on that connection. He insisted that at least the top five positions of every organization be loyal to him. Anything less was unacceptable. He needed devoted depth to serve his plans.

~~~

Cheyenne was getting worried about Marc. Had she asked him to do something that put him under suspicion or in serious trouble? He was supposed to call back last night. Maybe he just couldn't get with her boss yet. This box HAD to get processed, and the clock was ticking. Her stomach rolled and lurched. Was it the breakfast on top of nerves? Unusual. She had a digestive system that could handle anything, but this case just kept expanding; it was bigger than anything she'd ever done.

She filled her morning with busy work like cleaning Luke's room and changing the sheets to distract her fever-pitched thoughts. She talked with Gabe about setting up the salvation locations. When he left to meet with people who would start doing the work tomorrow, she was alone again. Gabe and Luke were meeting with pastors and ministers of other churches to fill them in on what had been covered in the church service last night. Everyone had something to do.

She felt so disconnected. Never had she been the prey, and this was torture. Until Manning and his demons were dead or put away forever, she was his target. She could never have known the assignment would turn out like this. If she did know, would she have taken it? The answer was 'Yes.'

Her phone rang. She checked the screen before answering, and it was Marc.

"Marc, I was so worried! What happened?"

"It was tough getting some time with your boss. Everyone is watching everyone else. I told her you were underground with important evidence and needed to know who to trust. She said you were right to question; she's weeding that out for herself right now. There are two people I'm sure you can trust, though, her and the ADD. He may be only second in command, but he can get this to the President, potentially saving his life. I found out that Manning is practically in your lap right now. He'll be looking for you. If you trust me to do this, I can leave for the airport now, rent a car to come to you, get the box, and take it directly to your boss. She's already met with the ADD. He knows she'll need to call on him early tomorrow, spur of the moment, to get a top priority item to the White House. He's a good man, and he's in. We can do this."

"Hold on, Marc, I have an idea that could save a lot of that time." She ran to the office where Jill was working. "Quick, Jill, I need your brain of the local terrain. Emergency!" Jill rushed into the hall with Cheyenne, out of earshot of the other volunteer. "I need to know if there are any airstrips around here big enough for a small private jet."

"Wow, I've lived here all my life but, let me think. Wait a minute, just before you cross the county line to the east on the main highway, less than ten miles from here, a developer started a fly-in residential neighborhood on about one hundred acres. It went bust a few years ago. They didn't build homes; just the airstrip got put in. I doubt it has any runway lights, but I'm sure it's big enough for a small jet. Many of those wealthy people have that kind of plane. I'll bet that would work for you."

"You are a lifesaver! Do you know the name of the development?"

"Ahhhh, something about planes and then Ranch. What's the name of those things they park them in?"

"Hangars!"

"That's it, Hidden Hangar Ranch."

Cheyenne ran back to the bedroom with the phone in her hand. "Did you hear that, Marc?"

"Yes, every word. I'm checking it out right now and will get the jet to land there ASAP. We might just make it before dark. If not, I'll need you to be in a vehicle that has very bright headlights. Look for my text. I'll meet you there."

"It gets dark early here, so hurry. And Marc, I'm coming back with you. I want to be the one that hands this to my boss, and maybe the ADD too. It's become my mission in life to finish this thing. I'm no good here anyway. If this gets processed through to POTUS on the fast track, we will all be back here tomorrow to take down Manning."

"OK, Cheyenne, see you shortly."

She had to call Gabe. Since Manning seemed to have eyes everywhere, she wondered if the Host could somehow shield their view of her in a vehicle leaving town and then getting on a jet. Otherwise, he could still get to her.

~~~

Pauley was so excited about Kasey's baby. It was a first for him in his sheltered life. They helped Kasey get checked into the hospital and waited while the staff set her up in her room. Within minutes after that, Crystal came hurrying in and took over. All was well, so David and Pauley left, promising to check back later.

At the front doors, David almost ran into the weird little guy who followed them here. Tom told them earlier that Kasey was under surveillance because of the possibility of Carlos showing up. He said a quick prayer that everyone would be safe from harm, mainly because this agent acted strangely erratic and nervous.

Gabe needed a few more things that David had in the shop, so they headed that way. Pauley was scanning the windows as if his eyes were radar.

"Everything OK out there, son?"

"So many demons, dad. It just keeps getting thicker. Angels are walking with people and sitting on rooftops. Demons stay clear of the angels, but they're holding tight to those who are still in darkness. If people could see this part, it would make a lot of them take this seriously."

"We walk around like we have something tied over our eyes, so wrapped up in our own little dramas that we don't see the big picture. I did it for years. I guess that's what the darkness is counting on." David sighed. "Let's hurry this up so we can get back to the church and help out."

They spent some time in the shop. David had some paperwork to do, bills to pay, mundane things. Pauley busied himself to organize shelves and display cases and do the much-needed dusting. Pausing what he was doing to observe his son, David realized he hadn't even asked for Pauley's assistance. The boy just pitched right in. Six days ago, while Pauley was physically present but not engaged, he was almost a non-entity. Today he was everything David could hope for and more. Miracles. They aren't just a thing of the bible. They happen every day.

"OK, son. We're finished here for now, and I appreciate your help. Time for us to go."

They locked the shop, got in the car, and pulled out onto the street.

"Dad, my Guardian just told me you have to call Cheyenne. She needs to go somewhere today, and the demons can't know, so she needs to be invisible. It's really important, about getting that box somewhere."

David picked up his cell phone and handed it to Pauley. "Push the button for Gabe. We'll tell him too."

Pauley got Gabe on the first ring and repeated what his angel said.

"Thanks, buddy. I'll call her right now." Gabe was with Luke, talking with some volunteers and setting up salvation stations where people could come to accept the light. As holy ground, they are off-limits for demons. Many of these positioned around the county would be ready by tomorrow afternoon. Prayer chains were already spreading the word of the locations and their importance as safe zones for people to seek out and assist.

~~~

Crystal arrived after Kasey was settled in her room and hooked up to a fetal heart monitor. The contractions were steady and regular but not that close yet. Her doctor said to relax; this would probably take several hours. So, they talked about their lives, about school, about falling in love, about disappointments, all the things girlfriends share with each other. They talked until two in the afternoon with only an interruption from Billy when he and Trisha came in at eleven. Trisha decided to go to the bar and grille for lunch and let Gran or Billy bring her back later.

Crystal enjoyed their talk and the fact that it was helping her friend through her first-time labor. But one thing was disturbing, Kasey seemed to emphasize the scenario of something terrible happening to her.

"Well, I just won't hear that kind of talk, sweet girl," she scolded. "This is supposed to be a joyous time for you. Not a sad time when you worry about not being here for this baby. You're young, healthy, and greatly loved and supported. No time for nervous jitters, you're bringing a new life into this world, and this little one needs its beautiful mama to be around for a very long time to come."

"But a wise woman covers all of her bases," Kasey sagely replied. "Crystal, I've put a lot of thought into this. Really. If anything happens to me, I want you to make sure everyone knows that I want my baby raised by Tom and Beth, I put it in writing, and it's in my bag. You met them last night. They want a baby so badly, and I can't think of anyone who could be better parents. I'm probably just being silly, but this is important to me. If I'm not here to protect my baby, I want to make sure that someone else will."

"Of course, it's a deal. I will make it known if anything happens, but it won't. Period." She held Kasey's hand and squeezed.

The door opened, and a weaselly man stuck his head in. "I'm with the maintenance department. I just wanted to make sure you had a phone hooked up in here. Or if you have a cell phone and don't want one."

"My friend here has a phone. I don't need one, thanks," Kasey answered, but something felt off. She let it go and attributed it to hormones.

The ex-FBI agent walked down the hallway with the attitude that he owned the place. So, no phone that Carlos could call. "Good. Then he has to come here if he wants to see her, and I'll be watching," he thought to himself.

The hospital was small and all on one floor. Every room had a window. Thirty minutes later, Crystal left to go to the public ladies' room again, leaving Kasey alone. There was a tap on the window, and Kasey looked up. At first, she didn't recognize the man with the beard and mustache, yet she felt no fear. But in an instant, she knew. Carlos!

Her only connection right now was the heart monitor, so she could still move around just a little, enough to take a step and open the window, but it still had a screen on it to separate them.

"I'm coming in. I'll be pretending to be an orderly and will have one of those masks on my face. But I have to know. Once the baby can travel, will you meet me somewhere?"

"Carlos! Wouldn't that mean that you'd have to be on the run all of your life? How could we raise a baby that way?"

"Do you still love me?" he asked hopefully.

"With all my heart," she whispered. "But you have to go now. Go somewhere safe and contact me later. Maybe in a couple of months after everything settles down, and they catch all the other escapees. Really, GO!" She shooed him away with frantic gestures and then whispered, "and my heart goes with you."

"I'll go, and we'll make it work. You, me, and our baby." He blew her a kiss, and she shut the window and crawled back onto the bed just as Crystal returned. Maybe she could imagine a future, after all. And then the first hard contraction hit her, and she prayed this part wouldn't take long.

~~~

When he left Kasey's apartment, Carlos first collected the fake IDs and paid the balance. They were ready. He had no trouble, and he was on his way in minutes. Looking at the documents, Carlos found that his new name was Jose and Kasey's name was Maria. Joseph and Mary in English. He smiled. Was there some symbolism here? He hoped so. While in prison, Carlos had been going to church services. He began feeling a lot different about faith and God than before. He and Kasey never discussed these things because she wasn't from a family that believed, and he hadn't been a practicing Catholic for years. Maybe these new ID names were a sign that it was time for this to be a part of their lives.

He arrived at the hospital and observed from afar for a time. There was that car that he saw following Kasey's friend. And that looked like the guy who was driving it. He was now pacing around the front door. Carlos went to the back and waited for his opportunity.

After talking with Kasey, he felt reassured that he was doing the right thing. She was his heart. He had been stupid but not a ten years' sentence worth of stupid on his first significant arrest. And not when there were guys committing rape who were getting scolded and sent back to college because they had great futures. The justice system in this country had no fair balance or consistent justice in it at all. Maybe they could leave the US and find another place that would be wonderful for raising children.

There was one thing he couldn't do for her yet, despite his promise. He couldn't leave until he saw the face of his baby. He planned to hang around in a wooded area behind the hospital and check back to see how she was doing. With that face etched in his memory, he could decide where to go.

~~~

It was after two p.m., and Tom had been nonstop busy with calls, reports, and emergencies. The FBI agents sent in hadn't gotten any useful information from the escaped con they'd captured, so he was awaiting transfer to the county jail until they determined he was ready to return to the prison.

A loud commotion was coming from the entry. One of the other officers rushed back to the Deputy stations and told them it was a massive crowd of reporters led by Senator Manning and his entourage, demanding to speak with the FBI Director. That's all they need now, a political photo-op show.

He remembered that he hadn't heard from Beth. He tried her cell phone again and got her voice mail. Now he was getting worried. She never went anywhere without her phone, and she hadn't told him about any plans for the day. He dialed dispatch and asked for a patrol unit to swing by his house to see if her car was there.

"We do have a unit in the area, Tom. I'll let you know momentarily."

"Thanks, Abby. It's just not like her not to answer either phone. I can't be too careful right now. Ring me on my cell, would you? I don't want to miss your call. I have to get out before the circus makes its way back here."

He waited. His phone rang a few times, but the calls went to the message system. His cell rang as he was exiting the building the back way.

"Dempsey here."

"Tom, it's Abby. Beth's car isn't in the driveway."

"Thanks again, Abby. I'll check with her folks."

Tom had a sick feeling in the pit of his stomach. He messaged Beth's mom to please call or message his cell, that he was having a hard time reaching Beth and thought she might be there. They each had apps downloaded that pinpointed the location of their phone. If Beth's mom didn't know her whereabouts, he would use it.

Less than five minutes later, a message came in from her mother. She had no idea where Beth was today. Now she was worried and asked him to call when he found her.

He opened the app and punched in the required information. A map came up on the screen with a small red dot in a local neighborhood. He hesitated but decided to take a quick ride to that address to check on her. OK, so he was being overprotective. She could be angry for a few minutes if she wanted.

It took him all of ten minutes to get to the location on the map. Beth's car was in the driveway behind another vehicle he didn't recognize. There was a real estate sign in the front yard, no signs of activity. He parked the patrol car two houses away and approached on foot, holding his weapon. No sounds. He took a deep breath and moved forward across the lawn instead of taking the sidewalk. He peeked in the front window of the living room. Beth and another woman were sitting on the floor, hands bound behind their backs, tied at the ankles, and duct tape over their mouths.

He burst through the unlocked front door and ran to her, ripping the tape from her mouth. "Beth! Are you hurt?"

She shook her head, "No, I'm OK. But please get us loose. I'm numb all over."

As he was releasing them from the tape, Beth explained, "When I got here to help Janet, she was already here and bound up. It was a big man with a beard and mustache wearing hunting clothes. But he didn't hurt us. He told me to be quiet and left as soon as he was sure we were taped up and couldn't move."

"I found him sleeping in the front bedroom. I guess I surprised the heck out of him," Janet added while Tom was placing a call to the dispatcher from his cell.

"Abby, this is Tom Dempsey. I need a unit and an FBI agent at the address I'm texting. I found Beth; she's fine. But we have a possible connection to the prison break."

"On the way, Tom."

~~~

That was the closest Lester had ever gotten to being caught because of his own negligence. This better come to an end soon; he was slipping badly. The other prisoners had whispered to each other about him losing his hard edge that had made him famous and feared. Maybe they were right. Maybe years ago, he would have killed those two women just for being there, but he had no beef with them today. He was just so tired of this, of running, of having to watch his back and get no sleep. Well, at least he was more refreshed than he had been in a long time after the hours of sleep he'd gotten in that house.

Five hours ago, he ran for deep cover and now found himself crossing heavily wooded land heading west. The final goal was still his son.

~~~

Excruciating pain! The waves were coming fast now. The nurse wheeled her into the delivery room, but she was conscious of the need to push. A vice grip from her lower back down sent waves of pain as all of her muscles contracted. "Almost there, dear." Said one of the nurses with a mask over her mouth and nose. She closed her eyes against the intensely bright lights. Knees up, heels on the stirrups, another gripping wave hit her.

"Push now, Kasey," said the doctor, calmly but in a slightly louder than normal voice.

The nurse helped raise her shoulders to push harder and then let her lean back when the wave ended.

"Only one or two more of these, and we should be able to call it a day here. Almost done." He was trying to assure her, but she really couldn't concentrate on anything but the pain. Seconds later, another wave hit.

"Again, Kasey, push hard." The nurse raised her shoulders. Kasey let out a part scream, part growl, loud and guttural enough to hurt her throat. The baby's head emerged, and she felt a great deal of relief already. The rest of the baby slid free, and the pain lessened considerably. She took a couple of deep breaths, and the remainder of the process took its course.

"Good work, my girl." The doctor praised her, pleased with the uncomplicated birth. "This is one beautiful baby! Nurse, please write her birth time as three thirteen p.m."

"Kasey, you have a beautiful baby girl, honey," smiled the nurse.

They swaddled the baby and gently handed her to Kasey, who held the tiny bundle to her chest. And as with most new mothers, she could see nothing else in the room but that perfect little face. "Hope, her name is Hope. Hello, my sweet little one. I've been waiting for you," she said softly. Kasey unwrapped her baby to count fingers and toes.

In the waiting room, Crystal paced. Outside of the labor room window, Carlos worried.

Twenty minutes later, with all the initial tests done, the baby was weighed, measured, and cleaned up. Both mother and baby returned to the labor room Kasey had been in, where they'd stay together until their release. Kasey was tired and sore but felt good. Hope just wanted to sleep.

Crystal came in to visit with tears of joy flowing down her face. Kasey saw her, laughed, and shed a few tears of her own. Hope snuggled in a rolling infant bassinet next to the bed, her face the only visible skin in the closely wrapped baby cocoon.

"She is so perfect. Look at that darling little nose and those perfect lips." Completely taken with Hope's preciousness, the two of them fawned over the sleeping baby until Kasey yawned.

"I'll let everyone know and get out of your hair, for now. It would be best if you had some sleep, you'll be getting more visitors soon. I'll be back in a little while." Crystal rose to leave, and Kasey took her hand.

"Thank you for being such a wonderful friend." She rested her head back on the pillow and smiled as Crystal left.

Outside, Carlos had been watching for signs of Kasey and the baby. He saw when the nurse brought her back to the room. He saw the baby in the bassinet. Both seemed to be OK. Then he saw the other lady come in. He would wait.

Time passed. It seemed like hours but was probably only twenty minutes when the lady left. Kasey looked so tired, but he'd been here too long and had to get moving. He tapped on the window. She opened her eyes, saw him, and her eyes widened in surprise. "Carlos!" she mouthed and sat upright. He put his finger up to his lips in a "Shhhh" and pointed to the baby, smiling.

She slid to the edge of the bed and lowered her legs. Just a little shaky but fine. She wheeled the bassinet over to the window, using it to help herself balance.

Carlos looked in the bassinet at the bundle that could fit into his two hands and marveled. She opened the window and whispered, "Her name is Hope. Isn't she beautiful?"

At that instant, a little man with a big gun walked around the exterior wall corner and stopped thirty feet behind Carlos. It all happened so fast; it was a blur to Kasey, and Carlos was barely aware of anything.

She screamed, Carlos half-turned, the man shouted, and the gun went off twice.

Outside, Carlos crumbled to the ground with a bullet in his shoulder. Blood gushed from the wound. He wanted to touch Kasey and see his baby, but the excruciating pain was all-consuming. He closed his eyes and lost consciousness.

Inside, where the second bullet had strayed, Kasey fell to the floor.

In the hallway, Billy and Trisha coming in had just passed Crystal leaving; they all heard the shots and ran to the room. Trisha screamed. Billy went to Kasey and cradled her in his arms, lying on the floor next to her, sobbing. She was alive. Crystal ran to the bassinet and picked up the baby, taking her out of the room while she too cried, and Trisha followed.

The nurse at the attendant station dialed 911 for the police while other nurses and doctors ran toward the sounds.

The little man outside, the ex-FBI agent, was paralyzed. He hadn't meant to shoot. His arm hung limply at his side, but he still gripped his weapon. The gun was out as a warning not to try anything. His heart raced, his head swam, the bile rose in his throat, but his feet wouldn't move. His demons were ecstatic.

Sirens screamed, tires screeched, and before he knew what was happening, he was in handcuffs, face down in the dirt.

Paramedics came running from the ER and expertly attended to Carlos, getting him onto a gurney and into the hospital for surgery.

Billy rocked Kasey, holding her protectively. He let go when the staff lifted her away from him and into the bed to examine her. She was not injured. The doctor said it was her weakened system, having just had the baby, and the shock made her pass out. They found the stray bullet lodged in the far wall and said how she was so lucky. Billy knew better, so did her Guardian Angel, who still hovered over her.

29

Thursday Evening

CRYSTAL SAT in the waiting room, holding and rocking newborn baby Hope, with Trisha by her side. The two of them were in shock, thinking Kasey was dead until Billy came out and assured them she had simply collapsed with no injuries from the bullet. Uniformed police and men in suits swarmed around and through the building. The staff evacuated most out-patients and secured in-patients in their rooms, but the danger here had passed, and no lives were lost this time.

Trisha finally had the mental clarity to pick up her cell phone and dial Gran. She let her know that Billy wouldn't be coming back today; Kasey and the baby were fine. She felt like a zombie talking, all energy drained with the adrenalin leaving her system. Gran could hear the whole story later.

Crystal called Luke. She could barely speak or breathe. "Please come to the hospital. Kasey, Carlos, shooting." He said he'd be right there and hung up on the run, shouting to Gabe. The volunteers just stood with open mouths, fearing how it sounded.

"Crystal called. Something bad at the hospital. No other details" was all he could say as he slammed the car into drive and spun gravel out of the parking area. Gabe called Cheyenne. She was waiting to hear again from her contact about a private jet landing time. He wanted her to know where he was going with Luke.

"Cheyenne, we're heading to the hospital. Something bad has happened with Kasey. Have you heard from your contact yet?"

"Nothing. Marc may be on his way. They were trying to be here before dark. Let me know what happened, and I'll call when I have more information."

Luke was practically taking corners on two wheels. They saw two ambulances, three squad cars, and several dark SUVs as they neared the hospital. Uniforms and suits were everywhere. An FBI agent put a handcuffed man into the back of a black SUV as a news van arrived.

Luke screeched to a halt and jumped out, running to the door. There was no tape cordoning off the front, so he went right in to see Crystal sitting near the admissions desk. She couldn't get up, her hands full. Was she holding a baby?

"Oh, Luke!" she cried. He hurried to her and held her. "Someone tried to kill Kasey."

"Calm, breathe, calm," he softly spoke to her while he rubbed her back. "Try to tell me what you know."

"The baby was born; everything was fine. She was tired, and I had just left her room when I passed Trisha; this is Trisha, Kasey's little sister. Trisha and Billy, you met him last night at the church meeting; they were coming in to visit. There were two shots. We all ran to her room. She was on the floor. Billy went to her, and then the doctors and nurses came in. We didn't know then, but Carlos was outside her window. He was shot, but only in the shoulder. He's in surgery, Luke. I heard the police talking. They said that there was an FBI agent outside who shot them. Why? Why would someone just shoot? Carlos didn't even have a weapon; he was no threat. And to shoot into a hospital window with a woman and newborn right there!"

Luke was angry and shocked but saw the miracle here - Kasey and the baby were OK. He quickly sent up prayers of thanks to God for protecting this mother and her newborn. Inside, his heart heaved, knowing there would be much more of this during the next thirty-six hours. Gabe soon caught up with him after hearing part of the story from the officers outside.

"Luke, I think she knew," Crystal sniffed. "She told me several times if anything happened to her, she wanted Tom and Beth to raise the baby." Trisha looked up. Could Kasey have really known something terrible would happen? She needed to know who Tom and Beth were and why Kasey would give them her baby. "Somehow, she knew." Crystal whispered, tears still streaming, "but she believed she was going to die."

A nurse walked over to Crystal. "I'll take the baby now and put her in the nursery. She needs to have a bottle. You can see her anytime there; we'll take care of her until Kasey is strong enough to have her again."

"Did Kasey name her? I didn't get to see her or ask." It was something Trisha needed to know, and Crystal hadn't said.

"Yes, dear, her name is Hope." The nurse did her best to contain her own emotions, her eyes welling with tears. Hope, precisely what we all need.

~~~

David treated Pauley to a hamburger and milkshake on the way back to the church. They'd worked through lunch at the store, and stomachs were growling. Pauley gave David instructions again just half of a block from the parking lot.

"We need to go back to the hospital, right now. Dad, someone shot Kasey."

311

"What do you mean, son?"

"She wasn't hit, but Carlos was. He's already a Christian. Kasey will be happy."

David took the next right and sped back to the building where they had dropped Kasey just a few hours ago.

~~~

Tom was wrapping it up with the officers and the FBI agent at the vacant house. They now surmised, by the description, that the man who'd bound the women and slept here in the empty house was one of the escaped cons, Lester Byrd. The others didn't know, but Tom did; this was the second time Byrd had the opportunity but didn't hurt innocent people. It was tough to figure some people. Was there indeed some good in everyone? He was just grateful his Beth was unharmed.

An officer walked into the house looking for Tom. Janet and Beth had finished giving their statements and were released to leave. "Deputy Dempsey, there's another crime scene at the county hospital, and they're asking for you.

"County hospital? Kasey is there to have her baby! Beth, can you get your car and meet me at the county hospital. Are you OK with driving? I may need you there."

He never asked her to help him with his work, let alone even sharing how his day had gone, so this had to be serious. She nervously grabbed her purse and keys, hugged Janet, and got to her car as quickly as she could. Tom was already in his patrol car, speeding to the hospital with a siren and lights on.

~~~

Cheyenne's phone rang, it was Marc. "I'm here, Marc. When are you landing?"

"ETA is forty-five minutes, close to five p.m. your time. Bring the box, and jump on board as soon as we come to a stop. We'll take off again immediately. Your boss is with me, and we're going straight to the ADD when we land in DC."

"OK, Marc, I'll be there waiting for you. Safe travels."

She clicked the end button and pushed the icon for Gabe.

"Cheyenne, news?"

"Yes, landing in forty-five minutes."

"I'll take Luke's car from the hospital and be there in ten. Won't take us long to get to the strip."

"I'll get the box and be ready to get in the car when you get here. Are you sure Pauley said we'd be cloaked? I'm so nervous, and Gabe, I didn't tell you, but I'm going with them to take the box to the Assistant Director and make sure it gets into the hands of the President."

"I had a feeling you would have to do that. I'm absolutely sure the cloak will work, and my additional fervent prayers will be with you too. And, since I'm driving a different vehicle, no camper for them to recognize either."

"Trusting someone other than myself is something I have to learn. But I'm watching out the window for you."

"Be right there." He hung up and started those fervent prayers right at that moment.

He turned to Luke, "I need your keys. Cheyenne has an appointment."

Luke handed him the keys. "Blessings on the success of this mission."

Gabe nodded and ran for the car, praying, "Lord, I trust that those angels are ready to hide us starting right now. Please make us invisible to the demons and the eyes watching for Manning. Cover the car and jet too, oh, and all of the activity in DC. Please protect all those fighting this battle now and the larger one we face. Thank you, Lord. Amen." He could tell Cheyenne the story of Kasey when they were on their way.

~~~

Gabe was already halfway to pick up Cheyenne when Tom pulled into the hospital, closely followed by David. Tom jumped out and jogged to the closest officer, one of the guys he knew well.

"What happened here? I just got the call on this."

"Double shooting, Tom. It looks like an ex-FBI agent shot at one of the escaped cons. One bullet hit the con; another went into a hospital room but missed the patient. They've got the shooter in cuffs on his way to the station. Apparently, he'd been fired and was trying to make a name for himself and get reinstated. Both of the victims are here. The patient is fine. She just had a baby and passed out from shock. The other victim is in surgery."

Tom was sick. He turned and began walking toward the door when Beth ran to him for her car. "What happened, Tom. What can I do?"

"Kasey had the baby, was shot at, but is OK. Carlos was here and is in surgery. Some cowboy thought shooting him would be a good idea." She gasped. He took her hand, and they entered the door. David and Pauley stood nearby. Crystal stood with Luke and a young girl. Billy, the big bartender, was there with his arm around the girl's shoulders. There were tears, lots of tears. Crystal turned and saw them as they approached.

"Tom, Beth, I'm so glad you're here." She sniffled, hiccupped, and gave each a hug.

"How's Kasey?" Tom asked in a monotone voice. Crystal told her story again, ending with the baby being in the nursery and Kasey being cared for by the medical staff.

"She told me on at least three different occasions, even today while she was in labor, that if anything happened to her, she wanted you and Beth to raise her baby. She was adamant that I make it known to anyone and everyone. She trusted you both with the most precious thing in her life. If she thought she was in danger, I'm sure she would have said so. I think she just had a premonition." Crystal took a deep breath. "She named her little girl Hope."

Crystal walked with Tom and Beth to the nursery where Hope had just been fed and changed. They watched her sleeping peacefully.

Tom's phone rang. "Dempsey."

"Tom, it's escalating and out of control. There are three pods of perps aggressively attacking people in the street with various weapons. We have a jewelry store robbery, several B and Es, two shootings, three auto thefts, and a half dozen car accidents. Add those to the hospital shooting, the Jake Bauer shooting, and the capture of the con. Hold on, another report of someone shot just coming in, and two of our officers tell me there is a parade of people walking into the county; many are armed, and they're seeing a lot of people with the same unusual tattoo. They're coming in on each of the four main highways. We don't have enough officers to handle this! Can you take some of these?"

"I'll be there asap. Has the Chief called for reinforcements? "Beth heard it all. She kissed him and left, praying for his strength and safety, then hurrying off to meet up with some of her church members at one of the salvation locations, which were starting to get busy.

~~~

He drove as close to the side door as he could get. Cheyenne ran out, the box under her arm, and jumped in the front seat.

"Should I be in the back, hiding?" she worried.

"No, the Host has us covered. Manning's eyes won't see us at all. Breathe!"

"While I'm breathing, tell me what happened."

He told her what had happened at the hospital. None but Beth and Tom yet knew about Beth's ordeal. She worried for Kasey and the baby, but her concentration was on the box. It could avert the national, perhaps a global, catastrophe of Manning's presidency and his planned dark agenda. Cheyenne checked her watch. Four thirty-five, and they were speeding to the landing site. The country, and more, was at stake in this battle against dark and evil powers.

Heading east, they passed a continuous line of people on foot walking toward town. Gabe kept telling himself that they were invisible to the strangers, and he almost missed the turnoff, climbing vines having claimed most of the sign for Hidden Hangar Ranch. He took a hard right on a yet unpaved but somewhat well-cleared road. It went about a mile back into fields and woods and opened onto a large expanse of green. The road split; each leg ran parallel to the other with a long grass landing strip in the middle. There were empty and overgrown lots marked around the perimeter. No landing lights either. This abandoned development was definitely in the very preliminary stages.

"As soon as they touch down and stop, I'm to run to the steps and board. We'll take off right away. I won't be in contact with you for a while. The goal is to get this tested with the ADD and then get the results to the President ASAP. If all goes well, we can come back in force and take Manning down tomorrow before he goes to DC and can do any more damage."

They heard a jet engine overhead. Marc was a bit early. The jet came swooping in, low and fast, and made a perfect landing, circling back near the car. She opened her door, leaned back in for a quick hug, and ran to the jet's opening as fast as she could. Engines screamed, and the plane tore off down the runway again. He watched it disappear into the clouds.

"Be safe, my warrior woman. Lord God, please help and protect Cheyenne as she enters into even more danger, trying to do Your will." He started the car and headed back to the church, picking up the phone to let Luke know about the crowds of people coming toward town.

Inside the jet, she handed the box to her boss. "There is blood evidence for Manning in here, including a rock that he used to bash in the heads of two young girls, smeared with their blood and his from the severe scratches he received in the struggle. Also, some costume jewelry from the two murdered girls twenty years ago. And a rag with Manning's sweat and blood from wiping off his hands. It should be enough for a conviction."

Her boss smiled, patted the box, and said, "Cheyenne, you've done an incredible job on this case which got bigger than any of us could have imagined. I think you ought to grab the next ninety minutes of flight to rest. Things are going to get hot and heavy until Manning is behind bars."

Marc patted her on the back. "Excellent work, agent. I'd be surprised if there weren't a promotion in this for you."

She smiled but didn't have the heart to tell either of them that this was her last mission. She had decided to quit the bureau. Her boss was right; they sorely needed the rest as fatigue screamed from every part of her body. Willing the tension to decrease, she nodded off against the headrest.

~~~

"...reporters on the scene at Henderson County Hospital. A young woman in her hospital room barely missed being shot this afternoon, just an hour after she gave birth, when an ex-FBI agent shot at an escaped convict, Carlos Martinez. She was inside the hospital building, near a window. We believe he was trying to contact her and that

the child is his. The shooter stalked her to find her boyfriend, even following her to the hospital when she went into labor. He shot twice, possibly without warning. Both the woman and Martinez are alive. Martinez was not armed. The ex-FBI agent is rumored to have been attempting a capture of the escaped convict so he would get his job reinstated."

The TV newscast was background noise to those in the hospital waiting room but not Lester Byrd. Five o'clock brought darkness these days, so he found a shed on the edge of a small property. A one-room log cabin was just twenty yards away, and someone was home, but there were no barking dogs, so he felt comfortable taking shelter. Someone inside was watching TV, and Lester listened.

When he heard the news, his shoulders sagged. Carlos. He had such hope for that kid. It hurt as if it was his own son who had just gotten shot and captured. An FBI agent fired with no warning and was reckless enough almost to kill both the kid and his girl when Carlos was unarmed and no threat? Someone needed to pay for this. The someone who orchestrated this whole thing. How many lives had it cost already, and what was the big plan?

He didn't hear his name mentioned at all. Hopefully, the two women had been found and released. Lester didn't want any harm to come to them on his account.

"Senator Gregory Manning has personally met with and congratulated the Director of the FBI and state law enforcement in Henderson County this afternoon for capturing yet another of the escaped convicts without firing a shot. Manning attributes it to a bill he pushed for senate approval. The escapee, caught in a country area of Gibson Glen in Henderson County, is the fourteenth capture.

"Eleven dangerous convicts are still on the loose. The FBI is on high alert nationwide."

"Senator Manning will be sworn in as Vice President

on Friday afternoon. A vice president has never been removed from office because of criminal charges in our nation's history. Even with less than twenty-four hours left of his visit to Henderson County, Manning's fans are following him into town on foot, on every highway in the county. In itself, this wouldn't be a problem. However, his supporters contain many sometimes violent, gun-carrying vigilantes, and emotions are running high. The FBI is already largely present due to the escaped prisoners, and local law enforcement leaders are putting on extra forces from adjoining counties. This usually peaceful and quiet county is already at the boiling point. We'll be back with more at eleven."

It sure sounded like a lot was going right for Manning, he loved the chaos, and he was doing some serious grandstanding too. Lester hoped the person in the house liked to watch a lot of news and stay up late. He wondered if the eleven p.m. edition would bring him more helpful facts. There was a decision to make. Should he turn around and make someone pay for the mayhem created for mere greed and power lust, hoping he might still escape to see his son, or should he keep going on his original goal and let Henderson County and Manning go their natural course?

30

Thursday Night

CRYSTAL'S CAR sat in the hospital parking lot. She handed her keys to Luke, and he opened the passenger door for her. After being allowed to talk with Kasey for just a moment, Crystal realized both she and Kasey were still recovering from the shock, and each just needed rest. It had been a day full of adrenaline, and it would take some time for it to wear off.

"Don't let the darkness pull you in when we have such a huge responsibility right ahead of us. Please stay with me," Luke pleaded with her as they drove. Sinking into gloom now was terrible for her and her baby. Tomorrow could be worse than today, and he wanted her to get through it with her sanity. "Let's get you some hot tea or chocolate and set you up for the night in my room at the church. Cheyenne left tonight, so the room is clean and ready, and I can keep using the other twin bed in the guest room. I'll be happier knowing we're under the same roof."

"I don't have any clothes," Crystal answered in a monotone.

"You can use one of my shirts for tonight, and either wash your things in the laundry at my apartment, or we'll run to your house in the morning for more clothes. There's a new toothbrush in the package in the sink drawer. No excuses." She nodded, too tired to speak but grateful for his caring.

Billy took Trisha back to the apartment she shared with Kasey and their grandma. He was going to stay there, so Trisha wasn't alone. Grandma Myrt knew the whole story. With Kasey unharmed, she remained at the bar and grill, promising to close early and come home to the apartment. As much of a tough old bird as she was, this close call was a blow to her. Billy didn't want her to be alone either; he'd stay and sleep on the couch.

Tom and Beth went home. It was a very long day filled with fear and tragedy for them too. They knew tomorrow would be even more strenuous.

David and Pauley went to the church to be with their friends. They arrived just behind Luke. Jill was gone, but she left the kitchen light on. Thanks to the devoted volunteers, everyone across the county had been instructed what was needed. They knew where to go and when to be there tonight and tomorrow. Tonight, they were activating the salvation centers, which were already gathering believers who were loudly singing praise songs while lines formed for prayers of salvation. Angels protected every center. Pauley told them he could hear the angel's songs beginning to come from numerous places. People were being saved, and demons were dying. But anything could happen tomorrow, as today had proved.

Everyone sat around the table, David and Luke with fresh coffee, Pauley and Crystal with hot cocoa. When the body has been in shock, it needs stillness, reflection, and something warm and soothing to bring it back to the present.

Gabe came through the door and went straight to the coffee for his own needs. "Cheyenne got off safely. They should be in DC by six forty-five our time and in the office of the Assistant Director by seven-fifteen. They've got amazing staff to run the necessary tests as fast as possible for the proof they need. She hopes to be back tomorrow with the cavalry to take Manning down." It was exciting news, but their focus was on the battle already begun around them. Alarm and exhaustion already nibbled at the edges of their spirits.

"Kasey and Carlos are both fine." Pauley had been quiet up to now, but it was time for him to speak. "I see everyone so sad because of what happened, but they're OK." No one spoke, but all were looking at him. "They have a beautiful baby named Hope! Kasey accepted Grace after hearing Pastor Luke last Sunday. Carlos accepted the light while he was in prison. We should be happy. And we have work to do. Open the front doors and stand back. There are angels ready to sing!"

Leave it to a child to remind them all what true faith was. A unique child who could hear the words and songs of the angels!

"Pauley is right. We won't often know why things happen. But we have to trust that even in the face of what we think is negative, God can turn bad into good for those who love Him and in accordance with His will. Our job is to keep the faith. His job is providing the strength. Let's keep that in mind for tomorrow too. It will be a trying day." Luke finished, looking around the table.

"I have a question about tomorrow. Where will David and Pauley be? I don't want this young man in any danger. You are a treasure, sweetheart." Crystal's gaze on Pauley was warm and maternal, momentarily restoring her and blocking out the shocks of the day.

"OK, let's go over the basic plan and end in prayer before we go home tonight, so we're all on the same page. Things will happen fast." Luke recapped the plan, and then they held hands and prayed before they all moved from the kitchen into the church and opened the double front doors. Ten people were already waiting for their turn to accept Grace. Another ten began singing, and Pauley sang with them. He had never sung before, and he sounded like an angel himself.

~~~

"....an eight o'clock update on local and national news. With the statements issued by Senator Manning's office that he will be returning to DC at noon tomorrow for his four p.m. swearing-in ceremony to the office of Vice President, there have also been many social media comments from his supporters. Rumors began of an announcement for his presidential run several months ago. A large contingent will greet him at the airport and follow him into the city. Several groups plan to line the route, and they too will join in the entourage. Still more will begin flowing into DC by early morning. They intend to show solidarity, to support the Senator as he becomes Vice President. And give him encouragement to run in next year's presidential election.

That was what Lester needed to hear to make up his mind. He couldn't wait till morning. He left the shed and began his trek back to town.

~~~

Their jet touched down on the runway of a private executive airport. A limo awaited to carry them to the bureau headquarters, where the ADD was on alert in the forensics lab with his team of specialists. A top-secret task force had been at work for the past week to discreetly collect fingerprints, saliva, and hair from Manning's office, private bathroom, and limo. Even without hearing from Cheyenne about the box, they had prepared for what was likely to come. Several high-ranking officials knew that this man was a terrible choice for the country. And many suspected a background of foul play. They all worked at hyperspeed through the night.

Cheyenne and Marc couldn't do much. They got coffee from the lab employee kitchen and waited.

However complicated the processes were to get DNA from an old rag and a rock, these scientists and technicians would do it. The DNA from the samples collected this week had already been analyzed and was ready to be matched.

When Cheyenne told her boss about the box, the FBI contacted the families of the murdered girls. They were told that some possible evidence had come to light. Photos were now being sent to them via the internet to see if they would recognize the jewelry. Each family identified a single piece of jewelry belonging to their lost child. Files on both girls contained dental records and skin tissue samples. Their DNA had been easy to identify and was also ready to match. The catalyst, in this case, was Cheyenne, and the fuel was the report filed before she went to Gibson Glen. The fact that Manning told her the time frame, the location, the type of crime, and the age and sex of the victims, led them directly to the murder case files.

Cheyenne could feel every tick of the clock in her molars. The suspense created a high anxiety level, and Marc wasn't doing any better. They moved to a lounge area next to the labs and settled into a comfortable couch. Cheyenne's boss and the ADD stayed in the labs to oversee every step of the process.

~~~

Beth sat next to her husband on the couch at two o'clock in the morning, both bone-weary.

"There are shifts of volunteers working the salvation centers around the clock. I'll be going back in the morning after catching a few winks. How are you, hon? How are things at the station?" Beth asked, rubbing his back.

"Insane. We got reinforcements from four more counties to do eight-hour shifts around the clock. Better but still not enough. There are parts of town that are in flames. First responder resources are stretched to the max. People keep marching into town, and now Manning and his men are having a huge stage put up so he can "talk to his people." He's losing his grasp since he can't get the box or find Cheyenne. You know what dangerous people do when they get desperate?"

324

"Over and above all of that, I thought I'd lost you today when I couldn't reach you. I don't think I've ever been so afraid. Now, I've got time for a few hours of sleep. Let's just go hold onto each other for a while before this craziness starts all over again. Are you with me?"

She smiled. They walked to the bedroom holding hands.

~~~

Her eyes opened. The sound of ambulances and police cars was background noise to her thoughts. She was fine. The baby moved and stretched in the bassinet beside her. Hope. Yes, Hope had given her renewal. Kasey was sure she was going to die or get killed. But Hope changed that. She could now envision Hope growing up. A future, something imaginable, was progress she could accept.

The nurses had told her that Carlos was fine too, and it was a minor surgery to remove the bullet from his shoulder. They also told her he would be in a guarded hospital room until tomorrow when the FBI would take him for interrogation before going back to prison.

There was a light tap on her door, and one of her favorite nurses peeked in.

"Just checking on you. Do you need anything?"

"Thanks, Meghan, we're fine."

"Then would you like a minute with company? Just a minute, though. I'm bending visiting rules."

"Sure. But who's up at this early hour to visit?"

Meghan backed out and wheeled Carlos in, leaving his wheelchair right next to Kasey's bed, and she left, shutting the door. He leaned over to give her warm hugs and kisses, grateful to sit next to Hope and to hold Kasey's hand as well.

"Oh, Carlos, are you OK now? I was so frightened for you and so afraid. Do you like the name I chose for her? Isn't she just the most beautiful thing?"

Carlos couldn't take his eyes off the child. "I'm going to be fine. I was so foolish to put you in danger but so thankful you weren't hurt. Her name is wonderful, and she is the most beautiful thing, only second to you."

"Do you want to hold her?" Kasey asked.

"No love, they promised me only a minute so I could see her. The agent guarding me and your nurse know each other and arranged this out of great kindness. I talked to FBI people today, though. I agreed to cooperate, and they said it would help me. I just want you to know I wasn't part of planning the prison break. I got dragged along at the last minute because the leader felt sorry for me. He took care of me and wanted me to have a new start with you. Otherwise, I'd still be there."

Her heart was satisfied. Carlos was still the man she knew and loved, and she'd wait for him for as long as it took.

Meghan opened the door. "Sorry, but the visit is over, kids. Let's get Carlos back before anyone knows he was gone."

He bent over and lightly kissed Hope and then Kasey. "We'll be OK. I believe now." He touched the cross she wore around her neck.

"Me too," she answered as her eyes welled with tears.

~~~

"Billy, are you awake?"

Trisha tiptoed into the living room. Billy was lying on the couch, staring at the ceiling, thinking for the thousandth time how close they came to losing Kasey and how devastated he'd been.

"Yeah, Trish, can't you sleep?"

"No. Too much to think about, Billy. I keep looking out the window at the church and seeing people going in and out. All night! Why didn't we ever know you go to church? I mean, I've known you my whole life. How could we not have known that?"

"Not something I talk about much, being a bartender. It's good for people to see me as a tough guy. Helps your Gran keep the place peaceful."

"If you go to church, do you understand God?"

"It's not for us to understand Him. More important to trust Him and know that He understands us and loves us just the way we are little one. We can understand how He wants us to be, and we can try to be that, but He and we know we keep falling and failing. The thing is, He loves us anyway." Billy explained.

"Pastor Luke said that you can pray, and God will save you. Does that mean to save us from the demons and bad guys out there?"

"More than that, it means to save your soul so that when this life is over, and this old body is all used up, we can spend the next life, the eternal one, with Him. No more pain, no more worries. All He asks is that we spread love while we're still here."

"I like that, Billy. Will you help me?"

The Guardians watching over them in the apartment began to glow the brightest gold, and their special song, the one loved by Pauley and hated by demons, flowed from their lips upward, shattering the screaming bat-like creatures into dust as it rose.

31

Friday Morning

HE SAT straight up in bed, eyes wide open, realizing the solution was so simple. Pauley must have received it in a dream. They'd all had the right idea, but a puzzle piece was still missing, and now he had it.

Pauley saw it was still dark, but this couldn't wait. He jumped from his bed and ran to his father.

"Dad! Dad! I know what to do! Wake up, dad! We have to call Gabe now."

David was awake, it was six a.m., and he'd been up for over an hour, thinking, preparing, wondering, and steeling himself for what was to come today. And praying, he was praying for his son's safety, for the protection of all of them.

"What, Pauley? What do you know, son?"

~~~

Cheyenne's watch alarm went off at six a.m. and startled her from sleep. She found her head was resting against Marc's shoulder. "Wake up, sleepyhead. We need to see how things are going." She gently shook him, and his bloodshot eyes opened.

They walked back into the lab. Cheyenne's boss was still present and turned with a smile when she heard them enter. "We've got it. The ADD just went to clear an immediate meeting with the President, which we will ALL attend."

Cheyenne was overjoyed! The ADD came in and said, "POTUS will see us in 30 minutes. Let's get our shit together and get over there." The heads of the specialist groups presented their documents and stored the evidence in a vault, giving the key to the ADD. "We're ready, now let's move it!"

They walked at a breakneck speed to the limo, waiting to take them to the White House. Staff led them to the President's private office, where they walked him through the evidence, facts, and conclusions. The District Attorney for DC was in attendance and concurred; there was no time or need for a Grand Jury indictment. Article 1 Section 6 of the Constitution allows for the arrest of members of Congress for committing a felony. There are no exceptions for time or location, and there was plenty of factual proof here for a felony arrest.

The President approved, Manning would be apprehended and brought into custody, then to justice.

The ADD phoned those he knew to be trustworthy; they couldn't arouse the suspicion of the Director. Undercover forces would converge on Gibson Glen in two hours at nine a.m., a necessary tactic because a large number of Manning's volatile supporters were also continuing to fill the town. They would take all precautions to control the situation. The bureau jet would leave the private strip outside DC at nine a.m. with an ETA of nine forty-five at the airstrip where they picked up Cheyenne. The four of them, Cheyenne, Marc, her boss, and the ADD, would need to be shielded and transported in safety to the rally location until Manning arrived.

Local law enforcement and FBI had reported earlier that the Director of the FBI and Manning would have their photo-ops and speeches at ten-thirty. The Governor and one junior state Senator would also be there, riding on Manning's coattails. Traffic on the main highway leading into town was likely to be thick, and Manning had already arranged a helicopter to whisk him away to his jet at eleven thirty for his flight back to DC.

Manning would plan to whip his followers into a frenzy. He'd have his men steal the box because they probably knew it was taken to the church by now and fly away with it in hand, securing his political career of dominance and tyranny. Manning had already spoken in interviews about his affinity for ending presidential term limits, so that would be a priority. He would be the first of a ruling dynasty to stretch ahead, perhaps for centuries, if that happened. He, and his manipulators, wanted an end to all democracy. None of this could be allowed to happen.

The ADD planned to use the media called in by Manning to destroy him with an arrest on the stage in front of the cameras before Manning could leave. It would be touchy since many in the crowd would be armed. But this had to be a complete takedown and fall from grace with no room for him or for his cronies and influential supporters to get him off the hook.

Cheyenne called Gabe. "We're good to go! Four of us will need a ride from where you left me back to the church. Anticipating a nine forty-five arrival. Are the shields still up?"

"Up and strong. I'll be there in a van. I saw one of the volunteers driving a nice one yesterday that will be perfect for this. Good guy, I'm sure we can borrow it for a few hours. I'll be there waiting. Oh, and good job, agent."

She took a minute to fill him in on the ADD's plan before ending the call.

Crowds began forming at the international airport where Manning would board his private jet as he transferred from the helicopter to go to DC. Trucks, campers, cars, motorcycles, and vans started forming in groups along the route. People wore logo t-shirts with racist or offensive messages, and many had handguns tucked in belts and long guns slung cross-body over shoulders. It was an open carry state, and these people took full advantage of it. Some carried flags displaying the symbol of the tattoos with the red eyes and strange writing as they fluttered in the occasional thick breeze. Others proudly waved signs with Nazi symbols. Not everyone in attendance was so deep into the cult, but their silent acceptance made them complicit.

A great deal of Manning's grooming for political advancement by the Princes encouraged him to be racist, sexist, and intolerant of all who were not white and wealthy. His speeches were full of fiery rhetoric, trashing people of color, people who followed alternate lifestyles, and anyone who disagreed with him on anything. The fact that his followers loved him for it made a bold statement of humanity's lack of compassion. Fortunately, he and his mobs were still the minority, though the media would have it look otherwise.

~~~

Gabe's phone rang as soon as he hung up with Cheyenne. It was David's number.

"Morning, David. What's up? I know already it's got to be important."

"Yeah, brother. Really important. Pauley got the solution, the last part of the puzzle. It doesn't make me comfortable because many good people will have to be in the middle of the whole thing this morning. But I trust they'll be protected. The angels' songs are just a part of this. We're on our way to the church in about ten minutes."

"I'll round everyone up. Lots to catch up on."

Luke walked into the kitchen, where Gabe sat. "Something big?"

"Yeah, that was David, and Pauley has something. They'll be here

331

shortly. Is Crystal up yet?"

"Up and ready to party!" she smiled as she walked in to join them, barefooted and wearing a long T-shirt of Luke's and a pair of his running shorts, which must have been slung low below her belly. "And I'm stylin' too!" she laughed.

Luke thought he'd never seen her more beautiful.

~~~

Lester no longer had to worry about being seen or recognized. It was still semi-dark, and the roads into town and the residential streets were full of people. Some partiers, some political supporters who thought their cause was just, some insurrectionists and terrorists, many armed, and few there for good reasons. His reason was no less heinous than theirs, but he felt a kind of right in his wrong. Manning was a plague on the country, so he planned to do a good thing.

He walked right to the center of town where the finishing touches were being made on a massive stage, presumably for Manning to work his crowd later today. The setup couldn't be more perfect. Whoever it was pulling the strings, Manning was blindingly confident that he wasn't able to be touched. He was wrong.

A little scouting showed Lester the place he was seeking. The entire stage was an open target, close enough for the handgun he had in his belt and easy enough to melt back into the crowd.

Now he just laid low and waited for the show to start.

~~~

Eyes bloodshot and sleep-deprived, Tom arrived at the station in the same condition as the rest of the force. He learned that they would put all they had today into crowd control. It sounded like trying to hold a tsunami at bay with one hand behind your back. Each Deputy got an itinerary for the show. It looked like there would be a lot of speech giving to suck up to Manning and to pump up the crowd until their idol stepped on stage at ten-thirty a.m. Then he would be whisked away by a copter at eleven-thirty. The masses would be released and encouraged to do what they saw fit in the town, an intentional demonstration of the "New Order," which meant chaos and destruction. Manning, of course, would be gone so that he held no responsibility for their actions.

Tom and Luke had a short phone conversation on his ride into the station. Luke caught him up on their plans with Cheyenne and the ADD. It was going to be crazy and dangerous, and he was already more exhausted than he'd ever been in his life. When it was over, he planned to sleep for a week. How had Gabe held up, repeating it over and over and constantly fighting these forces of flesh and principalities of evil? The man must be superhuman.

Beth was at their church volunteering another shift to help people who wanted to accept the Gift. It would be a long day lasting into the night, and the crowds of people might not entirely leave town for several days. His mind was working on twenty things at once. He had to stop and breathe—time to remember who was supplying the strength in this endeavor. God was directing; they just had to concentrate on one step at a time.

~~~

David pulled into the church parking lot faster than his usual speed. He and Pauley rushed to the door where Luke was already waiting.

"Come in. Sit. Catch your breath. Pauley, you start when you're ready." Luke handed David a hot cup of coffee, and Crystal gave Pauley some juice.

Pauley couldn't wait.

"I just woke up and knew this; I don't know how. But my angel told me about the song, and they told us about angels being able to keep singing the song for as long as they wanted, and all other angels around could sing it too. It's not just one angel per person. And that the song of each angel kills or drives off hundreds of demons. Gabe, you said that those smaller demons are the ones we have to deal with, so the warrior angels and you can deal with the really big mean ones, right?"

"Absolutely right."

"So, this morning, I just knew. We have to have a bunch of people actually in the crowd who want to be saved. People we put there. People ready to accept Grace as soon as one prayer is prayed. As many people as we can get there and more. We have to stop the salvation centers and move them to the crowd in front of the big stage in the middle of town. That's where the most demons will be. I'm supposed to tell you this part and one more thing, we have to use their loudspeaker system."

"Thank you, Lord, for the blessing of Pauley's gifts! We now have a powerful weapon, one I never had in twenty years of battles. It was there all the time, but I had no way to receive the message. Pauley's Gift is communication, and God knew that even before he was conceived. Your gifts are blessings to the whole world, son." Gabe finished with glistening eyes, proud of Pauley and so grateful.

Gabe explained the plan of the ADD to arrest Manning on stage in front of everyone and on national television at ten-thirty when he went on.

Luke's mind was working in hyperdrive, putting all this new information together.

"We have to coordinate with Tom and Cheyenne and the ADD forces. Gabe, can you do that? We have to get the volunteers notified of the change in plans. Crystal, can you get to Jill and the two of you put them on notice to stand by for further instructions? I'll get in touch with the boys in the band who play for our services. One of them is a whiz at electronics. We'll get him to covertly hook up a toggle and mic so that the prayer will be over the sound system. Maybe Tom and his officers can give the boy cover to get the connection made. The prayer will be short because we won't have much time."

Luke continued, "I have an idea to get everyone on their knees as Manning makes his entrance. They worship him, so that should be easy. The people waiting for the prayer will know ahead of time that they're on their knees for Christ, not Manning. With Manning's followers on their knees, we have less chance of them using the weapons they're carrying. They'll be disoriented, and so will their demons.

Once the angels' songs begin, the lesser demons will be dropping their charges anyway, so much of the danger will be gone. As Manning enters, I'll be on the mic to give the invitation. With any luck, his arrogance will make him think it's about him until it's already too late. In his confusion, the ADD can do his thing with the arrest.

The part that will be interesting is to see how this all comes out on film. Viewers won't hear any angel songs but will see people on their knees, crumpling as the demons let loose, and then the arrest and charges and Manning hauled off to an FBI car. They'll also see the reactions of the Director of the FBI, the Governor, and any other high-level people in attendance as they witness the takedown of Satan's favorite human son." Luke paused.

Crystal responded, "Who would have thought just a week ago that the handful of people in this room would be able to make a world-changing difference today? We're so blessed to be seeing a better future in the making. I'm outta here, boys. I have calls to make." She exited to dress in her freshly laundered clothes and get to work in Luke's office.

Luke called the number for the band and set it up for the boy to meet with Tom in thirty minutes.

David asked what he could do. Gabe had him call Tom to meet with the boy and explain and catch him up on what was happening with Pauley's latest vision. It was approaching time for Gabe to get the van, so he'd be there waiting for the jet. He'd bring them up to speed on the kitchen conversation as he drove them back to town; the van was the safest and most invisible place to be.

Luke asked Pauley to call the hospital to check on Kasey. It was something he knew Pauley would like. Kasey was part of the family and needed to realize they were thinking of her.

They had just about two hours to pull all of this together.

~~~

"I made this perfectly clear and shouldn't have to repeat myself! I want a highly proficient team to get the item before eleven a.m. today. They say they know where it is. Then there will be no screw-ups. None! I do not care what has to happen to get it. Any amount of collateral damage is acceptable. I want it in my hands when I'm sitting in my jet at eleven-thirty. Just get the damned thing!" Manning would have slammed down the receiver had he been in his office. Clicking an icon to end a call just gave no satisfaction at all.

Sitting cramped in the small room at Settle Inn, the four of them were going over final plans. Monstrous black beasts, looming by each man and heaving sulfurous breath, were calling the shots today. Manning only thought he was in charge. His beast was a High Prince with superiority over the others, and it emitted a toxic cloud through its pig-like nostrils, then stared at each of the three lower-ranking creatures with its burning eyes. Manning spoke as it spoke, and both the lower Princes and the humans in the room completely understood the words and tone. There was a hierarchy, and if they were to survive, they would respect and bow to it.

"I own each one of you because you decided to be owned by those in power. You will do whatever it takes to make this plan work because it benefits you. I am the chosen one, and you are my subordinates. I am the Vice President and will be the President in a matter of days. I am the leader of the free world. Stay in line, and you will reap your rewards. Fall out of line, and you will pay the dire consequences.

Understood?" They all nodded. The Director of the FBI, the Governor, and a junior Senator were his to command. They understood and accepted; the whispers of the Demon Princes who stood with them reinforced Manning's words. And there were so many more like them in line to kiss his ring.

"My appearance today will show my command of the public. It is the culmination of decades of planning and grooming and manipulating by the masters, on a path to put the world under one leader. Me." The thoughts made him heady and arrogant with power, exactly how he needed to be for everything to go right today.

"But if I am ever booked in this lowly kind of accommodation again, someone will be out of a job, or worse," he reminded them with disgust as he looked around the room. "I want the exact plan. What's taking place now? What is scheduled, right up to my entrance?"

The Director spoke first. "There are thousands of your followers in town and in front of your stage already, just waiting to see you and hear you speak. There are thousands more lining the roads through two counties and waiting at the international airport. They hope to catch a glimpse of you leaving in your private jet. The tower will hold all commercial traffic in and out for your departure, which is their priority. Your copter is ready to take off from here at eleven-thirty, or earlier if you desire, and your jet is fueled and ready to fly. There will be some speakers starting at ten a.m., mostly to keep the crowd pumped up for you."

"At ten-thirty, you will be announced and make your entrance. We have agents all around the center, in buildings, and on rooftops, for your security. Of course, we chose only those we know to be deeply loyal to your vision. You can speak as long as you desire between your entrance and eleven-thirty, and then you exit. The crowds will be further incited and entertained during the following hour and then will be told to return to the places where they came from so they can watch your swearing-in ceremony at four p.m. eastern time today. Of course, the numbers alone prevent them from leaving the town in a few short hours. We've placed many undercover agents within the crowds to instigate trouble after you've gone, especially against people of color and anyone who opposes you."

The Governor cut in so he could garner some of the attention. "All major television and cable stations are here, so your rally will have global viewing. You will outshine the President and every other world leader in your first rally, kicking off the campaign to your officially elected and unending presidency. Sir, I'd like to say I'm honored to be among your closest allies." The Governor bowed his head.

"You're not my ally. You're my subordinate. Please keep your perspective."

32

Crescendo

LONG LINES of people, sometimes five people deep, bordered the road to the airstrip cutoff. Their van got no attention moving out of town, and the road itself wasn't blocked. The total lack of frenzy with this number was unusual and disturbing, but the masses posed no problem to him now, so Gabe continued on his mission.

Right on time, nine forty-two, he could hear the jet approaching. He waited until the jet came to a standstill, then drove as close to it as possible. First to emerge was Cheyenne. She looked tired but determined. Behind her was a man, probably her contact, then a woman he presumed to be her boss. The last one out was unmistakably the ADD who was giving orders to the pilot as he disembarked. Cheyenne hurried them to the van. The rear van windows had dark tint; the second and third-row seats looked comfortable. After closing the back door, she climbed into the front passenger seat and reached over for Gabe's hand, giving it a warm squeeze.

"Are you sure no one will see and recognize us on the way there?" questioned the ADD.

"Sir, you're as good as invisible." Gabe smiled at him.

They arrived at the church just after ten. Gabe had explained as much as he could, leaving out the parts about Pauley, the angels' songs, and anything else that wasn't going to affect the performance of the ADD and his forces.

"Manning should be arriving backstage any time now. We're here to pick up Luke. David, Pauley, and Crystal are staying in the protection of the church."

Cheyenne opened her door to give Luke the front seat, and she got in the back. His was a more active role, and from here on out, she was an observer. It was bizarre to know that non-believers looking at the van would see only a nondescript driver and no one else. Gabe drove slowly to the town center, allowing time for those in the path to move without being harmed. He parked about fifty feet from the side of the stage.

The boy from the band approached Luke's window and passed him a cordless microphone. "It's good for about one hundred feet, sir. It works without you having to get out of the van. And there's no toggle. As soon as you hit the button to speak, it will override the system and then break off when you let it go."

"You're a genius, Joe. Stick around for the show, but please stay safe. Thank you." Luke was ready. His phone rang, and Crystal's name was on the screen.

"The volunteers have managed to get everyone waiting at the centers to relocate to the stage area of town. They know that they'll be asked to get on their knees if they can, but that it's for prayer, not for Manning. The invitation will come over the speaker system to accept Jesus and give thanks. Every one of them is eager and thrilled to be able to help. To win the battle while accepting God's Grace is exciting. Some even asked if they'd be able to hear the angels sing," Crystal reported excitedly, and he repeated it, in part, to those in the van.

"When do you want to exit the van, sir?" Gabe addressed the ADD.

"Just spoke to my coordinators for special forces and undercover agents. Give me a minute before you start your speaking part, Luke. Then we'll be ready at the side of the stage to use that confusion to catch Manning unaware, and the forces will move in as well."

~~~

Lester leaned against the tree and felt the gun in his waistband. He'd seen the limo pull up a few minutes ago and was watching the time. The shot had to happen during a lot of loud activity. He would prepare for the entrance but be ready to hold off. These rallies had numerous points of wild yelling and applause. No hurry. He felt oddly calm, deeply centered, and very sure. It was a mission, or maybe more than that. It was a calling.

Ten twenty-five.

The crowd was becoming electrified in anticipation. Some guy was on stage acting like he was a big shot and making a lot of talk about being on the right side and how the country would be so much better. "A New America" was the slogan. Clapping. Hooting. More clapping. The TV cameras were catching it all.

Ten twenty-nine. The ADD and his forces were on the move.

The clown on stage was getting ready to introduce Manning. His mic went mute—the look on his face, priceless.

"Ladies and gentlemen." A voice not attached to anyone visible rang out over the sound system.

"And now, please get down on your knees as a fitting welcome."

The crowd quieted, shuffled, and lowered themselves to the ground.

Backstage, Manning heard the instructions and was grinning, "What a great idea! Who thought of this?"

The techs in the sound system van were going crazy trying to figure out what was happening. Their system wasn't working, and they were locked in. A uniformed deputy with the Sheriff's Department stood outside of the door smiling, with his arms folded across his chest.

Manning walked forward to the rear drape of the stage.

The ADD approached the stage from Manning's blindside.

Over the loudspeaker, Luke's voice rang out again, "Father. Thank you for offering me your Grace and forgiving my sins. I accept your Son as my Savior. In the name of Jesus, Amen."

Those who came for salvation said 'Amen' after repeating the words. The angels began to sing loud and clear, the ethereal beauty of the sound filling the air of their dimension.

The warrior angels finally heard what they'd been waiting for; the horn for battle sounded by the Archangel Michael. In an instant, there were wings and swords everywhere. Clouds of demons attached to crowd members tried to flee, but most were turned to dust by song or sword. Gabe and Pauley witnessed that, Gabe from the front seat of the van, and Pauley on the church kitchen TV. It was a sight that rendered both of them speechless, but the sounds heard only by Pauley forced him to his knees with hands covering his ears. David rushed to his side.

Manning burst through the drape opening just as the ADD shot in from side stage and grabbed his arms. Four Special Forces agents took over holding and cuffing Manning. The ADD took the live mic and announced, "Senator Gregory Manning is under arrest for the murders of two girls in Henderson County. The President of the United States ordered this action after investigating the facts presented. The office of the Director of the FBI obtained the evidence."

Manning struggled and seethed, his eyes drilling holes in the face of the Director, who looked dumbstruck.

Angels continued to slash and sing. Demons died by the hundreds of thousands, soaring up into plumes of wispy smoke as their ashes and burning cinders fell to the ground.

Pauley, David, and Crystal watched it on TV in the church kitchen. Pauley heard the Angelic Host singing and the excruciating shrieks of the dying demons as they spiraled up and vaporized in their attempts to flee, but everyone else was deaf to that part of the drama.

~~~

The shrieking diminished as fewer and fewer demons remained, and Pauley was eventually able to remove his hands from his ears. Everywhere the cameras panned, people were being prayed over by saints within the crowd, though the cameras couldn't capture the images of dark drooling demons releasing them.

"Dad, we have to go to Gabe at the van. The angels are telling me to go now!" Pauley pleaded.

"You're not leaving me here by myself; get your car. We're ready." Crystal urged David.

David hesitated for less than a split second and then rushed them out the door. People filled the streets in confusion. Some were still trying to get closer; some were trying to flee. David proceeded cautiously as the crowds seemed to part to let them through.

~~~

Still on the stage, Manning's massive demon Prince was caught off guard, stunned, and about to detach itself and disappear, but Cheyenne's guardian angel was faster. With his sword, he swung an arc above Manning's head. He swiftly did the same over the Governor and Director, who had both rushed to the stage.

After this battle, the Demon Princes behind each man expected to receive praise and promotion. Instead, they received extinction. With the swing of the angel's sword, the heavenly blade sliced into them, and each in turn imploded, sucking lesser screaming demons around them into a momentary black hole and leaving only a flickering flame and the odor of sulfur in midair for a second afterward. Millions of their lesser comrades were gone or broken and fleeing in terror. All of this was beyond the capability of most human eyes and ears.

What the live cameras captured was Manning's arrest, the others on stage falling to the floor, massive crowds on their knees and with faces in the dirt, people with bibles praying over others, and some people running and screaming as if something was chasing them. Total chaos. Reporters on the scene were speechless as the cameras continued to record the melee.

~~~

David pulled up on the passenger side next to the van Gabe drove. Cheyenne jumped from the van's side door as Pauley and Crystal emerged from the car. They all gathered between the vehicles.

"What's wrong? Did something happen at the church?" Gabe asked with concern in his voice as he rushed around the front of the van to them.

"No, but the angels told me we needed to come here now, to be with you. They didn't say why," Pauley said, almost out of breath. David stood by his side with a protective arm around his shoulders.

The reporters were all talking into their cameras again. Gabe overheard them saying they were momentarily cutting over to the President making an emergency speech from the White House on all networks and radio stations. Gabe tuned in on the van radio and held the mic to it, clicking on the voice activation again for all to hear. And now, the President's voice rang out over the loudspeaker.

"My fellow Americans. Many of you have been watching a widely televised rally for Senator Manning. It was the start of his presidential campaign, just hours before becoming vice president of these United States. I want to assure you that the events taking place are real. It was a surprise sting conducted by many levels of law enforcement and multi-agency cooperation after a lengthy undercover operation to find and eliminate corruption at its worst. This arrest was necessary to derail an accused murderer from his political agenda. During my administration, no one is above the law, even high-ranking politicians in this country. I apologize to you for the dramatic way it had to happen. Still, I assure you that everything is under control, and the new Vice President, House Representative Amy Sutton, who I chose days ago, will be sworn in at four p.m. eastern time as planned. Thank you, and God Bless America."

People stood with mouths open, unsure of what to do next. Reporters cut back to the rally, panning the crowds for reactions.

No one paid attention to the big, bearded man leaning against a tree laughing. Oddly, no longer were any demons riding on his powerful shoulders.

With the destruction of the Klazyn demon forces which had gripped them, most of Manning's followers were left weak and disoriented. Those who came armed didn't raise a weapon. Those who wavered in their allegiance were prayed over and given the opportunity to accept the gift of Grace and Light. And yet, with the freedom of choice also being a divine gift that God would not take back, some chose to maintain their status with darkness, and so they fled the losing battle to regroup at a different time, in a different place.

FBI agents, the police department, and the Sheriff's office watched for unruly individuals who might have thought to take things into their own hands. But despite the presence of so much weaponry, no incident occurred. Tom couldn't have been more relieved.

Far away, in places scattered around the globe, members of a covert group of men watched their plans to rule the planet disintegrate. They lost forty years of planning and preparation in a matter of minutes. Their Demon Princes had nothing more to do as they waited for the Dark Lord to decide their fate. Their existence was tenuous.

This time, nothing felt the bite of Gabe's sword. He was no longer a warrior using his physical strength and weapon. The supernatural gifts Pauley received were the new weapons to fight the darkness, and with team planning and the help of Luke, Cheyenne, Crystal, Tom, and so many more, this had been accomplished with success here in Gibson Glen.

Gabe reached into his jacket and pulled out a wooden cross about the size of two of his large hands. He walked to the remaining crowd in front of the stage with Cheyenne and Pauley following. Some who were still on the ground looked up at his imposing stature. Others who were standing turned to see what he was going to do. Many still held the bibles in their hands which they brought to ward off demons and pray with the confused.

Gabe held the cross high. The meaning was clear and understood without words. It enveloped those watching, swelling their hearts; God was victorious. Turning back around, he faced his friends Luke, Crystal, and David, still with the cross held high. Pauley stood on Gabe's one side, Cheyenne on his other, and the people gathered behind him, first a dozen, then fifty, then hundreds.

David looked at them and saw the drawing Pauley had done in his mind's eye. His first thought was how God was so awesome, and then tears streamed down his face as he became overcome with love and admiration for his son and gratitude for all of their new friends.

Luke took Crystal's hand and began singing. One by one, they all joined in as many lit cigarette lighters, and cellphone flashlights, "This little light of mine, I'm gonna let it shine. This little light of mine, I'm gonna let it shine....". TV cameras were still recording as darkness and gloom faded and rays of the sun broke through the clouds.

The singing continued, but Gabe paused to give praise. He knew more battles were ahead, but he now had human allies, all with gifts, strengths, and strong faith. Gabe also had a partner, the one chosen for him, and in his future travels, they would be together. He was tired, but there was no weariness. Instead, a peace never experienced filled his heart. A smile crossed his face, and he raised his chin, looking upward. "Thank you, Father, for your light and direction, for your blessings and protection, for victory and perseverance, for new life, new friends, and for love," he prayed just loud enough for Pauley and Cheyenne to hear, putting one arm around Cheyenne's shoulders. In unison, they all said, 'Amen.'

~~~

It is not the final battle. Gabe's sword will be retired, but he won't. The Army of Satan will not end its quest for dominion until the day God declares it over and they, and their leader, are thrown into the fiery pit for eternity.

Others who now know about spiritual warfare and the existence of Angels and Demons engaged in the battles for good over evil will spread the word. The media had covered this battle if only the side most humans could see and hear, but maybe it will be enough to turn the tide going forward. People need to peel the scales from their eyes and see evil where it exists for what it is. The lust for power and the tremendous greed that has taken over has to be beaten back and replaced by caring, charity, hope, and love. Always love. For it is the greatest of all of these.

EPILOGUE

Epilogue

AFTER A time, Gibson Glen returned to normal, but residents would talk about this event for generations to come. Pauley's grandchildren would think it was a legend.

People had died. People had changed. Lives would never be the same, but decades of wrongs were made right, democracy got a reprieve, and families found closure. There will always be more work to be done. Though darkness continues to take advantage of every opportunity, new knowledge limits those opportunities. The Light is winning, for now.

Cheyenne turned in her resignation. She and Gabe became a team, traveling where God called and sharing the story of Henderson County. They taught others how to defeat demons with better weapons than swords. Pauley occasionally joined them during summer vacations.

David and Pauley went back to life at the pawnshop but with a new twist, to use what they had learned to help others and remain fully connected to their spiritual family. Pauley stayed in touch with Gabe to give insight when needed, but his highest priority was to spend a few years being a kid and going to school. His gifts wouldn't suffer; they would grow stronger. One day soon, God would call on him again.

Luke had the opportunity to move on to a bigger church in New York. He turned it down to stay in Henderson County with Crystal. They married and raised their family, one girl with sandy hair, green eyes, and freckles, and two very busy boys, in the town they both loved. But they did have to double the size of their little church building.

Kasey and Hope had to wait only two years for Carlos to join them. The judge who sentenced him went to jail for corruption, and a new judge was assigned to review the case. He reduced the sentence to three years in the county jail instead of the state prison, less his time served. When he was released, Carlos got a job in construction and then built his own business. They married and had one more child, a son they named William Luke.

Billy met a lovely lady who didn't care about his slight limp. He inherited the bar and grill when Gran passed the following year, and he happily stepped in to take care of all of his girls, Trisha, Kasey, and Hope, as long as they needed him. Billy finally got to be a dad and grandpa.

A month after the event, Beth told Tom she was pregnant. They had a set of twin boys with red curly hair seven months later. Within the year, Tom received his promotion to Detective.

And an old man with a thick gray-streaked beard and mustache bought a little cabin in the woods near a town not far away with cash he found somewhere. He stayed to himself mostly but sometimes ventured to the local high school football games. The boy he watched graduated and became a teacher and coach at that same high school. The man carried a small silver cross he kept in his wallet that he bought from a pawn shop in Gibson Glen a day after the event. He had that date engraved on the back. It was the day of his acceptance.

~~~

Over time, new demon lords rose in rank to replace the old ones. The world was changing, and they had to change with it because their time was not over. Their hold in the global political arena remained strong; it was a fertile place to plant the seeds of corruption. As they had done for all the ages of man, they continued to find and groom new "investments" among the humans.

"The critical question remains, how are we going to protect our battalions from death by the salvation songs of the angels?" one new Prince asked in a gravely raspy voice at a POETS summit.

"I'm not sure we can," replied another. "But politics in the US is dividing the population like never before. Many who call themselves Christians are often not true believers, and they will lead more astray. Greed is growing, and selfishness along with it. Young ones are growing up with no beliefs, so fewer are being saved, and with that, the angels sing fewer songs. Time is on our side," he chuckled. "One way or another, the New Ones will be corrupted or eliminated."

A third Demon Prince stood to speak. "To help all of that along, I have teams of human scientists working on a new plague that's about ready to be released in China. It's a virus. We're going to call it Corona."

~~~

For more of C.L. Ferrari's *In The Absence of Light* series, please follow her website

www.clf-words.com

The Inner Circle Newsletter keeps you up to date on everything coming from the desk of C.L. Ferrari and offers you first peeks and perks. Become a member

Inner Circle Connection | cherylynn (clf-words.com)

ABOUT THE AUTHOR

About the Author

From a very young age, C.L. Ferrari showed interest in writing stories and poems, drawing, painting, and photography. Today she encourages programs for youth to get early exposure and training in these fields believing that mentorship and availability will ensure a future for the arts.

When she was three, her family moved from Michigan to Florida where she lived for the next sixty three years, during which she married and had a family. Sporadic travel for business and pleasure took her to most of the U.S., the islands of Bermuda and the Caribbean, South America, Central America, and Italy.

Also a voracious reader, Ms. Ferrari was influenced by some favorite authors. Two Christian fiction novels by Frank E Peretti were especially important in creating a pivotal point in her life, only to be acted on years later when she became a grand jury member on a heinous murder case for seven months. The realization of evil in it's most raw form, and learning what human beings are capable of doing to each other on the darkest side, and what we are able to do for each other on the side of good, became vivid reality. Thus the inspiration for the *In the Absence of Light* trilogy, her first Christian fiction novels.

C.L. Ferrari, aka CheryLynn, began seriously writing and

publishing in her early sixties, just before retiring. Her first work was a non fiction, *Enriching Your Retirement,* to help those who didn't have a plan or any outside interests. She moved to Mexico in 2018 where she writes and paints from her small farm, surrounded by mountains and overlooking the beautiful Lake Chapala.

In 2022 Ms. Ferrari, formed the publishing house, Portal Publishing LLC, for her own books and to assist other new authors in their quest to publish. She encourages contact and feedback through her website and email. Members of her newsletter are her literary family, staying in touch with what is coming from her desk as soon as it happens, and getting advance peeks at new manuscripts.

www.portalpublishingllc.com

www.clf-words.com

Cheryl@clf-words.com

ACKNOWLEDGMENTS

Acknowledgments

Thank you to all those who helped me through the dark times which inspired this novel.

To those who, through words or actions, guided me back onto the right path when I strayed.

To my brothers and sisters in Christ who aren't afraid to spread the light into dark corners.

****

Thank you to my children and grandchildren who will carry on the faith to future generations.

To my family who so often said I never finish anything, not understanding that is a common attribute of a creative mind, and that with time, many things do get finished.

To my mom, who through it all still loves me.

To my favorite grandparents who are with Jesus, waiting for me to join.

***

And thank you to the wonderful support team who gave of their time and wisdom to make this book possible. This has been an incredible, very long, journey and I thank you for standing with me through the tough times, the dry times, and the victorious times. Friendships are golden.

***

Father, I hope I've delivered your message as you intended.